Death in a ball of fire

A million years seemed to pass as Lieutenant Logan Hunter waited for something to happen. The German Schmeiser cleared its throat and a big ball of fire rose from his last position, at the culvert. Logan Hunter gagged, "Oh, Jesus!" as he realized what it was. Men were screaming as the flame thrower hosed into the culvert at them. Somebody must have made it out the far side because the submachine gun hammered again in a long burst. Then it got very quiet for another eternity as Hunter squatted behind the bushes, heaving but unable to throw up his bile. In the distance someone called something out in German.

Hunter started running, trying to keep his head below the level of the hedge between him and the German mop-up unit. He realized he was running in blind panic when he tripped over something on the path and sprawled headlong, tearing up his hands. He rolled over and suddenly found himself looking into the grinning, awful face of *Death* itself. . . .

Armageddon in the West

Jonathan Scofield

A DELL/BRYANS BOOK

Published by
Dell Publishing Co., Inc.
1 Dag Hammarskjold Plaza
New York, New York 10017

Dell ® TM 681510, Dell Publishing Co., Inc.

ISBN: 0-440-00290-7

Printed in the United States of America

First printing—February 1982

Armageddon in the West

1

Normandy, June 6, 1944, D plus 0300 hours . . . First Lieutenant Logan Hunter of the U.S. 101st Airborne Division did not yell "Geronimo!" or anything else as he dove out the open hatchway of the low-flying C-47 into what seemed to be ice-cold ink.

The static line popped his chute open with a gut-wrenching jerk. Logan grasped the shrouds to control his descent as he stared down into total darkness and hoped the fly boys had dropped him and his I&R platoon in the right place. As the planes droned off the young S2 officer drifted earthward silent as a thistledown. Thirty of his men had jumped with him. But he'd never felt so alone in his life. Night jumps behind enemy lines were not supposed to be chatty affairs, so each man floated down through the darkness wrapped in his own cocoon of silence, cold, and fear.

In theory they'd jumped from three hundred feet. But how could you judge your altitude in total darkness? Logan braced himself to hit the sod of the DZ. But the next thing he knew he was being attacked by clawing branches. He grimaced in surprise and pain as he dropped through the branches of the tree in which he'd landed. A broken branch scraped his cheek open. Then he came to a whip-snap halt, still off the ground, and for God's sake, how far?

Off in the distance he heard the sound of broken glass. Closer in, another trooper swore mightily and called out, "Hey, I'm hung up in a durned old tree!"

Logan called out, softly, "As you were, goddamn it! Rally on my clicker. And the next man who yells can give his soul to Jesus, for his ass will belong to me!"

Suiting actions to his orders, the hung-up leader took the toy cricket they'd issued him from his pocket and made it chirp twice. The signal was repeated close at hand and a cautious voice whispered, "Steinmuller, here, sir. I can't make you out, Lieutenant."

"You see a tree, Sergeant?"

"Yessir. That's about all I *can* see."

"Well, I'm up in the damned thing with my shrouds caught in the limbs. See if you can tell me how far my heels are from Mother Earth."

There was an orange flare and Hunter snapped, "Not with your goddamn zippo, you maniac! Reach up and see if you can touch my boots!"

The abashed Steinmuller doused the light, but said, "I have you about six, seven feet up, Lieutenant. You're hanging well clear of the trunk."

Hunter nodded in satisfaction, reached for his jump knife, and started cutting through his nylon shrouds

8

as he muttered, "Move clear and gather in the sheep with your clicker. Let's try and keep this down to a roar if we can."

He suddenly dropped to the ground and fell on his side in his heavy gear, knocking some of his wind out as other troopers moved through the wet grass toward his unplanned command post. As Hunter rose he could make out about a dozen ghostly forms all around. He called a whispered roll and knew they were all from the stick who'd jumped from the same plane with him, minus three men.

Somebody whispered, "They never said nothing about trees in this DZ, Lieutenant. It was supposed to be an open meadow."

"I noticed," Hunter said. "Any ideas on what happened to Sergeant Flint's stick?"

"They must have come down somewhere else, Lieutenant," Steinmuller said.

Hunter wondered what else was new. He swore softly and said, "Okay, we obviously landed away from our assigned DZ. Flint and his guys will be waiting for us there if they came down the right way. Where's Compton and our R-300?"

There was no answer. Hunter was missing his radio as well as his radio man and two less important scouts. Hunter swore under his breath and looked at his radium-dialed watch. "Okay, thanks to that SNAFU back in England we loaded late and landed even later. It's going to be getting light soon and it's time to get this show on the road. Sergeant Steinmuller and most of you will stay here while I make a sweep with Arnold, Dugan, and Falco. I've got to find that R-300 and get our bearings before we do anything else."

Steinmuller cleared his throat and said, "Begging

the lieutenant's pardon, I might come in useful if you run into any Krauts. I speak a little German and—"

"Talk to them here," Hunter cut in, adding, "I'm not looking for a conversation with the Krauts right now. I'm looking for my R-300 and three of our guys. Give us half an hour and then start moving until you figure out where the hell they dropped us."

The tall lieutenant and the three scouts he'd picked moved out into the open to the east. The sky was a paler shade of slate now, and he could see the men around him better. "Corporal Falco," he said, "take the point. Arnold, to the left. Dugan, move out to the right flank. Keep me in sight but spread out as far as you can. Falco, you know the form. We'll move to the nearest edge of this whatever, and then sweep back. The missing guys will be on the ground if they're not in the trees. I heard breaking glass over to the northeast, so watch for a house or something. Anybody sees anything, I want him to freeze and not use his clicker. I'll move in on anybody I see standing still. Any questions?"

Arnold, a washed-out aviation cadet who was still a little eager, said, "Yessir. But in I&R class they told us a patrol leader took four guys with him. Ain't we supposed to have a getaway man, covering our rear?"

Hunter snorted in disgust. "Tell him, Falco."

"You only need a getaway man when there's some place for him to run for help, Arnold," the burly corporal explained. "No matter where the fly boys dropped us, we're miles behind the German lines."

"Oh," Arnold said.

"Let's move it out, damn it," Hunter growled. "This is hardly the time and place for on-the-job-training. We'll know soon enough how good we are. Spread it out and move it in!"

* * *

In the blacked-out West End of London a telephone was ringing next to the bed of Ramie DeWitt Davis, UPI. The ash-blonde war correspondent sat up and swung her bare feet to the floor as she answered the phone. A male voice at the other end said, "Hi, Ramie, did I wake you?"

Ramie glanced at the brass coach clock near her blacked-out window. "Heavens, no, I'm always bright-eyed and bushy-tailed at four A.M. Who is this?"

"Hey, baby, don't tell me you don't recognize my voice. It's Danny Boy, the airborne's gift to the girls of London Town, remember?"

Ramie grimaced and was suddenly aware of her nakedness. She knew it was silly to pull the sheet up over her breasts like that, but the voice of Major Dan Bradley had that effect on her. "I'm not a London girl, Dan. I thought you were down on the south coast with the 101st these days."

"Ahah, you *did* remember that night in Soho. Look, kitten, I just managed a three-day pass. I know it's a hell of an hour to call, but with only seventy-two hours to spend with you in London, I can't afford to waste any time. I'm calling from Charing Cross Station. I could make it over to your place in only a few minutes. Okay?"

Ramie shuddered. "Forget it, Dan. I told you I never wanted to see you again and I meant it."

"Come on, baby doll, don't play hard to get. God knows when I'll get another chance to be with you. I guess you reporters know D day's this summer for sure and—"

"Oh, for God's sake," she cut in. "Try that poor-soldier-off-to-the-front stuff with some ATS girl in a pub! You know you're a headquarters john, Dan." She glanced again at the clock. "And, I might add, not a very considerate one. I have to get up and go to work in just a few hours, Dan, so if you don't mind . . ."

"Aw, come on, honey, it's cruelty to animals to ask us both to sleep alone."

Ramie's face went Mona-Lisa serene as she hesitated, asked, "Who said I was sleeping alone?" and hung up. She was instantly ashamed of her easy dig, but if there was a man in England who deserved it, it was the smug young Major Bradley. She lay back down, frowning, as she realized the airborne wolf would probably repeat her crack to his buddies. But she didn't know anyone else in the 101st and Dan was the sort of man who larded his comments with gynecology in any case. She switched off the bed lamp and rolled over to try and get more sleep before the alarm went off. But sleep was out of the question now. That hated voice from the past had upset her more than it should have. She punched her pillow and told it, "Look, damn it, we had a very minor fling with a handsome louse and it's over. Forget about it."

The phone rang again.

Ramie tried to ignore it. There had to be some limits to Dan Bradley's smug self-assurance and she'd told him there was another man up here in bed with her. Was that why he'd rung back? To spoil things for her at what would have been a delicate time, had she been telling the truth? Knowing Dan Bradley, it was easy enough to believe.

On the seventh ring she gave up, grabbed the phone, and snapped, "See here, Dan, I've had just about enough of your sophomoric calls, you silly twit!"

A new male voice replied, "Is that you, Ramie? What are you talking about? Who's a silly twit?"

Ramie flushed as she recognized the voice of her

fellow UPI correspondent. "Sorry, Pete. I thought you were somebody I met in the blackout a million years ago. What's up?"

"You are, if you're still working for UPI. Get your pretty fanny over to SHAEF and see if Ike's still there. If he's not, chase him wherever they say he went. The balloon's gone up!"

Ramie sat up straighter and gasped. "You mean D day's here at last?"

"You got it, toots. The landing craft are out in mid-channel by now and both the Eighty-second and 101st Airborne have landed in Normandy ahead of the landing. I'll cover here while you run over to SHAEF, right?"

Ramie was on her feet groping for her underthings as she said, "Wrong. SHAEF will be handing out the usual press releases. I'm on my way south to flirt my way aboard an LST. Have Waterman meet me at the motor pool with our shortwave set. She and I will call the story in from the beachhead if she's half as good at flirting with dirty old staff officers as I am!"

It was still dark but threatening to get lighter as Hunter and his patrol stood over the huddled form in the weeds near a hedgerow. Falco spat and said, "That's O'Hanlon, all right. He landed facedown and you ain't supposed to do that with a streaming chute, but I recognize the new boots. He was the only guy in our stick with new boots."

"Arnold, pick up his ammo," Hunter said. "The glass I heard breaking was near here. I don't see anything. Let's check the far side of the hedge, Falco on point."

As Falco moved toward a gap in the hedges young Arnold asked, "Are we just gonna leave him here like this, sir?"

"Graves will find him if our guys get ashore," Hunter replied. "Let's go, men."

He followed Falco through the gap. The burly corporal was hunkered behind an overturned sedan in the middle of a dirt road running north and south. Beyond lay a stone house with scattered outbuildings all around. One was a glass greenhouse. The folds of a parachute were draped over the framework of the shattered glass roof. Hunter joined Falco and muttered, "What do you think?"

"This is a German staff car," Falco said. "Looks like one of our fly-boys shot it up. Nobody inside, so they must have lit out running. No sign of life over there, either."

Hunter grimaced as he noticed how easy it was getting to see things that far away now. "You'd think someone would have noticed if they'd been home when a guy crashed through their greenhouse. Cover me. I'll see who it was."

"I ain't afraid and I'm still on point, Lieutenant," Falco said.

But Hunter replied, "I know. I put you there. Your carbine carries farther than my .45 and we haven't time to do this by the book."

As he drew his pistol and moved across the open space toward the farmstead the older and more experienced Falco covered him with a grudging smile of approval. The new looie was okay, for one of them country-club guys you sometimes had to watch out for. Falco knew Hunter was taking a chance and that he wasn't the sort of officer who'd order one of his men to take one. Falco had been worried when the new looie arrived fresh from Benning. But Hunter wasn't one of them hoity-toity know-it-alls like Major Bradley. Boy, *there* was an asshole! Falco was glad he hadn't had to jump with old Danny Boy. They said he'd done all right in North Africa back in '42. But if he'd ever been a paratrooper, it didn't show these days.

Hunter moved across the farmyard to the shattered greenhouse. The door was locked from inside. He broke out a pane with his pistol barrel and reached through to open it. The interior was a whelter of overturned plants and upended wooden shelves. The sky was alarmingly bright now, and their radio man, Compton, looked awfully messy as he lay spreadeagled in the wreckage. His chute had opened, all right, but his descent through the glass roof had cut him to ribbons. Hunter put a hand to Compton's sticky throat to make sure he was dead. "Boy," he muttered, "you sure picked a swell place to land." Then he began to unbuckle the heavy R-300 from the dead trooper's webbing. The radio had landed atop the corpse. It hadn't helped Compton one hell of a lot, but hopefully his cut-up flesh had cushioned its tubes. The damned thing might still work, once he wiped it off with Compton's torn chute.

Hefting the soap-box-sized R-300 to his shoulder, Hunter turned to leave. But as he reached the doorway he heard Falco calling out, "Watch it, Lieutenant! There's something moving in that house!"

"Hold your fire," Hunter called back. "Are Dugan and Arnold with you?"

"Yessir. You want me to see if I can circle around the back?"

"Negative. We don't have the bodies to surround the place. Stay put. I'll work my way back to you some damned way."

He was still trying to figure out how when the door of the stone farmhouse popped open and somebody waved a white pillow case at them. Hunter thought quickly and called out, "*Nous sommes Américains! Qu'est vous?*" in high school French. There was a moment of silence. Then a large middle-aged woman in black dashed out, sobbing as she waved the pillow case at them wildly.

"Stay covered and watch the house for me," Hunter called to his men. He stepped out to meet the excited woman. As she ran at him, babbling high-speed French he couldn't follow, a younger and more sedate woman followed her from the house. The older woman threw her arms around Hunter as he put down the R-300 with a puzzled smile. The younger French-woman said, in English, "My mother is overwrought to see you, *m'sieu*. We were afraid you were the *boches* again!"

Hunter shook his head. "We're U.S. Army, *m'selle*. Are the two of you alone here?"

"*Oui, les boches* took my father and brothers away to work on their coast defenses. But now that you Americans have liberated us, they will be back soon, non?"

Hunter wasn't sure he'd liberated all that much, but he didn't think they wanted to hear that. He called across to Falco, "Send Arnold back to get Steinmuller and the others. But cover me while I have a look inside."

The younger Frenchwoman understood. She said, "*Oui*, I will lead you around the property, *m'sieu*. You will discover we are not traitors like a certain blonde in the village I could mention."

He left the radio and followed them toward the house, gun still drawn but politely down at his side. It only took him a few minutes to check out the house. He went to the door and called Falco in. As the corporal joined him, Hunter said, "Okay, they're alone and seem to be on our side. Watch for Steinmuller and the others and tell him I want a defense perimeter set up around this place for now."

"Are we going to use it for a base, sir?"

"Negative. I said for now. It's almost light and I want some cover long enough to contact the rest of the outfit and hopefully find out where the hell we are. Have Dugan bring the R-300 in. Meanwhile these ladies must know what part of France we landed in."

Falco saluted and moved off. Hunter rejoined the two women in their living-room-kitchen and spread his situation map on a plank table as he asked the younger one if she knew how to read a map.

She didn't but she said the nearest town was called Carentan. He found it on his map and sincerely hoped she was wrong. "We're near Ste. Mère Église," he said.

She made the sign of the cross and said, "Oh, no, *m'sieu. Les boches* are in Ste. Mère Église! It is their headquarters in this sector!"

The door opened. Hunter winced as he saw how the dawn light outlined Dugan as the trooper lugged the R-300 in. Hunter told Dugan to put it on the table and said to get Sergeant Steinmuller on the double. Then he turned back to the English-speaking Frenchwoman. In the ominously brighter light through the doorway he saw she was older and prettier than he'd first taken her for. He was probably wrong to call her *m'selle*, but it would be even ruder to say *madame* if she was an old maid. "They told us the Germans didn't have anything in Ste. Mère Église, *m'selle*. Are you sure it's not just a military police unit or something like that?"

She shook her head and insisted, *"Mais non, m'sieu!* There is at least a regiment of the beasts based there.

We, alas, have had enough experience in such matters to know where they are concentrated."

Sergeant Steinmuller came in. Hunter introduced him to the two farm women and said, "Somebody screwed up. These ladies say Ste. Mère Église is crawling with Krauts."

Steinmuller blinked and asked, "Ain't that where the Eighty-second was supposed to come down, Lieutenant?"

"Yeah. I said somebody screwed up. You're qualified with the R-300. So get on the air and see if you can raise Eighty-second Division."

Steinmuller took a seat near the battery-operated set, but as he started to fiddle with the dials he asked, "Don't you mean 101st, sir?"

Hunter snapped, "If I'd meant 101st I'd have said 101st, damn it! They dropped the same time we did, or maybe even earlier, thanks to that last minute SNAFU. By now they're down at Ste. Mère Église and if this lady is right they don't need a warning. They need *help!*"

Hunter went back to his map as Steinmuller held the ear phones to his head. He seemed to take forever with the R-300. Hunter used the blade of his jump knife as a map scale and muttered, "Damn, we landed miles from where we supposed to." He asked the French girl how far south of Carentan they were and she said five kilometers.

He went to the doorway. The sun would be up any minute and you could make out colors now. Normandy looked like the Land of Oz. Everything was too green. He didn't see any of his men as they covered the house on all sides. He'd have been annoyed with them if he had. He wet his finger to test the wind. It was from the southwest and Ste. Mère Église was to the north. But the sounds of gunfire should carry eight or twelve miles against the wind and he didn't hear anything but the chirping of a linnet in a nearby hedgerow. He stared thoughtfully at the hedgerow. It was high and thick. Every Norman field seemed surrounded by the same wall of heavy spinach green. You could lose a lot of sound in this peaceful-looking countryside, but, damn, they couldn't be that far from the beachhead. What if someone had really screwed up? What if D day had been called off at the last minute and they were *alone* on this side of the channel?

He went back inside and stared down at his map some more. They were only a few miles inland from the beach coded as Utah and the goddamned first wave should be landing right about now. So why was it so *still* outside? Did Ike think they could just wade ashore with no covering fire?

Sergeant Steinmuller started talking into his mike. That seemed reasonable. But Steinmuller was speaking in German, which didn't. As Hunter frowned down at him the sergeant switched frequencies with a grin and said, "That oughtta shake 'em up. I just told some Kraut to return to base and await further orders."

Hunter grimaced. "Swell. Now that you've had your laugh for the day, where the hell is Eighty-second Division?"

"I can't seem to raise them, Lieutenant. I'm on the right wavelength, but nobody's here but us chickens."

"Okay, they're probably maintaining radio silence. Start sending to them in Compton's code and see if they answer."

Steinmuller hesitated, then said, "I don't know the new code, sir."

Hunter swore and turned to go out to the greenhouse. Then he remembered he'd told Compton to memorize the S2 code and not to jump with it on him. "Okay," he said. "Send in the clear then."

"Clear, sir? What if some Kraut picks us up?"

"Can't be helped. We're here to gather intelligence and relay it to the brass. So far all we've collected is two dead and one missing and the fact that the Krauts may be in Ste. Mère Église. So get it on the air, damn it."

Steinmuller started calling "California I&R calling C.Q.," over and over. Hunter took out a pack of Chesterfields and offered them to the two women. The older woman took one with a smile of thanks. The younger one said, "No, thank you, *m'sieu*. My mother and I would offer you and your gallant men breakfast, but we have nothing. Some boche stopped here yesterday and took the last of our provisions."

He reached in the baggy side pocket of his pants, took out a K ration and handed it to her. "Try this. We'll leave you the rations of two of my men before we leave. It should last you until . . . things get better."

Steinmuller called to him and Hunter turned from the women. Steinmuller said, "They told me to shut up, sir. They said they know about the Krauts in Ste. Mère Église and said they'd court-martial me if I sounded off in clear again."

"Okay. What's the situation to the north?"

"Eighty-two didn't say, sir. They just told me to shut up about Ste. Mère Église. The guy at Eighty-two sounded excited."

Hunter nodded and went back to the doorway to call for Falco. Before there was any answer the sky was zippered open above him and he looked up to see a flight of P-51s going somewhere in a hurry. Falco broke cover and was moving his way when a thunderstorm broke to the northwest despite the clear dawn sky. Falco joined him, grinning, and said, "That sounds like big navy stuff, Lieutenant."

Hunter nodded. "They're landing, late as usual. Send runners for O'Hanlon. I'm leaving his body here with Compton's for now. We're giving their rations to the French ladies inside. We'll be moving out in five, so if you spot Sergeant Garson's body anywhere back there, bring him in too, but don't waste time looking."

Falco saluted, turned, and double-timed away as Hunter wondered if he was making the right moves. There were so damned many moves and any of them could be wrong. Jesus, he thought, they made a doctor study eight years before they let him take out a kid's tonsils. Then they give a guy ninety days of OCS and tell him to take a whole platoon into combat and make sure they all get out alive . . .

You weren't supposed to leave your dead behind. You weren't supposed to risk a living man for a dead one. They had a lot of swell double-binds like that in the book. It was probably so that the top brass could chew you out no matter what you did. He wasn't all that worried about being chewed out, but he'd already lost three men without hearing a shot fired in anger and the others were depending on him. Depending on an untried officer who simply didn't really know his trade yet.

He went inside and told Steinmuller to take the R-300 out and get someone to pack it, as if he knew what he was talking about. Then he sat at the bare table and began to fold his map away. The younger French woman came over to him and murmured, "M'sieu and his gallant men are to withdraw?"

"You'll be safer with us out of here," he said. "I have to leave two of my dead. I'm sorry about the greenhouse. If you see about having the bodies cared for the U.S. Army will reward you some day."

She made the sign of the cross and said, "There are things a Christian does not expect payment for. I will tell our priest in the village and he will know what is to be done, hein?"

He nodded his thanks, feeling foolish about the lump in his throat. She said, "My man was killed at the front in 1940. It was up near the Belgian border. One hopes he died among Christians. *Les boches* never told us where my Jean Pierre fell. Perhaps they really did not know."

She put a hand on his shoulder and added softly, "Be careful, *m'sieu.* Our prayers go with you, but sometimes prayers are not enough, *hein?*"

He rose and gravely took her hand. "My father fought here in France in the last war. He always spoke highly of your people. I . . . wish we didn't have to keep meeting like this."

She smiled wearily, and said, "Ah, perhaps someday when this is over *m'sieu* and his gallant men can return as tourists, non?"

"I'd like that, *m'selle.* Or should I say *madame?*"

"At my age, *m'sieu, m'selle* has a pleasant ring to it."

The older woman in the corner cackled something that sounded dirty. Her daughter blushed and said, "I fear my mother thinks we are flirting, *m'sieu.*"

He laughed. "I wish we had time to." Then he kissed her hand and went outside. Steinmuller and Falco had the men lined up across the road in the cover of the hedgerow. He asked about the bodies and Falco said, "Laid out beside the greenhouse, sir. You want to look at them?"

"Negative. We're moving north toward Ste. Mère Église. Falco on point. Steinmuller and the radio here with me in mid-column. The damned hedgerows make flank scouts more bother than they're worth, but let's not walk into anything blind, Falco."

Falco nodded, but said, "I ain't blind, sir. I already know there's supposed to be a mess of Krauts up in Ste. Mère Église."

Another trooper cracked, "Is this trip really necessary?"

The others laughed. That was supposed to be a good sign, according to the book. Maybe they were just stupid? "They dropped us to find the Krauts, and whether they're there or not, Ste. Mère Église is where the nearest outfit was supposed to land. So let's cut the bullshit and move it out."

Falco moved north along the deserted narrow road as the others followed, walking at wide intervals close to the hedges on their left. The hedges on the far side offered as much cover, but if a man had to dive sideways into brush he wanted his right-hand side clear to fire at whatever made him do so. It was eerily quiet in this sector as they crunched the gravel underfoot, but the muttering storm to the north-west seemed louder now. Every once in a while a louder crump of high explosives punctuated the sullen rumble of distant battle, and every time one did, Steinmuller whistled softly and said, "Incoming mail," until Hunter wanted to hit him.

But the tall lieutenant didn't say anything as they trudged on. He knew he was moving on the sound of the guns, like the book said he was supposed to. The book had been sort of vague about why. It was full of neat things like "Move on the guns" and "Take the high ground," and he supposed they made sense, in an OCS classroom. Out here in the field he wasn't so sure.

Could dad ever have felt like this? Dad never talked much about the last war. But Hunter knew he'd been a lieutenant too, and that he'd led them into battle and watched them die. Dad never marched in the Legion parades, back home on the Fourth of July. But he'd seen dad's campaign ribbons in that cigar box he kept them in. They were a little faded now, but there'd been a mess of them. So dad must have done something right. But how had dad *known* what was right? How did anybody know what was right? Jesus H. Christ, those generals and colonels back in England had been planning this invasion since the beginning of the freaking war and they'd dropped everybody in the wrong place!

Two of the men behind Hunter were talking about baseball. He called back, "As you were, damn it! You're being paid to worry about the Third Reich, not the goddamned Dodgers!"

They shut up, abashed by the authority in his voice. Boy, he thought, if only they knew. But they didn't know. Just as those doughboys back in the AEF couldn't have known that Lieutenant Duncan Hunter must have been scared skinny and worried sick as he led his men over the top in '18.

Logan Hunter scratched at the scab on his cheek as he suddenly knew his father for the first time. Not as a father, but as another soldier, and suddenly time took an odd twist and father and son seemed one as Logan Hunter led his stick on the guns, dry-mouthed with anxiety but wearing a crooked little smile of understanding. He knew that if he ever saw dad again they wouldn't have to talk about this. He'd always loved his father, but in years to come, if he made it, they'd share something more between them. He wouldn't have to tell dad much about today. He'd just say he saw the elephant on D day and dad would know what he meant.

He lost sight of the point as Falco rounded a turn. Hunter slowed but kept going. When he picked up the point again Falco was talking to two other men in paratroop kit. Hunter told Steinmuller to hold and moved on to join the trio. As they saw him coming, one of the troopers called out, "You're going the wrong way, sir! We just came from Ste. Mère Église. I don't think anybody else made it out!"

"What happened up that way?" Hunter asked.

"You mean what didn't, sir," the other trooper exclaimed. "We got the shit shot out of us! The fucking fly boys dropped us right over the fucking town instead of the DZ! Guys came down on church steeples and peaked rooftops. One guy took a cross right up the ass! Half the guys got busted up just landing, and then the goddamn Krauts boiled out of the buildings like hornets and that's all she wrote!"

"You two got out."

"Yeah, well, we both run pretty good. Tex, here, ain't from my company, but great minds run in the same channels and we met up outside of town, running like hell. I saw my platoon leader get it so I never waited for orders. It was pure hell, Lieutenant! There's nobody up ahead but a mess of Krauts and the last time we saw them they were acting about as friendly as spitting snakes!"

"We didn't hear any fire and we landed not far from here at 0300."

The one called Tex nodded and said, "You missed the good stuff, then. We landed and it was over in maybe fifteen minutes. They caught us in a sucker play they'll likely all get decorated for. We been running and hiding and running some more ever since.

Is this the road to that there Utah Beach they mentioned?"

"Maybe," Hunter said. "You don't want to go there if you're offended by noise. There's a German army between us and the beach. And unless it's the Fourth when the wind's right you can hear that somebody's still fighting like hell over there. You two move back and fall in with my men. Falco, you're still on point and I don't remember ordering a piss break."

Falco looked uncertain. Then he nodded and moved up the road as the one called Tex said, "We ain't going back to no Ste. Mère Église, sir!"

Hunter smiled pleasantly and said, "I didn't hear that. Didn't your mother ever tell you that they shoot men in this man's army for refusing to obey a commissioned officer?"

"But, sir, there's nothing but fucking Krauts up ahead! The Eighty-second's been Little-Big-Horned!"

"So you keep telling me. I like to see for myself."

"Lieutenant, you're fixing to get us all killed!"

"Maybe. You want to die right here and now as a deserter or do you want to straighten up and soldier, trooper?"

He didn't receive an answer. He nodded and, seeing Falco was well ahead now, signaled back to Steinmuller to resume the march. He told the two frightened troopers to fall in near the head of the column, where he could keep an eye on them.

The sun was up now, and Hunter moved his men to the right side of the roadway, giving up the edge with their carbines in favor of keeping them less visible in the shade of the hedges on the right hand side of the roadway. The wind had either shifted or the fighting down on the beaches was picking up. He heard the distant woodpecker rattle of a machine gun and when Steinmuller commented on it, he said, "Yeah, it was too rapid fire for one of ours, so the Krauts must be falling back from Utah. I make it a couple of miles away, though, so don't sweat it. They have to be aiming at somebody else."

He trudged on. Behind him, a man muttered, "Jesus, the looie sure is taking this all more cool than yours truly!" Another trooper laughed and answered, "Quit your bitching. You never had it so good. Me and the looie brush our teeth with brillo pads. That's 'cause we are paree-troopers. Didn't they tell you back in Benning that Superman was washed out of the paree-troopers for being too soft?"

The book said they were all right as long as they were bitching and joking. What the hell was he supposed to do when they stopped? The two stragglers he'd picked up were already on the verge of mutiny. What if they infected the other men? Maybe he should have let them run on. But the book said you couldn't let men break under fire and they'd have been captured for sure if he'd let them wander deeper into occupied France on their own. What would dad have done? What *could* dad have done? What if they were right and he was leading his stick into a Kraut ambush? What else was there to do? There were Krauts for *sure* in every other direction and Eighty-second Division had said they knew about the one in Ste. Mère Église, right?

Sure, and what if they meant they knew the Krauts still held the town and that there was nothing anybody could do about it until the main army moved in off the beachhead?

Hunter missed a step and stiffened as a plane whipped over, low and screaming with its superchargers. Then he saw it was a P-38 and moved on as the twin-tailed fighter-bomber zoomed skyward like a hornet looking for something in its sky worth stinging. The sunlight glinted on its wings and twin props as it banked with sinister beauty. Hunter grinned and said, "Go get 'em, fly-boy. I'm glad I'm not a Kraut this morning!"

The P-38 hung motionless for a moment at the peak of its climbing turn. Hunter frowned and murmured, "Hey fly-boy, you can't be *serious!*"

Then he shouted, "Off the road and take cover!" as the P-38 dove back toward them, nose guns spitting at the men the eager pilot had spotted on a road behind the German lines.

Not waiting to see if his command was obeyed, Logan Hunter dove headfirst through a thin place in the hedges, landed in high grass, and clawed though it on his belly to get as far from the road as possible. It suddenly hit him what a cockroach must feel like when somebody turns on the kitchen lights unexpectedly.

The earth heaved under Hunter as the P-38 dropped its wing bombs for good measure on the far side of the hedges. Hunter rolled over and looked up as the P-38 zoomed skyward, banked again, and reversed course to strafe them again.

Hunter stayed where he was, hoping the grass looked taller from up there than it did down here. But as the fighter-bomber made its second pass Sergeant Steinmuller was on his feet, waving his helmet at the oncoming plane as he shouted, "G.I.! G.I.! You crazy son of a bitch!"

"Steinmuller, *down!*" Hunter yelled. He saw the pilot had spotted the sergeant and was swinging his nose guns that way. Steinmuller saw too, and dropped to the ground, too late, as the spitting .50 chewed a

path of rising dust and clods across the open field
. . . and across Steinmuller.

Hunter groaned and buried his face in the sod as
the P-38 roared over, apparently not seeing him. As
the banshee wail of the twin engines faded he raised
his head, then cursed. The silly son of a bitch had
found a home. He was banking to come over them
again.

Hunter drew his pistol, even as he wondered why.
The stupid fly boy was American in the first place and
you couldn't hit a plane with a .45 in the second. But
he had to do *something*. His men were getting slaugh-
tered.

The P-38 roared over again, spitting death, then
once more climbed into the sky to chandelle around
for another pass. But at the peak of its climb, the right
engine suddenly burst into flames.

The men around Hunter cheered and he looked to
see why. Then he spotted the yellow-nosed ME-109
above and beyond the shot-up American plane. The
German pilot was an eager beaver too. He recovered
from his first pass and dove back to finish the P-38
off as it started to maple-seed down, trailing a cork-
screw of black smoke. The American pilot bailed out
just before the ME-109 opened fire again to finish it
off in a big ball of flame and flying debris. A man
stood up. Hunter yelled, "Down, damn it! That Kraut's
not on our side, either!"

But apparently the German thought he was. He flew
over them doing a victory roll before roaring off to the
south, waving bye-bye with his wing tips. Hunter
laughed despite himself and muttered, "I never
thought I'd be so glad to see one of *you* guys."

He got to his feet, walked over to where Steinmuller lay, and gagged. Others were getting to their

feet. "Okay," he called out, "reassemble on the road and let's have a roll call."

As he pushed through the hedges again he spotted Falco coming his way. The corporal stepped around a bomb crater in the roadway and said, "Jesus, I thought for a while I was all alone in the world, sir!"

"I know the feeling," Hunter said. "You just made sergeant, Falco. Steinmuller bought the farm out there. Let's get them lined up and see who else that crazy bastard got before the Kraut nailed him."

"He didn't nail him, sir. I saw him coming down over there to the northwest. He was a lousy parachutist, but I think he made it."

"That's his problem," Hunter growled, turning away as the others joined them on the road. Hunter waited a few moments to make sure. Then he counted again and said, "I see nine noses and we're supposed to have fourteen. What can anybody tell me about the other four, besides the sergeant?"

The stray called Tex said, "They got that guy that was with me, sir. I think his name was LeRoy."

"I was with Dugan. It was awful," Arnold said. "He took a round in his head and it even blew his helmet to shit."

The other two were swiftly accounted for and Hunter realized with mixed emotions that he had no wounded to worry about. Massed .50 fire didn't leave many wounded in its wake. He repressed a shudder and said, "Okay. Falco's the new sergeant. Arnold, you get out on point. Let's get out of here."

Young Arnold looked surprised. "You want *me* on point, sir?"

"Why not you, Arnold? Somebody has to take the point."

"Yessir, but I just got here. I've never been in combat before."

Hunter grimaced and said, "Welcome to the club. This is my first jump too. Move it out, Arnold. Thomas, you get to lug that R-300. So stay close to me or Sergeant Falco."

He had his decimated stick moving again when Falco, at his side, cleared his throat and observed, "Begging the lieutenant's pardon, that Arnold kid is pretty green."

"We're all green, Falco. You see any other men in this stick who've been around the block before?"

Falco nodded and said, "Yessir. Me. I made the Sicily jump with the Eighty-second back in '43."

Hunter didn't answer as he digested that. He knew he'd been caught not knowing what was in each of his men's 201 files. The book said a good officer knew the name of every one of his men's wives and children. But the asshole who'd written that had served in a peacetime army, when garrisons stayed together a while instead of playing musical replacements. He grimaced and said, "I should have known, Falco. But I didn't. How come you're still a two striper—or were until just now—if you were in combat a year ago?"

Falco shrugged. "I'm sort of a fuck-up, sir. I don't mind the soldiering, like right now. But there's something about me and inspecting officers that just don't go together. You know what I mean?"

Hunter chuckled. "I know what you mean. How many times have you been busted, Falco?"

"Gee, Lieutenant, who counts? It's like asking me how many dames I've laid in my time. The last time was for sort of bending a couple of MPs out of shape. I mean, Idda *shown* them my fucking pass if they'd asked me *polite*. But they never. I was with this nice-looking tomato in a pub when this jerk-off MP started up with me like I was dirt or something. I mean, a guy can't take no shit with a woman watching, right?"

Hunter nodded. "I get the picture. I hear the Eighty-second took a bad time in Sicily."

"Ninety-four percent casualties. Of course most of them was only wounded guys. I guess maybe half the outfit bought the farm. I was never even scratched. But my stick was so shot up they sent to the repo depot, and then when you guys reformed for this jump—"

Hunter cut in with a frown to say, "Jesus, they never told us you took casualties like that. If you came through alive you must know something."

Falco shrugged and said, "There ain't much to know, sir. You keep your ass down and your trap shut, and if they ain't killed you in two weeks you just keep making the same moves and *nobody* can kill you no more."

"Okay. Man to man, Falco—how do you like the moves I've made so far?"

Falco didn't answer.

"Come on, Falco," Hunter insisted.

Falco shook his head and said, "It ain't my place. You're an officer. I ain't."

"Damn it, Sergeant, don't pull reverse rank on me. You're the only man I have who knows his ass from his elbow. So level with me. What would you be doing right now if you were in command?"

Falco hesitated. Then he said, "Well, sir, I sure as hell wouldn't be headed into a town full of Krauts with nine men after hearing they'd shot up a couple of outfits."

"Then where would you go, Falco?"

"I ain't sure, sir. But it sure as shit wouldn't be Ste. Mère Église."

Hunter nodded as they walked on. He saw that Arnold, up ahead, was scouting the bends in the road by the book. Falso waited until they'd walked on a couple of hundred yards before he cleared his throat again and asked, "Lieutenant?"

"Yeah?"

"Are we still headed for Ste. Mère Église?"

"That's where they told me this road leads, Sergeant."

"I remember, sir. But what if Eighty-second ain't there? What if them stragglers was right and the outfit's been wiped out?"

"I, for one, will be very sorry. But I don't see that we have much choice, do you?"

Falco didn't answer. That was the trouble with officers. They asked for your fucking advice and then they never took it. But the looie had a point. Falco knew there were Krauts ahead no matter which way they went, and the one thing he liked about being an enlisted man was that you didn't have to think so hard. You just did like the fucking officers told you, and if they got you killed, it was *their* fault.

2

TRAFFIC WAS HEAVY south of London that morning and got worse as one neared the channel ports. Military vehicles hogged the narrow English roads like they owned them. That morning they did. Military and civilian police were shunting nonmilitary traffic on to dirt side roads or stopping them outright if they couldn't reach their destinations by detour. But Ramie Davis and her assistant, Beth Waterman, were driving a pretty good bluff. Ramie had selected an Austin sedan from the UPI motor pool that, like its two comely passengers, wore quasi-military kit. The Austin was painted the same olive drab as a military staff car and, while the legality was in question, it sported white stars and some meaningless letters and numerals on hood and bumpers. The two girls, of course, wore correspondent's uniforms the same color and cut as if they'd been WAC officers. For-bidden indications of rank, each wore a black UPI patch on her shoulder. Ramie was used to being saluted by soldiers on the street by now, but it still made Beth giggle.

Beth Waterman was younger and newer to the ETO than the experienced Ramie. Beth was a blue-eyed brunette who'd been told in her teens that she re-minded people of Betty Boop and sometimes she over-played the part. Ramie had selected her because men found her so cute. As far as Ramie knew, Beth didn't put out any more than the other girls they worked with, but she looked like she did.

As they rode with the shortwave set on the seat between them Beth pointed at a sign they were pass-ing and said, "Oh, you're going the wrong way, Ramie! That's the way to Southampton, but you missed the turn!"

"We'd never make Southampton, Beth. That's where everyone seems to be going. Didn't they tell you I've been covering the build-up down here for weeks?"

Beth popped her gum and said, "Well, you're the boss. But I still think we should have turned. This road we're on seems to be petering out."

Ramie switched on the car radio without answering. Ahead through the windshield the road was narrowing down to two-lane hard top. But she knew what she was doing. The sky ahead was lightly overcast and a flight of planes was moving across her line of vision. She couldn't make out their outlines too well. They were either bombers or transports. She wondered if that silly Major Bradley had made it back in time to go in with his men. She laughed and when Beth asked why, she said, "I was just thinking of a silly twit I used to date. He was always pulling that corny old line

35

about leaving for the front any minute. You know how it goes, of course?"

Beth popped her gum again. "Oh, do I ever! I had a quartermaster supply sergeant telling me that sob story just a few nights ago."

"You shouldn't date enlisted men," Ramie said, searching the dial with her free hand.

"Pooh," Beth pouted, "I don't see what's wrong with enlisted men. I'm not a snob. And some of them are cute."

"Yes, but they can't give you a scoop and we're supposed to be reporters. Hush, I think this is CBS!"

A high-pitched male voice crackled weakly from the radio under the dash against a background of what sounded like crackling cellophane. They'd picked him up in mid-sentence as he said, ". . . going up the sea wall now. I'm afraid things are a bit confusing on this stretch of beach, ladies and gentleman, but from where I'm crouching I can see the flash of German guns atop the cliffs seems to be lessening and . . . yes, there go the rangers! Oh, if only you could see this, ladies and gentlemen! It's just incredible! I make out five, six, no, eight men going up the cliffs on ropes like alpine climbers and here comes some more of our fighter planes and, oh, lovely, they're firing their wing rockets into those pill boxes up there and . . ." The voice was cut off as if by a switch and a moment of white static was followed by a new voice, saying, "Stand by, ladies and gentlemen. We seem to be experiencing some technical difficulties. But we'll be right back on the air with more of the incredible events of this historic occasion."

A singing commercial came on and Ramie switched off the radio. "There, you see? I told you they'd have reporters with them, Beth. All we have to do is find some officer I know with the rank to get us across."

She made a sudden turn onto a dirt lane. Beth, caught off guard, grabbed the door handle and gasped, "Christ! I'll have bruises for a week! What on earth are we going this way for?"

"Commando camp I know about. In peacetime it's a yacht basin. It's so hush-hush that most of our competition doesn't know about it. But I was down here interviewing a British rear admiral a while back, and from the way he kept staring at my boobs, I think he liked me."

"Oh. Does he have a friend?"

"Down, girl. Aside from being married, Admiral Kane is old enough to be our father. Come to think of it, he's old enough to be his wife's father. But he's a nice old man."

They topped a rise and Beth gasped "Help!" as the road dropped down a perilous incline toward a small harbor scooped out of the white chalk cliffs by the sea.

"We're in luck," Ramie said, spotting the landing craft lined up along the sea wall. "They haven't left yet!"

A British sentry tried to stop them as they hit the bottom of the incline and tore through the open gate with Ramie waving her press pass out the window. Beth hunched down in her seat and muttered, "Oh, you're going to get us shot!"

Ramie braked to a stop in front of a long nondescript wooden building. "Leave the radio for now and try to look sexy," she said as she opened her door and got out.

A startled-looking man in commando battle kit was coming out of the building. "Beg pardon, miss, but this is a restricted area."

"I'm Davis of UPI. Is the Admiral inside?"

"Yes, but I'm afraid he's dreadfully busy at the moment."

"That's what we want to talk to him about. Come on, Beth."

Commando training didn't cover unarmed combat with what seemed to be female Yank officers, so the commando could only mutter protests as they swept grandly by him and went inside.

He'd been right about the admiral being busy. The situation room was full of officers in RN and Commando kit moving what looked like Monopoly pieces on a big map table. There was an awkward pause as the two women barged in. Then a tall, lean man wearing white sideburns and a lot of gold on the sleeves of his navy blues rose and said, "I say, Miss Davis, this is a pleasure, but dash it all!"

Ramie dimpled and said, "We'll only take a minute of your time, Admiral Kane. UPI sent us down especially to cover your part in the invasion."

"Oh, dear . . . We'd better go into my office. Excuse me, gentlemen. Carry on with the plot."

Kane moved around the map table, took Ramie by the arm and led her and Beth out of the situation room, saying, "Nobody's supposed to see that without top clearance. How on earth did you ladies get on this base?"

"Pull," Ramie replied. She introduced her co-worker as the admiral took them to a small spartan office and firmly shut the door. He waved them to seats by his desk but said, "I say, what we're doing here is dreadfully hush-hush and all that. Actually, this unit isn't supposed to exist at all, so one would hardly want a story about it in the papers, what?"

"Your commandos are back-up reserves, right?" Ramie said.

Kane looked pained, sat on the edge of his desk, and said, "I'll let you in on a few things if you'll give me your word you won't print it in less than forty-eight hours. By then it won't do Jerry any good one way or the other, but he's not to know we're here until things become more settled on the other side of the channel. I shouldn't be talking to you at all, but I know how perishing persistent you can be, Ramie. So one hand washes the other, eh?"

Ramie nodded. "You have my word, sir."

"Oh, let's not go all bloody military, Ramie. You know my name is Ivor. By the way, Alexandra and I are having a cocktail party next week, weather and the Third Reich permitting. You have our address in Belgravia, don't you? They say Ike may be there, if he can get away."

Ramie nodded but said, "You were going to tell us what's going on, Ivor."

"Was I? Oh, dear, I really wish they'd let us fight this perishing war without you reporters looking over our shoulders. Makes a man look like a bloody ass at times."

He took out a gold cigarette case, offered Wood-bines all around, and stalled by gallantly lighting the women's cigarettes while he decided how much he should say. He finally sighed and said, "Can't tell you any details, but you've already guessed we're acting as a sort of fire brigade."

Ramie nodded. "Your lot goes in when and if the first wave on Sword or Juno gets bogged down, right?"

"My dear girl, you're not supposed to have the code names for our beaches! I can see you've been chatting with someone at SHAEF and the blighter really ought to be shot. But, very well, that's about the size of it. I can tell you, since the Jerries must certainly know it by now, that our lads landed rather neatly in their sector. You Yanks seem to have picked beaches the Jerries were inclined to be more difficult about. Utah seems to be going rather well at the moment, but I'm certainly unhappy about the latest dispatches from Omaha. Rather unexpected, since the Jerries there are farthest from their own main forces. By the way, you remember that Major Bradley you brought to the Chalmer's party that time?"

Ramie grimaced. "I haven't seen Dan Bradley for some time."

Kane said, "Good. Never could stand the chap. But from what I hear, he's earning his keep today. Last dispatches were rather grim. Their commanding officer broke his leg coming down and it seems the Jerries were expecting them."

When Ramie laughed, Kane looked blank and asked, "Did I say something funny?"

"No, I'm terribly sorry about those poor troopers, but you see, Danny Boy didn't jump with them last night. He was in London on leave. Making annoying telephone calls, as a matter of fact."

"Oh, I know who you're talking about," Beth said. "He's that good-looking blond major with all the medals. I think he's cute."

Ramie wrinkled her nose and said, "He's all yours. Can I quote you on the airborne SNAFU, Ivor?"

"Heaven, no! It's an American show. Besides, I don't really know the details. Our lot merely listened in an the shortwave back and forths. Your Bradley seems to have picked the right time to go on leave, though. From the little I know, the 101st seems to have blundered rather badly and Lord knows what's happened to them since they went off the air."

"He's not *my* Bradley," Ramie said firmly. "I gave

him back to the girls in Trafalgar Square some time ago. As to just what may or may not be going on across the channel, that's one of the things we wanted to talk to you about, Ivor. Beth and I need a ride. How do we go about boarding something that can take us across to the beachhead?"

"Now I know you're mad! It's out of the question! Our supply craft are still coming in under heavy fire and nobody would be responsible for civilians over there, male or female!"

Ramie shook her head stubbornly and said, "Oh, come now, we were just listening to a radio newscaster broadcasting from the beach over there, Ivor."

"Quite. That would be young Muller. Special dispensation from Ike. He's over there alone. Your major Yank broadcasting systems are pooling his dispatches. Ike says he can afford maybe one young and silly newscaster, but he's refused to allow any others to join Muller before the landings are secured. Maybe in a day or so, Ramie."

"In a day or so my old high school newspaper will have Muller's scoop on page one, Ivor! It's not fair! I've been over here since the blitz, waiting for a story like this! You have to get us across!"

"Out of the question. We just got a call from the palace. His Majesty got word that Winnie is motoring down with the same silly thought in mind and we've direct orders from the Crown that not even Churchill is to play in the sand over there until we're sure we're there to stay. It's still touch and go, old girl. Our lot could be pushed back in the water at any moment. If I were you I'd run over to Yank GHQ. They really have a better grasp on what's going on over there than we do here."

"You're not me, damn it," Ramie said. She rose to

her feet as she added, "Come on, Beth. I'll find some way to get you and that radio across, if we have to swim."

Beth rose with a sigh and said, "How do I get a transfer out of this chicken outfit?"

Trooper Arnold slowed down and hugged the hedgerow to his left as the narrow roadway wound around another bend. The sun was higher now, and even a green soldier could see they'd have him in a bowling alley situation if he walked into anything important on the far side. Arnold was learning to hate hedgerows. Some of the bushes were in bloom and the buzzing of bees mingled with the distant rumble of battle. Normandy was post-card pretty until a guy thought of all the places a German sniper could be hiding in all that bucolic scenery. Arnold resisted an impulse to look back. He knew the others were keeping him in sight. But he still felt alone out here on point. In all those war movies they were making, the hero always walked ahead of his men and they stayed close enough to *talk* to one another. He'd learned in basic why guys didn't move like that in real combat. But it still felt lonesome.

Arnold held his carbine muzzle pointed the way he was going like they'd taught him. But it still felt sort of dumb. He knew there wouldn't be anybody around the bend. The young trooper had enough humor to smile thinly at his own dramatics as he eased around the curve, looking like Errol Flynn in that dumb picture for God's sake. He was expecting more of the same sort of boring view down the gravel between the hedgerows. The Frogs didn't live on their farms like folks back home. They clustered together around a church and communal manure pit and walked or rode out a couple of miles or more to work the fields. On a day like this, the fields were empty, of course. But that farmstead where Compton bought it had been a good walk north of the main clump back there, if those women had been telling the truth. So they ought to be coming to more houses soon. The stick had been on this road for hours and how damned far could a Frog farmer walk?

He studied the road ahead for a time, then stepped clear of the hedge and signaled with his carbine that the bend was clear before he moved on. It felt like he had a pebble in his boot. How in hell could a guy get a pebble inside a paratroop boot? They were laced halfway up his shins and the pants were bloused below the tops, tucked under the rubber contraceptives most troopers used to keep them in place. Regulations said you were supposed to tuck the pants in the boot tops and use the three rubbers they issued you with every pass to keep from getting VD. But everyone knew the pants never stayed in the boots that way, and who the hell met that many dames, for Pete's sake?

A bird twittered at Arnold from the shrubbery and he said, "Aw, shut up." It was funny how the birds and bees didn't seem to know there was a war on. The rumble of big guns to the northeast was constant now. The looie said they were moving sort of in line with the coast. But nobody along this boring road seemed to give a damn. Didn't the damned road ever end?

"Count your blessings," he muttered aloud. He was getting used to being on point. It wasn't half as interesting as he'd expected. But that didn't mean he wanted to meet any damned Germans. He didn't know what the hell he'd do if he met any Germans. He'd never seen one, except in a war movie, and he still wasn't sure he believed in them. Germans were sort of like Eskimos. He knew who they were and what they looked like, but they weren't the sort of things you ever really expected to see in the flesh.

Arnold was half-aware he was falling into the sloppy mental state a soldier wasn't supposed to, but always did when the first excitement trailed off into dull routine. He knew he was supposed to stay alert and on his toes out there on point, but he was tired and drained and the dumb whatever in his boot was bothering him more than anything he expected to see up the road ahead in the next million years. So his stockless carbine was at port arms and he was looking down when a man suddenly burst out of the hedges up ahead, spotted Arnold, and froze in place, with one hand undecided about the pistol in the shoulder holster he wore outside his leather jacket. Arnold gasped, came unstuck, and dropped to one knee with the carbine muzzle trained on the unexpected target. Arnold's mouth was dry and his heart started hammering as if it wanted to come out and fly away. He didn't know if he should fire or not. He didn't know what to do. Like the other surprised man, Arnold was frozen with buck fever.

The leather-clad figure gave a resigned shrug and slowly raised his hands shoulder-high. Something clicked in Arnold's head and he nodded and called out, "Coming zee here, march snail!"

The man didn't move. But his hands were still up, so what the hell? Arnold looked back, saw the looie legging it his way, and moved in on the prisoner. As he got closer, the ex-aviation cadet frowned thoughtfully and said, "Hey, you ain't no German, are you?"

The other man shook his head. "I'm Eighth Air Force. What about you?"

"Airborne. Was that you in that fucking P-38?"

"Yeah, I had to bail out. Damned 109 jumped me while I was strafing some Krauts."

Hunter trotted up to Arnold's position, .45 drawn. He nodded and said, "Good work. What do we have here, Arnold?"

"He says he's that fly-boy that shot us up back there, sir. Do we get to shoot him?"

Hunter ran his eyes over the prisoner's U.S. flying togs and wearily shook his head. "You can put your hands down. Hunter, here. First John, 101st Airborne."

"I'm Captain Rowan, 557th Fighter. Are you guys trying to tell me that was *you* a few miles back?"

Hunter nodded grimly. "Not trying. Telling. Congratulations, Captain. You're one hell of a pilot. You cost us five men back there. You'd better stick close to me and my sergeant until the others get used to the idea. We'll drop you off in Ste. Mère Église. if regiment's there, and if we ever get there."

Rowan licked his lips and stammered, "I thought you were *Krauts*! Jesus, I sure feel lousy."

"Not as lousy as the troopers you nailed, but what the hell, I cheered when that Nazi shot you out of the sky, too." He turned to Arnold. "Before you take the point again, you didn't hear much of this conversation, right?"

Arnold nodded and said, "Yessir, I can see how it might be better to break it to them gently." Then he saluted and moved on. As Hunter signaled Falco to move the others up to them, Rowan asked, "What's my story?"

"If I were you, Captain, I'd keep my mouth shut. I'll handle my men. You stay close to me and do as you're told."

Rowan frowned thoughtfully. "Ah, you did say you were only a lieutenant, didn't you?"

"Yeah, you outrank me by one grade." Then Hunter holstered his .45, threw a vicious left hook and put the fly-boy on the ground with a split lip and dazed expression. As Rowan started to rise, Hunter kicked him flat on his back and snapped, "Listen and listen tight, you silly son of a bitch! Strafing us may have been an honest mistake. Pulling rank on an officer after you've just killed five of his men is more than a mistake. It's suicidal idiocy! Any further questions?"

The pilot didn't answer as he sat up, wiping his mouth with a palm and staring in wonder at the blood he saw there. Acting Sergeant Falco halted the others and came to join them. "Trouble, sir?"

"It's over," Hunter said. "Captain Rowan here was the pilot of that P-38 and I guess I got carried away as we were rehashing things. I'm making you responsible for him, Falco. We're taking him with us and nobody's allowed to hit him but me."

Hunter waved the men on after Arnold as Falco bent to help the pilot to his feet. Rowan's voice was more bewildered than annoyed as he told Falco, "He cold-cocked me! I said I was sorry and he just hauled off and cold-cocked me!"

Falco hauled him erect and said, "Yeah, Captain. I can see he gave you a real fat lip. But it could have been worse. If I'd been out on point instead of that kid Arnold, you'd be dead right now."

"I'm going to report this," Rowan muttered, shaking himself free of Falco.

"You do that, Captain. Are you wearing shoes under them fleece-lined boots?"

"No, of course not. Why?"

"You got a lot of walking to do. It's too bad we met

up so far from the place you strafed us. We left five pairs of paratroop boots back there and one of 'em might have fit you. Let's catch up with the others, okay?"

Rowan nodded and they started legging it to rejoin the column. Rowan didn't like the burly noncom's attitude. The way he spoke to a commissioned officer bordered on insubordination. But as he ran his tongue gingerly over his split lip the captain decided this was hardly the time to put Falco in his place. Instead, he said lightly, "I suppose you paratroopers know more than I do about fighting down here on the ground."

"That's right, Captain. You can always cut out on your own if you don't like our style."

Rowan kept his thoughts to himself. He wasn't about to cut out on his own deep in enemy territory. But he didn't like their style one little bit. Okay, maybe he'd made a mistake, but that gave them no right to cold-cock a superior officer and talk down to him like this. Rowan knew he was going to get hell for strafing the wrong men. But these things happen in a war and if he could save up enough counter-charges against that cocky Lieutenant Hunter . . .

Aloud, he said, "We were told friendly forces would have identification panels to spread out when we came over, Sergeant."

"They never issued us none. I don't think I'd have wanted to draw attention from the air in any case, Captain. There was some ME-109s up there too, re-member?"

"Maybe. But how the hell was I supposed to know you guys weren't Germans? You were moving on a road deep inside the German lines and my mission was to interdict all road traffic behind their lines."

"You sure interdicted the shit out of us, Captain. But let's drop it. What's done is done and we're more worried about the road ahead than what happened behind us."

They walked a time in silence. Then Falco said, "Hey, Captain, you must have flown over Ste. Mère Église, right?"

"I don't know. A town's a town from the air. Why?"

"It's the next good-sized town up the coast and that's where the looie's taking us. You sure you didn't fly over it?"

"We never fly over a town we don't have to. Flack can take years off your life. Now that I think back, though, there was a town I could see from topside. You say it's due north?"

"Close enough to due north, Captain. Why?"

"Hell, there's no sense in heading that way. The town was burning pretty good. I passed over close enough to catch some harassing fire. I only saw it from an angle, but it looked pretty shot up and I don't think the flack coming my way could have been fired from American guns, do you?"

Falco grimaced and said, "Hell, even I can recognize a P-38 going by! There ain't another plane on either side you could mistake for a P-38. You better tell the looie about that flack, Captain."

"You tell him. I don't think he likes me."

Falco grinned crookedly and was about to start jogging forward when Hunter stepped to the middle of the road and raised a hand. "Ten-minute break and piss call. Smoke if you got 'em but don't break out rations or benzedrine just now."

The men sighed wearily and moved over to the roadside to flop down. Only one man stayed on his feet to piss into the bushes. They'd only notice later, Falco thought, how seldom you had to go on a forced march.

Hunter waited until the men were settled before he sank down to rest his legs with his back to a sapling woven into the hedge behind him.

He was lighting a smoke when Falco joined him. Falco hunkered down and repeated what the pilot had told him. Hunter blew smoke out his nose and said, "That was hours ago. A lot can happen in a war in that time."

Falco sighed and said, "Begging the lieutenant's pardon, he's got wax in his ears! If Eighty-second was holding the town they'd be controlling the fires and they wouldn't be shooting at no P-38s, even with that asshole in the driver's seat!"

Hunter nodded and said, "I know. But, to repeat, it was a while back and there wouldn't *be* any fires if somebody hadn't hit that town good. Let's say our guys moved in and the Krauts pulled back to fire at Rowan from Indian country. Flack guns have wheels, remember?"

"Sir, I don't know shit about no flack guns. But I do know that only the Krauts shoot them at anybody, and if you're right about them hauling ass, that still puts them between our position and Eighty-second's, right?"

"No argument, Falco. But look at it this way. There are Krauts between us and *every* American position. At least we know our side is some damned where around Ste. Mère Église. So that's where we're headed. Any other questions?"

"Yeah, Lieutenant. What the fuck are we supposed to be doing here? I mean, since we jumped last night all we've been doing is floundering around and getting killed. Ain't there supposed to be some point to all this shit?"

It was a good question. Hunter wasn't sure he had any good answers. "It was simple enough at the briefing before we took off. From there on things get complicated. First the regimental S2 turned up missing and the colonel had to reshuffle the deck, delaying our take-off. It still would have worked if they'd dropped us anywhere near the right place. But you were there and you know they screwed that part up. I guess our mission now is just to stay alive until we can somehow get back to regiment and see what else the colonel has in mind for us to do."

Falco wanted to say that staying alive while advancing on a town everybody said was still held by the Krauts was a contradiction in terms, but they'd been over that ground, so what the hell.

Captain Rowan came over to them and sat down uninvited, complaining that he had no cigarettes. Hunter didn't offer him one. The army paid Rowan, and a guy was supposed to think ahead. Grubbing smokes was considered the mark of a raw recruit or a real slob.

Hunter looked up to see Trooper Arnold hunkered nearby. He asked, mildly, "Arnold, what the hell are you doing back here?"

Arnold blinked and said, "Didn't you call a break, sir?"

"I did. I put you out on point, too. I don't remember ordering anyone to relieve you. Who the hell's watching the road ahead?"

"Uh, I guess nobody is, sir."

"You're wrong, Arnold. You are. Get your ass up to the next bend and stay there until somebody tells you different. You can sit down, you can smoke, you can even jerk off, but if I catch you doping off again I'll court-martial your ass. On the double, Arnold!"

The chewed-out trooper got to his feet and moved wearily up the road as Captain Rowan chuckled and said, "I see you run a tight ship, Lieutenant."

"It's not a ship. It's what's left of an airborne stick and I've lost some of my best men."

There was no graceful way to answer that, so Rowan didn't try.

Trooper Arnold moved up to the bend and hunkered down where he could see both his comrades and the road beyond. He laid his carbine across his thighs and fumbled for the smokes in his jacket, muttering to himself. His head was down, but he looked up when he heard a tinny woodpecker noise. His jaw dropped and for a moment he just sat there as a motorcycle with a side car, carrying two men in black uniforms and coal-scuttle helmets, came down the road toward him trailing a cloud of dust.

The two Germans spotted him and the driver swung the handlebars and hit his brakes, sliding broadside toward Arnold as the man in the side car raised the Schmeiser machine pistol in his lap. Arnold rolled sideways off his rump in what would have been blind panic if the young trooper hadn't been making the right moves they'd drilled into him over and over again at Benning and ever since. The equally rattled German fired wildly with his Schmeiser, tearing the hedgerow above Arnold into wet green confetti as meanwhile the American wound up on his belly in the classic prone position of the rifle range. Later, Arnold would have no conscious memory of aiming or even squeezing the trigger. But as the motorcycle rig smashed into the far wall of brush and stalled,

Arnold emptied his magazine into them in one long burst of automatic fire.

Like every paratrooper wearing the wings, Arnold had been required to qualify with his weapon on the range and, now that it really counted, he fully justified his sharpshooter's rating by putting three out of four rounds into the screaming Krauts as they rolled off and out of their burning rig.

There was a hollow click and Arnold gasped, ears ringing, as he realized he'd emptied his weapon. Across the road the motorcycle lay burning on its side with the empty sidecar skyward, wheel still spinning. Arnold saw the two Krauts sprawled in the gravel like discarded rag dolls, but he gasped in panic and clawed at his ammo belt, sobbing and feeling dumb and helpless. He was trying to shove a spare clip in without removing the empty one when Lieutenant Hunter ran up, .45 drawn, and dropped beside Arnold, asking, "Are you hit, soldier?"

"I don't think so, sir. But I guess I hit *them* motherfuckers!"

Hunter stared across at the two figures sprawled in the road. "That's for damned sure."

He saw Arnold was still rattled. So as Falco and Tex ran up to them he snapped, "Falco, move somebody further up the road while I have a look at those Krauts."

Falco nodded. "I'll cover you, sir," he said, and ran up the road to the next bend. Hunter got up and moved across to the nearest German. He rolled the body over with his foot as Arnold and Tex joined him.

"That's the uniform them Krauts we dropped on top of was wearing, sir," Tex said. "Is he SS?"

Hunter shook his head as he knelt by the black-uniformed corpse. "Panzer. Rommel's guys like to look pretty, too. But that pink piping on his shoulder straps gives him away as just a tanker. You got an officer and his driver, Arnold. Those three silver pips make him a captain. Let's see what's in his pockets."

Arnold stared down soberly as Hunter went through the dead German's pockets. The only sound was the puttering of burning gasoline from the motorcycle, and a damn fool bird tweeting in the hedges. The German officer lay faceup, eyes open, with a bemused smile on his face. He didn't look dead. He looked like he should be saying something as Hunter searched his uniform. He didn't look like Nazis were supposed to look, either. He just looked like an ordinary guy of maybe thirty. Arnold licked his lips and wondered if he should feel sorry for the dead Kraut. He didn't feel anything much. Wasn't a guy supposed to feel some damned thing after he'd just killed two guys? Arnold swallowed and asked, "Did I do right, sir?"

Hunter handed up a grey cardboard passbook and said, "You sure did. Look how you punched his ticket, soldier."

Arnold took the passbook and saw there were two small neat bullet holes in it. He opened it. One of the rounds had gone through the German's ID photo. But you could see it was the same guy. The lettering under it read, "HOLZER, FRANZ, HAUPTMANN, PANZERKAMPFWAGEN OKW." Arnold wondered what he was supposed to do with the thing. It wasn't the sort of war trophy a guy might ever want to show his kids. One of those helmets would look nice on a den wall someday, but they were too heavy to worry about right now.

Hunter took out a letter-sized manila envelope and

opened it as he muttered, "Damn, I wish Steinmuller hadn't bought the farm back there!" He scanned the typewritten pages inside and added, "It's probably in code as well as Kraut, anyway. We'll let regiment worry about that. Arnold, see if there's a briefcase or anything in that side car. Watch out you don't burn yourself. That metal has to be hot. I'll see what the other Kraut was carrying."

He headed for the other body lying facedown in the road as Arnold moved to the wrecked motorcycle rig. As he knelt by the driver, Tex yelled, "Watch it! He's still alive!" Hunter flinched back and fired his .45 at point-blank range as the possum-playing German rolled over, pistol in hand.

Hunter's .45 round took the driver over the eyebrow and his head snapped back as if a ghostly hangman had yanked a noose around his neck. As the body went limp Hunter whistled and said, "That's one I owe you, Tex!"

Arnold ran over from the side car, gasping, "I thought I killed the bastard, sir!"

"You did," Hunter said. "He just didn't know it yet. I don't know how he came through it with all those carbine slugs in him either, but they say some guys are like that."

"Like a durned old rattlesnake," Tex added, as Hunter went through the fresh corpse's pockets and only found the ID of a panzer NCO.

Hunter stood up and said, "All right. I think what we have here was a staff officer going someplace else in a hurry with dispatches. You may have done something important, Arnold. We'll know when we get the captain's papers decoded. I'm writing you up for a Bronze Star either way. So let's both try to stay alive until I can get to a typewriter."

"Gee, I don't feel like I deserve no medal, Lieutenant."

"Shit, they giv them out for less. Why should you be left out?"

He became aware of other men moving to join them now, and called out, "Just where the hell do you men think you're going? Show's over. Take up your positions where Falco left you, damn it! Tex, run forward and relieve Falco on point. You've got eyes and I need the sergeant back here to keep these idiots in formation."

Most of the men moved back, abashed, but Thomas asked, "Don't you want to radio this in, sir?"

"Negative. I don't have the code memorized and I'm not about to brag about this in the clear for the Krauts to intercept. They might have been fond of their captain."

Hunter saw Rowan was coming up the road from where he'd left him. He ignored the fly-boy as he waited for Falco to get back so they could regroup and move on. His ten-minute break had stretched to more like twenty.

"Don't you want me out on point anymore, sir?" Arnold asked.

"Don't be piggy," Hunter replied. "You're supposed to take turns."

Falco rejoined them. Hunter said, "Sergeant Falco, meet Corporal Arnold. It's damned near noon and we have to get some damned place today. The others are getting sloppy. I want you with me and Arnold bringing up the rear. Thomas, stay near me with that R-300. Let's move it out."

As they started north again, Captain Rowan said, "I didn't know your men packed Tommy guns, Lieutenant."

"They don't. The carbine fires full automatic if you set it right. We started out with Thompsons. They look great in gangster movies, but they weigh a ton and jam if you don't treat them like expensive watches. You'd better fall back a ways, Captain. I don't like us bunched like this."

Rowan wrote another black mark in his mental shit list but didn't argue. As they slogged on without him, Falco said, "I'd watch that fly-boy, if I was the lieutenant. He ain't just overeager. He's one of them nasty officers you gotta worry about."

Hunter smiled thinly. "I noticed. I get along with most fly-boys, but he seems to take himself pretty serious."

"I wish that ME-109 had finished him off. He thinks he's the Red Baron," Falco said. "He oughtta be fighting for the other side." Falco spat and added, "Come to think of it, he was. The Nazi pilot who shot him down was probably a nicer guy."

Their conversation was interrupted by what sounded like someone rolling a garbage can across the sky above them. Hunter froze in place, knees bent and undecided until the incoming mail had obviously passed over. It seemed to take forever before they heard the shell land, far in the distance.

"Sounded like a navy eight-incher," Falco commented. "They used them in Sicily. Some cruiser off the coast is giving the Krauts some harassing fire with their big guns."

Another garbage can rolled over them and Falco added, "What did I tell you, sir? Listen, it came down way to the south of the first one. They ain't aiming at nothing in particular. Just lobbing HF ashore to shake the Krauts up and slow them down."

"I know what harassing fire is, Falco. Let's hope they keep throwing it well inland. Could we change the subject? You know there's not a damned thing we can do about those random shells."

Falco nodded and said, "Yeah, it's like lightning. It can hit you anywhere and any time. Uh . . . Lieutenant?"

"Yeah?"

"We ought to be getting pretty close to Ste. Mère Église by now, right?"

"So?"

"So aside from having met nobody but Krauts in the last couple of miles, the navy wouldn't be shelling so close to a town our guys were holding, would they?"

Hunter started to object. But fair was fair. He nodded and said, "We'd better take to Indian country before we move any closer. It'll slow us down, but better safe than sorry."

He raised his hand to halt his stick, then turned to the nearest trooper. "Mahoney, catch up with Tex and get him back here. We're going through the hedges to advance the rest of the way in off the road net."

As Mahoney jogged out of sight up the winding road Hunter made a circle in the air with his fist to gather in the men and explain the new tactic to them. "We're up against the devil we know and the devil we don't, men. We wouldn't be moving on Ste. Mère Église if I thought the Krauts still held it. But until we're sure they don't, we have to treat it as if it was an enemy position. You know skirmish drill, but for God's sake remember we're scouts, not assault troops. We could be advancing on other troopers, so forget what they said about shooting first and asking questions later! Captain Rowan here showed you how easy it is to make a mistake about such matters. So watch it. Our guys are better than the Krauts, and they didn't send us over here to take on the Eighty-second! Any questions?"

Inevitably, some wag said, "Yessir, May I please be excused for the rest of the afternoon?"

Hunter didn't find it all that funny, but he joined in the round of laughter. "We'll all get screwed, blewed and tattooed when this is over. Falco, divide the stick in two. Corporal Arnold with you. Thomas and Captain Rowan with me. We'll form rough diamonds and leapfrog SOP."

Trooper Mahoney rejoined them, alone. "Where's Tex?" Hunter asked.

"I couldn't find him, sir," Mahoney said. "I ran at least half a mile up the road and that's all she wrote!"

"Goddamn, he's deserted again!" somebody said.

Hunter wondered what else was new. He shrugged and said, "He wasn't from our outfit anyway. Move out, Sergeant Falco."

The noncom nodded and shoved through the hedgerow with Arnold and three other men. Hunter waited a few moments and followed them with his own larger group. Captain Rowan would be useless in a fire fight, armed only with his pistol and not trained to fight on the ground. So when they broke through the hedge into a fallow emerald-green field, Hunter said, "Thomas, give the R-300 to the captain."

"I don't know how to work that thing," Rowan protested.

"You don't have to work it. Just carry it so Thomas can use his carbine if he has to."

"Goddamn it, Lieutenant, do I look like a coolie?"

"Negative. Most of the Chinamen I've met seemed

pretty bright. I'm not asking you to pack the radio, Captain. I'm ordering you. We used to have enough guys to carry our own gear. But that was before we met you. So cut the bullshit and do something useful for a change. Give him the R-300, Thomas. If he drops it, shoot him."

Hunter turned to see that Falco and his men, on the far side of the field, had moved up to the first hedgerow across their line of passage. He nodded and said, "Okay, spread out and let's watch the spinach as we flank Falco."

Hunter's bunch moved north in a wide-spaced diamond with the two officers in the center as the relieved Thomas led on point. The fact that Thomas wasn't really covering him emboldened Rowan to croak, "I'll get you for this Lieutenant!"

"You already got us," Hunter snapped. "So shut up and let us soldier."

They moved up to the hedgeline. Thomas peered through to the next field and signaled it was clear. Falco was watching from the far side. So Hunter ordered his men to line up behind the hedgerow with their carbines shoved through to cover Falco's next move before he waved the acting sergeant forward. Interested despite himself, Rowan said, "Oh, I get it. If anybody hits those others out in the open, we give 'em hell from this cover, right?"

Hunter nodded. "Yeah. And if Falco makes it across to the next line, we get to be the target while he covers us. You're supposed to have more men if you want to do it right, but what the hell."

"Goddamn it, Lieutenant! I told you I thought you were Krauts!"

"Hey, relax. You only put the finishing touches on

the SNAFU, Captain. We were all screwed up before we hit the ground last night. I only landed with half my men, in the wrong place, and it's been a rapidly deteriorating situation ever since."

3

RAMIE DAVIS WATCHED the approaching cliffs above
Omaha Beach as she and Beth Waterman clung
to the bridge rail of the PT boat. They both wore
hastily acquired helmets and the men's fatigues that
nice quartermaster officer back there had insisted were
the smallest sizes he had in stock. They looked like
GI waifs even with the sleeves and pants rolled up.
Beth was seasick from the choppy channel crossing,
but she was bravely trying to bear up. Ramie was too
keyed up to think about the whitecaps they kept
slamming across. The PT boat had been stripped for
courier duty and was manned by U.S. Coast Guard
personnel. Its big Packard engines clawed them across
the waves at a frightening clip, but it seemed they'd
taken days to cross, even though it was more like
four and a half hours since they'd left England. The

shoreline ahead hung under a pall of smoke but Ramie was afraid they were too late. The last dispatches said most of the beaches were secure now, save for something called harassing fire. She knew the soldiers would never let them up those cliffs in these ridiculous outfits, and if it was all over by the time they got ashore . . .

A fatherly man in coast guard officer's kit joined Ramie at the rail with a sigh and said, "Well, little lady. I sure am feeling foolish right now."

Ramie smiled up at him. "Really? You don't look foolish, Captain."

"Honey, I told you I was only a lieutenant JG, and a World War One retread at that. But my rank's not the only thing you seem to have gotten confused in your pretty little head. I was just on the radio to flag and guess what they told me about you and this other little lady here."

Ramie grinned. "I've no idea, sir. Did your officers say something bad about us?"

The JG sighed. "Don't bat your eyes at me like that, girl. I've a daughter older than you and, come to think of it, she's slickered her old dad a few times, too. But you, Miss Davis, are a pure caution. Flag says they never heard of you. Let's see how you wiggle out of that one."

Ramie looked innocent and replied, "I don't know what you're talking about, sir. How could I possibly know anyone at Coast Guard headquarters? I showed you our press credentials and—"

"Now hold on, girl. You never would have boarded this vessel waving that fool press card at a grown man! You told us you were cleared with flag and that I could check if I liked—knowing, of course, that we'd be out here on the water before I'd get around to doing any such thing! You know what you two are, Miss Davis? You two little ladies are stowaways! You have boarded a U.S. vessel of war under false pretenses. So what have you to say for yourselves?"

"There must be some mistake. Maybe it was the U.S. Navy we cleared it with. You know how girls are about mixing up things like that, Captain."

He snorted and snapped, "Honey, you're about as mixed up as old Albert Einstein and as helpless as a basket of cobras! You lied to this poor old salt. Damn it, we're fixing to put in and I don't know what to do with you."

"Are you going to make us walk the plank, sir?"

"No, but if you were my daughter I'd purely spank your sassy bottom. Lord knows you deserve it! This is a serious business, Miss Davis. What on earth am I to tell flag about this mess you've gotten me into? They'll have me beached for carrying unauthorized civilian she-males aboard this vessel. Old 448 is supposed to be on high-priority dispatch duty and you've gone and turned us into an infernal ferry boat!"

Ramie tried to look contrite as she said, "I wouldn't want you to get in trouble over a little mix-up after you and your men have been so nice to us. But, look, we'll be landing in just a few minutes, right?"

"Not exactly. We ain't a landing craft. Things go ashore by rubber raft."

"The details are unimportant, just so we get ashore, Captain."

"I'm a JG and you'll do no such thing! It's bad enough we brought you across. I ain't about to put you sweet young things ashore on Omaha Beach!"

Ramie frowned and said, "Oh, dear. Won't that get you in even more trouble?"

He frowned back. "I don't follow you, little lady."

"Well, if Beth and I left your boat on this side, you wouldn't have to explain anything when you got back, would you? I mean, nobody told you what to do about us, did they?"

He started to object. Then he smiled craftily and said, "By Jimmies, I was wrong. You're even smarter than Einstein and meaner than them snakes! You knew all the time you had me by the short hairs once I let you aboard, didn't you?"

"Well, I can see you're just too smart for me to play games with."

The JG rolled his eyes heavenward. "Oh, Lord, give me strength! If my Sarah Lou had been as ornery I'd have drowned her at birth! You got me either way, you sassy thing! I can sure see the advantages of getting you off my vessel before you can get me in more trouble. But seriously, Miss Davis, that beach ahead ain't no place for ladies, even ladies as ornery as yourself. This is my second trip across and my stomach ain't settled from this morning. I mean, there's been a lot of fighting ashore and—"

"Lieutenant," Ramie said firmly, "I came over here during the Battle of Britain and I covered London under the blitz. I've seen my share of unpleasant sights. You just get us ashore and let us worry about our delicate feelings, all right?"

He hesitated, then shrugged. "Move aft and tell the bos'n I said it was okay for you to ride in the raft with the stuff we were supposed to be delivering. But don't never say I didn't warn you. And if you get your pretty head blown off, I'll never speak to you again!"

He grumped away to con his craft through the treacherous shallows from the wheelhouse. Ramie picked up the radio set and said, "Come on, Beth. We're almost there."

"Ramie, I think I'm going to throw up," Beth said. But she didn't. As they moved back to where some coast guardsmen were making the motor-driven raft ready, a geyser of white water rose like Old Faithful and drenched them all with spray, and there was the ear-splitting roar of high explosives. Both girls dove flat near the raft.

Beth gasped, "Oh, my God, what was that?"

"German 155," one of the seamen said. "You shouldda been with us at sunrise. They were coming down like raindrops."

Ramie saw the radio set had landed in the scuppers. She retrieved it and told the men the skipper had said it was all right for them to go ashore with them. The beefy bos'n shrugged, said the skipper was nuts, and told them to stand by. Another shell landed, further away, and then the boat slowed down and began to swing its stern broadside to the shoreline. "This is it," the bos'n said, and dropped the light raft over the side and then followed it.

Neither of the women had expected to board so casually. But there was no time to argue. Holding the radio with one hand and Beth's arm with the other, Ramie leaped down as Beth gasped, "Are you crazy?" But she had no choice but to go with her.

For a sickening moment Ramie was sure they were going to fall off between the bobbing raft and the PT's hull. Then male hands grabbed them, one pawing Ramie's breast, either by accident or design, as the seamen literally threw them atop the bales of dispatches and special supplies. When Ramie raised her head and pushed the helmet brim higher to see, they were bouncing across the surf in the flat-bottomed craft. Beth lay facedown, moaning. But Ramie was already making mental notes for what she hoped would be the scoop of her career.

The raft darted between two jagged tangles of up-ended railroad steel rising above the surface. Ramie asked a seaman what they were and he said, "I don't know what you call them, miss, but the Krauts sure left a mess of them out here in the shallows. The engineers were supposed to clear them, but you can see they missed a few. It's worse at high tide. Run a hull across that crud and it rips your bottom open like a can opener."

They crested a wave and dropped down the other side as Ramie sniffed and gagged. She didn't ask what she was smelling. She'd been in the East End of London after the fire bombings of '40, and one never forgot the odor of charred human flesh.

Mixed in with the sickly sweet roast pork stench, she could smell sea water, the acrid smell of burnt wool, the dry metallic scent of scorched steel, and the chemistry-set reek of exploded ammunition. How could the smell be so strong this far offshore? Ramie looked over the edge of the raft. Little jelly fish bobbed under the surface with an odd four-leaf clover design etched into their transparent discs as they went on doing whatever jellyfish do, oblivious to man and his wars. But there were other things bobbing in the shallows as they went in. She saw a floating orange and a totally unexplainable and unexpected rubber contraceptive. But most of all she saw paper. Hundreds of pieces of paper, floating soggily all around. She reached down to snag a square as the raft moved on. She hooked it but it fell apart in her hands as she lifted it for a better view. The one shred she managed to salvage had some writing on it in faded and barely legible ink. It read, "June 5, 1944 . . .

Dear Gloria: By the time you get . . ." and that was all. She wondered who Gloria was and how she'd feel when a black-edged telegram was delivered instead of that letter he'd never had the chance to mail.

A man called out, "Heads up, gang!" and Ramie was caught by surprise when the raft grounded in ankle-deep water. Some other men were coming their way to meet them. Ramie grabbed Beth and the radio and snapped, "Come on. I don't want to be sent back now!"

"I do," sighed Beth, as she rose to step over the side. A wave came in and soaked them to the knees as they moved up the gritty wet sand to dry ground. But before they got there, Beth clutched at Ramie and pointed, gasping, "Oh, God, is that a body?"

It was. A GI lay facedown in the shallows, legs moving sluggishly as the beach wash lifted and dropped them. Ramie swallowed and led Beth on as some detached part of her made a mental note of the blue and grey patch he'd been wearing. Wasn't that the patch of the Twenty-ninth Infantry? She wondered how she knew that, and why nobody seemed to care about the dead boy still lying there. The beach up from the water's edge was a milling confusion of men and vehicles. Everyone seemed in a dreadful hurry to be going anywhere but where they were. Ramie knew it had to make some sense, but she felt like a strange ant moving into an uncovered nest of other ants in olive drab.

"Not so fast!" Beth gasped. "Where are we going, Ramie?"

"I'm not sure. There's a sort of cement wall over there near the base of the cliffs. Let's set up there, for now. What time is it?"

"It's almost six and what if we're stuck here after dark?"

"Of course we'll be here after dark, silly. But it's summer and we don't have to worry about that for hours. Come on, this damned radio is heavy."

They slogged across the deep sand as passing GIs spotted them, blinked in surprise, and moved on. Ramie spotted a cluster of men near the sea wall they were making for. They were doing something with what seemed to be limp bags. Maybe barracks bags. Maybe she could get an interview.

Then, as the two girls got closer, Ramie gasped in horror. Those . . . things they were lining up along the base of the sea wall weren't barracks bags. They were dead GIs. A lot of dead GIs. Beth tugged at her sleeve and said, "No, Ramie. I don't want to look!"

Ramie didn't want to look either. But she steeled herself and moved on, saying, "We're reporters, Beth! What were you expecting over here, a fashion show?"

Ramie swallowed and approached closer. She could see what the living GIs were doing now. She paused to watch as the Graves Registration team slid a cotton mattress cover over the boots of a dead GI and tugged it up around his hips. The boy they were bagging looked too young to be a soldier and he seemed to be resisting them with his dead flesh as they lifted him into a sitting position to pull the bag up over his head and knot it shut before letting him flop limply back to the sand. She could still see his face. She knew nobody would ever see that teen-aged face again, but it was burned into her memory forever. They started to line up the legs of another dead man and then one of them spotted them and said something. An officer turned, stared at them, and asked, "What in hell, are you *nurses* down here?

These guys don't need nursing. Why aren't you up at the aid station?"

"We're not nurses, Captain," Ramie said. "We're with UPI."

"You're correspondents? That's crazy. You're both dames!"

Ramie smiled wanly and said, "I've noticed that lately. What's the story here, Captain?"

"What does it look like?" he growled. "These poor slobs bought the farm and there's more where they just came from, all up and down the beach. Why don't you go play somewhere else? We have a job to do here."

Ramie nodded and pointed with her chin as she told Beth, "Let's go down that way. That looks like some brass having a pow-wow near that wrecked weapons carrier."

Beth followed but protested, "Ramie, we're going to get in trouble. Can't you see they don't want us here?"

"They never want us anywhere, Beth. Come on. We have to find somebody who knows what on earth is going on."

They joined the men around the burned-out weapons carrier as a tall officer was yelling, "I don't give doodly shit what division wants by 2100! My men have had it and so have I! How much do those fat cats sitting on their fat asses think real people can take?"

Then he spotted the two girls and stopped, thunderstruck. An older man swung around to follow his gaze and gasped, "Jesus H. Christ! How did you dames get here? Don't you know this area's not secured yet?"

"I'm Ramie Davis, UPI. They sent me to get the big picture, Colonel."

"Oh, yeah? Well, I'm sending you the hell out of here on the double! There isn't any big picture. We're trying to figure out what the hell is going on too! No kidding, girls, this is no place for women—or even men if they don't have to be here."

"All right. Where's the front line, Colonel?" Ramie asked.

"Front line? You're *on* the damned front line! You think those are fire crackers going on all around us? I don't know how you got here, but for God's sake get away from it! We've got a fingerhold on the cliff tops, we hope, but we're in mortar range and every once in a while we run across a Nazi in a rabbit hole up there. We're not sure all the land mines are out of this sand yet either. So watch your step as you go, but for God's sake, *go!*"

Ramie shrugged and turned away, telling Beth, "Look, there, up the beach. It might be a command post."

As they made their way through the confusion of moving men and machines Ramie started sorting out the lay of the land at Omaha. It was three or four city blocks from the water's edge to the base of the eroded cliffs. Here and there the cliffs were cut open by a roadway leading down from the high ground above. But even a civilian could see they'd been natural death traps earlier. So the business about rangers scaling the cliffs on ropes under fire began to make more sense.

The incredible waste of war didn't. Omaha Beach was littered far worse than Coney Island after a long summer holiday. You could hardly put your foot down without stepping on spent brass, tin cans, those mysterious oranges and, for God's sake, more used contraceptives. Ramie had lived in wartime London long enough to know oranges were worth their weight in gold, but some got in, so they'd probably issued each man an orange as he boarded his landing craft. But the rubbers were just ridiculous.

Beth saw them too, and giggled, "They seem to have had an orgy here just before we arrived, darn it."

Ramie stepped over a helmet in the sand with a self-explanatory hole in it. There was all sorts of military issue strewn across the sand. She saw jerry cans and wooden crates with black crescents stenciled on them. There were other helmets and it made her shudder to see how many. Packs, shelter halves, and tent pegs lay everywhere. She saw what seemed to be hundreds of gas masks, each in its neat little canvas pack. She noticed not one man they passed carried a gas mask, and most of them no longer had packs. She knew each GI had boarded his landing craft with forty pounds of gear the taxpayers had bought for him. But now most had stripped down to little more than their ammo harness and canteen, with a mess kit and raincoat folded over the back of their ammo belts, period.

They had to step around the larger discarded toys of war. Burned-out trucks, jeeps, and those funny-looking wheeled boats they called "ducks" stood on burned-out wheels or lay on their sides like dead cows. The soft sand healed itself quickly with men and machinery moving across it, but you could see where shells had left craters earlier in the day. One saucer-shaped depression was filled with water the color of pea soup. A GI boot was floating in it. As they circled the crater a soldier walking like a drunk blocked Ramie and asked, eyes blank, "Hey, have you seen

Charlie Company? I gotta find Charlie Company! Where's Charlie Company?"

Ramie took him by the arm to steady him as she spotted a passing man with a red cross brassard on one sleeve. She shouted, "Medic!" and the other man looked their way, nodded, and came over. He looked at the dazed GI dubiously and Ramie murmured, "I think it's combat fatigue."

The medic shrugged and said, "There's a lot of that going around. I can't do nothing for him, lady. I ain't got hands enough for the ones who really need me. You ladies shouldn't be here."

Then, having done all he had time for, the medic moved on. Ramie looked helplessly at Beth as the dazed GI shook himself free and staggered off, shouting, "Hey, Charlie Company! Where the fuck is Charlie Company?"

"Ramie, I'm scared," Beth said.

"That makes two of us," Ramie answered, "but we have a job to do. For heaven's sake, will you carry this damned radio set for a while?"

The smaller girl took the set with a sigh and they moved on, drawing more curious glances and an occasional lewd comment. A line of vehicles was moving up a ramplike road cut in the cliffs. At the bottom, off to the side, a soldier in smoke-grimed tanker's kit sat on a jerry can smoking a cigarette and staring seaward with a bemused expression.

Ramie went over to him. "Hi, we're with UPI. Aren't you a tanker?"

He muttered, "I used to be. I got out. I don't think anybody else got out. But I got out."

Ramie looked around. There was no tank in sight. "What happened to your tank?"

"I told you. I got out. I was the TC. So I was in the

turret when they hit us and she started to brew. I yelled for the others to get out and then I rolled out the hatch and ran a million miles. I can't run no more. Where am I, anyway?"

"This is Omaha Beach, soldier."

"Oh, yeah, I remember Omaha. I remember Atlantis and Lemuria, too. Omaha was nothing. They never told us what it would be like up there in the hedgerows."

Ramie pointed to a C ration crate and told Beth to set up to send. Then she asked the tanker, "How far inland have our men pushed the Germans by now, soldier?"

The tanker took a drag on his cigarette. "Beats me. Our M-5 never made it all that far. They didn't warn us about the hedgerows. The goddamn Frogs are fruity for planting hedges. They got this wall of hedge around every goddamn five acres or so, see? We tried to just crash through. But they don't mess around with hedgerows in Normandy! They got a goddamn ditch on either side of the hedge, with the dirt piled up around the roots maybe three feet or more. The hedges are old. Some of the branches are thick enough to cut for timber and an M-5 can't go through stuff like that. We hadda look for gaps in the hedgerows, and every place you found a gap in the hedges you found some wise-ass Kraut waiting for you with a Panzerfaust. That's what got us, a Panzerfaust. It's like our bazooka, only bigger. Jesus, it was loud when that thing slammed into us! I yelled for the other guys to bail out and then I rolled out myself and started running. I could hear the Krauts laughing as I ran off. Ain't that a bitch?"

Ramie nodded and was about to speak when Beth broke in. "I can't get the radio to work, Ramie. I keep turning all the dials and nothing's happening. I don't hear a thing when I switch on and off. We must have broken it."

"Well, fix it, silly!"

Beth looked hurt and answered, "I only know how to work a radio, Ramie. I don't know anything about fixing one!"

"Great. All right. There's no sense carrying it any further." She turned back to the tanker. "Does this road lead up to the main show?"

"Guess it must. I just came down it, and if I wasn't in the main show, I don't know who that was, smoking up my old M-5!"

"Come on, Beth," Ramie said. "There's no fighting going on down here on the beach now."

Beth looked startled and protested, "You can't be serious! This soldier said they're *shooting* at people up there!"

"Well of course they are, you goose! They call that a battle, and that's what we came all this way to cover. Let's see if we can hitch a ride to the front."

They went over to the notch in the cliff and Ramie stuck her thumb out as a jeep approached. The four GIs in the jeep looked astounded, but they didn't stop. A couple of big six-by-six trucks passed them by and then a jeep with a major seated beside the enlisted driver stopped.

The major didn't offer them a ride. He said, "I don't know where you two madwomen came from, but get your tails back there. That's an order!"

Ramie smiled and said, "We're civilians, Major. We're covering the battle for UPI. How about a lift to the front?"

"You silly broad, this *is* the front! What were you expecting, a painted line on the ground? My CP, topside, is under fire at the moment and if you think I'm about to arrive with two dames in the back seat you've been smoking funny cigarettes! Drive on, Murphy. You two, get the hell out of here!"

As the irate officer left them behind Ramie shrugged and said, "Oh, hell, let's walk. It's just up the hill, right?"

Beth followed, but not happily. "Ramie, you're going to get us both hurt, and what if the Germans rape us?"

"Oh, for God's sake, we're not going that far. I just want to get close enough to the fighting to see what's going on. We'll find some officer who's not so excited and he can tell us what the situation is."

A truck honked its horn at them and they moved to the side of the cut as the six-by-six passed them, groaning up the incline in low gear with a bunch of GIs in the back. One of them spotted them and cat-called over the tailgate as Ramie waved.

"Gee, they're awfully fresh," Beth commented.

"They're awfully young too. God, I'm only twenty-six and I'm beginning to feel like their mother. Did you know I'm too old to be an aviation cadet, Beth?"

"That's silly. Twenty-six isn't old, even for a girl."

"The army seems to think so. They want their fly-boys young and eager. Sometimes I think they want them young and innocent, too. It's hard to get an adult to do the things they want them to. I remember back in '40 . . . " Then she grimaced and said, "Never mind. It was a long time ago. I know what that tanker means about Atlantis and Lemuria."

"Gee, Ramie, it was only four years."

"I know, but it was another time and another world. Come on, shake a leg."

The incline was less steep now, but Ramie's legs were feeling the climb from the beach. Had it really only been four years since she'd been an eager cub like Beth? God, it felt like forty since she'd covered that hot, dry fall. Someday she'd tell her grandchildren about a London when you could still dine out without standing in line and girls had thrown their stockings away when they got runs in them.

The London she'd first known wasn't there anymore. That funny little Chinese place in Limehouse had burned to the ground, along with Limehouse. And would there ever be a London Chinatown again? Everyone had looked so stylish, that first year. Even with the war on, the shops along Oxford Street had displayed the new fall fashions. She'd spent some of her first paycheck overseas on the new open-toed shoes that buckled around the ankles. She still had them, back at her Marlybone flat, repaired over and again, but still her best shoes to wear to a party.

They got to the top of the cliffs. Beth looked around and asked, "Where are the hedgerows that man was talking about?"

It was a good question. The top of the cliff was grassy and windswept. The road led toward a burned-out row of houses, swerving around a massive shell-pocked concrete bunker that looked like it had been designed for the 1939 World's Fair. The tube of a German coast defense gun pointed at the ground, like the penis of a heroically proportioned but exhausted bull. As they walked along the road shoulder, Ramie saw a helmet in the grass and realized with a start that it was German. It looked exactly like the ones in Hollywood war movies and she wondered why that disappointed her. She kept trying to tell herself that this was real, but it didn't *feel* real. Despite the noise of distant gunfire and the stench of death in the air, there was a dreamlike stage-set quality to everything that she could neither shake nor understand.

"I don't think we should go much farther without permission, Ramie," said Beth.

But Ramie insisted, "Come on. You can see the Germans have been pushed way back from the beaches now."

They started to move on. Then, with no warning at all, something exploded with an odd, hollow *crump* on the road behind them.

Beth said, "Oh," in a little-girl voice, as Ramie turned to stare at the slate blue smoke hanging in the air behind her. "That must have been one of those mortar things they told us about!" Ramie gasped. "We have to find cover!"

"You go, then," Beth said. "I . . . I think I'm hurt." Then Beth's legs buckled under her and she sank to the ground with an odd grace.

Ramie ran to her, dropped to her knees, and sobbed, "No, you can't be, Beth! It was such a little explosion!"

Beth's eyes were closed as she lay in the dust of the road shoulder, but she licked her lips and muttered, "I feel all mushy. I'm not having my period, but my panties are wet and sticky, you know?"

A jeep came up out of the cut from the beach. Ramie waved it down and shouted, "Help us! My friend seems to be wounded!"

A startled officer stared at the girl lying by the side of the road. He jumped out and ran to roll Beth over on her side. Beth moaned in pain and Ramie gagged as she saw that the mortar fragments had sliced into Beth's back in three places. The officer unhooked the first aid pouch from his ammo belt and rose to hand it to Ramie, saying, "Here. This is the best I can do, miss. I have to move on."

"You can't! You have a jeep! I have to get her down to the beach!"

He shook his head. "You'll have to wait here until you spot an ambulance going the other way." Then, before Ramie could stop him, he was back in the jeep and leaving them to their own resources.

Ramie dropped to her knees again and pillowed Beth's head in her lap as she fumbled to open the first aid kit. There was little more than a roll of gauze, a packet of sulfa powder, and a tiny disposable ampule of morphine, if the needle on the end meant anything.

Ramie tried to read the lettering on the ampule. It had somehow gotten water-soaked and the lettering had run. Besides, she didn't know if Beth needed the shot or not. Ramie reached in a pocket for the little pearl-handled penknife she'd thought might come in handy and began to gingerly cut open the back of Beth's borrowed fatigue shirt and the more substantial blouse under it. She stared dry-mouthed at the little square puncture under Beth's bra strap. It wasn't bleeding much, on the outside. It seemed pointless to bandage her there.

The other two wounds looked much the same. One fragment had hit Beth in the small of her back, far enough, she hoped, to the left of the spine. The other had entered under the right floating rib. Ramie didn't know what to do about any of them. She stared wildly around and saw a convoy of weapons carriers coming up from the beach. She stayed down with Beth's head in her lap as she took off her helmet and waved it frantically. The trucks tore by without slowing down. Ramie threw the helmet after them and screamed, "Bastards! Bastard sons of bitches!"

Beth murmured, "Are you mad at me?"

"Listen, Beth, they won't help us and we have to

get you down to the beach, okay? Wake up, Beth. It's only a little ways, honey."

Beth didn't answer.

Ramie sobbed, "No, please, God! It's not her fault! I was the one who was stupid! I was the know-it-all! Don't let her die, God! You can't let her die! I won't *let* you take her like this!"

Neither God nor the wounded girl answered, so Ramie struggled to her feet, with the smaller girl in her arms, and started staggering back down the road toward the beach. It was downhill. That helped, but even though Beth was a small woman, she seemed to get heavier with every step. Ramie couldn't believe the beach could be so far as she jogged down the long incline with one arm under Beth's knees and the other supporting her shoulders. Beth's helmet fell off and her black hair hung down as her head bobbed limply. Her mouth hung open and Ramie couldn't tell if she was still breathing or not. She staggered out of the cut and the tanker was still sitting there on his jerry can. Could that be possible, after all this time?

He rose, slack-jawed, as Ramie gasped, "Help me, please, for God's sake help me! She's been hit!"

The tanker nodded, took Beth from Ramie, and lowered her gently to the sand before he roared in a bull-like tone, "Medic! Medic! Medic on the fucking double!"

It seemed forever, but it was actually only a few minutes before a man with a red cross on his sleeve made his way to them through a gathering crowd of curious GIs. He took one look at Beth, nodded, and drove a morphine needle into her thigh, through the pants and all. Then he opened the cuts Ramie had made in her clothing and whistled. "Mortar, huh?"

"I think so," Ramie said. "Is she still alive?"

"Yeah. But she's in bad shape. Them little buggers make little holes, but they buzz all around inside. She's in shock and looks like she's bleeding internally. Just sit tight and I'll get some litter-bearers. I don't know what you dames thought you was doing here, but you're in luck. They're loading the wounded aboard just down the beach, so they'll be shoving off for England before that morphine wears off."

"How come you gave her that shot in the first place?" the tanker asked. "Even I can see she's out like a light."

"We give everybody a shot no matter what shape they're in when we get to 'em," the medic replied. "Saves a lot of screaming when and if they come to. Take a look at a mortar fragment sometime and you'll know why it smarts when the shock wears off. Look, you folks want a lecture or do you want a litter? I'll be right back."

As he elbowed his way through the crowd, Ramie got down to cradle Beth's head again. The tanker looked around and growled, "What's the matter with you guys? Is there something unusual about getting hit on Omaha Beach?"

A nearby GI muttered, "That's the first *dame* I've seen like that."

The tanker snorted in disgust, knelt by Ramie, and put his cigarette between her lips. She took a deep, shuddering drag and murmured, "Thanks."

"You'll be going back in the transport with her, huh?" he asked.

"I'll have to. I feel so stupid. We came all this way to get a story and all we managed to do was get her hurt . . ."

"I know what you mean. After all that training, they burned us out before we ever got to fire at anything. But look at it this way—a lot of poor slobs never even made it ashore. LST next to ours blew up a mile off shore. The tanks and all went to the bottom. At least all three of us are still alive."

Ramie nodded, but asked, "Is that all that matters in this war, just staying alive?"

The tanker took a drag of smoke and let it out thoughtfully. "It matters when you consider some of the alternatives, miss."

4

LOGAN HUNTER moved in the lengthening shadows of a hedgerow to join Falco's other group long enough to find out why the acting sergeant had signaled him. He hunkered down by Falco in the corner of the field they'd just crossed and asked, "What's up? There's nothing ahead in the next open field, Falco."

"I know, Lieutenant," Falco replied. "But look what's in the one on my flank!"

Hunter peered through the gap Falco indicated and whistled softly. A Waco U.S. Army glider lay on its back in the grass like a swatted insect. The wings had been pulled off as if by a mean little kid. The square fuselage lay on its back. The nose was a mass of tangled metal and plexiglas.

"That ain't the way I'd have landed, if I'd had any

choice, sir," Falco commented. "I thought you'd want to know about it before we moved on."

"Cover me," Hunter said. "I'm moving in for a look inside."

"Lieutenant, there ain't no way in hell anybody's still alive by now. That Waco crashed last night, a good fifteen hours ago. Anybody that lived through it is long gone by now, so why chance it?"

"We need two carbines. This .45 is keen for S2 bullshit, but things are turning out more serious than planned. Captain Rowan better have a carbine too, don't you think?"

"Since you asked me, sir, I don't. I wouldn't give that fly-boy shit."

Hunter drew his pistol and eased through the hedgerow. The book said not to expose yourself like this, if you were an officer, before you'd sent a scout ahead to make sure. But the book said lots of dumb things about officers, like carrying a pistol instead of a carbine. Hunter was learning to think for himself. If he'd started earlier he wouldn't have to be taking this chance. He'd have helped himself to one of his dead's carbines instead of abandoning them back there with the firing action messed up, like the same book said. He moved over to the glider, pulled some of the wrecked canvas and plexiglas out of the way, and peered inside. Then he gagged and turned away, trying not to throw up. He took a deep breath and looked again. They were still there. Maybe two full squads and all their gear, wadded in one big ball of metal, meat and rags in the nose of the wrecked glider. It had obviously lost its wings well above the ground and landed on its nose before falling on its back.

Hunter saw a carbine protruding from between two mangled torsos. He grabbed and pulled. It came out with a sickening sucking sound, covered with blood and feces. Hunter tossed it out on the grass. That one belonged to Rowan if he could find something less disgusting for himself.

He couldn't. That was funny. They couldn't have sent all those guys over without weapons. He steeled himself and grabbed a dead shoulder to pry it from the congealing mass. The crushed corpse of what seemed to be the glider pilot fell away to reveal only further pressed GIs.

Hunter frowned. Wait a minute, he thought. Maybe their guns were racked or something. You don't jump with your gear from a glider.

He couldn't get to the rear through the mounded bodies. He moved around to the side, took out his jump knife, and sliced open the canvas. He stuck his head in and looked forward. He saw now why the men in the nose had been so awesomely mangled. They'd been a heavy weapons section. The base plates of their mortars and the tripods of their big .50 caliber machine guns had smashed them like so much scrap metal when they hit. He could see it stuck to the pile from behind. But . . . where were the machine guns and the ammo boxes that should have been with them?

"Salvaged," he muttered, stepping away from the glider. The Waco hadn't been towed across alone. Some other glider troopers had made it and taken the stuff they could use.

But gliders were one-way disposable aircraft. They landed. They didn't take off again. Where the hell were the other gliders?

Hunter shrugged and walked back around to where he'd left the carbine in the grass. He wiped as much of the crud off in the grass as he could. Then he cut a triangle of canvas away and wrapped the carbine up to clean it properly later. As he started back, he heard Falco yell, "Cover!" He darted back to drop behind the glider without waiting to find out why.

He didn't want to give away his position by yelling questions at Falco. So he crawled the length of the fuselage on his belly and risked a peek around the smashed tail assembly. Three men in civilian clothes were moving toward him across the open field. They carried U.S. Army carbines and sported white armbands with red lettering on them. Hunter stayed under cover, but yelled to Falco, "Hold your fire! I think they're FFI!"

The men froze in place, arms at port. Then one of them called out, in a thickly accented and very nervous attempt at English, "*Allo*, are you *Américain, m'sieu*?"

Hunter called back, "Yeah. Who are you guys?"

"French Forces of the Interior, *m'sieu*! Dare we approach you?"

Hunter thought, decided the odds of it being a German trick were sort of weird, and called back, "Okay, but my men are covering you until we sort this out."

Hunter rose, gun in hand but down at his side as the three Frenchmen came over, grinning. The one who spoke English saluted and said, "Lieutenant Jacques Beaudouin, FFI, at your service, *M'sieu Américain*! We thought there might be more guns in this glider, hein?"

"I think you got most of them the first time you looted it," Hunter said.

Beaudouin looked hurt and replied, "*Mais non*, we did not *loot*! We took what we needed for *les boches*, *M'sieu*, ah, Parachute. That was this morning. Since then others have joined us. It is astounding how many of the men I suspected of admiring *les boches* have come forward to be in on the kill."

Hunter nodded and said, "That sounds reasonable. But just what are you guys doing? Are you just running around pissing in German gas tanks on your own or is somebody in charge of your operation?"

"We are in radio contact with the Free French Command across the channel, *M'sieu* Parachute. I assure you everything has been quite regular. Last night, as ordered, we cut as many telephone wires as we could. We have picked off many boche dispatch riders and, when they have been in *practique* numbers, we have had some fun with isolated units as well. Our command post is not far. Would you like to inspect it, *M'sieu* Parachute? We have tried to be *très* military, but, in truth, most of us are not soldiers in more settled times."

Hunter looked at his watch. "I'm sure you know what you're doing. My men and I have to get to Ste. Mère Église. How far are we?"

Beaudouin frowned and pointed in an unexpected direction as he said, "It is perhaps ten kilometers, *M'sieu* Parachute. But the last we heard, *les boches* were there in force."

Hunter blinked in surprise, started to reach in his jacket for his map, and then dropped the idea, since it was obvious without looking that if they weren't crazy, he'd taken a wrong turn somewhere in the hedgerows. "I thought we were a hell of a lot closer," he said. "Other airborne were supposed to land near there. Have you guys run across any other of ours?"

"Not alive, *M'sieu* Parachute. There are some other gliders like this one, here and there. Forgive me, I mean no disrespect, but we have been wondering why you people came down so spread out."

"I've been wondering about that myself, and if I ever get to talk to the air force somebody had better have a good answer."

"Ah, that is what we thought. The winds are treacherous across this peninsula, *non*? Some of our people said you *Américains* were *très* confused last night, but I, Beaudouin, said you just had the bad luck, hein?"

"Make it a lot of both," Hunter said as he took out the map and unfolded it. "Could you show me where the hell we are, Lieutenant?"

The Frenchman took the map, studied it a moment, then took a pencil stub from his breast pocket and made a little X, saying, "Here, *M'sieu* Parachute."

Hunter took the map back and saw that unless Beaudouin didn't know his own country, they were way the hell inland from Ste. Mère Église and would have overshot it entirely if he hadn't lucked into these guys. He put the map away, saying, "I think I know where I went wrong. I keep forgetting how the channel hooks north around here. My brain knows it, but my damned feet keep feeling like it runs east and west."

Beaudouin laughed. *"Oui, les boches* have always found things *très* confusing too. They think our fields are laid out in a regular checkerboard pattern, like the blocks of a city. It is amusing how often they get lost. And when they stop, alone, to ask question—*ooh la la!"*

Hunter said, "I've got to get back to my men. Good hunting, Lieutenant." Then he frowned and said, "Wait a minute. Did you say you guys have been intercepting German dispatch riders?"

"*Oui*, and sending their droll messages to DeGaulle instead of Rommel."

"That means you have guys who read German?"

"But of course. We have been occupied by the animals for five years, and one must be *practique* as well as patient, non? In more rational times, I am the village postmaster. I was reading German mail before they asked me to do it officially. My German is almost as good as my English. No doubt that is why they made me an officer, *non?*"

Hunter took out the envelope he'd taken from the officer young Arnold had killed and handed it to the Frenchman, explaining, "We shoot dispatch riders too. See if you can tell me what I have here."

Beaudouin slung his carbine, took a pair of bifocals from a breast pocket, and adjusted them on his nose before he opened the envelope and began reading the contents, moving his lips. He laughed and said, "How droll! This is not a dispatch, *M'sieu* Parachute. It is a birthday greeting, to Erwin Rommel himself! I did not know the triple-titted boches had birthdays. I thought they just crawled out from under wet rocks."

Hunter sighed. "Hell, I thought it was important. G2 will have Rommel's date of birth in their order of battle book. But wait a minute. The guy that was carrying this birthday message wasn't headed toward the coast. He was going the other way."

Beaudouin shrugged and said, "That is simple. The message is addressed to his home in Germany. No doubt our Erwin went there to celebrate his birthday with his family, *non?*"

"Yeah, but on D day? Wait a minute, what's the date on that message?"

"June the fifth. Does this matter?"

Hunter whistled softly. "Somebody up there likes

us after all. The angels couldn't have timed it neater. Don't you see what happened? Rommel wrote himself a furlough, just before D day! He couldn't have known we'd be landing just about the time he was blowing out his candles. So the slob's not here watching the store. He may be on his way back. He must be on his way back, by now! But it's going to take him a couple of days to grasp the situation and do something about it. And meanwhile, some second in command is sweating bullets at German GHQ!"

The FFI man laughed. "I told you it was droll. No boche is allowed to take the pee pee before he has permission from his superior officer. *Les boches* along this coast will simply try and hold their positions as well as they are able until our Erwin arrives to resume command, hein?"

"Yeah, but SHAEF thinks that's who they're fighting right now, and Rommel taught 'em in North Africa to handle him with kid gloves. It's been nice meeting you guys, but I've got to get this on the air!"

He dashed back to the hedgerow and told Falco, "It's okay. They're on our side. We're taking a chow break and holding for now. I have to get to the R-300 on the double."

He ran back to his own half of the stick, dropped to his knees near Captain Rowan and the R-300 and explained what he'd just learned to his fellow officer as he switched on the set. Hoping it was still on division's frequency, he let the tubes warm up and held the hand set to his face, sending, "California S2 calling division. Repeat, California S2 calling division. Come in division. Over."

All he heard was static. He cursed and said, "If they're still in the war they're on another wavelength." He turned the dial with his free hand until he intercepted a far-away-sounding conversation in coded English. He had no idea who Mississippi was, but Big Blue Ox wanted some eight-inchers two thousand feet in front of them, right now. Hunter waited for a lull in the exchange and cut in, saying, "Mississippi, this is California S2. Let me speak to your S2 officer. Over."

The reply was, "Who the fuck is California? Over."

"Listen, Mississippi, this is important. I'm airborne, calling from behind the Kraut lines and I've got vital scoop for you to relay. Over."

Another voice said, "Mississippi, this is Colonel Palmer with Big Blue Ox and I want those fucking eight-inchers here and now! Over!"

Hunter shouted, "Colonel Palmer, this is high-priority intelligence I'm trying to relay. It'll only take a minute. Over."

There was a moment of silence. Then Colonel Palmer said, "Up yours, you sneaky Kraut bastard! Ignore the asshole, Mississippi! I got high priorities too. The mothers are wearing German uniforms and I'm not *asking* for that salvo, I'm *ordering* it! We need 'em at eighteen hundred feet ahead of us now, and the gap is closing. Fire for effect and I'll range you. But for God's sake, *do* it! Over!"

Hunter swore in helpless rage. At his side, Captain Rowan asked, "Trouble?"

"They think I'm a Kraut. I can't say I blame them. But Jesus Christ!"

"Want me to try? I was in radio contact with my fighter wing when that ME-109 jumped me. So I know the score."

Hunter nodded and handed the pilot the hand set. Rowan turned the dial way off the ground forces band, cleared his throat, and said, "Mother Hen, this is Red

Four. Do you read me? Come in, Mother Hen. Over."

Hunter couldn't hear the other end of the conversation, but he saw the fly-boy was good with communications as well as nose guns when Rowan smiled thinly and said, "That's affirmative, Mother Hen. I'm down and behind enemy lines, but it only hurts when I laugh. I'll tell you about losing my kite later. Can you patch me through to Conway in S2? Over."

As he waited, Rowan nodded to Hunter and said, "S2's military intelligence."

Hunter repressed a snort of annoyance. Maybe Rowan meant air force S2 was the same as all other army S2. Maybe he was an asshole. It didn't matter, as long as they got through with the information about Rommel being AWOL. They'd told him at the briefing that everything depended on the invasion forces moving at least a couple of miles inland before the Krauts could move their reserves in where it mattered. Knowing the Kraut armored back-up might be late to the party could clear a few decks for action in the next vital hours.

Rowan was speaking again. "Yes, Conway, it's really me and I'm really still kicking. I know I called a mayday. But you can't keep a good man down. Listen, since you know my voice, we can cut the code crap. It doesn't matter if the Krauts are listening in. They know what I'm telling you, and it must have them shitting their pants. Get this through to Ike. Field Marshal Rommel is not, repeat, not at his command post in Normandy. He's home on leave, singing happy birthday to himself. SHAEF will know who that leaves in command and how he fights. How do you like it so far? Over."

Rowan glanced at Hunter, who nodded and made the thumbs-up sign. Then Rowan said, "You read me correctly, Conway. The information comes from FFI sources. I've been in contact with them. After I bailed out I picked up some airborne stragglers and we're trying to make our way back to our own lines. I can't give you our position for obvious reasons, but the poop is legit and you'd better stop asking dumb questions and get it through to the top brass. This is Uncle Don, your Uncle Don, good-night, little friends, good-night. Over and out."

He signed off and told Hunter, "I think I shook them up. They hadn't heard."

"You sort of shook me up too. I can see how you fly boys get all those pretty medals. What was that shit about Uncle Don?"

"Didn't you listen to that radio program when you were a kid? It's an inside joke. My first name's Donald, see?"

Hunter looked disgusted and said, "I don't care if it's Donald Duck, as long as your S2 man relays that message through to SHAEF."

"Oh, he will. Conway wants a medal, too."

Hunter grunted, took two K rations from his thigh pocket, and handed one to Rowan as he called out, "Chow call. Make it snappy, men. Its almost sundown and we have farther to go than I thought."

Trooper Mahoney asked, "Permission to pop the pep pills, sir? I'm just about beat."

There was a mutter of agreement from the others. Hunter knew they'd start sneaking the benzedrine anyway, once it was dark. So he shook his head and said, "Not yet. We may be up all night, so let's keep the bennies in reserve until we really need 'em. Dosage as required, after sundown."

As he opened his K ration Captain Rowan did the

same, with an expression of disgust, and said, "Christ, this is the breakfast pack. I've never figured out the contents of that can they put in the breakfast pack."

"Neither have I," Hunter said. "It looks like baby brains. But don't eat it if you're not hungry."

"I'm hungry. I'm just not hungry enough to eat shit. Someday somebody is going to have to answer for what they did to K rations, though, and I'd like to be the first witness!"

Hunter was surprised to find himself in agreement with the fly boy about anything. He'd never figured out K rations either. He suspected they'd been put together by a committee, with mixed results. Some of the contents were reasonable. Each compact box of water-resistant cardboard contained two cigarettes and some chewing gum. Some had tinfoil packets of Nescafe. The canned cheddar cheese in the noon pack was quite tasty, as a matter of fact. But Hunter doubted a pig would relish the can of so-called ham and eggs the fly-boy was bitching about. He wondered if the profiteers who made them for the army ever tasted the stuff they put in the packs. There was a fairly decent fruit bar in one pack, some tasty malted milk tablets in another, but you could wind up with something that was supposed to be a chocolate bar and tasted like brown cardboard. Each pack contained what looked like two sets of dog biscuits, wrapped in cellophane. One set tasted like saltine crackers, which was okay, and the other tasted like toilet paper, which wasn't. Knowledgeable GIs always tried to get the noon dinner pack as the lesser of three evils. Hunter had wrangled as many of these as he could for his men, but the rest of the division was smart too, and that was why he had the one breakfast pack to give to Rowan. It served the bastard right for sending that self-serving message. Hunter decided to keep the carbine for himself too.

Rowan poked disgustedly at the contents of the breakfast pack and settled on the dry biscuits. Hunter divided his few ounces of cheddar with his jump knife and handed half to the fly-boy. "Here, we have to keep you on your feet. How are those flying boots holding up?"

Rowan shrugged and said, "They're ruined. But I'm not quite barefooted yet. I should have thought to take the boots from one of those Germans back there.'

"Yeah, I guess you were still too shook up to look out for Uncle Don."

Rowan sighed and said, "That's for damned sure. Are we square about that little trouble I had identifying you guys from the air?"

"No, but forget it. I'm getting to love you more by the hour, now that I know your style."

Rowan didn't get it. He swallowed some cheese and asked, "Is it true you guys have benzedrine?"

"Yes, but you can't have any. You make me nervous enough as it is. I don't know who sold the army on the stuff. I guess it was the same chemist who invented dehydrated eggs. I'd swap either for their weight in ammo."

"Well, they must know what they're doing. Pep pills make more sense than letting a paratrooper fall asleep in combat, right?"

"I'm not sure about that. I'd rather have a sleepyhead than a doped-up trooper anywhere near me with a gun. These guys were good specimens when the airborne accepted them, and they've trained like athletes ever since. It seems to me a guy in good shape could go a couple of nights without sleep if he had to without artificial stimulants."

"What if the action lasts longer?"

"Shit, how long can anything last? A healthy man can stay awake seventy-two hours if anything at all exciting is going on around him. In three days an outfit should have won or lost, for God's sake."

'They're your men, but if you ask me, you sound a little puritanical. You may not drink or take benzedrine yourself, but—"

"I've tried the issue benzedrine," Hunter cut in. "That's why I'm afraid of the stuff. We used them on a training exercise back at Benning. It scared the shit out of me. Not while I was on them. Later, when I came to my senses and remembered some of the funny ideas I'd had and some of the things I'd almost done. We had one man who must have taken more than me, or maybe just didn't have as much tolerance. He decided that a real paratrooper didn't need no sissy parachute if he was really tough. So he hollered Geronimo and jumped, without his parachute. The hell of it was, none of the rest tried to stop him. It seemed so . . . reasonable, at the time."

Across the clearing, Acting Corporal Arnold washed down the last of his dog biscuits with canteen water and told Falco, "Jesus, the rations taste like shit and my water tastes like piss!"

"Come on, kid," Falco said. "You've found your home in the U.S. Army."

Another trooper called Tennessee snorted and said, "That's the pure truth and I've never doubted it. But when this war is over, I'm aiming to move so fur up the hollow that nobody will ever be able to tell me about it if there's another one!"

Falco said, "Bullshit, Tennessee. You've found a home, too. You never had it so good. You gotta admit there's more shoes in your duffle bag than in your whole home town."

Arnold joined in the round of laughter, but Falco could see something more than the K rations was bothering him. He stood up, stretched, and looked across to where Hunter was sitting with the other officer. He caught Arnold's eye and motioned him over. Drawing the young ex-cadet aside, Falco asked, "Okay, what's eating you? You still shook up about them Krauts back there?"

Arnold nodded. "Yeah, how did you know?"

"I jumped in Sicily. Look, it was you or them, right?"

"Hell, I'm not shook up about killing them. They damned near killed me before I came unstuck."

"Yeah, a lot of guys go through that the first time. Maybe some guys who bought the farm in this war never *did* come unstuck in time. Don't worry. Next time you won't take as long. It gets sort of like swatting flies after you've done it a few times."

"That's what's been bothering me," Arnold said. "That's all it felt like. Like I was swatting flies or maybe slapping at a mosquito before it could bite me.'

"That's the way a soldier's supposed to feel. What are you bitching about, Arnold?"

"The way nothing happened to me back there. I mean, up to then, I'd never killed anything bigger than a rabbit. But now I can say I killed two guys. One, anyway. The looie finished the driver off."

Falco stared blankly at him and Arnold insisted, "A guy who's just killed a guy ought to feel, well, different. I mean, the first time a kid *comes*, even if it's only with his hand, he sort of passes through to a whole new outlook on life, right?"

Falco laughed. "Well, yeah, he knows his pecker's not just for pissing and the girls don't just look like soft boys anymore. But shooting a Kraut ain't like losing your virginity, kid."

"I thought it would be. I used to wonder, if the time came, if I could do it. I thought if I ever got up the nerve to really kill some guy I'd be a different person afterwards. But it's been hours now, and I don't feel any different than I ever did. Ain't something supposed to happen to you?"

"Not unless the other guy shoots first. What were you expecting, Arnold, horns and a tail? Killing a guy don't make you taller or grow more hair on your chest. I hate to have to tell you this, kid, but you're the same slob now you always were."

Arnold laughed, but said, "That's what's so weird about it. It didn't feel awful and it wasn't a thrill. Don't some guys get a thrill out of killing people, Falco? That's what I've always heard."

Falco frowned thoughtfully and said, "Maybe if a guy was sick in the head he'd get a charge out of it. I never have. I know you're supposed to have bad dreams about it, afterwards. But the only nightmares I ever have about Krauts is like when I shoot at one in my sleep and the bastard won't go down. The ones I got in Sicily never bother me."

"Jesus, do you think we're both cold-blooded killers?"

Falco snorted in disgust. "Hey, come on, stop making such a big deal out of it. You know what you are, Arnold? You're a frustrated bullshit artist. You were looking forward to telling your grandchildren war stories, like them old farts around the legion hall back home. You can always tell an old soldier who never heard a shot fired in anger when he starts that shit. Them Krauts you shot up spoiled your future for you. You'll never be able to play the vet who went through hell with a straight face, and you're looking for something to make what you done sound like Hollywood."

"Maybe you're right," Arnold said slowly. "It did seem like a sort of letdown back there. It was all over so fast, like the way you feel after you've been up an alley with a hooker. No matter how hard-up you started out, you never feel it was worth what she asked when it's over. Maybe if they'd died slower, making a speech or something . . ."

Falco snorted and shook his head. "I'll give you a speech. Run over there and ask the looie when he wants to push on. We got less than an hour to go before sundown and these hedgerows are spooky enough in the daylight."

Arnold nodded and dog-trotted along the hedge toward Hunter's position. Falco watched him, eyes narrowed thoughtfully. What was that crap about wanting guys to die slow and talking about it to you? Falco had shot maybe a dozen men in Sicily. It was hard to tell when a guy dropped if you'd really nailed him or not. Nobody had ever died too slow for Falco. When he had to shoot at a guy, he wanted the jerk to just lie down and say no more about it.

There was something funny going on in Arnold's head. The kid said he felt weird because he'd gotten no thrill from gunning those Krauts. But what in the hell made a guy want to feel a thrill? Who said they'd sent you over here to enjoy the fucking war?

Falco muttered, "Cajun. That's who he reminds me of."

Falco turned away and hunkered down, hoping he was wrong. Cajun was what they'd called that guy in Sicily. The one who'd chalked up thirty-nine Krauts before they were pulled out. The one who'd kept bitching and bitching about not getting the chance to make it an even forty. The one they'd hung for murder after he went nuts and shot the supply sergeant that night to make up for his missing Kraut.

5

THE ROOM was semidark, save for the situation map taking up one whole wall like a movie screen. The acetate over the map was marked with red and blue crayon. Red for enemy positions and blue for Allied. There was a lot more blue, of course, since Rommel didn't report the disposition of his forces to Eisenhower on a regular basis. Seats had been provided for the small group of top brass in the room. But the only man sitting down was a Free French brigadier who walked with a cane.

The American officer standing by the map with a long wooden pointer swept it in an arc from Calais to Cherbourg and said, "The RAF and Fighter Command have done a lovely job on the enemy's air cover and it's safe to assume they don't have our present positions at all. Montgomery reports he landed in good order, and while the British don't have as many wheels as we do, nobody can hold like the British Tommy. So our northeast flank should be pretty secure. The Omaha landing, as you gentlemen know, could have gone better. But our people have the situation stable along that stretch of coast now, and Utah landing at the base of the Cherbourg Peninsula is in even better shape. The enemy there seems to have made one hell of a tactical error unless he knows something we don't know."

He moved the tip of the pointer across the base of the peninsula in a throat-cutting gesture and added, "They've withdrawn to dig in around those big fortifications around Cherbourg. So a thrust along this road from Utah to Carteret on the far side will cut them off from the rest of the war. Once they're pinned down in Cherbourg a modest amount of armor should be enough to starve them into surrender. Our tankers are meeting no real resistance in that area now, and they're ready to go as soon as they get the go sign."

He fell silent and all eyes turned on a balding man wearing a short field jacket and four silver stars. Dwight David Eisenhower swallowed the green taste in his mouth. He knew he was expected to say something, and he wished he was somewhere else. He was aware that some of them thought he was indecisive, but, Jesus, there were so many things to decide, and half of them had to be blind guesses.

Ike cleared his throat. "What about that German armor concentrated up near Calais?"

The man at the map laughed and said, "Yes, we really suckered Rommel into thinking we'd come across the narrow part of the channel. He's got heavy hardware north of the Seine. It's starting to move, too. But we own the sky and you move slow and sneaky without air cover. Besides, there's that rumor that Rommel's not in command. Hitler only has two tank commanders who move as fast as our guys, and Guderian is on the Russian front. It's simple math, General. We only have to move our armor twenty-odd miles tonight to cut the Cherbourg garrison off. The heavy enemy reserves have to move over a hundred, and by the time they can, Montgomery will be well dug in around Caen."

"Without enough armor," Ike remarked, adding wearily, "There's never enough armor. Run that part about Rommel being home on leave by me again."

"We have two reports on that, General. British intelligence has him home to celebrate his wife's birthday and the FFI says he went home to attend his own birthday party. I don't think it matters whose candles are on the cake, as long as he's not here in Normandy."

Ike frowned. "Either way, it would be a break for us, if only we could be sure. By now he knows we've landed, but even if he flies in he's going to need time to get a handle on things and . . ." Ike turned to a man with wings over his medals and said, "I want all your interdiction pilots to give top priority to anything that looks like a staff car."

The air force general nodded and moved to the bank of phones near a side wall. Ike turned back to the map and said, "I don't know. We could take the chance and chew a hell of a bite out of Hitler's friendly neighborhood army, or we could wait for George Patton. How long would that take, Colonel?"

The man with the pointer said, "At least a few days, sir. General Patton is on his way down from Scotland, but he won't have his armor sorted out and in shape to move for some time."

Another officer said, "Harmon's Second Armored is ready to go, General."

Ike sighed. "Hell on Wheels has had ants in its pants since Harmon took command. The question is which way we move our heavy stuff, not whether they want to fight or not."

A phone rang and an aide picked up as Ike paced back and forth, looking like he was about to vomit. The others waited. You waited a lot with Ike.

The aide cupped a hand over the receiver and called out, "General, there's another report on Rommel. Some brown-nosing German officer sent a birthday message to Rommel in Germany. It was sent this morning."

Ike turned with a frown and demanded, "Where's that scoop coming from?"

"Fighter Command S2, sir. Apparently one of their downed pilots gathered together some FFI and scattered airborne stragglers behind the enemy lines and has been fighting a private war on the Cherbourg Peninsula. They intercepted German dispatches earlier in the day and—"

"That's the third strike," Ike said, turning back to the map. Taking a deep breath, he added, "All right, the word is go. Our tanks can be across the base of the peninsula before dawn and once our own armored infantry is dug in along that east-west highway the hedgerows will be on *our* side for a change!"

As other officers moved to the phones Ike added, "With Hitler's pet field commander AWOL, old Von Rundstedt will get to run his Army Group B his own way for a change. We know that Rommel was for fighting in close and that Von Rundstedt's been insisting all along on a defense in depth. He's a good but cautious soldier. He'll pull back and dig in to do it like the books says, and this time the book's wrong. I want the name of the pilot who confirmed that rumor about Rommel. If he's right he gets the Silver Star. If he's wrong he'll be peeling spuds as a private—assuming we have any army left, of course."

He turned to stare morosely at the situation map as he complained, "I wish we had more red up there. Our airborne may as well have stayed home for all the good they seem to have done. What's the latest on our jumping jacks?"

An embarrassed-looking officer with parachutist's wings over his breast pocket said, "The Eighty-second came down more or less together, in the wrong place, and took a mauling. I'm afraid the 101st was spread from hell to breakfast and the situation hasn't stabilized yet."

A British officer in a red beret with wings on it said, "Our Red Devils landed in good order, sir. The First British Airborne and the Free Polish Brigade have consolidated their positions near Monty."

Ike growled, "Good show. It's becoming increasingly obvious that someone at Fort Benning left something out. As soon as things settle down a bit I want a full investigation on what went wrong with the U.S. Airborne. Some officer in pretty boots has one hell of a mess to answer for!"

6

RAMIE DAVIS moved unsteadily along the passage-
way as the hospital transport sluggishly crested
a ground swell. She entered the tiny cabin to see
Beth propped up and awake with a plasma tube in
her arm and her make-up a mess.

Beth smiled. "Isn't this neat? They gave me a private
room. I guess they didn't want a girl sleeping with all
those men they loaded aboard, huh?"

Ramie didn't answer as she sat on the edge of the
bed. She didn't think Beth wanted to hear about some
of the wounded she'd seen back there. She was trying
not to think about a couple herself. She'd heard those
animal whimpers in the ruins of the East End during
the blitz, but they still made her heartsick.

As she took Beth's hand, Beth asked, "Have you
been crying, Ramie? Your eyes are all red."

"I'm all right. How about you?"

Beth giggled. "I'm feeling horny. Isn't that silly? One of the nurses said that happens a lot to wounded people. She said lots of the wounded men masturbate, even after an amputation. She said she'd understand if I wanted a candle or something, but I'd be too embarrassed.'

Ramie laughed. "Well, you're obviously going to live. How do you feel about your other parts?"

"Itchy. The doctor says that's a good sign. Look over there in that ash tray. They said I could keep them for souvenirs and when we get back to England I'm going to start a charm bracelet with them."

Ramie leaned forward to stare down at the three ugly little shards of twisted metal they'd dug out of Beth's flesh and repressed a shudder.

"Beth, you know I'm sorry. I owe you an explanation, at the very least."

"Oh, pooh, I'm not angry, Ramie. I was, when that silly thing went off right next to my poor fanny. I remember wanting to really tell you off when I realized I'd been hurt. But then they turned the lights off before I could really get good and mad. Uh . . . Ramie?"

"Yes, dear?"

"They told me you saved me. They said you carried me all the way back like I was Fay Wray and you were King Kong. How did you ever manage to do that? I've been meaning to go on a diet, but . . ."

"You don't need to diet. Listen to me, Beth. I have to tell you why I acted so foolishly back there. You were right and I was wrong. Neither of us had any business being so close to the fighting."

"I knew that before we landed. But it's okay. We

lived through it and you had to get your story, right?"

"Wrong. I guess you could say I was overcompensating for an inferiority complex instead of using the brain I was born with. I've always done that a lot, Beth. Up until now, nobody but me ever got hurt. I had no right to expose you to danger like that to prove myself to the world."

Beth shook her head, puzzled. "Gee, you don't act like you have feelings of inferiority, Ramie."

"I know. I'm a pretty cocky broad when people are watching. I know it's dumb. Any first-year psychology student could pigeonhole me as a classic case of rejected bastardy."

"Oh, pooh, I don't think you're a bastard. Maybe a little pushy, but—"

"They go together," Ramie cut in. "I was in my early teens when I found out I was the by-blow of a sordid backstairs affair between master and servant. My father was a rich old man who couldn't keep his hands off the hired help. My mother, of course, was the young servant girl. They packed her off with a tidy sum and a generous allowance that would stop if ever she opened her mouth about the grand and ever-so-social Lowell DeWitt!"

"DeWitt's the middle name you use, right?"

"Yes. I guess it was my mother's pathetic idea. When I was little, we naturally lived well. I was told she was a widow and that my father had died in an accident. I never lacked for anything and I was sent to the best schools. As a matter of fact, for an ex-servant, my mother became quite grand. Then, when I was fourteen, she was gravely ill for a time and one night, semi-delirious, she played True Confessions for me as I held her hand. You might say it shook me up."

Beth nodded gravely. "You should have heard it earlier or not at all. Fourteen's a lousy age without even more surprises. God, I had such pimples when I was fourteen. But you're all grown up now, Ramie. I don't see what all the fuss is about. Your father did right by you and your mother, which is more than a lot of men can say. Nobody would ever know, if you'd just stop telling everyone about it."

"I've never told anyone but you, Beth. I wanted you to understand why I behaved so terribly stupid back there on Omaha."

Beth looked totally confused as she replied, "I don't understand at all! Your mother and father weren't really married. Big deal. That's no reason for a girl to go around chinning herself and trying to beat the U.S. Army at their own game, is it?"

"No. Not logically. Everything you say is true, Beth. My wealthy father did all he could to clean up his sordid little domestic scandal and I must say I never lacked for anything. But it *burns* me, Beth! I grew up in a good neighborhood and went to Wellesley, but the DeWitts are social! I have half-sisters and half-brothers you see in the society section all the time and they don't know I exist. Can you understand how that eats at me?"

"You want to top them," Beth said, nodding. "They sent your pregnant mamma off to limbo and now you're as good as them and better. But you are good, Ramie. You're one of the best woman reporters in the field and you've got the bylines to prove it."

"It's never been enough." Ramie sighed. "I don't think a Pulitzer would even be enough. I don't know what would make me feel like . . . like a real DeWitt."

Beth laughed. "Maybe you could look up one of

your brothers and marry him? That would really jar your real father and he wouldn't be able to say anything! Hey, wouldn't that be neat?"

"For God's sake, that would be incest!"

"Sure it would. That's what would be so neat about it! Why have a *tiny* little skeleton in the closet when you could give those hoity-toity DeWitts a *real* gasser to keep under wraps? Gee, you'd be rich as well as sneaky. They'd have to call you Mrs. DeWitt DeWitt, right?"

Ramie laughed and said, "You're nuts. But you're cute and I admire your astonishingly filthy mind. Am I forgiven, Beth?"

"Oh, pooh, stop padding your part. That cute doctor with the red hair says I'll be up and around in no time and now that I'm a wounded vet I'm putting in for a raise."

A nurse came in and Beth cracked, "Who goes there, friend or enema?"

"Both," the nurse said. "Miss Waterman's had enough excitement for now, Miss Davis. The officers are serving cocktails topside, so . . ."

Ramie nodded, squeezed Beth's hand, and got up to leave. Outside in the corridor she hesitated, then decided she'd rather smoke alone out on deck than flirt with anybody. She found a hatchway and stepped outside to fumble out a pack of Woodbines in the lee of a lifeboat. As she lit up she suddenly realized she felt good. She took a drag and let it out with a soft smile. Beth's right, she thought. I've been padding my part.

She knew she didn't want to marry any half-brother. She wasn't sure now that she ever wanted to even meet one. What *did* it matter, at this late date? She was a grown woman and a respected pro. Maybe it was about time she put the past aside and began to *act* that way.

7

THE SUN was down. The sky was still light enough to read by as trooper Mahoney stepped through a gap in yet another hedgerow and caught a burst of machine gun fire full in the face. The German bullets chopped Mahoney to hash and sent his helmet and some of him back through the hedgerow in a blizzard of twigs and leaves.

Logan Hunter shouted, "Spread out and hug the bank!" as he rolled away to the left, found a small gap between two heavy trunks of hazel bush and risked a peek. The next field was empty. But a haze of blue smoke against the hedges on the far side betrayed the position of the German machine gun crew. Hunter emptied the clip of his carbine at it in one long burst of automatic, then rolled away as the return fire he'd expected to draw smashed through where he'd just been. The hedge he and his people were pinned down behind was old and had a good solid bank of earth up around its roots. They were okay for the moment if they kept their butts down. But they couldn't move away from the hedgerow. And if the Krauts had the manpower, they'd be trying to flank him by now.

Hunter raised his head from the dirt to look for Falco's half of the decimated stick. He could see where Falco should have been, down at the far end, but Falco wasn't there.

Hunter nodded and muttered, "Good thinking." Then he turned his head and shouted to the men with him, "Listen sharp! Stay down and fire your carbines straight up at interval. Don't try to play Dan'l Boone. Just keep making some noise where they can't hit you. I'm moving down a ways to play periscope, so don't anybody else try it!"

He started crawling on knees and elbows as the three troopers and one fly-boy left proceeded to pop their weapons in a ragged fusillade behind him. The machine gun opened up again, hashing greenery just above them as Hunter muttered, "Jerks. Didn't Adolf send you to basic?"

Apparently Adolf hadn't. When Hunter crawled clear and risked another look the blue haze was thicker and still in the same place. He knew from the sound it was a heavy MG-43. They probably had its bipod sandbagged and were playing World War One. From where Hunter lay, he could see all sides of the big green box they were in. He had no idea what he could possibly do about it if Krauts popped out of the bushes in any numbers. He saw Captain Rowan crawling his way and shouted, "Have you gone nuts again? Get back there and send some more .45 rounds at the moon!"

Rowan looked confused, raised his pistol and fired it twice, from the wrong position.

Hunter cursed and dropped below the level of the bank as the MG-43 drummed slugs along the other side of it. The fat was in the fire. So he sighed, raised his muzzle, and fired a burst from his fresh clip to make them think there were a lot of guys, spreading out. Rowan crawled to where he lay and asked, "What in the hell are we doing?"

"Drawing their fire. Haven't you noticed? The next time I tell you to do something, if you screw up I intend to shoot you on the spot. Have you got that much down, fly-boy, or am I talking too fast for you?"

"This doesn't make any sense," Rowan said. "We're wasting ammo."

"So are they. You haven't been hit lately, have you?"

"No, but you sure sent that point man of yours the wrong way."

"I noticed. His mother gets a free flag. If I thought you had the brains of a gnat I'd explain basic infantry tactics to you, but just keep your ass down and your mouth shut and maybe it will all sink in someday—if we make it."

He ordered Rowan to stay put and started crawling again as, on the far side of his cover, he heard a new rattle of carbine fire and a rebel yell. The machine gun fell silent. Hunter called to his own men, "Cease fire and hold!" He found another loophole and raised his head for a look.

There was nothing to be seen but the far wall of green and the fading haze of gunsmoke. Then Acting Corporal Arnold popped out of the bushes the Krauts

113

used to own over there and came running across as Hunter got to his feet, smiling thinly. He walked back to the gap where Mahoney had bought it. Mahoney was still there. What was left of him, anyway. He stepped out to retrieve Mahoney's carbine as Arnold ran up to him, saluted, and said, "Falco sent me to tell you we done it, sir!"

"I knew that. Any casualties?"

"Uh, yessir. Tennessee's dead. Falco said we don't yell before we break cover in this war."

"Falco's right. What did you outflank over there?"

"We don't know, sir. They're wearing funny uniforms. There were six of them. Falco said they must have been green. They had this regular machine gun nest set up and Falco says it made no sense. He told me to tell you the area's secured, sir."

Hunter nodded, signaled his other men to follow, and started across the field with Arnold. On the far side, he found Falco and his two remaining troopers smoking by an awful mess. The Germans lay in a pile inside a ring of sandbags. One was sprawled across the MG-43 he'd thought they had. Their uniforms were Luftwaffe blue, with pink piping. Second growth alder and poplar grew all around. There was a slight slope to the ground and as Hunter looked down through the trees he could make out what seemed a single-lane secondary road down there.

"The way I see it, sir," said Falco, "they were put here to cover that road. Only they could see both ways through this fucking hedge and we got lucky. They didn't have no perimeter or nothing. Just a half-ass machine gun section out here all alone. Ain't that a bitch?"

"They were Panzer Grenadiers," Hunter said. "Maybe their weapons carrier broke down or got shot up, so they pulled back in these trees hoping somebody on their side would come along."

Falco spat and said, "Panzer Grenadiers, huh? Begging the lieutenant's pardon, but they look like Kraut fly-boys to me."

"I know. Ask Hermann Goering why he dressed them up like that. The point is they were mechanized troops, without the mechanized. They were probably as confused as we are. Have you scouted that road down there?"

"Just a quarter mile each way, sir. It don't look too important."

"Nobody builds unimportant roads, Falco. And it runs east and west."

He took out his map, unfolded it, and said, "Jackpot. It's a farm lane running to Ste. Mère Église and it's starting to get dark. Let's go back to the old way. Arnold, take the point and let's move it out."

Falco hesitated, then shrugged and said, "You heard him, Arnold."

A few minutes later they were slogging east on the unexpected narrow roadway. What was left of them. Even Falco was too tired to give a damn what lay ahead. But he kept listening for the sound of gunfire and as crickets began to sing from the bushes all around he knew that whoever held the town had it nailed down pretty good.

Less than an hour later, as the light was giving out, Arnold rounded a bend, spotted logs across the road ahead, and was about to move back when a voice called out, "Freeze, you mother fucker, and if you don't answer me sudden and in English you can say your prayers!"

"GI! GI!" yelled Arnold, throwing in the password for good measure. One of the paratroopers behind the roadblock threw back the countersign and added, "Advance and be recognized." As he got a better look at the approaching trooper, he added, "What happened to you, boy? You look like somebody drug you through the keyhole backwards."

"Listen, I got some guys behind me. Okay if I call them in?"

"Hell, sure, the more the merrier. God knows there ain't as many of us as there used to be and tonight we'll all have second helpings."

Arnold ran back and found that the others had overheard enough to be moving in on the double. He stopped until Hunter joined him and they all moved in together. As they climbed over the logs the troopers on the other side spotted the silver bar and came to attention. Hunter said, "As you were. What's the situation here in town?"

A perimeter guard said, "The Eighty-second owns it, sir. But the fucking Krauts sure made us earn it! The first wave was about wiped out. Then we had us a serious discussion on the matter and the Krauts took off like big-ass birds. Some of 'em, anyway. We killed us a mess of Krauts here. You want one of us to take you to the CP, sir?"

Hunter nodded numbly. Now that it was over, he felt drained and as he followed the guide into the ruins of Ste. Mère Église he kept expecting to wake up and find it had all been a dream. There was something wrong here. It couldn't be over, just like that. It was like watching a movie when the reel broke in the middle of the story.

It was less than twenty-four hours since he'd taken off from England with a full platoon, and now he was down to a handful of tired men and he still didn't know what had happened. He started to ask the guide how the landings had gone. But they'd tell him that at the CP and he wasn't sure he really gave a damn.

The airborne had done what it had been sent to do, more or less, and the rest of the army could worry about their own damned jobs. He just wanted to lie down somewhere and sleep a million years.

Behind him, Arnold said, "Hey, wait up. I got a rock in my boot and it's killing me."

Hunter turned wearily. "I'm not about to wait up. You'll just have to leave the damned thing in your boot for now, Arnold."

The acting corporal muttered and kept walking, albeit limping badly. At Arnold's side, Falco said, "You should have took it out when you first felt it, kid."

Arnold said, "I know. I was going to, but somehow I sort of forgot all about it for a while."

8

A FTER A FEW days rest Logan Hunter was starting to feel like a human being instead of a zombie as he strode into regimental HQ in freshly polished boots. A tall blond man with oak leaves on his shoulder met him just inside the doorway and said, "A word of warning before you report to the new CO, old buddy. Watch out for him. He snaps."

Hunter nodded. "So I've heard, Dan. What seems to be his problem?"

Dan Bradley answered, "Senility, I think. He's a retread from the last war and he talks like Victor McLaglen playing the tough old top kick. He just reamed me good for being on pass when the balloon went up. And let's face it, old buddy. *You* sort of screwed up on D day, too."

Hunter smiled thinly. "I know. Maybe if you'd been with us things would have gone smoother."

The regimental S2 frowned and said, "Hey, let's not be getting snotty, old buddy! I had an excuse for missing the drop. You jumped and blew it. Do you read me, *Lieutenant?*"

"Loud and clear, Major. I'll never call you Danny Boy again."

Bradley laughed and corked his junior officer on the shoulder. "Come on, let's not tense up on each other, buddy boy. Us peasants have to stick together against the fucking brass, right?"

Hunter nodded and moved past him to report in. He didn't know about that boyish major. Bradley was a hard guy to figure. One minute he was smiling at you and the next he was pulling rank. Hunter wished his superior would make up his mind, if he had one.

He found the regimental sergeant major in an alcove, guarding a door with a desk and his life. He told the sergeant major who he was and the noncom said, "Yessir. The colonel is expecting you. Go right in."

Hunter removed his cunt cap, tucked it under his left elbow, and went in to hit the balk line on the floor in front of the field desk as he saluted the feisty-looking little grey-haired man glaring up at him. The new CO wore a lot of fruit salad under his paratroop wings. A couple of them were completely new to Hunter, but he recognized the World War One Victory ribbon. The bird colonel snapped, "My name is Sam Bell and I'm a whale of destruction. When I holler froggie I expect everyone to jump. Do we understand each other, Lieutenant?"

"Yessir. I'm reporting as ordered, sir."

"Good. In case you're wondering, I earned these wings the hard way at Benning when the troops were first forming up before Pearl. What have you to say about the way you fucked up on D day?"

"No excuse, sir. I did what I could with what I had where they dropped me."

"That's the first honest answer I've heard all day. But let's face it, you didn't do a hell of a lot, and neither did anyone else, and they're on my ass about it. What's this shit about you being insubordinate to an air force captain?"

Hunter blinked in surprise. "I didn't expect the mother to make that charge, sir. If you've read my report, you'll see he was lucky we didn't shoot him."

Colonel Bell glanced down at the papers on his desk. "Yeah, I think I'd have shot him, too. But you still busted a superior officer in the chops, and he's supposed to be some kind of nine-day wonder. They just hung a Silver Star on him for some reason and I've been told to give you an official reprimand. Do you feel reprimanded, Lieutenant?"

"Yessir. No excuse, sir."

"Good enough. I served under another Lieutenant Hunter in the last war. First Lieutenant Duncan Hunter, AEF. Mean anything to you?"

"Yessir. He's my father, sir."

The older man laughed incredulously and rose from behind his desk. "For God's sake! Put her there, son! I thought I'd seen your face before. You're the spitting image of my old CO and we're going to drink on it! Didn't your father ever tell you about his old corporal, Sam Bell?"

"Corporal, Colonel?" Hunter frowned, glancing at the eagle on Bell's shirt.

Bell took a bottle of Canadian from the file cabinet

as he nodded and said, "That was last war. Your dad
and I saw some heavy action not far from here. I
came out with the rank of sergeant and, well, remember the Depression? Naw, if your folks managed to
feed you you don't remember the Depression. I had a
wife and two kids of my own to feed, so I reupped in
the regular army in '32. I was a warrant SG when the
Japs hit Pearl and you can't beat getting in on the
ground floor. My own son, Gil, is a little too young
for this one, knock wood. I guess they thought they
were humoring an old vet when they let me qualify at
Benning. But field grade officers who aren't afraid to
leap out of C-47s break a lot of legs, and the rest is
history. Here, drink up."

Hunter took a sip of Canadian and handed the
bottle back. Bell took a healthier swig and put the
booze away as he said, "It feels good to have another
Hunter with me against the Krauts. If you're half the
man your father was, the Krauts will be well advised
to steer clear of this regiment. I wish there was some
way to leave that black mark off your records, but . . ."

"I don't expect any favors, sir," Hunter cut in.

Sam Bell nodded. "I know. I told you I served under
your father. But I'd do it anyway, if I could. They say
Ike wants to scrap the whole idea of airborne. So this
is not the time to bend any rules."

"I understand, sir. I know I shouldn't have slugged
that fly-boy. But if I ever run into him again I'm going
to kick the shit out of him just the same."

"Yeah, I read about what he called a natural mistake. But the next time you see him, act polite. That's
an order. They get excited when you hit a hero. I
know he stole that Silver Star from you. I mentioned
it, sort of loud, to SHAEF. But right now we're in the
dog house and Ike himself signed the bastard's com-

mendation, so it's too late to change the official records. On paper, you and your few survivors don't look so hot right now. You didn't take out enough Krauts to balance the books. Some transport command mother has friends in high place too, and they're insisting they dropped all you kids in the DZ and don't want to hear any more about it."

Hunter snorted derisively. "I'd like to give them something to hear about, sir. The Krauts didn't kill us all, and I've got witnesses that they dropped us miles from our DZ. And apparently they dropped my other stick in the channel, since nobody's seen one of them since."

Bell grinned craftily and said, "By God, I like your style, son, and I may just give you the chance to sound off about the SNAFU. They're pulling us out to lick our wounds and replace all the eggs we dropped. Ike's ordered a complete review of what went wrong and I've been making up a list of officers to send in for us. Do you have any good telephone numbers in London, son?"

"A few, sir."

"Good. I'll send you with Major Bradley to give our side of the story. You'll be on detached duty and checked into Brown's Hotel on per diem while they rehash things there. It'll take 'em weeks, if I know the fat cats who do their fighting on paper. What's the matter? You don't look happy. Don't you want to go to London?"

"Of course, sir. It's . . . yes, of course."

Colonel Bell nodded and said, "I think Major Bradley is an asshole, too, and I just told him so. But as regimental S2 he has to appear before the board and he's pretty good at covering his own tracks. The son of a bitch was getting laid in London when he was supposed to be jumping in Normandy, and there's not a thing anybody can do about it. Believe you me, I read every bit of the fine print trying to put him in the coffin, too! But, what the hell, a born politician may come in handy before the board. I'm expecting you to stand up to those field grade officers and stick to your story no matter how transport command tries to trip you up. Are you sure you have your map co-ordinates right?"

Hunter smiled and said, "Better than that, sir. I can call a hero with the Silver Star as a witness. Rowan sent a mayday when he was shot down after strafing us. So fighter command has it on record when and where his P-38 went down. The wreckage should still be there."

Colonel Bell grinned from ear to ear. "God almighty, you *are* your father's son! He was an officer who could think on his feet, too! There's no way in hell they can get around the provable fact that you and your men were nowhere near your assigned DZ that morning!"

Hunter nodded in agreement. "There's just no way we could have gotten that far from where they were supposed to drop us in less than a full day, and, assuming we got lost on bikes, the DZ's not behind the enemy lines anymore. The 101st has recovered all its dead and not one sign of my men who jumped with Sergeant Flint has even been found. So Flint and half my platoon had to have come down either in the channel or much deeper into enemy territory. Either way, there's no way transport's about to put them over the DZ when they jumped."

Bell cackled gleefully. "Hot damn, we're back in business. Even a chairborne commando can follow *that* line of reasoning. I'll see if some of the other units who dropped in the wrong areas can nail those damned transport pilots in the box for us with similar reasoning. Meanwhile, you're my star witness. So we'd better arrange some transportation and expense vouchers on the double."

Bell reached for his desk phone. Then he hesitated and asked, "How do you get along with Major Bradley, son?"

"Danny Boy? I guess he's all right, sir. They say he did pretty good in North Africa and Sicily, before my time."

"It was before my time, too. I just got here from the Z of I. I'm not supposed to talk like this to junior officers, but watch him, Logan. I've been in this man's army long enough for my dog tags to vote, and your S2 superior is a back biter if ever I saw one."

Hunter frowned and said, "I'm afraid I don't understand, sir."

"I've never understood the breed, either. But you don't have to understand a shark to know you don't want to go swimming with it."

"I don't expect to do much swimming with old Danny Boy, sir. I just have to work under him."

"Yeah, and I'm sorry as hell about that, Logan. Why do they call him Danny Boy, anyway? Is he a tenor?"

Hunter laughed. "I've never heard him sing, sir. He gave the nickname to himself for some reason. He tells everyone to call him Danny Boy—unless he's pulling rank on them, of course."

"I know the type. Don't ever let him get anything on you, Logan. I don't claim to be a sweetheart, and if I have to be a bastard I'm damned good at it. But officers like Bradley don't act like bastards because they *have* to. They do it for practice! I wish I didn't have to send you both to London together, but I've no choice. They've sent for him and I need you there to make sure he doesn't blame me for the SNAFU on D day."

"That's impossible, sir! Nobody could possibly hang anything on you. You weren't in command at the time. There's no way you could be blamed for what happened."

Bell grimaced and said, "You don't think so, son? I can see you still have a lot to learn about this man's army."

9

Londondon was still officially blacked out, but it hardly mattered in high summer because the sky stayed light until eleven at this latitude. Ramie Davis, as an American, had never really gotten used to the pattern of day and night in Northern Europe. As she walked over to Baker Street to hail a cab she thought of Stevenson's poem.

> *In Winter I get up at night*
> *And have to dress by candle light*
> *In Summer quite the other way*
> *I have to go to bed by Day.*

She'd learned that as a child back in the States, but until she'd left her office late in the afternoon to find herself groping through the blackout, or come out of a pub after closing time at ten to blink owlishly in the dazzling light like a kid coming out of a matinee double feature, she'd never grasped Stevenson's meaning in full.

Near the corner of Wigmore and Baker two British soldiers saluted Ramie. She smiled and saluted back at them as they passed. GIs seemed to think she was a nurse or WAC officer too, but seldom saluted even a male officer in town on leave. After all this time in London Ramie really felt more comfortable with British manners. The British caste system had its drawbacks, especially for one near the bottom of the totem pole, but she sometimes suspected there was more hidden hostility in the "Democratic" pecking order of her fellow Americans.

She lucked onto an antiquated taxi coming down Baker. As she got in and gave the driver the Kanes' Belgravia address she glanced at her wrist and saw she was early, so she told the driver there was no hurry. He nodded and threw the ancient wreck in gear to rattle down the street with the little engine apparently doing double duty as a coffee grinder. The cab had been a relic even when civilian auto production had stopped near the beginning of the war, but all the other cars they passed were getting long in the tooth, too. Had there really been a time when new models came out every summer?

Ramie took her compact from the musette bag she wore slung on her left shoulder and examined herself in the mirror. Her hair and makeup were okay. But just okay, like the rest of London. Ramie was on her way to the fashionable cocktail party in her UPI uniform instead of the dress she'd planned on wearing because the skirt of her civvies was getting shiny and a strap on her one pair of decent shoes had given up the ghost again and was probably beyond repair this time. She had clean underwear and there were no ladders in her rayon stockings, but she felt crummy anyway. Even her makeup and perfume felt used.

The driver swung west on Oxford and Ramie stared out, depressed, at the passing shop windows. The plate glass was taped and even the window dummies in their dated dresses seemed bloody weary of keeping a stiff upper lip.

They swung toward the Thames at Marble Arch to drive down Hyde Park's east side. Even the park was war weary. Grass grew greener over here than in the States and someone kept trimming it as neatly as a golf course, but the antiaircraft guns squatting in a park detracted from the overall effect. A neatly dressed little girl was skipping along a path under the watchful eye of a prim-looking nanny. The child seemed oblivious of the grim toys of war around her or the grey barrage balloons hovering overhead. Ramie knew they'd been a part of the child's life since she'd been old enough to play in the park.

They swung around Hyde Park Corner, where a manic-looking man on a box was addressing a crowd of bored-looking people, and then they were on Grosvenor Place behind the palace grounds and Ramie told the driver to stop and let her off. She was still too early. How could she have known she'd have no trouble getting a cab? Things like that weren't supposed to happen anymore.

She paid the fare and walked slowly toward the Kanes' town house. She smiled wryly at her own annoyance, knowing she was overreacting to another of the little annoyances of her long stay in London. It was strange how it seemed to be the *little* things that really got you down. The West End had come through the bombings in good shape. The ruins had been bull-dozed into brick-shard vacant lots or neatly boarded over, depending. With a little effort and ingenuity one could still eat, drink, and fornicate at will in London. But, like the last-minute compromise in costume, everything seemed to turn out third rate. The best restaurants served fish and chips these days and you had to drink arf-and-arf whether you liked beer or not because hard liquor was rationed and the only Coca Cola in town seemed to be at the Rainbow Corner Canteen, if one could call what they served there Coca Cola.

She saw the entrance to the Kanes' town house ahead and considereed walking back to the palace to kill time. But then she saw some people getting out of another miraculous taxi and decided that if they could go in, she could too.

Ramie waited until the earlier arrivals were inside before she walked up to the house and mounted the stone steps. The butler who greeted her had apparently come with the house. The "servant problem" in London wasn't finding a maid who'd do windows. By now the British had drafted almost every young person who looked healthy, male or female. Ramie wondered how many working girls would return to service after a few years in the ATS or even the Land Army. The Land Army girls, despite their dress uniform, were agriculture workers, driving tractors or digging spuds in some of the strangest places. They enjoyed an even wilder reputation than the military ATS, reputed to stand for Army Tail Service, although Ramie had looked it up and found it really stood for Army Transport Service. They said Ike was very pleased with the female driver they'd given him. But, alas, UPI could hardly print that.

Ramie followed the sound of clinking glass into a drawing room off the main hall and saw to her relief that she wasn't too early after all. A woman in a low-cut rust silk dress apparently left over from an old Joan Crawford movie was leaning on the grand piano in the bay window when she spotted Ramie in the doorway. She smiled and came over as Ramie suddenly recognized her hostess. Admiral Kane's young wife, Alexandra, had changed her hair color again. It was henna rinsed to match her dress. Alexandra Kane held out her hand in greeting. "Ramie, dear, so good of you to come. Are you on duty this weekend? I notice you're in uniform. It's very becoming, though."

Ramie managed to smile back as she murmured some lie and added, "Is your husband still at Admiralty, Mrs. Kane? I don't see him and I wanted to ask him about what his lot did on D day."

The redhead said, "Please call me Sandy, dear. I have no idea what Ivor's up to at the moment. I don't allow him to bring the war home with him. Do you want me to introduce you around or would you rather do your own mixing?"

"I'm fine, ah, Sandy. Nobody ever remembers each other's names at these affairs anyway."

"Oh, you're so right, dear. I think mixing is more civilized, too. But let's get you a drink, shall we?"

She led Ramie to a portable bar in another corner, still smiling. Didn't she ever stop smiling? Alexandra was one of those women who always looked like they'd just stepped out of a shop window, with her expression painted on a hollow plaster head. A bored-looking British petty officer stood behind the bar as they approached. Alexandra Kane asked, "What would you like, Ramie dear?"

Ramie saw they had an astounding and probably

illegal variety on tap. She smiled at the bartender and asked him if he could make her a tall, very tall highball. "I'd like something I could sort of nurse."

The CPO nodded sagely and took a Zombie glass from his rack. Mrs. Kane managed to look like she was yawning and smiling at the same time while she patted Ramie on the arm and said, "Evans will take care of you, dear. Excuse me, I have to mix."

But as she started to turn, she hesitated to ask, "By the way, isn't Davis a Welsh name?"

"I guess it was, once," Ramie said. "We've been American for quite some time, Sandy. Why?"

"I thought it was a Welsh name. You and Evans here have a lot in common." And then she was moving languidly away. Ramie looked blankly at the bartender and said, "I don't get it. Was that a crack, chief?"

His face was neutral as he replied, "Yes, miss. Scotch or Canadian with your highball?"

Ramie laughed. "Scotch, please, unless you have Welsh."

One corner of his mouth twitched, but he kept his place as he gravely poured a little Scotch and a lot of water in the tall slim glass and said, dryly, "We *make* the creature in the Valley, look you. But we've never told the Saxons about the *good* stuff!"

She smiled and said, "I see I have a lot to learn about my heritage, chief. It's funny, but back in the States, nobody seems to know the difference between being Welsh and English."

"So I've heard, miss. Will that be all, miss?"

She realized she was putting the enlisted man in a spot by chatting with him, so she nodded thanks and moved away with her highball, looking for some place to use as a base. She never would have come had she known the admiral wouldn't be at his own party. She knew there'd be no news fit to print from the poor man's silly wife and her friends. Ramie liked Admiral Kane. He'd always been very sweet to her about such war information as anyone connected with Mountbatten's rather hush-hush staff could give. And unlike some officers she'd interviewed, he'd never gotten silly about the differences in their genders. A man who led commando operations had to have some brains, no matter how he talked. So how on earth could Ivor Kane be so blind about his young wife?

It wasn't just that Alexandra Kane was a silly little bitch. She had a reputation to rival that of Messalina, and even if one discounted the gossip about her and those colored quartermasters in the back of her car, there was so much gossip about her that *some* of it had to have gotten back to her husband by now.

Ramie grimaced as she sipped her drink. The highball was just right, but now she regretted ordering it. Unless she gulped it or left it somewhere like a sneak she had to stay at least a few more minutes.

Outside in the bright evening light, two tall men in paratroop boots turned the corner. Major Dan Bradley told Lieutenant Logan Hunter, "This must be de blaze, nicht wahr?"

"Don't you know, Danny Boy?"

"It's a joke, son. Everybody knows where Sandy Kane holds court. Wait 'til you meet her. She's blonde, all over, and she really digs Yanks. You know what I mean?"

"You said she was married, Dan."

"Big deal. Her old man's one of them Noel Coward types who have to sit down to piss, and he's hardly ever home besides. But don't worry about old Sandy's sleeping arrangements, buddy boy. I saw her first."

"Why are you telling me about her, then?"

"Just wanted you to know what sort of a party I'm taking you to, buddy boy. You're new over here, so I have to fill you in about these English broads. Everybody back home thinks they're snooty and cold, but let me tell you a secret, buddy boy. These West End society broads put out quicker than any American girl. They can throw a greenhorn with that hoity-toity way they talk, but get one alone, and be prepared to take your beating like a man."

"I've dated some English girls, Dan."

"Yeah, ain't they something? I thought I'd shit the first time I made one. I was moving in slow and easy, see? I mean, I didn't know the rules over here, and she was pretty as hell, so I didn't want to blow it on the first date. We had dinner and a show and I kept my hands to myself all evening. We talked about the war and when she said her husband was a POW in Burma I figured I'd been wasting my time. But then we get to her place and I figure, what the hell, I'll settle for a good-night kiss."

"That sounds reasonable, Danny Boy."

"Hey, no shit, I was really being a nice little gent, once she'd told me her old man was being held by the Japs. I never even Frenched her. I mean, I gave her my best Jack Armstrong at Hudson High nighty-night in the doorway of her flat. And then she says, 'You will use a rubber, won't you?' and I was so surprised I wasn't sure I could get it up!"

Hunter grinned crookedly and said, "But you managed to, right?"

"Oh, did I ever! I guess she was sort of hard up, too. She said the Japs had had her old man since '42. We spent one wild weekend, buddy boy. We hardly got out of bed to take a leak. She even fed me tea and toast in bed, sitting there bare ass and talking like a fucking duchess. So don't let the way they talk throw you. They're all sex maniacs over here."

Hunter repressed a crack about it taking one to know one. Since the colonel had billetted them together at Brown's Hotel and they'd been attending those interminable hearings at Grosvenor Square together day after day, it was hard to avoid Danny Boy and, what the hell, Colonel Bell had said not to let him run loose snapping at car tires.

To change the subject, Hunter asked, "How come that street sign back there said Grosvenor Place? Grosvenor Square is way the hell on the other side of the park."

Bradley said, "How the hell should I know? The square's in Mayfair and this is Belgravia. Maybe they repeat the names in each district or something. Here's the place they're giving the brawl. Just follow my lead and we'll find out if old Sandy has a friend for you."

They were let in by the butler and Hunter caught the guarded look of distaste on the old man's face. So Danny Boy was telling the truth about having been here before, it would seem. Hunter wondered why the major worked so hard at being obnoxious. Bradley wasn't a bad-looking guy and there was no reason for him to have an inferiority complex. The jerk had field grade rank and the troops were the cream of the U.S. Army. But you always expected Danny Boy to start walking on his hands or doing an Al Jolson imitation.

Alexandra Kane greeted them inside by leaving a smear of her orange lipstick on Bradley's lips, although all Hunter got was a handshake as he was introduced to her. He didn't like her. There was something funny about her eyes as she smiled up at him, looking at him as if he was something she was thinking about trying on for size. She took each of the paratroopers by one arm and led them to the bar. Bradley nodded to the CPO as if they'd met before and said he'd have Canadian on the rocks. Hunter ordered a tall scotch highball to nurse while he got his bearings. As the bartender filled their orders, Bradley nudged him and said, "Gangbusters! See that blonde in the war correspondent's outfit?"

Hunter followed his gaze to see a quietly pretty ash blonde near the fireplace, with her profile turned to them. Bradley said, "This is your lucky night, kid. Her name's Ramie Davis and she's fantastic in the feathers. I'd introduce you, but I think she's sore at me. Just go over and tell her you use lubricated Guardians.

Hunter knew the bartender was listening. He sighed and said, "Jesus, Danny Boy, watch the mouth, huh?"

"Hey, I'm just trying to put you on to a good lay, buddy boy. You don't want her, find somebody else. I gotta stick close to old Sandy. Don't want some other guy to head her off at the pass."

Bradley moved away to join Alexandra Kane and her friends around the piano. Hunter took a sip of his drink and told the bartender, "Sorry about that, chief."

"I understand, sir. Rank has it privileges in the RN, too."

Hunter smiled wearily and moved away. The ash blonde was pretty and there didn't seem to be any better place to stand, so he moved over by Ramie and waited until their eyes met. He was surprised when they did. It seemed so natural to say, "Hi, I see great minds run in the same channels."

She knew what he meant. She nodded and said,

"These zombie glasses are a godsend, aren't they? Do you know the Kanes, or did Major Bradley draft you?"

"The latter. We're here to attend a rehash of D day together. The brass can't seem to understand how supermen like us could have made so many mistakes. After talking to them all day I'm starting to wonder how we did so *well*."

"I was on Omaha that day," she said. "If your 101st was anywhere near as confused as the boys around me, it's a wonder you're still alive. But I heard you did pretty well."

"Not as well as they wanted, apparently. Hey, I read a story the other day about two girl reporters on Omaha. One of them was wounded."

"I'm the one who wasn't. It was my story you read. I'm Ramie Davis." Then she shot a look at the group near the piano and wryly added, "But of course Dan Bradley already told you my name, didn't he?"

"I don't remember if he did. I'm Logan Hunter. That was a pretty good story you wrote, Ramie. It smelled like the real thing. I liked that bit about the tanker sitting on the jerry can. It was just right. You didn't overdo it, like Pyle."

She laughed and said, "Let's not get sickening, Logan! Ernie Pyle's the best reporter covering this war!"

"Yeah, he's good. But now that I've been there, I think he lays it on a little. Not the battle details. He's accurate as hell about them. But don't you think he makes the GIs sound a little sorry for themselves?"

She took a sip of her highball, considering her answer. "I'm not sure. I really only saw a very small corner of the war and God knows those boys over there had plenty to feel sorry about."

"Yeah, we took some casualties where I was too.

But nobobdy seemed to blubber about them. Maybe things are different on the Italian front."

Ramie looked up at him thoughtfully. "I think I see what you mean, Logan. There *was* a sort of graveyard humor over there across the channel, like they were holding their real feelings in. Come to think of it, I don't remember any of those GIs mooning about mom's apple pie or their old dog, Spot . . . Did Dan Bradley tell you I put out?"

Taken aback, Hunter laughed incredulously and didn't answer.

"You'd make a lousy poker player," Ramie said reprovingly. "I saw you both come in. I was hoping he'd be good, but we both know Danny Boy."

She hadn't answered the question she'd posed either, and Hunter wasn't about to seek confirmation or denial. It didn't seem likely that any man who'd been in bed with this one would be messing around with that cheap redhead over there. He said, "The only woman I remember him mentioning was our hostess, and he seems to have gotten his facts wrong there, too. He told me she was a blonde."

"That was last week. He'll probably sleep with her tonight, if he can get her alone long enough to proposition her. But as you see, it's not that easy."

Hunter followed her gaze. The crowd was getting bigger and Dan Bradley was seated at the piano now. He struck a chord and as some of the others chimed in, he bgan to sing and play "Roll Me Over in the Clover."

"Oh, for God's sake!" Ramie muttered.

"Would you like to go somewhere else?" Hunter asked.

"Anywhere else would be an improvement, but . . . can I trust you?"

"That's up to you. I know they never caught Jack the Ripper, but didn't he hang out in the *East* End of London?"

"Those were the good old days. Let's get out of here."

Nobody but the butler seemed to notice as they left. It was still light outside, of course. Hunter said, "I don't know my way around London so well. I think our best move is something to eat. I don't know about you, but I'm hungry."

Ramie had eaten earlier, but she said, "I know the only place in London that doesn't serve fish and chips with those papier-mâché brussels sprouts. Are you game for Indian cooking?"

He laughed and said, "I've never tried it, but anything's better than brussels sprouts." So they walked up to the corner and hailed a passing cab.

Ramie gave the driver the address and as they settled back, she said, "This is getting weird. You can get cabs again. I notice the streets don't seem as crowded tonight."

"Well, a lot of GI and Allied forces aren't here anymore."

She gasped and said, "Of course, and I'm supposed to be the reporter! I can use that in a feature, Logan."

"I guess so. Might be human interest as things change for better or worse. How long have you been over here, Ramie?"

"Since the blitz."

"Boy, you *have* seen some changes, haven't you?"

"Yes, there used to be a city, east of Saint Paul's. I'm afraid poor Jack the Ripper wouldn't recognize White Chapel these days. Limehouse is gone. So much of it's gone. What were you doing during the blitz, Logan?"

"Listening to it on the radio, of course. It sounded pretty grim, but it was far away and Roosevelt was running on a promise that no American boy would ever die on foreign soil again."

"Did you really believe that?"

"No. I voted for Wilkie. It was the first election I could vote in and I didn't want to throw it away. I don't know what kind of a president Wilkie would have made, but at least he didn't insult my intelligence. We knew it was coming. '40 was a good year, in the States. The Depression was winding down and the big bands were great to dance to, but we knew it was coming."

She nodded and said, "I was over here on Pearl Harbor Day, of course. It felt pretty strange to be an American in London that day. As the reports came in about how bad it had been, the people around me were almost ready to dance in the streets—Oh! Here's where we get out."

The cab stopped and Hunter paid the driver before following Ramie over to a narrow doorway between two closed shops. He looked around and asked where they were.

"Soho," she said. "If you're a good boy and eat your din din I know a private club that's open after ten and then you can walk me home."

"You live in Soho?"

"No, Marlybone, but that's just up a few blocks. By the way, the night is going to be Dutch, agreed?"

"Negative. I'm on an expense account too, and I wouldn't want people to think I'm being kept by a woman."

She laughed. "I tried." They went up the stairs to a second-story East Indian place. It was nearly empty and the waiter seemed overjoyed to see them. Ramie ordered for them. As the waiter left she looked around and said, "Brr, this is getting creepy. Before D day you had to wait in line to get a table."

"Don't London civilians eat out, Ramie?"

"They must. This place was built before the war. But Soho was pretty dependent on transient trade even before the food got so terrible, and after all, one can brew better tea at home, if one has a home. We're going to see a lot of closings between now and the day tourists come to London again. Do you think the war will be over this year, Logan?"

He shook his head. "I don't see how. When I left the front we were taking France back five acres at a time. They keep talking about a breakthrough, but now that the Krauts have moved in their reserves it seems to be settling down to a slugging match, like the last war."

"Oh. That doesn't give much scope for airborne operations, does it?"

"No, but who's complaining? I don't know where they'll use us again. As we were leaving there was some rumor about dropping us into Paris ahead to keep the Krauts from burning it. But that doesn't make much sense, even on paper."

"Then you'll be here for a while?"

"A little while, maybe. I don't know what we're trying to prove at those hearings. I've told the same story over and over until it's even starting to sound stupid and boring to me."

As the waiter was bringing their curry Ramie quietly asked, "Was it . . . bad, Logan?"

"Let's not spoil our appetites with war stories over dinner, huh? War stories are bore stories unless you tart them up with lots of gore."

He took an experimental taste. "Hey, this is good, even if I can't pronounce it."

By coffee and dessert they'd told each other the official stories of their lives. So they went to the private club Ramie could get into to see if they'd like to let down their guard some more.

Like the Indian eatery, the club was a second-story walk-up near Regent Street. It was much more crowded and the atmosphere was dark and smoky. They found a corner table and ordered arf-and-arfs. Near the piano a lady wearing nothing but a hula skirt and some wax fruit atop her dishwater blonde hair was singing the "Hawaiian War Chant" in a cockney accent amid considerable merriment. The colored piano player knew the tune a lot better than the singer. But she moved enthusiastically and had a nice pair of exposed breasts, so what the hell.

"Sorry about the entertainment," Ramie said, "but the pubs are closed."

"Her act is cleaner than the one we left at that party."

Ramie nodded soberly. "You do think a lot like me, don't you? But I must say I've never wanted to bail out of a C-47. Do you suppose it's a sex gene trait?"

He laughed and said, "Nobody wants to jump out of a C-47, unless they're missing some marbles."

"Why do you do it, then?"

"I've been wondering about that for some time. I guess it's because I'm a snob and they don't have horse cavalry anymore."

She sipped her beer and said, "You're going to think this is weird, but I understood that. What do you think is going on here, Logan?"

He stared thoughtfully into her eyes across the

little table. "I don't know. But I feel it, too. Maybe we're related or something. Do you have any long lost cousins?"

She literally flinched and he saw pain in her eyes. "What's wrong? Did I say something wrong, Ramie?"

She shook her head and stared down at her drink as she replied, "No, of course not. Someday we'll have to go to the library and look up our family trees together."

"Yeah, someday. Someday there'll be blue birds over the white cliffs of Dover and everybody will have a gyrocopter parked in their garage, right?"

"I'd settle for just the blue birds, right now."

They fell silent. Neither knew what they could say that would make any sense, but both of them felt what was happening. It was a crazy time and place to be falling in love. The beer was flat, the air was stale, and the crazy naked lady was singing truly dreadfully. He reached across the table to take her hand as he murmured, "I wonder if she knows the words to Berkely Square. I never really understood them until tonight."

"Neither did I," she answered, her voice almost a whisper.

The air seemed to tingle around them as they held hands across the table, looking into each other's eyes. And then Hunter realized that the air was *really* tingling. As the others felt and heard it, the piano fell silent and the half-nude singer stared up at the ceiling and said, "Coo!" frozen in mid-grind.

The buzz bomb's nerve-grating growl got louder and louder. Ramie gripped Hunter's hand, unaware she was digging him with her nails. A girl across the room stood up, but her escort pulled her down, saying, "Too late, love. It's going over us, I hope."

The overhead flying bomb's ram jet cut off, plunging them all in silence as the man across the room added, "Jesus!" and the half-naked singer covered her breasts with her hands and began counting, "One, two, free," in a little girl voice. Hunter knew why. The buzz bombs took four or five seconds to glide down after the ram jet cut out.

The vapidly pretty singer sobbed, "Please, God, five!" and then the whole building shook to the roar of the explosion. But, though the lights flicked off and the room was filled with the sound of screams and falling glass, Ramie and Hunter were still there, and they knew the bomb had landed somewhere else.

The colored pianist began to play "God Save the King" in the darkness and the crowd fell silent as someone produced a flickering candle. Then the lights went back on and everybody cheered. Hunter found himself looking at a grinning British sailor, who nodded and made a thumbs-up sign at him. Hunter nodded back to him. They both knew they were war buddies now, even if they never met again.

Ramie said, "Oh, heavens, I've made your hand bleed!"

"Did you? I'll put in for the Purple Heart."

She took a handkerchief out, dipped it in beer, and began to wipe off his hand as she apologized for being so hysterical.

"Hey, forget it, Ramie. It wasn't a fun thing to have happen, but we're okay." He squeezed her fingers as he added, "Maybe better than okay, okay?"

She said, "I have to cover that buzz bomb for UPI. They don't come down in the heart of London every night."

He nodded and signaled the waiter for their tab. But as they got up he muttered, "God damn you,

Adolf. You might have had a little consideration about your timing, for once!"

They went downstairs. There was no doubt about where the buzz bomb had landed. Everyone on the street was either looking or heading that way. Ramie took Hunter's arm and they headed down the street as an ambulance tore by. They didn't have far to go. As they approached a sudden gap in what had hitherto been wall-to-wall buildings the fire brigade and air defense wardens were already in position. They stepped over a fire hose and were told, "You can't go any farther. This is Situation Red. You'll have to go around."

When Ramie flashed her press pass the warden nodded and stood aside, saying, "Watch your feet, then. Lots of glass about."

They moved closer to the explosion site in the gathering twilight. It looked like a building excavation, filled with dust clouds and debris. A fireman was trying to hose out a rising plume of burning gas on the far side, but as they approached a superior snapped, "Let it burn, you fool! You want the whole bloody neighborhood filled with gas? You'll see one bloody bang if you do that, my lad!"

Ramie found a police officer, identified herself, and asked if there were any survivors. The bobbie shook his head. "No bodies even, miss. They may find something under all that wreckage in a day or so. No ruddy survivors, though. Jerry puts a ton or so of HE in them buzz bombs, you know."

Hunter asked if there was anything he could do. The bobbie seemed astonished by the notion. Figuring out Hunter's silver bars, he touched his hand to the bill of his hat and said, "No thank you, sir. Our lads have things under control. What control there *is*, after one of them things come down."

So Hunter stood by, feeling in the way, while Ramie asked questions moving from one busy man to another until she saw there really wasn't much one could say about a big smoking hole in the ground.

She rejoined Hunter and sighed. "There isn't any story, I'm afraid. Not a story UPI could use, anyway. I guess what happened was important enough to the poor people who lived or worked there though."

"Yeah, you can't even tell if it was a business building or an apartment house anymore. Where do you want to go now, Ramie?"

"Home. This really hasn't done much for my nerves."

"Yeah, I was talking to Hitler about that. Let's see if we can find a cab."

But she said she'd rather walk and so they did. It was less than a half mile to her place in Marlybone. No street lights were lit and the sky was darkening, but he could see her well enough as they stopped in her doorway. She licked her lips and said, "I don't know how to put this, Logan. I know I should invite you up for a nightcap. But I don't think I want to. The hell of it is, I don't know why."

"Don't worry about it, then. I'm a big enough boy not to cry."

She laughed and held out her hand.

"Hey, let's not go totally Harold Teen," he said, and took her in his arms to kiss her.

She responded, and for a moment he thought it was going to be all right, but when they came up for air, she murmured, "Please stop, Logan, we're just teasing ourselves. You can't come upstairs with me tonight and—"

"When will I see you again?" he asked, still holding her in his arms.

"I have to go up to Scotland in the morning on an interview. I'll be in Achnacarry for a few days, finding out what the commandos will be up to now that there's no French coast for them to play on. That's the only reason I was at that party tonight. Admiral Kane is connected with the commandos."

He kissed her again, albeit more lightly to let her get used to the idea. "I almost didn't come to the party either, but I did and you were there and now *we're* here and when will you be back in London?"

"This weekend?"

He thought and said, "I'm not sure. They could wind those hearings up any day and we could be on our way back to the outfit. I'm sure I'm here *tonight*, Ramie."

She suddenly pulled away and opened the door behind her. "That tears it! Get a better line!"

And then he was standing there with the door slammed in his face.

He thought about knocking to ask her what in the hell she'd meant by that. Then he shrugged and turned away, taking out a pack of Chesterfields and lighting up as he walked away.

She's nuts, he told himself, as he got his bearings and headed for the center of town. But that wasn't it, he knew. He'd somehow pushed the wrong button again, like he had back there at the club. He tried to remember just what he'd been saying when her eyes had gone opaque and he'd started to lose her the first time. Nothing came to him and as he saw a cab coming he flagged it down and told the driver to take him to Brown's. It beat trying to find the place in the damned blackout. As he settled back, he tried to forget about

Ramie. He knew he'd probably never see her again.

The brass had about finished raking him and Danny Boy over the coals for mistakes neither of them had made. Even that fat S4 colonel had to know by this time that there wasn't any more equipment that would have helped. There was already too much shit to carry and it wouldn't really help all that much to drop each trooper in his own private tank, if you dropped him in the wrong place with orders that were impossible to carry out.

Traffic was light and they arrived soon at his hotel. Hunter got out and went upstairs. He drew the blackout curtains and switched on the light. It was one of the best hotels in London and the room was okay, but it looked like the place was somehow haunted. He stared morosely at his B-4 bag at the foot of the made-up bed and said, "You should have come along. It was a bundle of laughs."

The phone rang as he was hanging up his jacket. Hunter sat on the bed and answered it. Dan Bradley asked, "What the hell are you doing home so early, buddy boy?"

"That's a pretty dumb question, Dan. If I wasn't here I wouldn't be talking to you, right?"

"Ah, that's the point, buddy boy. I was giving you the old bed check. I see you didn't score with Ramie after all, eh?"

"No, and if you'd gotten anywhere with the redhead you wouldn't be making obscene phone calls at this hour. Is there any point to this conversation, Dan?"

"I know I'm in with old Sandy as soon as I can get her alone. But it's sort of hard to get her alone with all those Limeys sniffing around, you know?"

"Sort of like a bitch in heat running down the alley, eh?"

"That's not delicate, but it sure is accurate. How did you manage to bomb out with Ramie, anyway? I told you she puts out, buddy boy!"

"Not for me, Danny Boy. Can we knock this off? I was about to turn in."

"Alone? It's too early! What say we go hunting, buddy boy? If all else fails there's always that penny arcade off Piccadilly."

"You go there and give them my love, then. I want to hit the hearings wide awake in the morning and see if we can get them over with."

Bradley told him he didn't know what he was missing and hung up. Hunter stared in distaste at the phone in his hand and put it back on the cradle. He stripped and was just getting ready to bathe when the phone rang again.

He picked it up, ready to swear, but it was Ramie. She said, "I'm sorry about that cringing virgin act, Logan. Did I awaken you?"

"I'm awake now. What did I do to upset you like that, Ramie?"

"It wasn't you. It was me. I think I was starting to fall in love with you, Logan. It's been a long time since I've felt like that and I guess it shook me up."

He sat down, nude, and said, "It shook me up, too. What do you think we ought to do about it, Ramie?"

"I don't know. The sensible thing would be to forget it. I don't think I could handle it again, Logan."

"Again? You're not talking about Dan Bradley, I hope."

She gave a sharp laugh and answered, "You have to be kidding. I'd go out with Adolf Hitler first!"

"But you did go out with him, right?"

There was a pause. Then Ramie asked, "What if I did? What if everything he says about me is true, Logan?"

"I wouldn't like it. But it wouldn't change the way I feel about you, Ramie."

"I wish you hadn't said that. I wish I'd never gone to that damned party. I can hardly claim to be Little Goody Two Shoes at this late date and I could have handled it if you'd just been a good-looking stud. But magic shakes me up. It's hard to say goodby to magic, and when you do it leaves burn marks on a girl's heart."

"I think I understand. That part about this maybe being my last night in London was the tactical blunder, right?"

She hesitated before she said, "I wouldn't use that line on any girl in London this late in the war, Logan."

"Ramie, it wasn't a line."

"I know, dear. All too often it's been the simple truth. And all too often it's worked."

"Oh? Has it ever worked on anyone I know?"

This time there was a long pause before Ramie said, very softly, "His name was Scott. He was a Spitfighter pilot in the Eagle Squadron. I was doing a feature on the Yanks in the RAF and . . ."

"Things got magical?"

"Don't cheapen his memory, Logan! He was over here fighting for the sky over London when a lot of people I know were dancing the jitterbug and stirring all the sugar they wanted in their coffee!"

"Some of us were looking for jobs. But I had that coming. A guy gets jealous, but I think I understand, Ramie."

"He was shot down over the channel and they never recovered his body. It was probably just as well. They said he went down in flames. I went down in flames too. I guess I went crazy for a while. I drank too much and fornicated with strangers until I either came to my senses or got over it."

He grimaced and asked, "Are you bragging or complaining, Ramie?"

"I know I'm shocking you. But I wanted you to understand why I acted so silly this evening. I knew you wanted me. I wanted you, too. If you'd just been a . . . guy, we'd probably be in bed together this minute."

"Gee, thanks. You tell swell bedtime stories, Ramie. Do we have to beat it to death like this? I said I understand. Once upon a time a little girl spent a magic night with a guy going back to the war. Only it turned out that the last night they'd have a chance to make it was really the last night. Have I left anything out?"

"Don't be angry, darling. I know I've hurt you. I've hurt us both. But I don't think I could go through it a second time."

He laughed bitterly, and said, "I knew I should have joined the quartermaster corps. It was nice falling in love with you. But you've made your point. Have a nice life, Ramie."

She didn't answer. He gently hung up the phone, and sighed, "Women. I'll just never understand them."

But he did understand, and he was sort of glad it had ended this way. A guy leaving a C-47 at three hundred feet had enough on his mind without worrying about "the girl he left behind." So it was over and he should forget her. That was going to be easy, right?

Hunter swore and rose to get dressed again. He had to be at the hearing in the morning, but the odds on his falling asleep right now were zero. He was no spring chicken either, and everybody had a few burns on the rug. He'd long ago discovered that the best way to put a torch out was to light another. Preferably one that didn't burn as bright. They said that nobody had to sleep alone in London unless they wanted to. And right now he didn't want to.

After sprucing up, Hunter went down to the lobby. They told him the hotel bar was officially closed. But as he fumbled casually with a ten-bob note a bellhop suddenly remembered a back room where guests could sort of discover the decanters on a sideboard near the fireplace on their own. It was definitely to be understood that no drinks were to be *served*, of course. He had no idea how they worked that on the bill, but he didn't doubt they would.

He found the small cozy sitting room and sure enough, there were unsupervised decanters and glasses where the modest crowd could get at them. There were maybe a dozen people in the room. It was hard to count them with the light so dim. Hunter poured himself a glass and moved over to sit in an unoccupied leather chair under some coaching prints. The woman seated next to him turned and said, "Oh, it's you."

He turned to see Alexandra Kane smiling archly at him with a glass in one hand and a cigarette in the other. The redhead said, "We met at my cocktail party earlier this evening, remember?"

"Of course, Mrs. Kane."

"Silly, call me Sandy. Where's Danny Boy? I was sure he'd come in by this time. It's nearly midnight."

Could it really be that early? Hunter said, "Dan and I split up early, Sandy. I've no idea where he went."

She sighed. "Probably looking for a bread-and-breakfast tart over in Trafalger Square, if I know Danny Boy. You left early with that Yank thing who works for UPI, didn't you?"

"I ran Miss Davis home."

"And she left you out in the cold? Oh, you poor thing. You must feel devastated. Or is it frustrated?"

He sipped his drink and said, "There seems to be a lot of that going around. Does Dan know you're waiting for him here?"

Her laugh was brittle as she said, "I was, but I'm not used to waiting for anybody. I thought he understood my signals while I was trying to get rid of that RN commander. The silly sod was terribly persistent, and I think Dan was annoyed about his gallantries. He couldn't have thought I'd be indiscreet with a navy officer, could he?"

Hunter grimaced and said, "That *would* be indiscreet, for an admiral's wife, wouldn't it?" He was just making small talk. There was a nice-looking little brunette sitting alone across the room and if only he could get rid of this silly tramp without hurting her feelings . . .

Alexandra Kane put her drink on the little rosewood table between their knees and leaned back again with her hand on Hunter's thigh as she said, "I see you know the rules. Never go to bed with your husband's ship-mates, what?"

He would have felt stupid removing her hand as if she were a nice girl caught by surprise in a rumble seat. He tried to stay light as he said, "Dan should be back almost any time, Sandy."

"That's his problem. Not ours. I'm not used to being stood up. And besides, you're prettier. How do we go about getting me to your room without frightening the horses? I wish you weren't staying here at Brown's. Lord knows when someone I know will pop in on us, if we do all our sparring about down here in public!"

"It's too late," he said. "I'm already caught. Now

that my eyes are used to the light in here I see some-body I know. I think you may know her, too. Wasn't that girl over there at your party tonight?"

Sandy followed his gaze and stared thoughtfully at the brunette across the room. "I don't think so. It's so hard to remember everyone who shows up these days. My husband will persist in inviting people I don't know?"

"I'd better check her out," he said, getting to his feet before Sandy could reply. He walked over and sat down beside the brunette, saying, "Listen, I need a favor."

She turned to stare at him curiously and he could see she was a little tipsy. She said, "I'm particular about that sort of favor, Yank. What's the matter with that redhead across the room?"

"Relax. I'm not making a pass at you, miss."

"Oh? Pity. What on earth are we talking about?"

He smiled and said, "I'm trying to ditch that red-head. I told her I knew you. If I promise to be good, can I sit and talk with you until she gives up and goes after somebody else?"

The brunette laughed and took his hand as she asked, "How's this for openers? But what's wrong with her? She's more attractive than me, and I can see her motor running from here. Don't you like girls, Yank?"

He squeezed her hand and said, "I sure do. But that one's playing too close to home. Aside from being married to a guy who could have me on KP for the forseeable future, she's fooling around with my su-perior officer and he could show up any minute."

"Oh, my, you do have a problem. I thought it was just my perfume. What shall we do to discourage her—within reason, of course?"

"I told her you'd been to a cocktail party with her

earlier this evening. What if you were to back me up on that?"

The brunette thought. Then she nodded, turned, and waved at Sandy. The redhead kept smiling, but her smile was strained as she nodded back, rose to her feet, and sauntered out of the room.

The brunette laughed and said, "That was fun. I think you're safe, if she doesn't know how to pick the lock on your door. Are you staying here?"

"Of course. Aren't you?"

"Lord, no, I can't afford Brown's. I just come here after hours to get drunk. You may have noticed I'm rather good at that. My flat's just down the street."

He realized they were still holding hands as she took a healthy swig, stared at the empty glass, and said, "It doesn't help."

"Why are you doing it, then? You don't look like an alcoholic."

"I'm not. I've just been drinking a lot lately. Would you fill this up for me again, please?"

He rose and took their glasses over to the sideboard. Nobody seemed to be keeping tabs. It must be some sort of flat fee thing. He'd have some service charge added to his bill and she must have an arrangement with that bellhop out front. He went back with the weak highballs he'd built for them and sat down again, saying, "By the way, I'm Logan Hunter."

"I don't like names. Call me Pat. I knew a Pat once, and it's easy to say. I think I'll call you Joe."

"That sounds reasonable."

"This drink doesn't. I didn't ask for a drink of *wate*r, damn it!"

"I'll make it stronger if you'll tell me what's eating you, ah, Pat."

She shook her head ruefully. "There's nothing you

can do about it. Nothing anybody can do about it, now."

"I'd like to try, Pat. I owe you a favor."

"You do, don't you? All right, how are you at raising the dead, Joe?"

He whistled softly, and said, "Not very good. What happened to him?"

"D day happened to him. He landed on Juno and they say he never made it up the cliffs. Can I have a decent drink now?"

"You know it won't help, Pat. You've already had more than enough and getting sick won't bring him back."

"Nothing will bring him back. What am I going to do, Joe?"

He shook his head wearily. "There's nothing any of us can do, except to go on. This is no good for you. Why don't you let me take you home?"

"All right. But you will use a rubber, won't you?"

He looked at her in surprise. "That wasn't what I had in mind, but if you want me to, I will."

"I don't know what I want. Yes I do, I want Joe back. But he's not coming back and—hell, let's get out of here."

He helped her to her feet and they left. It was black outside and she was unsteady on her feet, but she knew the way to her place and it wasn't far. As she fumbled for her key he knew he'd probably never be able to find his way here again. Even if he wanted to.

He half-expected her to say goodnight at the door. But when she finally got the door open she led him inside and shut it, saying, "Let's leave the lights out. Make-believe is better in the dark. Don't you think?"

He took her in his arms and kissed her. It felt nothing like kissing Ramie, but she responded eagerly and thrust her pelvis against him until they came up for air and she murmured, "The bed's this way. You do have rubbers, don't you?"

He sheepishly muttered something about them being regulation issue on leave as she led him by the hand until his knees were against the bed. She moved away in the dark and as he heard the rustle of her clothes coming off he started taking off his own. He sat on the bed to unlace his boots and felt the mattress sag under him and heard her voice pleading, "Hurry." So he did. He took out the tinfoil pack of contraceptives with a grimace of distaste. The stuffy little room smelled of lubricating jelly mixed with her lilac perfume as he unrolled the clammy thing onto his surprising erection. It was all happening so fast he hadn't had time to become fully aroused. But when he rolled over to join her nude body with his in the musky darkness he suddenly wanted her very badly. He'd never seen her in full light and he wasn't sure just what she looked like, but it didn't seem to matter as he entered her warm clean flesh and she gasped, "Oh, you have a lovely body. Will you do me a favor, Joe?"

He kissed her and asked, "What do you call this, an act of war?"

She suddenly sobbed and said, "That is what we're doing, isn't it? I want you to pound me. I want you to do everything to me. But I don't want you to say a word. And when we're done, I want you to leave without saying anything. I know it's crazy, but . . ."

"It's all right. I understand." And then he kissed her, hard, and let himself go as she arched her spine and responded savagely to his thrusts. It was good, even though they both knew what they were doing.

Hunter hadn't had a woman in some time and although she wasn't the one he wanted, or even anyone he knew, there was bitter truth to the cynical old saw about all cats being grey in the dark. The girl who wanted to be remembered as Pat had a firm young body and as he thrust in and out of it he couldn't conceive any possible improvement to her physical form or experienced movements. He knew she enjoyed sex and that she was used to a lot of it. He wondered if the guy she'd lost had been her husband or just a Tommy who'd spent a lot of leave with her. He knew he couldn't ask and he knew it didn't really matter. They were just two lonely strangers masturbating with each other's bodies, and while the magic was missing, everything else was there. He ejaculated and kept moving, still hotter than he'd expected to be and aware she was about to climax too. She groaned, "Oh, take that silly rubber thing off and do it right."

He hesitated. "Are you sure?"

"Shut up. I don't want *you* here. Just take that thing off and do it right!"

So he withdrew and discarded the used contraceptive. As he entered her again he didn't answer when she sobbed. "Oh, Christ, that's lovely. Why did you have to leave me, Joe? Didn't you know what we had was more important than your damned war?"

He grimaced and kissed her roughly to shut her up as he pounded her into climax. Substituting for a ghost left much to be desired and now that he'd taken the raw edge off his own physical needs he was starting to feel sorry he'd started this crazy business. What was he doing here in a musky little room with a woman he might not recognize on the street if he ever passed her again?

But the girl who wanted to be remembered as Pat

had needs too, and as he did his best to comfort her his own lust slowly regrouped for another assault. This time they climaxed together and went limp in each other's arms for a long sweet moment in eternity.

As they breathed in time and began to recover, Hunter understood more fully what Ramie had meant. And it was better that she not have any memories of him at all than to think of her trying to recapture them with another man someday. He felt used and more than a little crummy as he enjoyed the flesh of this lost little stranger. But, being young, healthy, and lonely himself, he enjoyed her just the same.

10

W HAT WAS your experience with our gliders,
Lieutenant?" asked one of the stuffed owls
seated behind the long table as Hunter faced
them stiff-backed in a bentwood chair. He stared
blankly at the board officer who'd asked the dumb
question and said, "I didn't have any experience with
gliders, sir. My men and I jumped with chutes."

"But you reported seeing crashed gliders, didn't you,
Lieutenant?"

"Yessir. We came upon one during my S2 sweep,
and of course, later, as we were securing the area we
found others that had crashed. I don't know what the
percentage of bad landings might have been, though."

Another officer snorted. "I can answer that. Over
half the damned things crashed on landing. That
won't do, Lieutenant. The glider troops suffered fifty

percent casualties before the purple pissing Nazis knew they were on the ground over there!"

Hunter didn't answer. He hadn't been sent to defend the glider troops.

The two-star general chairing the hearing said, "We've agreed gliders should be phased out, gentlemen. Let's get on with the way the parachutists dropped the ball."

He frowned at Hunter and added, "Considering all the training you and your men had, you seem to have gotten lost like green troops, Lieutenant."

Hunter flushed, and snapped, "We did no such thing, General. I had my position figured out soon after we landed."

"But you landed miles away from where you were supposed to."

"Yessir. We did, and I have no apology to make about that. Our chutes carry us straight down. We can't fly like superman to the DZ if the fly-boys drop us somewhere else!"

"Then you want to go on record as accusing the transport pilots of being responsible for your failed mission, Lieutenant?"

Hunter shook his head. "I'm not accusing anyone of anything, sir. I'm not a pilot. In all fairness, if I was I don't know if I'd have done any better at finding the DZ in the dark over unfamiliar territory while I worried about flack and enemy fighters. But I do take objection to the statement that my particular mission was a failure too. We did gather some intelligence and we did kill some Germans doing it."

"Yes, and you lost nearly two thirds of your platoon in the process. But let's not argue about that, Lieutenant. You and your platoon did a hell of a lot better than some of the others we've been going over. We're not here to convict anyone, Lieutenant. We're trying to make sure it never happens again."

"I understand, sir."

Another officer put down a paper he'd been reading and said, "Lieutenant Hunter, are we to understand you and your men had no other weapons but those little sawed-off carbines?"

"Yes, Colonel. We're an S2 platoon, not a heavy weapons company."

"Perhaps not, but you only carried a pistol, and those light pea-shooters are hardly enough to go up against German line outfits with."

Hunter took a deep breath and said, "We're not suppose to go up against enemy anything, sir. We're S2 scouts. Our mission is to locate enemy positions for the rifle companies to fight. We're supposed to move fast and only fight if we have to."

"Perhaps. But on your last mission you *did* have to fight. I notice you had to find yourself a carbine, too."

"Yessir. I intend to carry one with me if I jump again. It's true that D day showed us some bugs to be worked out, but—"

"You airborne have jumped before," another officer interrupted. "I must say I'd have thought by now you'd know what you were doing. God knows you got mauled in North Africa and Sicily. How many jumps do you think it will take to work out all these bugs you're talking about?"

"I've no idea, sir. This is the first war anyone's used airborne. The German paratroopers have had heavy casualties too."

"Let's not worry about what the enemy is doing wrong, Lieutenant! The army can't accept the waste you people have shown so far. I've been wondering about those carbines. What ever happened to the Tommy guns you people started out with?"

"Those were some of the bugs I was talking about, sir," Hunter said.

"Why? The Thompson's a very good weapon."

"Yessir, and it's also heavy. We don't just save the weight of the gun by jumping with stockless carbines set for full auto. We save the weight of those big fat .45 rounds, too."

A bald officer who obviously liked noise chimed in, "I *like* to see a Kraut get hit with a big fat round. Those little carbine slugs don't have half the stopping power of the .45, dammit!"

Hunter grimaced. "I'd be perfectly happy to hit them with a 75mm if a trooper could jump with a field gun strapped on, sir. In a fire fight the thing that counts is who throws the most fire, and the .30s we use in our carbines are light enough for a trooper to carry a mess of them. And for the record, my patrol was very low on ammo when we finally made it to our own lines."

The chair held up a hand for silence. "All right, the lieutenant is not in command of airborne S4 and he'll no doubt fight with anything they issue him, next time. I want to go over tactics with a man who's really been there and managed to get back. But I see it's almost chow time, gentlemen. So I'm calling a recess until 1500 hours."

Everybody rose. Hunter got up, saluted nobody in particular and left by the front door. Out in the corridor he found Major Dan Bradley pacing nervously. Bradley asked, "How did it go, buddy boy?"

"They're taking a three-hour lunch, for God's sake.

I thought this was supposed to be serious business."

"They're just going through the motions," Bradley said. "Let's go grab some chow ourselves. There's a Greek joint over a couple of blocks where you can get real eggs if they know you."

"I thought I'd eat here at the officer's mess."

"Come on, I'm buying. Never miss a chance to take a leak or eat civilian food. Besides, I want to talk to you. I think we've got a bone to pick."

Hunter nodded and followed the major out. Danny Boy made small talk as they walked to the place he knew. It was a clear day and the trees were emerald green between the smoke-grimed building fronts. London would be sort of pretty if anybody ever cleaned it up a little.

The Greek joint was in a basement, with murals of what looked like naked people running around in fig leaves and fireman's helmets. It smelled like a fish-and-chips shop, like most of the other restaurants in London these days.

Bradley waited until they'd ordered before he toyed with a paper napkin, eyes down, and said, "I've heard of bird dogging, buddy boy. But don't you think you were a little out of line last night?"

"Say again, Danny boy?"

"I might make you call me *sir* if you don't watch it, Hunter. I believe in sharing the wealth, but you've been acting like a real pig about it."

Hunter stared across the table at him. "What in the hell are you talking about?"

"Come on, don't play Shirley Temple with me, buddy boy. I've got spies. First I put you on to a sure lay, like your pal. But Ramie wasn't enough for you, right? You go zim-zam-thank-you-ma'am with the one

I told you was yours, and then you whip back to the hotel and bang my date! Who do you think you are, Errol Flynn?"

Hunter looked at him incredulously. "As a matter of fact, Sandy was at the hotel last night, looking for you, you chump."

"I know. My spies told me you were back in the private rooms holding hands with her."

"I wasn't holding her hand and she wasn't holding mine, exactly."

"Whatever. I checked with the chamber maid this morning. You didn't spend the night in your bed like you told me you were fixing to. Where did you and Sandy go?"

Hunter frowned and said, "Listen, Bradley, I don't owe you any explanations and, come to think of it, neither does Sandy. But if it will relieve your mind, I did score last night. But it wasn't with Ramie and it wasn't with Sandy, okay?"

"Look, it's not like I'm planning to marry Sandy but—"

"I know, she's already done that," Hunter cut in. "And neither of us have the rank if her husband decides to talk to Ike about it. You don't have to believe me, Bradley. But believe it or not, I finished off the evening with another lady. I know you had your cap set for Sandy, so when I spotted this other dame I left her on her own and went to meet my maker."

The waiter brought what looked like dishes of potato chips, but sure enough there were omelets under the chips, and if they were made from powdered eggs you couldn't tell. As they dug in, Bradley said, "The other dame must have been some dish, if you ditched Sandy for her. How was it?"

"It was okay. What can I tell you? The boy gets on

top. For Christ's sake, do we have to file three copies, Danny Boy?"

Bradley laughed and said, "I thought I'd checked out all the talent flying solo at the hotel."

Hunter started to explain about Pat living down the street, but decided it was none of his business. He'd half-forgotten where she lived and just what she looked like since he'd dressed in the dark and left her there asleep. But he was eternally grateful to the girl who wanted to be called Pat. And the last guy she needed to meet was this jerk across the table.

Bradley seemed more interested in the fact that Sandy had been at the hotel anyway, and insisted on the full story of Hunter's meeting her there. Hunter told it more or less truthfully, leaving out the part about her offering him the same opportunities. Bradley took the last bite of his meal and said, "Hot damn. If only we can stall things here in London a few more days. I can't call her at the house and just ask. She says her servants listen in. But look, buddy boy, you're in the clear. Everybody knows you're dating Ramie, see?"

"I'm doing no such thing. She said she had to go up to Scotland this morning."

"So what? You left with her and everybody knows she's a nympho. My point is that you could run over there and play John Alden for me. You make up some dumb excuse to get her alone a few minutes and set us up. I can cover for you here this aft. I'll say I sent you on a secret mission or something."

"It would be a secret mission at that, but no thanks, Miles Standish. I'm not going anywhere near that red-headed tramp."

Bradley frowned like a schoolyard bully trying to

impress the little kids. "Yes you are. Have you forgotten you're working for me, Hunter?"

Hunter put down his fork and stared thunderstruck at the major. "Are you pulling rank on me, you asshole?"

"If I have to. And watch that mouth of yours, Lieutenant."

"Why, you silly bastard. I've a good mind to go over to Belgravia and screw her bowlegged with the servants watching! But that would make me an asshole too."

"See here, Hunter, I'm your superior officer and—"

"No, *you* see here, Major Bradley! That bullshit about rank only applies to military duty. I'll be damned if I've ever seen ARs about sending a junior officer on patrol as a pimp."

"You're steaming me, buddy boy. That's not the way the game is played in this man's army."

"What are you going to do, charge me with refusing to obey a direct order to assist a superior in adultery with the wife of an admiral? I'd like that, Danny Boy. These hearings have been pretty boring, but my court-martial would be worth selling tickets to."

Bradley stared at him a long unblinking moment. Then something flickered in his eyes, like the turn of a shark in deep water. "Don't get your shit hot. Eat your damned old eggs. I was just kidding."

Hunter knew Bradley hadn't been kidding. Colonel Bell was right about the guy. He wasn't just a jerk. He was a real bastard under all that jolly buddy boy bullshit. While it seemed to be a Mexican standoff at the moment, he'd be serving under Bradley the next time they went into combat, and Bradley didn't owe him any favors.

Hunter shrugged and resumed eating. The omelet

suddenly tasted lousy. Across the table Bradley was making small talk about the hearing later that afternoon. Hunter wasn't listening. He wasn't worried about the hearings. Those brass hats would be doing him a favor if they grounded him. He knew they knew it, and that they had no intention of doing so. But Hunter could think of a hundred ways to screw up a junior officer in combat if you didn't like him, and Hunter considered himself a nice guy. Just think how many ways a guy like Bradley could come up with.

11

HUNTER WAS HOPING against hope that the hearings would last into the following week, when Ramie would be back from Scotland. But the brass hats got tired of hearing the same questions and answers too, and when they knocked off Friday afternoon they told Hunter and Bradley they wouldn't be needed any further. So it was their last night in London and in the morning they'd be going back to the 101st in Normandy.

The 101st wasn't fighting at the moment. They didn't have enough men left to fight. They'd been told to just hold their positions as the other outfits pushed the Krauts back a hedgerow at a time. Meanwhile other kids were training as replacements and being told how great an outfit they'd be going to in their new boots and wings if they paid attention to their instructors. Instructors had all the answers in this war.

Transportation had been arranged for the following morning, so that left Hunter, at least, with nothing much to do as the long summer evening waned. He called Ramie's number and got no answer. He hadn't expected to, but it had been worth a shot. He didn't know how to get hold of the girl who wanted to be called Pat. It was probably a lousy notion anyway. They'd parted friendly strangers and it seemed cleaner to leave it like that.

Hunter ate alone at the hotel and wandered over to Piccadilly to see what all the excitement was about. He found it depressing. Sweet but shabby little V girls were hanging around looking for a GI or Tommy who'd spring for a movie or a milk-bar shake. As an officer he felt out of place. He saw *Snow White and the Seven Dwarves* was playing down the street, but he'd seen it many times, and settled on a new Betty Grable film with an old familiar plot. He left before the ending. A pretty ATS girl was staring down at the cigarettes in the theatre's tobacco case. Cigarettes cost an outrageous half crown, or fifty cents, over here.

Hunter knew the ATS girl got half the pay of an American WAC of the same rank and the WAC got her smokes for four cents a pack at the PX. The girl was carrying a rucksack and was obviously on leave with nobody of her own in London either. But where could an officer take an enlisted woman with the pubs about to close? He passed up the silently offered opening and went out to the street again to see what else was lonesome. By the time he'd looked over some of the civilian talent still left he mildly regretted passing up that ATS girl back there. She'd been kind of cute and she might still be there.

But he wasn't in the mood for kind of cute. That

dreamlike hit-and-run affair with the girl he'd picked up at the hotel had left him unsatisfied, even though he'd vented his lust completely with her. He knew he could find another quick uncomplicated lay in London if he really tried, but these damned jump boots took almost as long to lace off and on as the fleeting pleasure itself, and he didn't just want to come. He wanted it to *mean* something.

As he walked alone through the crowded streets of London he heard a radio somewhere playing that British version of "Lili Marlene." It was funny how popular that dumb little song had become for both sides. But maybe it wasn't funny or dumb. The simple story of the lyrics was about a Kraut GI who'd been going to meet his girl under the lantern by the barracks gate, only orders came to pull out for the front and he'd had to go, leaving her there, stood up. Things like that kept happening to GIs, no matter which side they were on. And somehow you always remembered the ones you'd had to leave before anything happened more than you did the ones you'd spent a weekend with.

He tried to tell himself that was all that was bothering him about Ramie Davis. He had to go back to France and leave her under the barracks gate, with nothing settled between them one way or the other. Hell, if he only had more time, he'd be able to find out how the story ended. For all he really knew, she snored in her sleep and nagged at breakfast. No real dame could be as good in bed or out as the way he was starting to imagine the way it might have been. And what if she had been great as well as willing? The girl who wanted to be called Pat had been all any man could desire, if it had meant anything. Once it had meant something to Pat, and look at the mess it had made of her, right?

He wondered if Ramie had acted like that when she lost that RAF guy. She'd said she'd acted pretty wild for a time and in fairness to the girl who wanted to be called Pat, D day hadn't been all that long ago. She'd probably snap out of it and someday she'd wonder how in hell she'd ever taken a paratrooper home like that, if she remembered him at all. He knew she was probably with some other guy tonight, and he wondered why that should make him feel so shitty. He wasn't jealous. He hardly remembered what she looked like, and that had been part of the deal.

But when he got to the hotel he checked the back room anyhow. Neither Sandy Kane nor the girl who wanted to be called Pat were there, and the only woman sitting alone was sour faced and unattractive. He went up to his room alone and decided it wouldn't kill him. He didn't know when he'd get to sleep in such luxurious surroundings again, and it felt good enough to just take a long hot bath and slip naked between clean linen sheets.

Hunter felt drained, now that the hearings were over and he didn't have to think about saying the wrong thing or blowing up at those smug assholes asking all those stupid questions. He knew he was developing a nasty tendency to flare up. He wondered where that was coming from. He'd always been a pretty level-headed guy. He'd always gotten along with his teachers and bosses, back in the States. He'd have to start watching it. He'd been dumb to flare at Bradley like that, even if the jerk had had it coming. He thought back to socking that air force captain; it was funny, but he had no conscious memory of *decid-*

ing to do any such thing. The jerk had just said one dumb thing too often and there went the old left hook, as if it had a life of its own. He'd been tested for quick reflexes when he put in for the troops. But they were getting out of hand. You didn't have to be a medic to see that tear-assing around in combat and then tear-assing around on leave could make a guy nervous in the service.

He was determined to get a good night's sleep. But fortunately he was still awake when the phone rang. He reached out with an annoyed frown and picked it up. A female voice that sounded sort of Betty Boop said, "This is Beth Waterman, Lieutenant. I'm calling from Greenwich Hospital. Uh, is Ramie Davis there?"

Hunter blinked in surprise and sat up on one elbow as he replied, "Hardly, unfortunately. But while we're on the subject, what made you think she would be, Miss Waterman?"

"Call me Beth. I'm on your side. One of the girls from the UPI office said you were Ramie's new boyfriend and I've been trying and trying to reach her. I'm in a jam."

"There's been a lot of that going around, I hear. But you heard wrong about Ramie and me. I took her home from a party a few nights ago. Period. The last time she spoke to me she said something about going up to Scotland. The commando layout near Ben Nevis."

"I tried there. They said she was staying off base at some icky old inn and they didn't have the number. Hoping she might be back I've been trying her flat all evening. You were my last hope. These darned old English doctors want to send me back to the States."

He remembered something Ramie had told him as

they held hands across the table. "Oh, you must be that girl who caught the mortar round on Omaha! What on earth is an American chick doing in a British hospital?"

"I wish I knew. I guess they didn't have room for me when they loaded the GIs in the ambulances at Southampton. Anyway, I'm feeling great and I don't want to go home. The office says I have to do what my doctors say, but I thought Ramie could pull some strings. Ramie knows everybody."

He paused momentarily before saying, "So I hear. But I don't seem to be in her little black book, Beth. She's still carrying a torch for that fly-boy. Did you know him?"

There was a moment of silence. Then Beth said, "No, I never heard about *that* problem!"

"She has other problems?"

"Oboy, does she ever! But I don't gossip about my friends, so you'll have to ask her about them. Listen, Lieutenant, I can keep a secret, so if the two of you are sort of avoiding publicity—"

"She's not here," he said flatly. "I really don't have any way to get in touch with her, Beth."

"Oh, damn! They're putting me on a ship this coming Monday if I don't pull some strings. Well, I have to hang up now. Got other calls to try."

They said goodnight and he hung up the phone to flop back down as he wondered what she looked like. She'd had a cute voice, but nobody really looked like Betty Boop.

He closed his eyes and put the call out of his mind. He was just dozing off when the phone rang again. He muttered, "Jesus H. Christ, it's nearly midnight!" as he sat up again to answer the damned thing.

It was Sandy Kane. "Oh, there you are, Logan. I called earlier but they said you were out. Dare I hope you're still alone and turgid?"

"Sandy, it's awfully late to be making silly phone calls."

A male voice cut in, "It certainly is. Who is this, anyway?"

Hunter stiffened in dismay and didn't answer. He heard Sandy saying in a desperately casual tone, "Ivor, dear, is that you? Where are you calling from?"

Her husband replied, "My study downstairs, of course. I didn't want to waken you when I got in just now. But I see you're up and on the phone. Who are we talking to, old girl?"

Before Sandy could answer, Hunter said, "This is Lieutenant Hunter of the U.S. Army, sir. I took the liberty of calling your wife to see if she could give me a number where you could be reached in Scotland."

"You wanted to speak to *me*, Lieutenant?"

"Yessir. Actually I'm really trying to reach Ramie Davis. I heard she was up in Scotland with you and—"

"Logan and Ramie met at the party we gave the other day, Ivor," Sandy explained, catching on fast. Hunter suspected she did that a lot.

"Ah, one begins to see the light," said Admiral Kane. "I don't have the number where she's staying in Fort William, Lieutenant. But I can patch through a message to the commandos, and when she returns to base to watch the lads go through their paces they can give it to her. What's the message? I say, I'm not being asked to play Cupid, am I?"

Hunter laughed, seeing light at the end of the tunnel. "If only you were, sir. It's about her co-worker, Beth Waterman. It seems Miss Waterman managed to get herself wounded on D day and she's been calling rather desperately about being sent home. She doesn't want to go home and she seems to think Ramie can do something about it."

"Oh, I say, Ramie couldn't do all that perishing much even if we could call her tonight. Military doctors can be frightfully stubborn. Ramie told me about her friend getting hit and I remember meeting Miss Waterman. I know she only took a few splinters, but she's a rather tiny creature and no doubt the doctors don't want to take chances. Besides, with the hospitals full up, they probably want to get rid of her, as well they should. Where do they have the dear girl, should Ramie have more friends in high places than one suspects?"

"She called from Greenwich Hospital, sir."

"Greenwich? I say, that's a wonky place for lady Yanks to wind up. But we're in luck, dear boy. Greenwich is a Royal Navy hospital!"

"You mean *you* can stall her evacuation, sir?"

"Stall? My dear boy, rear admirals don't stall. They give orders! I'll give them a call at once and . . . No, better yet, I'm down here wagging my tail between Admiralty and Whitehall, and I was about to go over and burn some midnight oil as soon as I recovered from that bloody train ride. As soon as I reach Admiralty I'll call from there. More impressive if the hospital gets it on the official phone line, what?"

"That's very kind of you, sir."

"Say no more about it. Always glad to help a friend of Ramie's."

Hunter thanked him anyway and hung up. He sounded like a hell of a nice old guy. It was too bad he was stuck with that little redheaded tramp for a wife. He wondered if he should warn Dan Bradley about the extension phones all over the house in Belgravia. Then he remembered Danny Boy had mentioned them. Even Danny Boy was smarter than the round heeled bimbo poor old Kane was married to. They were both playing with matches, but it wasn't any of his business, so what the hell.

The next time the phone rang he was really asleep. So his voice was groggy when he rolled over with a groan and picked it up a third time.

Sandy Kane said, "Well, the old fool's gone out again. As I was saying before we were so rudely interrupted, darling—"

He swore and hung up. Wide awake again. The dame wasn't just a stupid bimbo. She was nuts.

He sat up and reached for a smoke as he wondered what he should do about it. But there wasn't anything a rational man could do about a woman like Alexandra Kane except to stay as far away from her as possible. He knew he'd better tell Dan Bradley about her dangerous sense of timing. Danny Boy already knew she'd screw a snake if somebody would only hold its head. But he owed it to any guy in his own outfit to warn him the silly broad seemed to be trying to get caught. And a husband who could stop the war with a telephone call wasn't really the guy you wanted catching you.

12

THEY RETURNED to their Normandy bivouac to find half the outfit gone and what was left totally confused. The regimental sergeant major said Ike had ordered all airborne units back to England for recovery and retraining. Half the units had already left and nobody knew where anybody was at a given moment. When the sergeant said he hadn't seen the colonel all day Dan Bradley said, "Hell, he's probably on his way then. Cover for me, buddy boy. I've got to see if any of these Normandy blondes like the cigarettes I smoke."

The sergeant cleared his throat. "Begging the major's pardon, we've been told the local French girls are off limits for now. Some of them seem to have had German blankets and field rations that army intelligence wants to talk to them about."

Bradley grinned and cracked, "Hell, I'm an intelligence officer, right? I'll just be doing my duty. See you around the BOQ if I strike out, old buddy boy."

Hunter waited until Danny Boy sauntered out before he turned back to the sergeant and asked what the situation at the front seemed to be at the moment. The noncom said, "We seem to be here to stay, sir. Those hedgerows are a bigger bitch than SHEAF planned for, but the Big Red One just grabbed a lot of real estate and I hear the Limeys under Montgomery have things nailed down pretty good on our north flank. Naturally, we're too close here to do any training exercises, so they're sending us back to Newbury, west of London. Uh, could I ask how those hearings went, Lieutenant?"

Hunter nodded and said, "We're keeping the gliders until somebody figures out a way to jump out of a C-47 with a jeep strapped on. The fly boys are going to be retrained and they've doped out better recognition signals for the pathfinders. This time the scouts are jumping twelve minutes ahead of the first wave instead of forty-five and, oh yeah, they think we'd better jump in daylight next time."

"Daylight, sir? That sounds like suicide to me!"

"It does to me too, and I told them so, loudly and more than once. They seem to think a little ground fire swinging in your shrouds beats landing a little safer and a whole lot lost. They may have a point."

He was about to leave to hunt up his HQ & HQ CO to find out where he'd be spending the night when a jeep braked to a stop out front and Colonel Sam Bell came in. The older man nodded and said, "You're just the man I wanted to see, Logan. Let's take it in my office."

Hunter followed the colonel and when they were

alone the old man waved him to a seat and got out the bottle, as Hunter filled him in on the London hearings.

Colonel Bell handed him a drink and took his own seat. "I'd already gotten most of that on the phone while they were chewing me for still being here. Where's Bradley? I need some staff work and I could have used it yesterday."

Hunter swallowed before he replied, "He went to check something out, sir. I can handle any S2 for you."

Bell frowned at him. "I know you can. His clerk typist knows more about his job by now than he does. You can't beat spending some time at a desk to find out where the paper clips are. Okay, I want your scouts and the heavy weapons companies to cover our evacuation from a strong perimeter. We're not that far behind the lines and I'd feel stupid taking sniper fire as I loaded up. You know the SOP, don't you?"

"Of course, sir. I'll post the heavy weapons on high ground around the evacuation points and move a screen of scouts out into the Indian country. I could use some extra hands from the rifle companies, though. We don't have quite as many scouts right now as the TO calls for."

"Tell my adjutant I'm making you our security CO with an acting rank of major. That'll make the froggies jump when you yell froggie. I, uh, wish I could make it a permanent rank, son, but you're still officially in the doghouse for smacking inferior superiors."

"I understand, sir."

"You do, eh? Well understand me something else, Logan. Why are you still covering for that asshole major of yours?"

"Covering, sir?"

"Don't look Bo Peep at me, damn it! I was covering for *good* officers before you were a twinkle in your daddy's eye. I learned a long time ago not to cover for guys like Bradley."

"He's all right, sir."

"You think so, huh? Let me tell you a little story. Happened back in the Depression army when I still thought the world was run on the level."

He took a slug of Canadian and continued, "I was pulling CQ one night while most of the outfit was on a training exercise in the field. It was raining cats and dogs, so I guess our company CO decided they weren't paying him enough to get that wet. He sneaked back to the company area to catch a few winks in a dry bed. But he'd been drinking and he wandered into the wrong barracks. Flopped in a noncom's quarters instead of his own. He must have been soused to the gills."

"What happened then, sir?"

"It gets sillier. Of all the goddamn barracks the fool could have picked to goldbrick in, he picked one the reserve platoon was using. So the guy who belonged in the bed wasn't out in the field. He'd been over in the PX drinking 3.2 until closing time. So he was feeling no pain either, when he got back to his quarters to sleep it off. Naturally he found it sort of mysterious to discover his door locked. He knocked on the door and the captain woke up, called him a dirty name, and put a round of .45 through the door, missing him by maybe an inch."

Hunter whistled. Colonel Bell nodded and said, "The guy came to the orderly room to get me. Having heard gunfire in the company area I was already on my feet anyway. So I went over with my own .45 and flash to see what the hell was going on. You get the picture, son?"

"Yessir. You found yourself in a position to arrest your own CO if I remember the ARs correctly."

"I should have," Bell growled. "I didn't. Blowing holes in doors had sobered him up enough to talk to by the time I got to him. So, like a chump, I got him to his quarters and we covered for the son of a bitch. You'd have probably done the same, right?"

When Hunter pursed his lips and nodded, Bell said, "There's more. You can't sound off with .45s on a post without the OD noticing. So when the OD arrived with a brace of MPs I told him I had no idea who'd been shooting off fire crackers. Next day they called me down to regiment. A guy wearing these same eagles on his shoulders asked me the same dumb questions and added he'd heard some rumors about the captain. I toughed it through. I covered for the prick even with my own ass on the line. So in the end it all blew over. It was about the dumbest thing I ever did, and I've done a lot of dumb things in my time, Logan."

"I'm afraid I don't understand, sir. Did they ever find out you'd lied for your superior?"

"No. I lie good when I lie at all. He had me by the nuts, once it was too late to go back and tell on him. I don't have to tell you how many ways a company CO can lean on a junior, do I?"

"He *leaned* on you, sir? What the hell for? You'd just saved his ass."

Sam Bell nodded bitterly. "Yeah. You'd think he'd have been a little grateful, right? Nine out of ten men would have been. But you have to watch that tenth son of a bitch! I guess he figured that now that

I had something on him, I'd abuse it. Maybe he was just like a kid with a hole in his tooth who can't keep from sticking his tongue in it to see if it's still there. Anyway, he rode my ass damned near into the guardhouse before I managed to transfer out. He wrote me up for every shit detail known to science and a couple he must have just made up. I think if there'd been some way to have me shot he'd have done that too, but lucky for me, it was the peacetime army. Is any of this sinking in, Lieutenant?"

Hunter nodded, but said, "Yessir. I'd better see about planning that defense perimeter, sir."

"You don't have anything to tell me about our Danny Boy, eh?"

"No sir. I assure you he's never pulled anything as raw as that drunken captain you just told me about."

"Maybe. But if I had something to use against him I could do the regiment as well as you a favor by getting rid of him. You won't always be in the doghouse for smacking that fly boy, son. If I had you manning the S2 post here at HQ when the next promotions list was being typed up—"

"I don't want the major's job, sir. Not that way, at least."

Sam Bell sighed wearily. "All right. We'll drop it for now. But when you leave here send a runner into the village for Bradley and ask him if he could please this once keep his pants on and do a little work around here."

As Hunter rose, the older man added, "You really are a lot like your father, aren't you? What's my old AEF buddy, Duncan doing with himself these days?"

"Dad's in Washington, working for the government on one of those dollar-a-year deals, sir. He tried to reenlist for this war, but my mother and the army doctors told him not to be silly."

Bell chuckled fondly and said, "That doesn't surprise me. Is he really in poor health, though?"

"You'll never get him to admit it, sir. Dad's always been a pretty feisty old bird. But his hearing's not what it was in the last war."

"Yeah, it was pretty noisy as I recall. I sure could use an officer like your father, tin ear or not." Then he smiled wistfully and added, "But come to think of it, I seem to have one. Now get out of here and soldier, before I blubber up all over you!"

13

L OGAN HUNTER may not have wanted Dan Bradley's job. But in the weeks that followed he got to do a lot of it anyway. The decimated 101st was stationed in and around Newbury, eighty miles west of London. The nearby Salisbury Plains were a great place to conduct airborne exercises for the replacements coming in from the Z of I. But it was a hell of a chore to get to London and back, so Danny Boy didn't try too hard. Unlike the enlisted men, officers were not required to have passes to leave the base. They carried ID cards, but the MPs never checked out an officer unless he was in obvious trouble and while Bradley abused his rank, he was very good about keeping his buttons buttoned and never showed his liquor walking past a brace of white helmets.

On the TO Hunter was the platoon leader of the

regimental scouts and the assistant of the staff officer who kept telling him to take over while he drove off in a staff car on some vague S2 mission or other. Hunter wondered just how Danny Boy worded those trip tickets for the motor pool. He obviously couldn't put Sandy Kane down as his destination.

The hell of it was, the chain of command was vague enough on the duties of both men so that there was no way Bradley could get caught unless Hunter simply ratted on him. An assistant is empowered, under the ARs, to take over a superior's duties in his absence. Most of the extra work was dull routine that attracted no attention, as long as somebody did it. Hunter knew he was being taken advantage of, but after he'd called Ramie's number a couple of times and gotten no answer, it didn't seem important. The only girl he was really interested in was either very busy with her work or with some other guy lately. It seemed stupid to go all the way to London to meet some other woman. The area around Newbury seemed to be crawling with them.

Aside from the local Berkshire maids and the whores and teen-aged V girls who always materialized around military installations, there were hundreds of Land Army girls working on the surrounding farms that summer. They tended to be strapping country girls who wore quasi-military jodhpurs that were said to come off with astonishing ease. So the bored and virile troopers of the 101st discovered there were better uses for the free rubber contraceptives than blousing one's jump pants with them.

But there was a complication the British Agriculture Office had overlooked in its desire to make Britain more self-sufficient in time of war. The Land Army girls were not the only extra helpers they sent the local farmers.

Thanks to the British Eighth Army's efforts in North Africa, the POW cages in England had been crowded even before D day. Turning German POWs loose seemed a bit much, but there were thousands of Italians captured back in the desert before Italy had surrendered in '43. It seemed pointless to keep former Fascist soldiers locked up when space was in short supply for current enemies, so Italian POWs were issued British work uniforms, dyed maroon to avoid confusion, and turned loose to work on English farms.

Unfortunately, many British and American soldiers remained confused indeed and more than a little resentful to see these recent enemies wandering about in rather spiffy uniforms, some wearing Fascist campaign ribbons, and all enjoying more freedom than Tommy or GI Joe.

Most of the Italian soldiers behaved decently and justified the trust placed in them by working hard and trying to stay out of trouble. But they were young and virile men too, and the results that followed, while sad, were inevitable.

The English girls were neither better nor worse than any other kind, and in truth most of them refused to date the exotic Italian North African vets. But some were pragmatic and there were obvious advantages to a bloke who had money to spend, didn't have to make bed check, and wasn't likely to transfer out just as you were growing fond of him. The effect it had on an English civilian male was bad enough. It drove the British and American soldiers nuts.

Major Bradley was doping off somewhere when the MPs brought Sergeant Falco back to the base. Hunter didn't have the rank to pull on the provost marshal. So he went to see Colonel Bell about it.

He caught the old man in the officer's club, alone at the bar, so he wasn't officially going over anyone's head as he joined the colonel and said, "I shouldn't be coming to you with this, sir. But my platoon sergeant got in a little scrape in town last night and I can't seem to make his company CO or the provost marshal see reason."

Colonel Bell signaled the enlisted barkeep and then turned to Hunter with a quizzical look. "I heard about what your Sergeant Falco did to that poor Italian slob in the Mermaid. You call hospitalizing a POW trustee and two MPs a little scrape, son? Your man's a homicidal maniac!"

Hunter told the barkeep to make his Scotch and water and turned back to Bell to object, "He didn't kill anybody, sir. As he tells it, the Italian passed a remark about the Land Army girl Falco was with. Unfortunately, Falco speaks Italian and—"

"I read the arrest report. Up to stomping the Italian's face half off we could say our man was within his airborne rights. But busting a chair over one MP and throwing another through a window was almost certainly against the ARs."

"There were six MPs fighting with him, sir. Falco wasn't in such great shape when I saw him in the guard house just now and neither of the guys he roughed up were permanently injured."

Bell took a sip of his drink before he sighed and said, "We could likely wash our own linen, if it was just the regimental MPs, Logan. But the British are sort of making a fuss about all the silver wire they'll need to hold that Italian's jaw together from now on.

The guy was in town on a British pass. Falco had no right to bust him up like that."

"He passed a remark about Falco's date, sir."

"So what? She was with Falco, not the other guy, and she couldn't have known what he was saying anyhow. You'd think Falco could have been a little more understanding with another Italian, right?"

Hunter frowned and said, "Begging the colonel's pardon, Sergeant Falco's not Italian. His folks may have been, once, but he was born in New Jersey and he jumped in Sicily. On our side."

"You're right. I shouldn't have said that. But your man's patriotism isn't the issue here. We can't have our men just running around kicking the shit out of everybody. He's got to be punished, damn it."

Hunter nodded and said, "I agree, sir. I suggested company punishment to Captain Walters at HQ but Walters says it's out of his hands and that the TJA is insisting on a special. If Falco's court-martialed he'll lose his stripes."

"I know," Bell said. "It seems to be a habit of his, judging from his 201 file. Do you mind telling me why you're going to bat for this fuck-up, son?"

"He's a good soldier, sir. I don't mean here on garrison duty. He's a lousy garrison soldier. But out on the line he's the kind of man you want covering your flank."

The colonel nodded and said, "Yeah, I remember your D day report. I've got that Bronze Star you wrote him up for somewhere in my files. Division turned it down. They only give us so many medals a battle and there were a lot of guys in the outfit who deserved them on D day who aren't going to get 'em, either."

"That machine gun nest he wiped out for me ought to count for one brawl in town, though, Colonel."

Bell thought, took another sip, and said, "I'd have to butter up my opposite number in the British army and I don't like to owe any officer, Lieutenant."

"I don't like to either, sir. But have you seen the replacements we've been getting in from Benning? I've got one seasoned combat vet I can count on in my platoon, and S2 will be going in ahead for the whole regiment the next time we jump."

Bell snorted. "*If* we jump, you mean. That crazy George Patton's just busted through the hedgerows across the channel and at the rate he's going the war will be over before we get ourselves back in shape to do anything."

Hunter said, "Yessir. I said my replacements were piss poor. Meanwhile my best man's sitting in the guardhouse, facing a special."

"You're overstating your case, son. I'll see what I can do. But I'm not promising anything." He glanced down at his wrist and added, "Weren't you to make a practice jump this afternoon, Lieutenant?"

"I called it off, sir. That's another problem, but I can hack it out with S4, I hope."

"Quartermaster giving you a rough time?"

"Not the ones here, sir. Some asshole back in the Z of I issued a mess of those weird infantry combat boots to the replacements I just got."

Colonel Bell gave a sour smile. "I've seen them. Raised some hell about it too. But we seem to be stuck with the damned things. There's no way we're going to get regular jump boots for the next six weeks or so, and I want those men trained, Lieutenant."

"I want them trained too, sir. But I don't want them

killed on practice jumps. If a man were to snag one of his lines with the buckles on the sides of those stupid boots—"

"It would smart like hell," Bell interrupted, but insisted, "You're just going to have to be careful, son. General Taylor wants his division combat ready and you don't get ready sitting on the ground."

Hunter saw the old man meant it. So he finished his drink and went back to the company area. He found Corporal Arnold lecturing them on map reading in the day room. They'd been taught map reading, many many times. But a scout had to know the subject better than any trooper in one of the rifle companies.

Naturally, when Arnold saw an officer in the doorway he stopped in mid-sentence and called them to attention. Hunter said, "As you were, men. We're going to jump this afternoon after all, so pay attention. How many of you are wearing those fucking infantry boots?"

More than half of them raised their hands. More than half of them looked too young to be in the army, too. Where the hell were they getting them these days? "Okay, here's the play," Hunter said. "Before we load up to go out to the air strip I want each of you to wrap electrician's tape around your boot tops. Make sure those damned buckles are flat as you can get them and taped down with no rough edges."

He saw one of the new men had his hand up. "Yes, Colson?"

"Where are we supposed to get this here tape, sir?"

"You don't have to get it. Corporal Arnold is going to requisition a couple of rolls from supply and issue it to you. Next time, wait until you have a real question, Colson. I'm not in the habit of ordering you men to do anything you won't be able to. It's 1300 now and we'll be jumping at 1600. So there's no excuse for wrapping that tape sloppy. Corporal Arnold?"

"Yessir?"

"Take the platoon back to their barracks and see about that tape. I'm holding inspection in one hour so I'll expect the leather that shows on those boots to be spit shined. And if any man here expects to go to town this weekend he'd better not show me a carbine I wouldn't want to sip my soda through. I'll be at the BOQ if you need me. Carry on."

Hunter went to his quarters to strap his own gear on. Each man kept everything but his main and reserve chutes on hand at all times. They'd pick up the silk over at the Ramsbury strip before they boarded the planes.

He took his time, but he realized he'd been over-eager when he glanced down at his watch and saw it was too early to check his men out. He tried whenever possible to avoid the "hurry up and wait" routine that made an officer look like a jerk. He knew his men actually had time to PX before the scheduled after-noon training jump. But once you had them scattered there was always some silly son of a bitch you had to look for. "Hurry up and wait" was a necessary evil of army life because while nine out of ten men managed to go through life on time, there was always that tenth jerk. So you had to allow for SNAFU and give yourself more time than you really needed.

Suited up with no place to go, Hunter went down the hallway to the day room, sat down, fished out a smoke, and decided he may as well try his luck with the damned phone again. He didn't have Ramie's office number and it seemed unlikely she'd be at her London flat at this hour, but it didn't cost to find out. He got the English male long distance operator and after endless clicks and buzzes he heard the phone ringing at her end. He let it ring four times and was about to pack it in when someone picked up and a Betty Boop voice said, "Hello, Miss Davis's residence."

Hunter knew there couldn't be two women in the ETO who talked like that. "Beth, is that you? This is Logan Hunter."

Beth Waterman replied, "Oh, I remember you. You saved my life one night. Whatever did you tell those people at Greenwich Hospital, Lieutenant?"

He laughed and said, "Lieutenants don't tell them anything, Beth. I got a brass hat in the British navy for you and I see he must have pulled the right strings. How are you feeling?"

"I'm ready to take on Clark Gable. But I'm still on sick leave. Ramie's letting me stay here for now. A buzz bomb got the place where I was staying while I was in the hospital. It's sort of spooky when you think about it. I mean, if I hadn't been wounded on Omaha I'd have been home there when the buzz bomb hit, you know?"

"Some girls were just born lucky, I guess. Is, ah, Ramie there, Beth?"

"Oh, didn't you know? She's back in Normandy, covering the big breakout. I think she's in St. Lo. It's hard to keep track these days, the way they keep moving the lines forward. Where are you calling from, Logan?"

"The middle of nowhere. We're out near the Salisbury Plains at a dump called Newbury."

"But that's in England, isn't it?"

"I'm glad you noticed. We've been pulled out of the war for now. Uh, St. Lo's pretty deep in France, if I remember my war, Beth."

"I'm worried about her too, but Ramie's safer right

now than those fresh Krauts. The last I heard, Patton's gone crazy, miles beyond St. Lo, and the Germans are still running from him. He's swinging north to hook up with the Limeys at Falais, so our girl's practically in the rear area and she seemed mad as anything about it in her last dispatches. You know Ramie. She tried to hitch a ride with Third Army but they said all their tanks were full up."

Hunter said something about having lunch with Beth the next time he made it to London and hung up, scowling. It felt dumb as hell to be sitting here in England when even girls were over there with the big show. But that was the army for you.

The men were ready and waiting when he arrived to inspect them. Their gear was okay. There didn't seem to be anything he could do about the scared look on some of those all-too-young faces. He knew they'd dropped the draft age to eighteen now. Allied propaganda was making a big deal out of the kids Hitler was sending to the front these days. Didn't they ever look at the GIs they were sending over now? Half the kids in his platoon were too young to vote or buy a drink, out of uniform. And airborne got the cream of the crop.

They drove out to the airstrip and got to wait some more. As they picked up their silk some of the replacements made the same dumb cracks about taking a chute back to get a new one if it didn't open. Hunter had found that sort of stale before he'd finished at Benning a million years ago.

He thought about that as they waited, smoked, bitched, and waited some more. Ramie had said something about how long it seemed since the blitz of '40 and he understood her all too well. Time did a funny thing in a war. Four years could zip past a civilian working at some peacetime job. But when one measured a life in seventy-two-hour passes and could lose old friends in minutes, every month seemed a peacetime year. Hunter knew, objectively, that he was only a few real years older than these kids, and that Corporal Arnold, down there at the end, was only twenty. Twenty was a young guy, even in the army, and Arnold had only made one combat jump. Yet he seemed like he was old enough to be half these kids' father now. It made no sense. D day was in the very recent past, on the calendar. Yet it was already ancient history over across the channel. Grim-faced GIs were slugging their way to meet the Canadians punching out of Caen to link up with them and by now they were feeling like hardened vets. Yet he knew some of them, and probably some of the Germans too, had been recruits on their way through the repo depos the night he and the few old-timers here had dropped in Normandy. Guys like poor Falco must feel they rated a gold watch from the company by now.

An S3 NCO came over to Hunter carrying a clip board as a couple of C-47s taxied along the runway toward the apron they were lined up on. The training noncom waited until Hunter had signed his men for the practice jump before he said, "The wind's from the northwest over the DZ, sir. It's gusting a bit, but we're game if you are."

Hunter handed him back the clipboard. "I don't have much choice. I tried to cancel out, but regiment says not to do that no more."

The sergeant replied, "Yessir. I see your serial has taped boots. I guess you heard, eh?"

"Heard what, Sergeant?"

"Oh, one of the guys with Able Company bought the

farm this morning. Caught a line in his boot buckle and came down streamer. Head first."

Hunter grimaced and said, "It smarts no matter how you hit. Thanks for cheering me up. I hadn't heard. I was drinking with the colonel earlier, too."

"Yessir. We were told to keep it quiet, but I figured you knew."

The C-47s were waiting, props ticking over. Hunter stared morosely out across the grassy airfield for a moment, took a deep breath and let it half out so his voice wouldn't crack, and yelled, "All right, Corporal Arnold, load your stick. I'll follow with mine."

As Arnold called his fifteen troopers to attention and gave them a left face one man stepped out of line and headed over to Hunter. Hunter snapped, "You're in ranks and at attention, soldier!" But the kid kept coming. Arnold looked back, confused, and Hunter called, "Load up, Arnold. I'll deal with this." So Arnold moved his stick toward the nearest transport as Hunter put his own stick at ease and warned the stray trooper, "You'd better have a reason for dropping out of ranks, soldier."

Then he saw the boy was crying.

Hunter took him out of earshot and said, "We're all scared, Murphy. Didn't anybody tell you back at Benning that someday you might have to board a C-47?"

"I can't jump today, sir," Murphy pleaded. "Maybe tomorrow, but not today! I just can't!"

"Murphy, I don't know how to tell you this, but you don't jump when you feel like it. You're supposed to jump when we tell you to, and I just told you to."

Murphy hung his head and sobbed, "I can't, sir. I'm feeling sick."

"Were you on base when they held sick call this morning, soldier?"

"Yessir, but—"

"But me no buts, soldier! You had your chance to tell the medics you were having your period before you ate chow, twice, on the taxpayers. You did make five jumps at Benning to qualify for those pretty wings the girls admire, didn't you?"

"Yessir. But only 'cause the jumpmaster pushed me out the last time. It gets worse every time. They told us we'd get used to it. But it gets worse every time. I shit my pants the last time."

"You're allowed to shit your pants, Murphy. But if you want to wear those wings you've got to earn them. If you hurry you can still make it to that C-47 and we'll say no more about it."

The boy shook his head stubbornly and blurted, "I can't. I won't."

Hunter hesitated. Then he let out a long breath and said, "All right. Go back to the shed and turn in your silk. Then hitch a ride back to the base as best you can and report to your first sergeant."

Murphy looked up like a condemned man receiving a last-minute pardon from the governor. "What should I say to the first sergeant, sir?"

"You won't have to say much, kid. You won't be the first wash-out he's had to type up the papers on."

"You want to wash me out of the troops, sir?"

"Don't want to, Murphy. Have to. It's been nice talking to you, but I have a C-47 to catch. So move it out, infantry."

As the abashed ex-trooper walked away, head down, Hunter turned to the others, watching in bemusement, and snapped, "First Stick, Tensh-hut! Left hace! Fortt ho!"

They were at attention, but one of them muttered, "He chickened," in a voice of wonder as they moved out to the plane.

"As you were!" Hunter snapped, shutting them up as he loaded them aboard. He knew they thought he was being hard-ass. But every time a soldier carried out a foolish order it made him more sure of himself and the other idiots around him who could be counted on to obey commands. He knew how Murphy had gotten through Benning. Back in the Z of I they could afford to coddle and coax a reluctant jumper and if he froze in the hatchway it wouldn't get anybody else killed. But if he ever led these rookies into the real thing, he wanted scouts he could count on. If that poor kid shit his pants at the thought of a training jump, what would he do the first time some Kraut took a shot at him?

As he settled in his bucket seat and the plane began to taxi, Hunter put Murphy out of his mind. He knew he'd never see him again. He had to make sure the fifteen kids who'd been dumb enough to follow him aboard this kite got out and down to the ground again okay.

Across the aisle, their knees aimed at Hunter's, two of them were talking about what had just happened. Their voices were almost drowned out by the roar of the twin engines, but Hunter was used to reading enough lip aboard a plane to know what they were saying.

One asked, "What do you think they'll do to Murphy, Spud?"

His companion shrugged and said, "Beats me. I guess he'll wind up on permanent KP."

"Yeah. Maybe he knows something the rest of us

don't know, huh? I mean, KP's not so bad, when you consider."

The one called Spud laughed and said, "Hey, don't go getting nervous in the service. Eight'll get you ten the fucking war's over before any of us see combat."

Hunter didn't know if Spud was right or not. He wasn't sure he wanted to know.

14

SERGEANT ROBERT S. FALCO was still showing the effects of his fight in the Mermaid as he stood at attention in Colonel Bell's office. The office door was closed, so Sam Bell didn't have to worry about nit picking IG reports as he snorted in disgust and asked, "All right, you dumb wop bastard, I want you to listen to me good."

"Nobody calls me a wop in this man's army, Colonel!" Falco flared.

"I just did and you're at attention, damn your eyes!" He saw the look in Falco's unswollen eye and added, "I know about that shavetail you smacked in the Eighty-second and I'm not impressed. In the first place I think I could whip your ass. In the second place I'd have you shot whether I won or lost. So I'll call you a dumb wop bastard until you can show me one fucking reason why I shouldn't."

Falco's face kept getting redder, but he didn't answer. Bell said, "You're going to grind your fillings loose if you don't watch it. You don't like to be called a wop, do you?"

"No, Colonel, I don't. But I guess rank has its privileges."

"You're damned right. But let me ask you something, Falco. If other folks can't call *you* a wop, what gives you the right to hit *other* guys for being wops? That's what you did, you know. You busted a guy's nose and then you broke his jaw with your jump boot, simply because his name ended with a vowel."

Falco shook his head stubbornly. "Begging the colonel's pardon, I jumped that jerk-off for passing a remark in Italian, not for being Italian."

"Bullshit, Falco. In the first place all he said was that the Land Army girl you were with was some dish, and he was saying it to another Italian POW. Not to you and not to the lady. I've got the full report here, and I don't mind tell you I did not enjoy kissing the King's ass to get it. The British questioned the guy you clobbered, together with other witnesses. Are you saying anything else was said to or about you in the Mermaid before you proceeded to wreck the joint?"

When Falco shrugged and didn't answer, Bell sat back and looked him in the eye. "Listen, Falco, I used to have an inferiority complex too, before I grew up. So I'll tell you why you smacked that guy, Falco. You were trying to prove you weren't a wop, like him."

"Goddamn it, Colonel, I'm not a wop. I'm as good an American as you are!"

"Yeah, yeah, I have your 201 file here, and nobody can say you're not one hell of a GI. An asshole, of course, but you get brownie points on fighting for mom's blueberry pie. We all know you're a fighting son of a bitch, Falco. When are you going to start acting like a grown man?"

"I guess I'm as much a man as anybody in this chickenshit outfit, Colonel," Falco growled.

"Bullshit. Grown men don't run around busting up pubs to show the world they're not really like those other wops the Limeys kicked the shit out of in North Africa. What part of Jersey do you come from, Falco?"

"Newark, sir. The North Ward. Toughest part of town."

"Yeah, well I grew up in a tough neighborhood too, and I stopped trying to prove it before you were born. I've got your number, Falco. I know what kind of guy you are. Ignorant, sensitive about at least one grandparent who doesn't speak English, and overcompensating for it with a loud mouth and a chip on your shoulder. You're a reverse snob who jeers at anyone with an education or good manners. You think if only you can bust enough heads nobody will notice what a slob you are. But it's no use, Falco. You are a slob, and you always will be."

Falco didn't answer. What did the old fart want from him, tears?

Bell leaned back and made a tent with his fingers as he stared up at the sergeant with a disgusted expression and added, "In my opinion you're not worth the powder to blow you to hell. But Lieutenant Hunter seems to think I'm wrong. So tell me something, Falco, am I wrong?"

Falco shrugged and replied, "That's for the colonel to say."

Bell snapped, "Damned A. All right, your platoon leader went to bat for you and I've been on the horn to a lot of people who don't know any better either. Here's what we're going to do. You're going to sign away two thirds of your base pay until the regimental slush fund's paid back."

"Paid back, sir?"

"Come on, you asshole, did you think the owner of the Mermaid was about to drop the charges unless somebody paid for the damages? You owe His Majesty some medical bills too. I told them we'd pick up the tab and they were pretty decent about it, considering."

Falco frowned and asked, "Do I have to pay for medicine in a military hospital, sir?"

"Who the hell were you expecting to, the British government? They didn't put that guy in the plastic surgery ward, Falco. You did. Fortunately for you, the British surgeons were officers and don't get to send us a bill."

He spotted the look of relief in Falco's one good eye and quickly added, "The deduction from your pay is just for openers. You're confined to the base until further notice. I don't want to see you in the PX with anything stronger than a Lucky Strike in your hand if you don't want me to put the PX off limits to you too. Meanwhile we have some grown men in the outfit who can go on leave without acting like Peck's Bad Boy, so be prepared to spend some nights as CQ and/or sergeant of the guard. How do you like it so far?"

Falco looked astonished as he asked, "Will I still have the stripes to pull sergeant of the guard, sir?"

Bell nodded grimly. "Affirmative. Busting you doesn't seem to make any impression, so this time I mean to work your ass off *wearing* those stripes! You don't deserve them, Falco. You don't deserve PFC. But Lieutenant Hunter says he wants you as his platoon sergeant and he's liable to need one any day now.

I told him he's making a big mistake about you, Falco. Do you think you're man enough to prove me wrong?"

Falco stood straighter as he replied soberly, "If the lieutenant thinks I can I'll give it my best shot, sir. Will that be all, sir?"

Sam Bell nodded, but then, as Falco saluted and prepared to leave, Bell said, "No. I know you're an asshole, but I'm going to tell you anyway—it looks like Operation Comet is on. And if you tell me you haven't heard latrine rumors about Operation Comet I'll puke."

Falco hesitated, then said, "A guy hears things answering phones for S2, sir."

"Yeah, well, it's still top secret and I shouldn't be talking to an asshole like you about it, but Lieutenant Hunter will be counting on you to lead the second stick. He's put that Corporal Arnold in for more stripes, too. I know Hunter's wrong about you, so what can you tell me about this Arnold boy?"

"Boy's the word that fits him, Colonel."

"Hunter said he did okay on D day."

"I guess all of us that got back must have done something right, sir. Arnold has to know more than the replacements we'll be jumping with."

"I know what you mean. We lost a lot of good men on D day, and Comet figures to be wilder. Even General Taylor bitched to Ike about it and we all know Maxwell Taylor eats razor blades for breakfast. But ours not to reason why and all that shit. You're dismissed, Sergeant, and so help me, next time—"

"There won't be a next time, Colonel."

"Bullshit. We both know you're a born fuck-up, Falco. But, ah, Sergeant?"

"Yessir?"

"Look out for Lieutenant Hunter, will you? I owe

his father for another war." In about the same way that you, Falco, owe the lieutenant, if you only knew it, Sam Bell added silently.

Bell smiled to himself after Falco saluted and left. He had had a habit of getting into trouble and getting stripped of rank too, until he had come under Duncan Hunter's command. Logan Hunter's old man was the first officer he'd met who'd been a human being instead of a martinet or a goldbrick. And Logan was following in his father's footsteps, all right. He liked Logan, no doubt about it. He sort of liked Falco too. The burly sergeant was like a magnified version of himself—at a much younger age, of course.

15

I N ALL THE 101st would be alerted for seventeen
missions that never came off that summer as the
dubious Eisenhower tried to figure out some use
for his airborne in a war that seemed to be an armored
blitz in reverse. A raging George Patton was bitching
that he would have wiped out the German Group West
had not Montgomery dragged his feet at the Falais
Gap, although, in fairness, the Canadians who dressed
like British Tommies showed the confused Germans
some very GI fighting indeed at Falais, and while
some German armor managed to escape the trap, a
hell of a lot didn't. Those who were still rolling were
rolling fast to the north and east as grim-faced Frenchmen began to dig up guns and ammo buried in '40
under Paris while underground fighters in occupied
Holland, Denmark and Norway began to knock off

Germans dumb enough to be alone on the streets at night.

But the Germans still held Holland as well as most of the fortified French channel ports and Hitler was screaming for someone to for God's sake do something. His battered ground forces were having enough trouble just staying alive as the Allies pushed them back in one savage skirmish after the other. The RAF and Eighth Air Force owned the sky now. The badly shot up Luftwaffe was sweating out the new jet fighters Berlin kept promising them, and meanwhile, there were so many British and American fighters up there that the RAF was able to divert a few squadrons to intercept the pilotless buzz bombs over the channel and thus make them even less bothersome as pure terror weapons.

But terror was a German cottage industry. So as the V-1 buzz bomb proved to be a frightening but strategically worthless weapon the Nazis unveiled the V-2, a Buck Rogers rocket that stood on its fins to go straight up, sixty miles, and arc down on England like a huge artillery shell. There was no way for a fighter to intercept the V-2 and, worse, they were lobbing them across the channel from occupied Holland, and the methodical Montgomery couldn't promise to move his British and Canadian forces through Belgium before September at the earliest.

Churchill and the British public couldn't wait that long. As the V-2 rockets slammed down all over the south of England, Operation Comet was thrown together to counter the rocket attacks. It was to be a joint mission for the British commandoes and American and British airborne units. The paratroopers would drop on the German V-2 positions in Holland to put them out of business as the commandos stormed

the Dutch coast, both to draw attention from the airborne operation and, they hoped, to evacuate the survivors. It was obvious that no paratrooper was about
to *walk* out of occupied Holland after blowing up
Adolf's new toys.

Operation Comet was simple in theory. On the
planning tables it was one impossible bitch. S4 complained that the logistics were impossible. S3 said the
combined operation was too complicated and S1 said
they didn't have the manpower. S2 was ordered to
work out the intelligence angles, and they were a
bitch too.

It wasn't that there was no intelligence on occupied
Holland. There was too much. The Free Dutch government in London had its agents reporting from
behind the German lines. British and American intelligence had their own agents doing the same. There
was a large and undetermined force of Nazi-hating
and independent Dutch men and women who seemed
to be operating on their own to make life rough on
their unwanted guests. And just to complicate life, a
small but fanatic and now desperate portion of the
Dutch citizens who'd bet on the wrong horse earlier
in the war were now working for the Nazis. Some
openly. All too many as double agents.

Neither Hunter nor Major Bradley, as regimental S2
officers, were privvy to the cloak-and-dagger high-level
details. They had enough to worry about. Or, rather,
Logan Hunter did. When the colonel sent them to
London to sit in with their opposite numbers at
SHAEF, Danny Boy seemed to take it as a golden
opportunity to get laid. He sat in at the first briefing.
But later, back at the hotel, he bought Hunter a drink
in the bar and said, "You can cover for me tomorrow,
buddy boy. I'm, ah, hopefully going to be tied up."

Hunter looked at him aghast. "Have you gone completely nuts? You must have been paying *some* attention back there, Danny Boy. The man said we get to jump out of airplanes, coming down on guys who go boom boom boom."

Bradley sipped his drink and said, "Hey, they're just shitting around. You remember Rear Admiral Kane, on Mountbatten's staff?"

"Yeah, I remember his wife too. Honest to God, Bradley, she's a nice looking head, but if Operation Comet is for real, don't you think the regimental S2 officer ought to know something about it?"

"I already know more than those brass hats back there, buddy boy. Operation Comet's not for real. It's just a gag for old Winnie's morale. Mountbatten's already said he won't play. He's sort of fond of his commandos and you don't need a crystal ball to see the whole plan's suicidal stupidity."

Hunter sipped his Scotch with a grimace as he considered the maps he'd been looking at all afternoon. He nodded, but said, "Mountbatten's smart and I guess a guy who's related to the Crown gets to put his two cents in. But where did you get that latrine rumor from? You don't know Mountbatten, do you?"

"Don't have to. Old Kane's on his staff, like I said, and he talks in bed. Old Sandy doesn't usually pay much attention, but this time, knowing the 101st is in on it, she did."

"Jesus H. Christ! She repeated a top secret like that!"

"What can I tell you? She likes me. The old fart she's married to is going off on some mission or other and she was afraid I'd be going with him until she found out it was just a lot of hot air. I don't know what Kane and the commandos are up to, but Operation

Comet ain't it. And without the boats to take us off, we can't go either, so what the hell."

He finished his drink, put the glass on the bar, and clapped his hand against Hunter's arm, saying, "I said I'd drive up to the Midlands with her tonight, so I'm counting on you, buddy boy. Tell 'em I'm on a secret mission or something, huh?"

"Secret from everybody but the admiral, you mean. What the hell's so important about the Midlands?"

"Nothing. That's why we're going there, buddy boy. Sandy says there's a swell little inn where she spent her honeymoon, and it's the last place in England we'd be likely to run into anyone her old man knows, see?"

Hunter saw. Most guys would feel sort of shitty taking a woman to a place she'd been to on her honeymoon with another man. But apparently they both found the grotesque idea perversely romantic. Hunter supposed a guy who liked to play musical beds with a slut like Sandy would find his own delicate feelings on the subject amusing. He said, "I won't turn you in. But you sure like to play with matches, Danny Boy. Leaving the adultery out of it, you could wind up facing an AWOL rap if anyone else ever found out about it."

"Hey, who knows about it but us, buddy boy? I know what I'm doing, and you're so right about the matches. That redhead has one hot little snatch, and tonight it'll be all mine!"

"Kiss it once for me, then," sighed Hunter. "I should think by now you'd had enough of it. God knows you haven't been paying much attention to anything else all summer."

Bradley looked at his wristwatch as he replied, "I can never get enough of old randy Sandy, buddy boy.

If it's any comfort, half the time I've left you to tuck the troops in beddy-bye I've been striking out. Her old man's been home on leave a lot, the bastard. But he's not there now, so adios and remember I'm counting on you at the briefing mañana, buddy boy."

Hunter found himself alone as well as disgusted. He started to order another drink, but thought better of it. It was too early to turn in and he didn't feel like prowling. It was his first night in London in quite a while, but despite what Bradley might think, he had to be at SHAEF in the morning wide awake. Comet might or might not be coming off, but he sure didn't want to lead two sticks in not knowing all the gory details.

He found a pay phone in the lobby and tried Ramie's number. Beth Waterman answered. She said her wounds had about healed and that Ramie was still tear-assing across France with Patton. Beth asked him what he was doing and when he said he wasn't doing much of anything Beth said, "I haven't eaten yet. Do you like Kosher food?"

Hunter laughed and said, "I haven't eaten enough to know. Are you Jewish, Beth?"

"No, but there's a Kosher restaurant over near Baker Street that I've been meaning to try. I've no idea what Kosher fish and chips could be like, but it smelled good when I walked by the other day. So how about it? Dutch, of course."

Hunter agreed, went out to hail a cab, and picked Beth up at Ramie's doorway. It seemed he was never going to find out what the flat looked like.

He'd kept the cab, but Beth said she'd rather walk. It was a clear warm evening and Beth looked even more like Betty Boop in her rather tight black civilian dress than Hunter had expected. When he commented on it, she took his arm and said, "June is busting out all over, right? I haven't gotten my new correspondent's kit and I seem to have gained a ton since I bought this dress at Bonwit's a million years ago. I've looked at some of the clothes you can still buy over here. Don't ever do that if you can possibly avoid it."

The summer sky was still light, but a street lamp was burning near the corner. "I feel so good about the brownout," Beth said. "It makes you feel like the war might end some day after all."

"Yeah, I guess they figure since the rockets don't have pilots there's no point in stumbling around in the blackout. Is that the place, with the Hebrew sign over the door?"

"Yes. Isn't this fun? I never expected to find a Jewish restaurant in the middle of London, did you?"

"I hadn't thought about it. It's a lot closer to Palestine than New York, so it figures, once you think about it."

They went in and took a booth. Beth couldn't look at him when a waiter wearing a skull cap and speaking pure Cockney came over to take their order. Hunter said, "I don't know too much about your food, so I'm placing our stomachs in your hands. What do you suggest?"

The waiter said he'd see what he could do and left. Beth giggled and said, "I know I'm being silly, but that Cockney accent is hitting my funny bone."

He smiled and said, "Yeah, it takes some getting used to. But fair is fair. If Jewish guys in New York can talk New York, they ought to be allowed to sound English in England, right?"

"I thought the New York accent *was* Jewish, Logan."

He shook his head. "Nope. Mixture of old Holland Dutch and Irish brogue, if my English teacher knew what he was talking about. You say Ramie's with Patton tonight, Beth?"

"Well, not *right* with him. He keeps running ahead of everybody. Ramie wrote she's trying to switch over to First Army HQ. General Hodges is much nicer to correspondents and she says he doesn't use as many four-letter words when girls are at the news briefings. Besides, Leclerc's Free French Second Armored is with the First Army and Ramie is sure that's who Ike will send in to liberate Paris." Beth pouted as she added, "Damn, I won't be there no matter who takes Paris back from the damned old Nazis. I'm so mad."

"Relax, our guys have a way to go before they can even think about Paris, and I'm expecting Ike to bypass it anyway. We were briefed a while back on the idea of dropping in ahead of the ground forces to keep the Krauts from burning the place as they left. SHAEF finally gave up on the idea. Why risk a blood bath when you don't have to? So far the Krauts have pulled out of every town they thought they might get trapped in. If I was Ike I'd let Patton drive by to the south, send Hodges around to the north, and watch the Krauts evacuate before I could close my pincers on them."

The waiter brought their noodle soup. Beth tasted and said, "Oh, I knew I was right," and proceeded to demolish hers. Hunter liked his too, but ate slower. Everybody ate slower than Beth Waterman. He could see why she had a weight problem, even though the curves she was packing at the moment were very attractive indeed. She had the merest beginning of what promised to be a double chin by the time she was thirty at the rate she was going. Meanwhile she was one of those cute little things made out of round bubbles, like she'd been drawn by a Disney artist. Her breasts were perfect spheres under the tight bodice of her black dress.

Her table manners were okay, considering. He could see she took a direct approach to satisfying her appetite. He somehow knew she'd satisfy any other appetites as directly and with as little hesitation. Her lusty little Betty Boop mouth looked interesting as hell, if a man liked his kissing uncomplicated. He liked her. You couldn't help liking girls like Beth Waterman. So why the hell did men carry torches for the complicated ones, for God's sake?

They finished their meal with such unseemly haste that though he hadn't planned on any pub crawling, it seemed sort of boorish to run her home this early. So after a dumb argument about the check—which he paid, of course—they wound up just down the street in a strategically placed pub she knew. The pub would close at ten and they'd wind up on the sidewalk close enough to the flat to run her home and say goodnight at a reasonable as well as polite hour.

They found a corner table and he found Beth drank her arf-and-arf the way she ate. No woman that little could put away that much beer without going once to the powder room. Someone in the past must have once commented on Beth's astounding capacity, because she said, "I think I'm dehydrated or something. Ever since I got wounded I can't seem to get enough liquids."

"Oh? I thought you were pretty well recovered, Beth."

She shot an arch look at him over the rim of her beer mug as she said, "Maybe I'll show you my old scars, if you're good. But I'm still thirsty as anything."

Hunter had no idea how to answer that, so he didn't try. The arf-and-arf he was drinking didn't seem strong enough to affect him, but he was a lot bigger than the tiny brunette, and he wasn't drinking nearly as much.

She didn't seem to be getting drunk, but he began to suspect she must be when she asked for a cigarette and, as he lit it for her, placed her fingertips on his wrist and gravely asked, "By the way, did Ramie tell you I put out?"

He managed to hold his lighter steady as he replied, "No. Do you?"

Beth took a deep drag and eyed him clinically as she let it out slowly through her nostrils. "I think I'm a nymphomaniac, and you're awfully cute, but I have to think about this. Are you and Ramie an item, Logan?"

He laughed and asked, "Do you always come right to the point like this?"

"It can save a lot of time, when the time is right. That's the only part I'm still trying to work out. I can see you're not one of those kiss-and-tell types, so let me put it another way. Are you in love with Ramie, Logan?"

He started to shake his head. Then he smiled sheepishly and said, "I'm working on that, too. And for the record, Ramie and I have never been lovers."

"She must be out of her mind. I think she's got the hots for you, too. What on earth seems to be the problem with you two idiots?"

"Are you trying to seduce me or be my mother, for God's sake?"

Beth sighed and said, "I'm trying to make up my mind. I haven't had a real affair since I've been back in shape to take my clothes off around a man and if those shoulders are real you're just what I've been saving up my fair white body for. On the other hand,

Ramie's my friend. Even if she hadn't ever saved my life it seems kind of dirty, you know?"

He reached across the table and took her hand. "I like you, Beth Waterman. You're good people. You want it level?"

"Hell, honey, I like it level or standing up. What you're trying to say is that you're carrying a big dopey torch for Ramie, right?"

"It's not that simple, Beth. I am, and I'm not. You see, Ramie and I agreed we didn't work. It's just not practical for either one of us. Maybe if there wasn't a war on—"

"But there *is* a war on, you jerk! Yeah, yeah, I know about her getting burned betting on a dashing RAF pilot and I know the figures on you jumping jacks. But damn it, how many times does the real thing happen, Logan? God, if I was in love with a guy and he made some dumb remark about being practical I'd hit him with a broom! What are you supposed to do about your *feelings*, Logan? Do they make you paratroopers take a vow of celibacy too?"

He smiled sheepishly. "Hardly. I've been trying to be practical about that, too. I mean, you don't hurt anybody when you don't take your heart to bed with you, right?"

She shrugged, looked at her watch, and said, "It's getting late. If I understand you correctly, Logan, you'd be perfectly willing to sleep with me tonight if there were no strings attached?"

He hesitated before he said, "Okay, it's level time again. You're a hell of a nice-looking girl and, more important, I like you. If I'd met you tonight as a stranger, by now I don't think we'd be having this conversation in such a dumb vertical position. But . . ."

"But we're not strangers," she finished for him. "I

don't think I could handle it either. Since we're playing True Confessions, Logan, I've been gushing for you since noodle soup, and it would be easy to convince myself, and maybe you, that we could just go on back to the flat and tear off a friendly, well, platonic piece. I know we'd enjoy it, too. But we'd be doing it in Ramie's bed, and Ramie would be there with us, wouldn't she?"

He nodded and said, "I'm afraid so, Beth. Shall I order another round?"

The little brunette shook her head. "No, I think you'd better take me home before I change my mind about seducing you."

So he helped her to her feet and they left. Beth was a little unsteady on her feet and by the time he got her to Ramie's door she was crying. He asked her what was wrong and she said, "Nothing, you big dope. I guess you think I'm a pretty brassy little tramp, right?"

He turned her gently, kissed her on the cheek. "No, Beth. I think you're one of the finest ladies I've met so far."

"Hah, some lady. My best friend's out of town and I—"

"You didn't do anything, Beth. But that's not why you're a lady in my book. Like I said, you're real people."

He kissed her again and walked away as Beth stood there, rubbing her cheek as she murmured to herself, "Damn it. Ramie, this is just too much. First you get me all shot up and now you have me all shook up! I think all three of us must be out of our stupid minds!"

16

As Hunter was undressing for bed at Brown's Hotel in London a phone was ringing in a small discreet country inn in the Midlands. Dan Bradley started in surprise. He was sharing a post-coital smoke with Sandy Kane at the moment and the last thing he'd been expecting to hear was a phone ring. He started to reach for it, but Sandy, although farthest from the phone on the bed table, slid her naked breasts across his chest to pick up, saying, "I'll get it, darling. It's probably for me."

It was. Dan listened, bemused, as the woman half atop him held a short one-sided conversation and hung up. As she cradled the phone, Sandy said, "Damn. Ivor just phoned the house from Southampton. He'll be in London tomorrow-aft and we're giving another bloody get-together tomorrow night."

She helped herself to the cigarette between his lips as she rolled off, muttering, "Silly old fool!"

"Who the hell was that just now and how the hell did they ever get this number, Sandy?"

"It was Evans, our man Friday. I gave him the number, of course. A girl has to take certain precautions when she's married to a leap frog who pops in and out on such short notice."

"Evans is that CPO you use as a bartender, right? He must like you a lot. Have you ever given him any?"

"Don't be beastly, darling. He's an Other Rank. Actually, I think old Evans rather dislikes me. We're both West Country, you know, albeit from opposite sides of the border. When I was in school we used to twit the Taffy girls from Radnor a bit, and Evans comes from Presteigne. Besides, he's old enough to be my father, even if he was an officer."

Not even Danny Boy Bradley, the airborne's gift to the ladies, was tactless enough to point out that Sandy's husband was older than Evans. So he took back his cigarette and asked, "How come he's covering for you if you've never laid him and he doesn't like you?"

"I told him to. He knows he'd only hurt poor old Ivor if he peached on me, and of course after I calmed Ivor down I'd bloody well see that he was sent back to sea duty, preferably in a leaky boat. Servants know their place, you see. Half the fashionable women in London would be divorced by now if their house staff didn't know which side their bread was buttered on."

"You'd have made a swell spy, honey. I thought I was pretty slick at this game, but you take the cake. I guess we'd better start thinking about getting back to London, huh?"

"Why? Ivor won't be back tonight. I wish you'd

put out that silly cigarette and make me come some more. God knows when I'll be able to see you again and masturbation is so poor a substitute for the real thing."

He snubbed out the butt and took her in his arms, but the phone call and this grotesque conversation had put him off his feed. So he fondled her as he tried to work himself back up. He couldn't help picturing the woman in his arms as she'd be tomorrow night, and his curiosity made him ask, "How come you have to jerk off when your husband's home? Doesn't he, ah, have what it takes?"

She shrugged and said, "He fucks me, if that's what you mean."

"I would have put it a little more delicately, but that's what I meant."

Sandy reached for Bradley's penis and began to stroke it as she considered. "I don't know why Ivor's such a dull thud in bed, dear. He's quite vigorous for a man his age and I suppose his old tool is average. But I just don't enjoy it with him. Half the nights he's home I wind up coming with my own hand." She giggled and added, "We have twin beds, you see. It's rather amusing, listening to him breathing next to me in the dark as I masturbate and think about other men."

Bradley laughed and said, "You know what you are, Sandy? You're a dirty little girl. I'll bet you liked to play doctor when you were a kid, right?"

She jerked his growing erection teasingly and said, "It takes a dirty little boy to know a dirty little girl. But isn't it fun? Let's French each other this time. I like to come feeling utterly depraved, don't you?"

Dan Bradley liked to come feeling anything, but as Sandy started kissing her way down his belly it seemed a little gamey, even for him. He'd noticed Sandy didn't seem to bathe as often as one might expect for a woman in her social position. Her armpits were rank despite the perfume she doused herself with in lieu of soap and water. Her groin, after sex with him and God only knew who else that afternoon, reeked like a fish market. But as she took his erection between her lips and cocked a thigh over his chest to settle on his face he didn't want her to think he was a prude. So he took a deep breath and, as the old joke said, once you got used to the smell you had it half licked.

Dan Bradley enjoyed dirty sex. He was hardly aware any other kind existed. But in truth Sandy was so childishly dirty that it seemed more like showing off than pleasure. As he parted her vaginal lips with his fingers to tongue her clit skillfully albeit with almost clinical detachment, he found himself examining her psychologically as well as gynecologically. He wondered how many other men she'd taken in that throbbing pink slit—or in the winking rectal opening above it, as far as that went. Sandy seemed to think every encounter called for a total orgy and wasn't satisfied until she'd filled every body opening with forbidden semen.

Was she satisfied then? That bit about jerking off next to her sleeping husband was pretty weird. Even a man as crude about sex as Bradley could see that was another form of perverse adultery. He somehow knew that if he and Sandy were married, she wouldn't be enjoying what they were doing right now. She was one of those dames who got her real thrill from the risk and betrayal in her dirty little game, not the cock she was using at the moment.

But whatever twisted reasons she had for being with him like this, Sandy was damned good in any position and now that he was fully aroused and she was taking him deep in her throat it didn't seem to matter that she was probably nuts and undoubtedly needed a bath. Bradley groaned with pleasure as he grabbed her naked buttocks to pull her open groin down against his face as he ran his tongue all the way inside her salty vagina and ran a wet finger up her rectum. He could tell she was coming too, whatever her mad reasons were, and for a long shuddering moment Bradley soared to heaven as he ejaculated down her wind pipe with her lips pursed over her teeth around the base of his shaft. But then it was over, and he gagged in disgust on the cod-fish wetness on his own lips. She moved her hips from side to side, pleading, "More, more, don't stop!" But Bradley knew he was going to vomit if he didn't, and he didn't want anyone to think he was a sissy. So he rolled her off and over to switch ends and as he drove his still turgid shaft into her she kissed him wetly and laughed, "Your face smells like pussy."

He figured she'd probably tried that in her time, too. But he didn't say so as he rinsed his mouth out with her salivating tongue and pounded her. She raised her legs to lock her ankles around the nape of his neck as she purred, "Stick it up my arse, lover! We have to do it *all* tonight!"

So he did, but even as he sodomized her Bradley was wondering how he was going to get out of this affair gracefully. Aside from being a little rich for his blood in bed, she was timing things so dangerously that even Dan Bradley could see they had to get caught sooner or later. By the time he'd ejaculated in her bowls, with her yelling nutty things as she played with her own clit, Bradley was sure he'd had all he could ever want of Sandy Kane.

But an hour later, as they cuddled together, planning when and how to meet like this again, Bradley knew that by the time they could he'd be out of his head with desire again. The little bitch was no good, so dirty in every way that she almost made him puke. And so exciting he knew he just couldn't stay away from her.

17

DESPITE THE FACT that Operation Comet seemed likely to get him and his men killed, Logan Hunter found the logistical details surprisingly boring once they got past the part where he came in. As the afternoon wore on he somehow found himself paying more attention to the female officer seated next to him than anything else the brass were screwing around with. He didn't know if any of them were screwing around with her. Her name was Hendrika Penseel and she seemed to be a captain in the Free Dutch Air Force. Hunter hadn't known there was a Free Dutch Air Force and he'd certainly never expected to find a woman flying for it. But as he paid more attention to her it developed she was an intelligence officer of some kind. The reason he hadn't paid much attention to her at first was that she wasn't really so great to look at.

Her figure wasn't bad, assuming that her uniform hadn't been tailored so hot. Her face was plain, neither homely nor really pretty, and she wore her dishwater blonde hair in a severe bun. The horn-rimmed glasses and the pencil stuck in her hair didn't inspire wolf whistles either. She was passable, just. But she outranked him and he was a little grown up for office romances. He'd have ignored her despite his boredom, had she not seemed to be playing footsies with him under the table.

The first time it happened, he put it down as an accident. The second time he shot her a curious glance. She was looking in utter fascination at the field grade officer at the map board, as if butter wouldn't melt in her mouth.

He decided he was developing a dirty mind. Going to sleep with an erection could do that to a guy. He was glad he and Beth had been sensible the night before, but Hunter was young, virile, and a man. A man very seldom got a shot at anything as nice as Beth Waterman and he was still wondering if he'd been a fool. He'd probably never see Ramie again, and even if he did, she'd said no. What had he been trying to prove? The girl he'd turned his back on had been willing and damned attractive.

The girl sitting next to him at SHAEF seemed to be nuts. When he failed to respond to her shy shod nudges, Hendrika slipped off her shoe and seemed to be trying to polish his jump boots with her stocking.

He turned to her with a frown. She wasn't looking at him. He tried to ignore her as the man with the pointer droned, "You'd better ignore any offers of help from the local civilians. The Dutch Underground has been giving the enemy a hell of a lot of trouble, but you can't tell a Gestapo man wearing an orange arm band just by looking at him. The Free Dutch guides who'll be landing with you will be all the help you'll need in that department in any case."

Hendrika rested her stockinged foot on Hunter's instep as she placed a casual hand in his lap under the table. It was embarrassing as hell even before she began to fondle his dawning erection. He grimaced, dropped his hand down to grab her wrist, and muttered, "What's the matter with you, Captain?"

"Nothing I don't think you can't cure for me quite nicely," she murmured, "unless that's a gun you're carrying inside your pants, Lieutenant."

He turned to stare at her, aghast, but she was looking at the man with the pointer as they struggled silently for possession of his crotch.

The total insanity of his predicament made it hard for him to keep a straight face. But he got her hand in a less indiscreet position as he warned her in a mocking tone, "I'll get you for this."

"Oh, I hope so," she sighed.

So they finished the meeting holding hands under the table. It seemed to take hours and felt dumb as hell. But then at last the general in charge called it a day and they let go of each other to rise, sedately, from the table. She walked over to talk to some older officers as he frowned after her, picturing her rather ample hips without that blue serge covering them. Then he shrugged and turned to get the hell out of there. So far nobody seemed to have missed Danny Boy, and if he could clear the building before anyone got around to asking Danny Boy was safe for at least another night. As he walked down the corridor he wondered why the hell he was doing this for Bradley.

A female voice to his right asked, "Where are you going in such a hurry? I thought we had a date."

He turned his head to make sure it was old Hendrika and not some other madwoman as he replied, "Is that what you called what you were doing? I was getting ready to kill you, Captain."

"Please, I am Hendrika to all my friends."

"I'll bet you have a lot of 'em, right?"

"Don't be nasty, Logan. I saw the way you were looking at me yesterday. But I could see you were too shy. And in a war, one does not have time for such things. My place is nearby. You are taking me to a party I must go to later. But we don't have to be there until eight and I think we'd better get the sexual tension out of the way first, don't you?"

He stared at her incredulously and asked, "Is that an order, Captain?"

She had no detectable accent, but her sense of humor didn't seem British or American. She remained straight-faced as she said, "You can put it that way if you like. I will be jumping with your serial on Comet D. So we have much to talk about and you may as well be my escort until then. I have no beau in London at the moment and I dislike attending social functions unescorted. But come, we can talk about our future plans later. You had better not take my arm as we leave. People will gossip about officers of the opposite sex and I have my reputation to consider."

She was definitely crazy, he decided, as they went out together. But one thing was for sure. He wasn't about to become emotionally involved with this Amazon.

As they walked toward her place he said, "I'm not

sure I like the idea of a woman jumping with me, Hendrika."

"I know. That is why I want to be on familiar footing with you when we do. I confess I am not looking forward to bailing out with or without a man, lover or otherwise. But one must do what one must do."

He'd never heard anything in the ARs about orders covering a situation like this, but the sheer cold-bloodedness of her approach intrigued him.

Her flat was on the second floor of a three-story walk-up. She led him into a starkly furnished bedroom and he decided protocol called for a kiss. But as he took her in his arms, Hendrika said, "I don't like to be pawed with my uniform on. Put your things over there on that chair. I shall be right back. There are certain precautions one must take at times like these."

She walked into the bath. Hunter just stood there, frowning. He put a hand up to his tie, and then decided he'd have to think about this weird situation a little more.

What was that bullshit about not wanting to be pawed, for God's sake? He hadn't started up with the crazy broad. She'd started up with him, and then as soon as he tried to act a little friendly he got that superior "Down, boy" crap!

Like all men, Hunter had run into that before, and, like all men, he didn't like it. Who the hell did she think she was? What made her think she was doing him such a big favor? He wasn't an animal who had to be serviced to keep it from kicking down the barn wall. He had a good mind to just walk out the damned door before she got back.

But, naturally, he didn't. As he sat down on the bed to light a cigarette he told himself he had to wait and see how the picture turned out. He didn't care one way or the other if she was on the level or if this was some new crazy tease. He'd thought he knew them all by now, but old Hendrika was a pisser.

Old Hendrika came back in the bedroom to say, "You're still dressed."

She wasn't. Her hair hung down loosely, softening her plain but not unattractive face as she stood there stark naked, hands on hips. Her body was fantastic. The Dutch woman was firm and Junoesque, like a model for Peter Paul Rubens, who kept in shape. She'd shaved her pubic hairs as if aware she resembled a nude painting in the Flemish School. She walked over to the bed with absolutely no hint of shyness despite the bright evening light through the open window curtains and sat down at his side, soberly asking, "What's the matter? Don't you enjoy sex?"

Hunter laughed and took her in his arms as he replied, "I think you just talked me into it."

This time she let him kiss her. She kissed skillfully although a bit dispassionately for his taste, and as he cupped one of her heroic breasts in his palm she pulled away from his lips to calmly say, "That wool itches. Take off your clothes if you want to fuck."

He wasn't sure he could. He undressed, feeling foolish. As he bent to unlace his jump boots he asked, "Are you always this, ah, professional, Hendrika?"

"Don't talk dirty. I'm a fellow officer, not a whore. I suggested we go to bed together because in a few days we will have more important things to worry about. No doubt behind the German lines we shall be forced to share the same shelter and latrine facilities. We may have to doctor one another's wounds. I don't know about you, but I am uneasy in intimate situations with a man I've never been in bed with."

He shucked his last boot as he laughed and said,

"Well, I wouldn't want to have you uneasy in a fox hole with me." Then he got rid of his pants as well and stretched out beside her. "What's my first general order, Captain? Do I get to get on top?"

She laughed and this time when they kissed she responded with more warmth and reached down between them to fondle him. "My," she said, "there certainly is more to you than meets the eye. We have to go to that party this evening, so we can save the vice for later. Let's just do it old-fashioned for now."

He grinned. "You're really weird, Hendrika," he said as he rolled into the saddle of her ample thighs. But then, as he entered her, he gasped and added, "Jesus, you're just what the doctor ordered, too!"

He hadn't realized how badly he needed a woman until the strangely detached Dutch blonde began to cater to his needs with skill as well as surprising strength. Despite her size, Hendrika was built small, or perhaps able to contract at will to suit any partner. She wrapped her strong arms around him to pillow his chest on her big breasts as she braced a heel on the mattress on either side of his thighs to move her Junoesque pelvis in perfect response to his thrusts. He exploded in her almost at once and, not wanting to disappoint her, slid a hand down between them to finger her clit as he tried to keep moving in her. Her shaven mons was intriguingly childlike, but no child molester had ever gotten anything like this. He could tell he was treating her right as her clit began to swell against his lubricated fingers and her kisses grew more passionate. By the time she was ready to climax he was getting there himself a second time and he was afraid they'd break the bed springs for a time. They were both big people and she'd dropped her rather alarming military bearing to respond to his lovemaking in a way he was sure the neighbors could hear and probably feel in the surrounding flats. She screamed aloud in her own tongue as she dug her nails into his back and tried to break him off inside her. He let himself go in her almost painfully tight vagina. Then, as if someone had pulled a switch, Hendrika went limp, took a deep breath, and said, "That was nice. Now we'd better bathe and dress if we are to make the party in Belgravia."

He laughed and said, "Screw the party in Belgravia. Do we really have to go?"

"Yes. It's business. I was invited by the British Admiral Kane. And as you know, he will be in charge of the commandos during Operation Comet. I like to be on friendly terms with my comrades in arms."

"Oh? I know Admiral Kane. I'm not sure I know him as well as you do, though."

"Don't be ridiculous. He's married. You are the only officer on the mission I will have made love to. Let me up. I have to douche and bathe. You can use the tub as I get dressed."

He fondled her teasingly as he grinned and said, "I notice you have a thing on cleanliness. Is that why you shave down here?"

"Of course. Crab lice are disgusting and one never knows when one will have the chance to bathe, once one is in enemy territory."

"Glugh! You just killed a lot of romance, kid. You seem to know a lot about conditions in occupied Holland, Hendrika. Have you been back there since the Nazis marched in back in '40?"

"Of course. This will be my third parachute drop behind the German lines. Why did you think I'd been assigned to your series? To keep you from having to masturbate in Holland?"

"You do have a way with words. But seriously, how the hell did you ever get out of Holland the last couple of missions, Hendrika?"

"Via the underground, of course. It is not difficult for one person to move about occupied Europe with the proper forged papers. It is even easier for a woman, of course. Naturally, such a thing would be out of the question for a parachute regiment, so this time we shall need Admiral Kane's boats. And speaking of Admiral Kane, let me up."

He did, admiring the view as she walked naked toward the bath. Now that he'd broken the ice he wanted more of Hendrika. He was ready to make love to her again right now. But she was right about quitting while they still felt up to going out again and he knew he'd have her later that night. He grinned as he reached for a smoke. She was a salty old broad and there was no way in hell he could really fall for her. But she offered exactly what he and little Beth Waterman had been talking about the night before. Operation Comet was pretty hairy, but he liked the fringe benefits. He and Hendrika could take care of each other's sex needs with no emotional problems, and if she could fight anything like she could fuck, the Germans were in big trouble.

The Kanes' town house looked the same, even without Ramie over there by the fireplace as Hunter and Hendrika came in. Chief Evans behind the bar betrayed no emotion on his phlegmatic Welsh face if he wondered what Hunter was doing with another blonde, but he remembered Hunter wanted a tall Scotch and water in a zombie glass, and since Hendrika had been there before Evans built her a gin and tonic without being asked.

231

The place was more crowded than the last time. Most of the people looking for some place to stand were men in various uniforms. A tall distinguished older man in British navy blue came over to greet Hendrika and when she introduced Hunter to Rear Admiral Kane they both looked pleasantly surprised. Kane said, "The lieutenant and I have spoken on the telephone, Captain Penceel. What ever happened to that American girl at Greenwich Hospital, Hunter?"

"Thanks to you, I had dinner with her last night, sir. She asked me to thank you for helping her stay over here. It was very thoughtful of you."

"Rubbish. Just doing a favor for a friend of Ramie Davis. She's not here this evening, is she?"

"No, sir. Beth Waterman says she's somewhere in France, with Patton."

"Ah, yes, Patton. Bit of a maniac, but a fine soldier. I take it you're here with Hendrika this evening?"

"Logan is with Operation Comet, sir," Hendrika explained. "It seems we'll be jumping together on Comet D."

Kane said, "Good Lord! You're not still intent on leaping about like that, are you, old girl? I mean, dash it all, in a few weeks you ought to be able to visit your family and friends over there less athletically. Our Monty's almost at the Belgian border, you know."

Hendrika went a little grim as she answered, "My home is not in Belgium, sir. I come from Rotterdam. That is, I used to come from Rotterdam. The house I was born in and the schools I attended are no longer there, courtesy of the Third Reich."

Kane looked uncomfortable and said, "Quite. One still wishes there was a way to leave women and children out of these wars. Forgive me, I have to go over and greet that ass of a general who just came in."

As he left them, Hunter turned back to Hendrika. "He doesn't sound too enthusiastic about Comet."

"You're right. If it was up to him, the mission would be aborted. But it is not up to him. Aside from Churchill, my government in exile is insisting on it. Our underground reports the people of Holland don't have enough food to last much longer. The Germans have been looting even neighborhood groceries, and if my country is not liberated soon—"

"Hey, Hendrika, back up. Comet's not a liberation mission. We're supposed to get in, knock off those V-2 rocket sites, and get the hell out before the Krauts wake up to the fact we're there."

She sniffed and said, "That may be the plan. On paper. But you'll see, once we are on the ground over there. My people can be as nasty as the Germans, once they've had time to brood under the Nazi heel for four years."

"Jesus, do you think there'll be a general uprising, once we land among them?"

"I don't think. I know. In all fairness, the Danish underground is good. But nobody in occupied Europe has put more Nazis in their graves as the Dutch underground. And that was with the Germans in full control. Can you imagine what will happen when they see British and American soldiers among them?"

He could. It sounded awful. He knew the final orders of Operation Comet called for a hasty evacuation. That would leave a hell of a lot of Dutch resistance fighters standing there with guns in their hands and egg on their faces when the Krauts massed for the inevitable counterattack. Admiral Kane had left some people out. There really had be a way to leave the *men* as well as women and children out.

Before he could brood further Hunter heard his

name being called and turned to see Sandy Kane smiling at him in another new dress. He wondered where the hell she managed to shop and, more important, what the hell she was doing here. Had Danny Boy been bullshitting about that inn in the Midlands? It was bad enough to cover for a prick who leveled with you. If Bradley had covered up some other seamy romance with a false adultery tale, Hunter had definitely had it.

As if she'd read his mind, Sandy said, "I saw your friend Dan Bradley earlier today."

"He didn't want to come to the party, eh?"

"It seems he'd already been to one. Who are you with this evening, that awful Dutch cow?"

Hunter glanced around, but mercifully Hendrika had drifted off to chew the fat with some British officer with a red beret stuck in his belt. He turned back to Sandy and said, "I'd hardly call Captain Penceel a cow."

"Well, everyone to his own taste. They say she's an easy lay."

"Takes one to know one?"

"Ouch! Has Danny Boy been telling tales out of school, dear?"

Hunter shook his head as he lied, "No. But when a lady calls a man on the phone to proposition him he can figure out the rest."

She laughed easily, and said, "That's right, I did proposition you one night, didn't I? I'd forgotten. One meets so many people in London during the season."

He took a swallow of his highball and said, "Let's both forget it, then."

"Why? My offer is still good, you know."

Hunter glanced around to make sure he wasn't being overheard as he growled, "Goddamn it, Sandy, how many guys from the 101st do you think you can handle?"

"Well, maybe not *all* of them, although it might be an interesting experiment. How many men are there in an American division, Logan?"

"About twenty thousand."

"Oh, dear, that would be a bit much. Perhaps I'd better just stick to the junior officers."

"Not *this* junior officer, toots. Aside from the fact that I don't bird dog other guys from my outfit, I'm sort of particular where I stick my dick."

She flushed crimson but managed to keep smiling, dripping honey and venom as she said, "I'm not used to being spoken to that way, Logan dear."

"Stay the hell away from me, then. I know this is going to come as a great surprise to you, but I don't like you very much."

"How do you know before you've sampled my, ah, wares?"

"Honey, there are girls over on Trafalgar Square selling cleaner wares for a quid, and I'd rather go to bed with any one of them than mess around with you."

Still smiling, she said, "You'll pay for that remark, I promise you. Then she turned to slink away. He washed the taste of the conversation away with another sip of his highball and moved to rejoin Hendrika. But the Dutch woman was having an intense discussion of logistics with the British paratroop officer and he'd heard all the logistics he'd wanted to for the day, so he wandered off to find someone else to talk to.

A vapidly pretty English girl was alone in a corner. So he nodded down at her and said something banal to break the ice. "You're very pretty," she said severely, "but I'm not looking for a bloke tonight. I already have one."

"I'm carrying a torch, too. But they're not showing home movies, so what the hell."

She laughed, gave him a name he'd never remember, and they made small talk for a while before Hendrika joined them and said, "The admiral is leaving for Whitehall. We don't have to stay here any longer."

Hunter smiled down at the English girl and said, "Sorry to have to leave you in this sticky wicket. But c'est la goddamn guerre."

She laughed and said she'd find a magazine or something. As Hunter and Hendrika left together, the Dutch woman asked in a casual tone, "Did I spoil something for you back there, Logan?"

"Hell, no. I've already forgotten her name. You're not jealous, are you?"

"Of course not. We are comrades in arms, not lovers."

Then she took him home and proceeded to fornicate him to death.

As they made lusty dispassionate love in Hendrika's flat, two British intelligence agents were recording every gasp and squeak from the room above. The technician with the headphones smiled wryly at his superior seated nearby as he marveled, "Gool Lord, she seems to be wringing the poor Yank out like a ruddy dish rag!"

The man in charge lit a smoke with an expression of distaste. "Never mind the rutting. What are they *talking* about?"

"He just said she had a lovely bunch of coconuts and she said she wanted to try it dog style. You know what people talk like in bed, chief. God knows we've had to listen to that German pig in heat often enough.'

The agent who was smoking shook his head. "We don't know for certain she's a double agent. It just seems bloody likely. We know they have one agent spying on Operation Comet and we seem to have eliminated most of the other likely suspects. But you know why you're recording Captain Penceel's astounding sex life, Collins. So listen in, damn it."

"I'm listening, and it's giving me one hell of an erection. She's not a bad-looking old bawd, and if you ever need a volunteer for interrogation in depth . . ."

"It's no laughing matter, Collins. The admiral gave specific orders about that Lieutenant Hunter she's with tonight. He says he wants the recordings as well as a full report in the morning."

The man with the earphones shrugged. "I can report the Yank has amazing stamina. But what the bloody hell is the admiral expecting down there, a full confession? We already knew Captain Penceel rutted like a mink and the Yank she's with tonight has security clearance. She just told him he had a loverly great dong. But I'm going to be very surprised if she tells him she's a Germany spy!"

"Haven't they said anything about Operation Comet?"

"Coo, of course they have. But what of it? They've both been at the same bloody briefings, and she's slated to guide him and his pathfinders when they jump. What the bloody hell could the Yank know that she wouldn't know already? She's his bloody fellow officer. By the way, they just turned over and I think she's going down on him."

His superior frowned and tried to come up with an answer. Despite his flippancy, Collins was a good agent and his remarks made sense. Whether a double agent or not, Hendrika Penceel had been in on Operation Comet almost from the beginning. There obviously wasn't a thing that young paratrooper could tell her that she didn't already know.

"They've stopped for a smoke and their second wind down there," Collins said.

"What's the Yank telling her?"

"He isn't saying much of anything. She's telling him about how nice her old neighborhood in Rotterdam used to be, before the Nazi buggers bombed it flat. If you want my frank opinion, she sounds like a lonely woman who's found somebody she can talk to. If she's a flaming spy, she doesn't ask many flaming military questions. If you ask me, we're wasting our time on this suspect."

"Nobody's asking you, Collins. It's not for us to say if she's a double agent or not. Admiral Kane has asked for every word they exchange in bed or otherwise down there."

"He must enjoy pornography, then. What the bloody hell is Kane expecting to hear out of those two?"

"I've no idea. But whatever either of them has to say to the other, the admiral wants to hear it."

18

BETH WATERMAN was back to work at the London UPI when Ramie Davis came in, a helmet strapped to her musette bag, and said, "Well, wounded veteress, are you ready to hit the dusty trail if I promise not to get you shot again?"

Beth jumped up, grinning, to hug Ramie. "I didn't know you were back from the front. I've been watering your plants, but I guess you'll want your flat back, huh?"

Ramie shook her head. "No. I'll only be in London twenty-four hours and we can have a pajama party. I came back with some Free French wounded and the feature's already filed. The front office says you can go back with me if you like. I'm with the French Second Armored now, and I remembered you spoke fractured French. I thought I did, but I'm going to need help finding my way about Paris."

"Paris has been liberated, Ramie? The last I hear, Ike wanted to bypass it."

"He still does, poor man. But De Gaulle's going to push in anyway, and if we don't get back to Leclerc's column on the double we're going to miss the scoop of the war."

"I'm ready! I'm ready! You say it's all right with Pete? What about your plants at the flat, Ramie?"

"Let them droop. Maybe I can give them to the landlady. Pete's giving you the rest of the day off, so we'll go back to my place and watch you pack. Our plane leaves tomorrow morning, so we've plenty of time. But let's get out of here anyway. My God, you've no idea how civilized London looks to me after all those rinky-dink villages we've been busting through."

As they went out to the street and hailed a cab Ramie filled Beth in on her transfer to the French Second Armored. "I don't know who was more relieved," she concluded, "me or Flash Gordon."

"Who's Flash Gordon, Ramie?"

They got in the cab and Ramie gave the driver her address before she laughed bitterly, and said, "Oh, I forgot, that was another military secret we're not supposed to print. George Patton wants everyone to call him Old Blood and Guts. But behind his back they call him Flash Gordon. One of the nicest things he called me was 'silly cunt.'"

Beth gasped, "Ooh, he sounds like a meanie."

"I think lunatic is the word you're groping for. To give the devil his due, the last time I saw Third Army they were doing dreadful things to the Krauts near Sens. But I just couldn't take any more of that glory-hogging buffoon and, as I said, he didn't like me all that much either. He threatened to shoot me when I tried to file a story on the new German tanks."

Beth asked what about the new German tanks and Ramie said, "They're good. Their Panther eats our Sherman M-4s for breakfast no matter what Flash Gordon says. But he said it was bad for morale to print the truth. Pete says we have to sit on it too. General Leclerc's probably keeping a few secrets, but at least he's a gentleman about it. You've no idea how nice it feels to be called m'selle instead of cunt."

Beth giggled and said, "Oh, I can hardly wait to meet all those Frenchmen! Is it true what they say about Frenchmen in the feathers, Ramie?"

"I wouldn't know. I haven't been with them that long and they seemed sort of busy. I may have a prince lined up for you, if you're good. I've met the Prince of Monaco, serving as a second lieutenant over there. He's a little young for you, but he's awfully nice, and single."

"If they're big enough they're old enough. What do I call him when I meet him? Prince? That sounds sort of like calling a dog, doesn't it?"

Ramie laughed and said, "You'd probably better start with Lieutenant Grimaldi. I think his first name's Rainier."

"That's cute. Speaking of lieutenants, I had dinner with your Logan Hunter a few nights ago. He's here in London, at Brown's Hotel."

Ramie looked away as she murmured, "Oh?"

"Don't be silly. Of course we didn't. I'm your old war buddy and the big goof's in love with you."

"You're the one who's being silly, Beth. I hardly know the man. We only spent one evening together, and nothing happened."

"Like hell it didn't, Ramie. We were pure, but you

came up in the conversation a lot. He's here in London on some sort of mission thing. But you can catch him at Brown's if you call after the meeting breaks up this aft."

Ramie hesitated. Then she said, "Why rub salt in old wounds? Besides, we have a plane to catch in the morning."

"Yes, but you'll be here all night and I can always bunk with Mabel if you get lucky. Don't be a chump, Ramie. The guy has it bad for you and he's awfully cute."

Ramie shook her head stubbornly. "He's all yours, if you want him. I've been around that block. It makes me nervous to date men from outfits running eighty percent casualty lists."

"Oh, for God's sake, Ramie. You're the one who's going back to the front, not him! Wouldn't you feel dumb if you wound up dead in France while he was here safe and sound in Blighty?"

"At least I wouldn't feel it," Ramie sighed. "Can we change the subject, Beth? I told you a long time ago why Logan and me won't work."

"Well, if you don't want to look Logan up, I've been invited to cocktails with Ike tonight."

"My, you certainly get around. What happened to that pretty English driver he seems so fond of?"

"Nothing. She's still, ah, giving him rides. I meant I was invited to the party at SHAEF, silly. Do you want to come along? Everyone will be there."

She saw the hesitation in her friend's eyes and added, "Not junior officers, of course. What do you say? It'll do you good to mingle with people again."

Ramie said, "Well, I've already seen *Snow White and the Seven Dwarves.*"

❄   ❄   ❄

Logan Hunter hadn't been invited to the brass hat's cocktail party. But Rear Admiral Kane had, and Kane had brought his wife, Sandy. The redhead spotted Ramie in the crowd and smiled her way over, glass in hand. "Ramie, dear, I see you're still wearing the same shade of olive drab. It's not really your color, you know."

Ramie debated tossing her drink in Sandy's face, decided she had enough generals mad at her, and replied, "I see you've redone your hair, Sandy dear. Or did someone just set your head on fire?"

Sandy managed to keep smiling as she said, "We really shouldn't sharpen our claws on one another like this, dear. It's an even match and, after all, we have so much in common."

Puzzled, Ramie asked, "We do?"

Sandy tossed her head to answer, meeting Ramie's puzzled gaze. "Yes, we seem to share the same tastes in men. I found Logan Hunter very virile, didn't you?"

Ramie reddened and said, "I've never made love to Logan Hunter, Sandy."

"You didn't? Pity. He's fantastic in the feathers. You really ought to try him on for size—some night when you're feeling up to not getting much sleep, of course."

Ramie didn't believe it. Logan wouldn't wipe his feet on a pig like Sandy Kane . . . would he? How did she know that? What did she really know about Logan Hunter, except that for some strange reason he shook her up?

Since Sandy seemed to be waiting for a reply, Ramie looked beyond her to where Admiral Kane was chatting with an American officer. "It's too bad your husband takes up so much of your time."

"Yes, isn't it? It was ever so much nicer to be married to him back when he had raids and such to lead. He's been spending far too many nights at home lately. Our poor Logan's had to console himself with a rather ordinary Dutch peasant woman these days."

Ramie frowned and asked, "What on earth is a Dutch peasant doing in London?"

"It does sound a bit grotesque, doesn't it? I understand she's with the Dutch Government in Exile. Logan obviously likes blondes, but I understand she's a great cow."

"Oh, you've never met her?"

"Hardly. But naturally, when I heard our Logan was shacking up with her, I made inquiries. Her name's Hendrika Penceel, in case you're interested."

"I'm not interested," Ramie flared. "Can't you find a car tire to chase or something?" she said, moving away from the laughing Sandy.

She told herself she wasn't interested. But she was still thinking about the spiteful redhead's words when the party began to break up. Ramie found a phone, debated with herself for a time, then rang up Brown's Hotel. They told her Lieutenant Hunter had checked out a few nights ago. So she obviously had no message to leave. As she hung up, she told herself there were all sorts of hotels he could have moved to, and Brown's was probably just too expensive. She told herself good reporters could always find out where somebody was, if they had the time and put their mind to it.

But she didn't have time. She was leaving in the morning, and she wasn't sure she wanted to put her mind to it.

19

L OGAN HUNTER was never to learn that the big blonde he'd slept away a few weeks and a lot of hurt with had ever been suspected as a German double agent. British intelligence was very discreet as well as very good. So they saw no need to inform Hendrika of the trouble they'd gone to to clear her, or that they'd finally captured the real German spy reporting on Operation Comet.

Admiral Kane's face was white-lipped with repressed anger as he confronted his erstwhile servant, Evans, in the interrogation room. Evans was seated, his expression fatalistic as he lit and smoked a cigarette. The British didn't use the rather childish as well as brutal methods of their German counterparts, so there was no light shining in Evans' face and his hands were not cuffed. There were far too many other men in the room for Evans to consider trying anything foolish.

"I can't believe you betrayed me under my very own roof, Evans," Kane said.

The captured spy laughed and shot back, "A lot you know about what goes under your roof, mate."

One of the men who'd made the arrest explained, "He still talks like a Taff because he is a Taff, Admiral. His father was a Welsh Nationalist and his mother, needless to say, was German. He had a quite good cover story, but in the end it seems one does leave a bit of paper behind as one wanders about. He was born in Wales, but he spent his formative years and a lot of summer vacations before the war with his mother's relations in Kiel. One of his maternal uncles seems to be a flag officer in the Kreigsmarine. Bit of nepotism, no doubt."

Kane shook his head and said, "Dash it all, Evans has been with me since before the war. And as far as that goes, I've visited Kiel myself."

Another agent said, "Yessir. But you were there as a British naval officer. Evans was visiting, quite often, with a false passport made out by the German printers who specialize in that sort of thing. He was what we call a sleeper, Admiral. Jerry seems to have been planning this war long before we suspected they really wanted another. We didn't arrest your bat man on his untidy record, though. We intercepted the microfilm he was trying to pass on to another German spy who's no longer with us. Would you like a copy of the blowups, sir? You already have the maps and papers he photographed on file, but we'd like you to verify that he had most of Operation Comet on film when we arrested him."

"I'm afraid I've been a trusting fool, gentlemen. My God, when I think back to how many nights I've been away, with this perishing German spy under the very same roof as my poor wife!"

Two of the agents exchanged glances. One of them shook his head slightly and the other said, "Your wife was never in any real danger, sir. His mission was to spy on you, not to trifle with your silverware or anything else."

"It still gives one a bit of a turn, just the same. Does my wife know you just arrested Evans here?"

"No sir. We called your home shortly after we picked him up, but Mrs. Kane wasn't in. She told the other servants she was driving up to the country."

Kane looked relieved and turned back to Evans. "Well, Evans, what have you to say for yourself?"

Evans didn't answer. He knew he was dead. But he considered himself a brave man. So as long as they were going to shoot him anyway, what was the best move he had left to mess things up further for the bloody sods?

Kane said accusingly, "Dash it all, man, my wife and I trusted you!"

Evans gave him a crooked smile and replied, "I know. I was raised on both sides to consider you bloody Saxons fools, look you."

"Is that all you have to say to me, after all these years?"

Evans had plenty to say. But he'd decided not to. He didn't owe any damned British officer juicy gossip in the first place, and the more Kane's wife whored around the bigger the mess would be when it finally blew up in the fool's smug face.

Evans took a deep drag on his cigarette. "Stuff it,

mate. I don't have to pretend to like you anymore. And for the record, it's been a bloody bore."

Kane started to say something, then nodded silently and marched out of the room. There was a moment of silence. Then one of the British agents said, "I say, that was rather decent of you, all things considered."

Evans laughed bitterly. "You're going to shoot me anyway, right?"

"As a matter of fact, we hang spies. But it was still a rather gallant gesture on your part."

Evans shrugged and said, "Fuck him. You can tell him if you like. I've always enjoyed the way she puts those horns on the old sod. And what the hell, I've nothing against her. She was a hell of a lay."

They never told anyone below the rank of general why Operation Comet had been canceled. They just did it. Partly because there was no way of knowing how much the enemy had on the already risky idea and partly because the V-2 rocket attacks seemed to be tapering off. The Germans still held Holland and most of Belgium as Montgomery moved northeast with all the deliberate speed of a lava flow—which speed drove both American and German generals nuts. Since El Alamein nobody on either side had ever figured out a way to either stop Montgomery or make him move a mile an hour faster than he felt like moving. There wasn't an army on earth that seemed capable of moving Monty *back* an inch either, so while he drove even the tolerant Eisenhower crazy with his maddeningly slow progress, Ike needed him there to guard the north flank as his other troops ran wild across France.

And so, as it seemed unlikely any important action

was going to take place in the low countries until Monty got jolly well ready for it, the 101st and other outfits alerted for Operation Comet were told to stand down. Hunter and Hendrika parted good friends, if perhaps a little saddle sore, and he went back to Newbury to resume his training and administrative duties.

Major Dan Bradley was supposed to do most of the administrative work for regimental S2, but rank still had its privileges and Sandy Kane had found another charming inn midway from London. Her husband, the admiral, seemed to be very busy these days. So Bradley was getting away with a lot of AWOL as well as murder.

Logan Hunter didn't really give a damn. Danny Boy was a bigger pain in the ass when he was on the base than when he was doping off with other people's wives. Hunter suspected Sandy had been talking about him in bed with Bradley, because on the rare occasions he saw fit to show up he gave everyone a hard time.

One morning as the I&R Platoon was preparing for a general inspection Bradley barged into their barracks unannounced. Hunter was over in his office and since an officer is always supposed to be proceeded into enlisted territory by a noncom to call the men to attention, nobody noticed when the major materialized among them.

Bradley zeroed in on Sergeant Arnold, seated on a footlocker as he cleaned his carbine. Young Arnold flinched in surprise as the major yelled in his ear, "Is there something wrong with your eyes, Sergeant?"

Arnold leaped to his feet and bawled, "Ten-hutt!"

As the other men in the barracks snapped to attention Bradley said, "As you were," in a disgusted voice. He turned back to Arnold and said, "If you want to keep those stripes, sonny boy, you'd better start showing a little military courtesy. What's going on around here?"

Arnold looked blank. Then he said, "We're getting ready for inspection, sir. General Taylor's coming down the line and—"

"Oh, yeah, inspection." Bradley moved on with a thoughtful look in his eye.

Arnold turned to the trooper nearest him and whispered, "Colson, go get the looie." The replacement didn't ask dumb questions. Arnold was still worried about the nut frothing at the mouth in his barracks but the new men were shaping up. Old Colson slipped out like an Indian and took off running.

Bradley stopped by an older trooper's bunk, stared down and snapped, "What's that picture doing in your footlocker, soldier?"

The trooper looked sincerely bewildered as he answered, "Uh, it's my wife's picture, sir."

"Your wife is very pretty. Get her the hell out of that footlocker. The general doesn't want to know what your wife looks like. He wants to see if you have all your shit lined up pretty."

Bradley moved on, looking for nits to pick. He stopped by an otherwise immaculate trooper, pointed down at his open footlocker and said, "What do you mean by having a half-used tube of toothpaste showing, soldier?"

"It's the only tube I got, sir. It's half-used because I've been brushing my teeth."

"Well, goody for you. Run over to the PX and get a fresh tube. These lockers are all supposed to be uniform."

The trooper stammered, "Begging the major's pardon, the PX is closed. It's Saturday and they're getting ready for inspection too."

"I know what day it is, damn it! Get that toothpaste anyway. I don't care how and I don't care where. That's an order, soldier!"

Not waiting for an answer, Bradley turned away to zero in on a carbine lying on a bunk with an open cleaning kit. Next to it he spotted a square of sandpaper and his eyes gleamed wolfishly as he stepped over to the trooper who went with the weapon. Bradley snapped, "What's your name, soldier?"

The recruit, fresh from Benning, answered, "Saunder, Harold J. Junior, sir!"

"Well, Junior. What have we to say about that sandpaper?"

"Sandpaper, sir? I was using it to rub down my carbine wood."

"I can see that. Are you aware that's willful destruction of government property?"

Saunders was puzzled as he replied, "I had gunk on my wood, sir."

"Tough shit. Ordnance ARs specifically forbid the use of sandpaper, glass shards, razor blades, or any other wood-cutting tools on U.S. ordnance. You just committed a court-martial offense, Saunders. What have you to say for yourself?"

"Uh, I was told to get ready for inspection, sir."

"Who told you to sandpaper that weapon?"

Saunders hesitated. An old soldier at Benning had shown him how to get the accumulated gun oil off his wood with sandpaper and he knew he hadn't been dumb enough to scrape down to the bare wood. He licked his lips and blurted, "My platoon leader, sir."

Bradley raised an eyebrow. "Oh, Lieutenant Hunter told you to sandpaper your carbine?"

Saunders gulped, trapped, and stammered, "I guess so, sir."

"What do you mean you guess so? You were destroying government property on your own or under orders. So what's it going to be?"

Saunders hadn't even been thinking about the looie when he'd said platoon leader. He didn't think it was a good idea to accuse Sergeant Arnold either. Arnold has seen action on D day and they said he was pretty tough. The major said, "I'm waiting for an answer. Did Lieutenant Hunter tell you you could sandpaper your carbine?"

"Uh, yessir."

And then Saunders thought he was about to wet his jump boots, for Colson was yelling attention in the doorway and Lieutenant Hunter was coming in and he was caught for sure between two officers.

Hunter said, "As you were, men," and moved down the line to join Bradley, wearing a puzzled frown. He nodded and asked, "Can I help you, Major?"

"I'm doing just fine. I don't see Sergeant Falco. Isn't he supposed to be confined to the post?"

"He is, sir. He's pulling color guard by the gate."

"I hope he waves the flags pretty for the general. We have a sort of court-martial problem here, Lieutenant."

"Court-martial, sir?"

"Yes. Saunders here tells me you told him it was okay to use sandpaper on his carbine. Is that true, Lieutenant?"

It wasn't, but they all knew that if Hunter accused Saunders of lying to a field grade officer he was on his way to the guard house for certain.

Hunter stared soberly at the frightened trooper as he nodded and said, "Affirmative, Major. I told him to get that crud off his wood no matter how."

"I see. Were you aware the use of abrasives is absolutely forbidden?"

"I was, sir. No excuse, sir."

This wasn't going the way Bradley had intended. He frowned at Hunter and said, "You're putting me in a spot, Lieutenant. I hate to turn a fellow officer in, but this is a pretty serious offense."

Hunter met his eyes, unblinking, as he said, "Understood, sir. If you want to take me to the colonel I guess we'll both just have to take our medicine."

The threat was veiled indeed, but there it was, like spit on the floor between them. Bradley reddened, snapped, "See that it doesn't happen again!" and stalked out as the men heaved a collective sigh of relief.

Arnold was moving toward Hunter and Saunders with blood in his eye. "I'll take care of this, Sergeant," Hunter said. Then he stared coldly at Saunders. "You owe me a hundred push-ups, soldier."

"Push-ups, sir?"

"You know what push-ups are, Saunders. I want fifty for your carbine and fifty for me. If you ever put me in a spot like that again you're going to pull a thousand. Do we understand each other?"

"I'm sorry, sir. I just didn't know what to say when that asshole—"

"Stop right there! You're talking about a superior officer and that's going to cost you another fifty!" Then Hunter's mouth twitched and he added, "Okay, make it ten for calling the major an asshole," and the men around laughed too.

Hunter sobered and snapped, "As you were, damn it! I have to get back to my own inspection work. Sergeant Arnold, see that Saunders pulls a hundred and ten push-ups. I guess you'd better give him a break every twenty-five. He's not quite a grown man yet."

Hunter turned and walked out as, behind him, someone muttered, "You sure got a buy on that rabbit's foot, Saunders. I've never seen a fucking officer cover for a private before."

"The looie's not a fucking officer," Arnold said. "He's a man. And you can forget that part about rest breaks, Saunders. He said a hundred and ten and I want them now!"

Outside, Dan Bradley was waiting for Hunter. He fell in step beside him as he said jovially, "You shouldn't have done that, buddy boy."

"You didn't give me much choice, pussy-footing around my platoon, Major."

"Come on, it's my platoon too, you know."

Hunter stopped, turned to Bradley, and snapped, "You're the administrative officer and I command the scouts in the field. I don't go through your desk at regiment and I'd appreciate it if you'd stay the hell away from my barracks!"

"Come on, it's my ass too if they don't pass inspection, buddy boy."

"I have three enlisted squad leaders to make sure they do, Danny Boy. Officers pussy-footing around hours before inspection don't help them get ready. They just shake them up. As a field grade officer you of course have the right to go anywhere on the base, but you might do it right by sending a noncom ahead of you to give them time to hide their comic books.

We're supposed to be leading these kids, not harassing them, Dan."

"Okay, okay, case closed. Listen, I don't see any reason for me to be hanging around while Maxwell Taylor looks for lint under the bunks his afternoon. Could you sort of cover for me while I, ah, run over to the air strip or something?"

"Jesus, you've got balls."

Bradley grinned. "Yeah, and they're about to explode in my pants. Look, I know I maybe got a little out of line back there, buddy boy. But we're still buddies, right?"

Hunter thought about that. Then he shrugged and said, "Okay. I'll tell anyone who asks that you're checking out the new gliders we got from the British. But for Chrissake take a *look* at a Horsa at least once in case the old man asks what you think of them."

Bradley laughed and said, "What's to think about a Horsa? It's bigger than a Waco and you can pack a field gun along in one. Big deal, S2 doesn't use heavy weapons."

"If you're not even going to look at a Horsa, remember it has wheel racks running the length of the fuselage and loads from the front. You can say you wanted to familiarize with British equipment."

"I'm off to get familiar indeed with British equipment. Sandy's found this place in Kingsclere with a connecting bath and, Jesus, you've never had a redhead until you've tried it standing in a shower all soaped up."

Hunter grimaced and started to say he didn't want the gory details. But then he frowned and said, "You asshole, Kingsclere is between here and Aldershot!"

"So what?"

"So Aldershot is where the Brits are training and they might like to screw in showers too! What if you crazy mixed-up kids run into some British officers at that inn?"

"I'll tell 'em I saw Sandy first. Relax, buddy boy. Aldershot's an army training center. Her old man's navy."

"Yeah, and working with Royal Marines and army commandos. But we've had this conversation before, so go ahead with your Russian roulette. But don't expect me to cover for you when the admiral catches you."

Bradley laughed harshly and said, "He won't, but what the hell can he do if he does, stand me in the corner?"

"He might kick the shit out of you. I've met him and he's no shrimp, Bradley."

"You're wrong. Sandy says I got a couple of inches on him, where it counts. I don't think he's man enough to fight anybody either."

"Danny Boy, the man is a *commando.*"

"Bullshit. He's just a ferryboat skipper for the commandos, and he's old enough to be my father even if I wasn't a paratrooper. You're not afraid of prissy old Limeys, are you, buddy boy?"

"I don't have to be. I haven't been screwing their wives."

"You don't know what you've been missing then. There's a lot of it floating around. Those hoity-toity Limeys just don't know how to take care of a woman in bed and half the dames in London are looking for a nice young Yankee boy they can take home to raise."

Hunter shook his head wearily. "Run along to meet

your maker, then. I've got an inspection to pass this afternoon."

"Yeah, it's rough in the ETO. Maybe we ought to get General Taylor fixed up too. We're not going to jump this summer and the war should be over by fall. You GI types are just wasting your time with all this chocolate soldier bullshit."

20

ONE MORNING the most beautiful city in the world
woke up sensing something odd was in the air.
Summer was almost over but the sky above her
chimney pots seemed far too clear for that thunder
rumbling in the distance. The streets were oddly deserted, save for German vehicles running back and
forth like disturbed ants. Rumors started running
back and forth too. The Germans were pulling out.
No, the Germans were digging in. No, the Germans
were getting ready to burn the city on Hitler's orders.
Paris didn't know what the hell was going on as she
rubbed the sleep from her eyes. Nothing the boches
did could surprise Paris anymore. But she hoped she
wouldn't burn to the ground.

She didn't. She had sons and daughters who worried
about her. In twos and threes men and women met in

odd corners with arm bands on and assorted weapons in their hands. To avoid detection by the Gestapo, the Paris underground had been organized in small cells, so that few people in the wide-spread organization had ever known, during the occupation, whether their neighbors were working for the boches or were fellow patriots. So as the word went out that this seemed to be it, men who'd eyed one another with mutual suspicion for four long years suddenly gasped, "What, you too?" as they met with armbands and rifles.

Then, being French, they tended to have a drink on it before going out to get themselves a boche.

Their leaders on both sides of the German lines tried to keep a lid on it. It was too soon. They were asking for a blood bath if they jumped the gun. But they didn't listen. From windows, alleyways, rooftops, and boldly in the streets the people of Paris started picking off the boches.

At German headquarters an officer and gentleman who knew what the words meant had some hard choices to make. His name was Von Choltitz, General Von Choltitz, and he was one of the very few people in Paris who knew what in the hell was going on. The American Third Army was flanking Paris to the south. The American First was moving around to the north to close the pincers. Leclerc's Free French were coming straight at him from the west and no matter what he did, Von Choltitz knew he was in trouble. Hitler had ordered him to hold Paris to the last man and put it to the torch before letting the Allies have it. It was the hitherto obscure German general's chance to go down in history. As the man who burned Paris.

Be it recorded to his credit that despite the uniform he wore and the cause he served, Dietrich Von Choltitz was a sensible civilized man. He ordered his forces to evacuate the city in as orderly a manner as possible, and to forget what Hitler said about playing with matches.

And so, as the Germans streamed out to the east, the bells of Paris began to ring as, up the broad Champs-Elysées rolled the American M-4 tanks of the Free French Second Armored, the Cross of Lorraine painted in red over the white American stars on their turrets.

And as the rattle of scattered gun fighting faded away in her streets, Paris blinked away the last cobwebs of that awful nightmare she'd been having, jumped out of bed, and put on her best dress to go deliriously nuts.

The party lasted for days, and up near the Belgian border, Bernard Law Montgomery was feeling very left out. So he started moving with a new enthusiasm that surprised the other Allied generals as much as it dismayed the Germans. Monty was still the most cautious commander on Patton's side. But he'd be bloody dashed if Patton was going to beat *him* across the Rhine, and Patton kept threatening to piss in it any day now.

So Monte called his staff to the big trailer he used as rolling quarters and field office and gave them new orders that shocked them as much as if the prudish teetotaler had appeared before them drunk and performing a naked fan dance. But his Canadian and British junior officers were more than willing to take the gloves off and go for broke, and, thanks to Monty's meticulous attention to logistics, they were up to full strength and had plenty of fuel and ammo in reserve despite the fighting they'd done up to now.

So the northern front exploded in the Germans'

faces as the Canadian First Army and the British Second steamrollered forward with the speed and guts hitherto reserved for Erwin Rommel or George Patton, and by September third the British had liberated Brussels. The people of Belgium started going nuts, too. But instead of kissing the girls the British slammed into Antwerp the next day. As the panic-stricken Germans reeled back toward the Dutch border Monty was able to tell Ike, rather smugly, that the major seaport with all its deep-water facilities was open for Allied business and that he expected to cross the Rhine shortly in the process of liberating Holland.

Then Monty had another look at the maps in his rolling command post.

The River Rhine does not empty into the North Sea like a kitchen tap. The Netherlands got their name because the delta of the Rhine is a vast marshland, braided into countless islands and outlets by the sluggish lower Rhine. As most people know, Holland is a manufactured land, created over the years by stubborn hard-working Dutchmen who tamed the natural quagmire with their dikes and canals. As a very good military historian, Monty knew how easy it was for anyone to hold Holland against an invasion from the south by blowing dikes and bridges. The Dutch were on Monty's side, to the extent they allowed the Gestapo to know about it. But the Germans who seemed to think they owned Holland at the moment had read their history books too. They knew that if Monty's blitz carried across the Rhine before winter there was no place to stop him on the dead flat North European plain that stretched from the Rhine to Russia. So holding Holland meant more to Germany than mere pride of possession. It was life or death for the Third Reich.

Back in July, after the German generals had tried unsuccessfully to get rid of Hitler, Hitler had ruthlessly rolled heads, including Rommel's. After a lot of reshuffling, a man named Walter Model had wound up in command of the German forces holding Holland and the lower Rhine crossings. Like all Hitler's pet generals, Model was a lickspittle and a toady. Unfortunately, he was also a very good field commander, and Monty knew it.

The British and Canadian tanks, spearheaded by the deadly Irish Guards, could handle almost anything they ran into on dry open ground. But they couldn't swim. The ruthless and efficient Model would most certainly turn every bottleneck bridge across the many streams into zeroed-in death traps. So Monty told his boys to slow down while he rethought the matter. For a time it looked like he was reverting to the cautious fuddy-duddy Monty of old.

Then he went to Eisenhower with his plans for Operation Market Garden. Ike was dumbfounded. The plan was awesomely daring for the dry and cold-sober Monty of all people to have come up with. But on paper it had at least a fifty-fifty chance. Ike was getting pretty sick of the war too, so he gave it the green light and the airborne was back in business.

Logan Hunter sat near Colonel Bell at the briefing held at General Taylor's division HQ. But if Dan Bradley was there Hunter couldn't see him in the crowd. The operations officer running his pointer over the large-scale map of Holland was saying, "After take-off from our various strips we'll rendezvous over Hatfield, here, just north of London. British and American rescue ships will be lined up across the North Sea to the Rhine delta. The British First Airborne Division and the Free Polish Brigade will land to the north at Arnhem to seize and hold the main bridges across the Rhine's main mouth. The U.S. Eighty-second Airborne lands here at Nijmegen to grab the bridges across the Waal. Our mission, gentlemen, is to land here, at Eindhoven."

He nodded to his enlisted assistant and a map of an even larger scale rolled down. "Okay," he said, "here comes the fun part. The 101st's DZs are here, here, and here, just north of Eindhoven. Our objectives are the bridges across Wilhelmina and Willems canals as well as these bridges over the Dommel and Aar rivers. We'll be holding the road net too. As Operation Market Garden lands, the British and Canadian ground forces are to roll up from the south to join us. So I don't have to tell you how vital your mission is. If the 101st can't hold at Eindhoven until the tanks arrive the tanks won't be able to reach the Eighty-second. If the Eighty-second can't hold out at Nijmegan until the tanks get there to cross *their* bridges, the British Red Devils will be cut off and Little Big Horned at Arnhem, and we wouldn't want that to happen, would we?"

He stabbed the map near a forested area and continued, "Division HQ, signals, medics, transport, and heavy weapons will land here, in gliders. A full regiment will drop by chute north and south of General Taylor's CP. The 501st Regiment lands here, north of the Dommel River, with their First Battalion dropping just north of these swamps along the Aar to hit any Krauts trying to secure the village of Veghel from both sides."

There was an uneasy murmur from the officers in the room. The operations man nodded and said, "I know we're coming down spread thin. The 501st will be spread even thinner with a river between them. But that's the point of Market Garden. Holland is a very soggy country. You think you have problems, wait 'till you see the mess the British airborne faces to our north at Arnhem! G2 and Radio Orange report the Krauts are retreating in disorder across Holland and we'll be the first troopers relieved by the Irish Guards, if they can get across those effing waterways. So make sure they can. The crossings you have to sieze and hold at all costs are here on the Wilhelmina. The British combat engineers may negotiate the skinny Willems Canal and the shallow rivers. But we'll all be out of business if they can't reach us across the damned Wilhelmina. The Dutch give their places funny names. So think Son Of A Bitch for the crossing at Son, and Best Bet for the bridge at Best. Are there any questions?"

Somebody muttered, "May I be excused for the rest of the afternoon?" but nobody paid any attention. A rifle company commander stood up and said, "I've got one. How come we're all landing *north* of two crossings on the Krauts' side of the water?"

The operations officer looked disgusted and said, "Because the British advance doesn't need us on *their* side of those crossings. We're supposed to keep the retreating enemy from blowing the effing bridges as they back north. That's pretty basic airborne tactics, Captain."

"Yeah, well I've got a couple of hundred kids depending on me to get them through basically alive. What happens if the armor doesn't reach us while we're futzing around on the Krauts' side of the rivers and canals?"

"That's a good question. You should have asked

yourself that before you signed up for the airborne, Captain. Are there any important questions?"

Logan Hunter stood up. "I'd like a breakdown on the disposition of German troops around Eindhoven, sir. My scouts and I will be landing ahead of the rest of you."

"I'd like to know more about them too," the operations officer said. "The situation is extremely fluid at the moment. The last G2 reports had the German Fifteenth Army retreating from Montgomery in disorder. Field Marshal Model's main Army Group B is intact and being beefed with reinforcements cannibalized from other German forces. Model's last known HQ was just west of Eindhoven but by now he should have fallen back to dig in north of the Rhine."

Hunter nodded and said, "In other words, we could face light resistance from scattered German stragglers or we could land smack in the middle of Army Group B."

It was a statement rather than a question. But the operations officer said, "That's about the size of it, Lieutenant. If we knew the Germans didn't mean to make a fight for Holland there'd be no point in our drop."

"Yessir," Hunter said, "but if they do mean to fight us for real estate, we're dropping in on more than one German army with three divisions and a half!"

"I already told you that, Lieutenant. Have you any suggestions about doing it a better way?"

Hunter didn't. He knew all the Allied airborne there was in the ETO was already committed to Market Garden and it seemed a little late to teach the Big Red One to jump. So he sat down.

Another worried officer rose to say, "I'm with the

First Battalion of 501 that you're being so good to. Three quarters of the kids you want me to land with out in Indian country have never heard a shot fired in anger, and a lot of my men have those fucking infantry boots nobody in his right mind would jump with!"

"You'll have to take that up with S1 and S4, Major. I'm S3 and we only plan the operations."

Another man shot to his feet to demand, "Okay, where is somebody from S4, then? They just issued us new harnesses none of my men have ever had a chance to train with! Who the hell thought up those stupid leg holsters for our automatic weapons, and what the hell was wrong with the carbines we trained with?"

A weary-looking field grade officer seated near the map board got to his feet. "I can answer that, Captain. It wasn't our idea. Somebody at SHAEF said to pass out the heavier submachine guns to the first wave and that's all she wrote."

A couple of other junior officers got up to air their gripes. Then General Maxwell Taylor moved to the front of the room, held up a hand for silence, and said, "As you were, gentlemen. This is the 101st Airborne, not a debating society. We're here because we're here, and we're jumping there because it's there. Every man in the outfit is a volunteer and I have definite views about shoving anyone out of a C-47 against his will. So if any of you find Operation Market Garden too rich for your blood, I'll be only too happy to arrange a transfer to the ground troops. Is there any man here who doesn't want to follow me to the DZ?"

There were no takers.

Maxwell Taylor smiled thinly and said, "All right, now that we've separated the men from the boys, all leaves are canceled and all units are confined to base until Market Garden D. I'll be happy to discuss any further problems that come up, personally, in my office. But this briefing is over. Go back to your units and work out the details with your people. Warn your noncoms that nobody below the rank of squad leader is to know the exact location of their DZs and I see no reason for any enlisted man to ever hear of Eindhoven before he gets there. You gentlemen are dismissed."

As they started to file out, Colonel Sam Bell caught up with Hunter and murmured, "Where the hell is Major Bradley, son?"

Hunter knew, but he said, "I'm not sure, sir. I think he said something about inspecting the glider line."

"What the hell for? We're not going across in any goddamn gliders. He'll be jumping with me, from my C-47, if he's anywhere near here when we take off. Give it to me straight, Logan. Is that silly son of a bitch on the base or is he shacked up with some Limey broad?"

"I'll look into it, Colonel."

The old man grunted and turned to join some other field graders as Hunter slipped away from him. He knew where Dan Bradley was. But how the hell was he to get word to him, now that he was confined to base, without going AWOL himself?

21

H UNTER WAS ONE of those rare officers who were
aware of "the sergeants' club" which, like the
Mafia, was not supposed to exist if anybody who
didn't belong to it ever asked. Many noncoms as well
as most officers were unaware of the sergeants' club,
for membership was limited to those good buddies in
key positions who made it work. Unlike the dubiously
ethical Mafia, the sergeants' club was a patriotic organization, designed to make the army run smoothly
despite the efforts of the "fucking officers" or silly regulations or commands. The professional noncoms, who
sometimes had more to do with running the army than
anyone above them suspected, had no written rules or
formal organization. They accomplished whatever
needed doing via a network of favors owed or minor
transgressions unreported. In most companies the first

sergeant, supply sergeant, mess sergeant, and certain trusted platoon sergeants conspired to make things happen that the brass might or might not approve of. Logan Hunter suspected his Sergeant Falco was in good standing with the army underground, so he went to Falco with his problem.

"I dunno, Lieutenant," Falco replied. "They got a lot of chickenshit MPs watching to see that nobody leaves the base."

Hunter nodded and said, "I know. I haven't slipped through a fence since I was an OCS cadet and I damned near got caught that time."

"Sneaking through fences is for recruits, sir," Falco chuckled. "Get caught doing that, and they got you like a big-ass bird. No way you're gonna explain it to the MPs if they catch you with your ass hung up on barbed wire."

"I know. And I need to get outside with a jeep, too. The major's shacked up over twelve miles from here and there's no way anyone's going to walk that far and back with the roads being patrolled. How would you go about it, Falco?"

"For Major Bradley? I wouldn't, sir. Begging the lieutenant's pardon, he wouldn't, neither, if he had any brains. The major's a fucking creep. Nobody owes him the right time."

"You may be right. But he missed D day doping off when the outfit jumped and this time they'll court-martial him for sure."

"Is that such an awful thing to think about, sir? You know he wouldn't lift a finger to help you if your ass was in the sling."

Hunter sighed wearily, and said, "When you're right you're right. But it gets complicated. He asked me to cover for him and I said I would. Don't ask me why

I said I would. I'm still trying to figure that out. The point is that he's counting on me. If I let him down he'll think I ratted on him."

Falco grinned and said, "Jesus, I wish *I* got chances like that. I could rat on that guy easy."

"You won't help me, Falco? Okay, I'll just have to see if I can bluff my way through with my officer's ID."

"Hey, Lieutenant, who said I wouldn't help you? Speaking man to man, I think you're nuts. But I'm not gonna let them fucking MPs nail you. They could replace you with somebody that's *really* chickenshit."

Hunter laughed. "You're a good man, Falco. How are we to work it?"

"Wait here, Lieutenant. I'll get us a jeep. No offense, but it's better if I sort of talk to the guys in the motor pool alone."

Hunter said he understood and as Falco took off Hunter moved over to a Waco parked on the grass and hunkered down in the shade of its wing to have a smoke while he waited.

He'd smoked four butts when Falco braked to a stop in the jeep, a broad smile on his face. Hunter got up and went over to climb in beside Falco, asking, "So what do we do now?"

Falco showed him an officious-looking trip ticket as he threw the jeep in gear. "This ought to get us past the gate, sir."

"I should say it should, considering the name somebody saw fit to sign on it! Are you aware of the penalties for forgery, Sergeant?"

"Hey, *I* never signed it. *You* never signed it. How the hell are *we* supposed to know if General Taylor signed it or not, right?"

Hunter grimaced. "All right, I asked for help and I'm trying not to cry. But what on earth is the general supposed to be sending us for?"

Falco reached down between the seats and handed Hunter a brown manila envelope with TOP SECRET stamped on it in red. "You better hang on to this, Lieutenant. We can use it going and coming, see?"

Hunter took the envelope but asked, "What's in this?"

"How are *we* supposed to know, Lieutenant? You're a junior officer and I'm only a fucking noncom. Would General Taylor tell us what he wanted us to run over to Aldershot for the Limey army?"

Hunter hefted the mysterious envelope. "Oh, my God, it's probably a comic book! This is raw as hell, Falco!"

"Yessir. That's why it usually works. Nobody ever asks you to let 'em look inside anything marked Top Secret. Lots of times when a GI who knows the ropes wants to goof off he just finds himself a brown envelope and starts walking. Nobody ever stops a guy to ask where he's going if he's carrying something that looks important, see? You leave your company area and go to a PX another outfit uses. That way nobody bothers you while you have your coffee and cake. The thing is to never *look* like you're doping off around any officer or noncom who knows you well enough to ask dumb questions. Goddamn goldbricking rookies always get caught, looking sneaky. A real fuck-off knows you gotta walk fast and military, throwing sharp salutes, until you can find some quiet place to relax."

Falco reached the end of the long line of gliders and hung a hard left turn down a narrow road running between hedges. Hunter asked where they were going and Falco said, "Fu Manchu road that takes us over to the gate the 501st usually uses, sir. We don't run into any brass from our regiment near that gate, see?"

Hunter grinned. "The MPs there won't know our faces either, right? Funny, I never noticed this little side lane."

"That's why it's a Fu Manchu, Lieutenant. It's just left over from when this was Limey farmland. So naturally you officers never use it. Guys who don't carry class-A passes gotta think ahead."

"Just between us girls, have you been AWOL often from this base, Falco?"

"What AWOL, sir? I always have a pass in case anybody asks in town. I, uh, picked up a pad of blanks a while back and your name ain't hard to sign."

"*My* name? I don't issue passes to you scouts, Falco. You're supposed to get them from your company officer, Captain Walters."

"Yessir, I know that and you know that, but do the fucking MPs know that? A guy could get in trouble signing his company CO's name on a pass. MPs in town could check that out with one phone call."

"I see. I wouldn't be in the orderly room when anyone from the provost marshal's called."

"You're learning, sir. Stick with me and I'll have you a real fuck-up in no time!"

"That's what I'm afraid of. Uh, this little adventure sort of puts me in a new situation with you, doesn't it?"

"Hey, don't sweat it, Lieutenant. I know my place. I'm doing this 'cause you're a regular guy. Not 'cause I want you to get me in no officer's club."

Before Hunter could reply Falco drove out onto

hardtop and swung a sharp left, warning, "Look important, Lieutenant. Gate's coming up."

Hunter sat straighter as Falco braked to a stop near two white-helmeted troopers. Falco handed one of them the forged trip ticket as he said, "Let's snap it up, huh? We're due in Aldershot five minutes ago."

The MP said, "Our orders say all leaves are canceled."

Falco spat and shot back, "What leave, you asshole? We got dispatches and you're holding up the war! You want to call and check, call and check, but make it sudden. Me and the lieutenant here ain't got all day."

The MP looked over at Hunter, spotted the silver bar on his shirt collar under the jump jacket and threw him a salute, saying, "Sorry, sir. I didn't recognize you."

Falco reached out to grab the trip ticket back as he said, "Okay, if you wanna know the truth, we're German spies. How about opening that fucking gate?"

The nearest MP nodded to his comrade, who swung the pole gate out of the way as Falco threw the jeep in gear and drove out into the forbidden world. As they sped away, he asked Hunter, "How'd you like that, Lieutenant?"

"I thought I'd wet my pants. What's to stop them from calling General Taylor?"

"Nothing. But they won't, sir. Buck-ass privates don't call generals up all that much. It's no skin off their asses if it turns out we were really German spies. They let us through with a trip ticket made out SOP and dispatches they ain't allowed to read anyhow."

"I'm not worried about their asses. I'm thinking about ours. What if we run into some MPs who won't buy our bluff?"

"I guess we'll be caught, sir. But what the hell, I told you you were taking a hell of a chance for that asshole of a major."

Dan Bradley and Sandy Kane were going at it dog style when Hunter burst in on them. Admiral Kane's wife was on her hands and knees across the bed as Bradley gripped her hips and gave it to her from the rear with his naked feet on the rug. As Hunter stepped inside and shut the door behind him, Bradley withdrew from the redhead and came at him head down and swinging. Hunter stiff-armed the major back and snapped, "Knock it off, I'm on *your* side, you jerk!"

Sandy had sprawled forward and instinctively groped for a pillow to cover her nudity until she grasped the situation and lay propped on one elbow, staring up at Hunter like a spoiled house cat lazing in front of the hearth. Bradley focused on Hunter and blurted, "Oh, it's you! What the hell do you mean by barging in on us like that, Hunter?"

"I had to. You don't answer phones. I called from the base and I called from downstairs. I'll explain it on the way back. Get dressed. Sergeant Falco's downstairs with our jeep running and *we're* both AWOL, too!"

"What the hell are you talking about? I told you to cover for me, buddy boy."

"I did. But it's wearing thin. The outfit's on the alert and confined to base. The colonel's looking for you. Are you coming with us or not? I'm not hanging around here all that long, Danny Boy!"

Bradley gasped, "Jesus!" and reached for his pants.

On the bed, Sandy sighed and said, "Oh, rats, I suppose I may as well get dressed too. I do so hope you were discreet with names, Logan dear?"

"Relax," Hunter said. "I just told my enlisted driver the major was shacked up with a local tart."

She got it, but Danny Boy didn't. He pulled on his boots with a grunt and said, "I knew I could count on you, buddy boy. But for God's sake, next time knock! I'd have knocked your block off if the lights hadn't been on. How serious is this damned alert, anyway?"

Hunter looked away as Sandy rose like Venus from the foam to saunter past him in search of her dress. "We'll talk about it in the jeep," he said. "For Chrissake, don't lace those damned boots *here*! Falco's exposed to passing traffic downstairs and if he and our transportation are arrested all three of us will spend the rest of the war in the stockade!"

Bradley nodded and rose to his feet, boot tops flopping as he shucked on his shirt and grabbed his jacket and cunt cap from the chair near the foot of the bed. Sandy, still nude, was seated on the edge of the bed with one leg raised as she rolled on her nylons. Bradley bent to kiss her goodbye as Hunter opened the door and snapped, "Let's go, Danny Boy."

As they went down the stairs together, Bradley chuckled and said, "I think she's a little sore at us both. She was coming when you charged in on us. I think I was too, but you couldn't have cooled me off any faster with a bucket of water!"

Hunter didn't answer. They *had* reminded him of a couple of hung-up alley strays, but Bradley outranked him by two grades, so what the hell.

22

SOMEONE ONCE DEFINED the difference between strategy and tactics by saying the decision to take the castle was strategy, and where you put the ladders and battering ram was tactics. Having been given the big picture, each unit of the division was left to work out their own tactical details, so the next few days at regimental HQ saw a lot of discussion around the sand table Colonel Bell had ordered set up.

It was Sam Bell's second war, so the old man favored simple foolproof tactics and shot down any razzle-dazzle ideas presented by his junior commanders. He'd learned the hard way that in combat nothing ever went quite the way it was supposed to on paper. Old soldiers repeat old bromides like "Take the high ground!" or "When in doubt, move on the guns," because experience had shown that, like the sea, war was a treacherous and unforgiving mistress. Had he been a clipper ship skipper, Sam Bell would have rounded the horn with shortened sails and taken the swells on his quarter. As regimental CO he wanted all his people on the ground in well-secured positions before they got around to doing anything dramatic. Their main mission was to secure division HQ from a German counterattack until the general got a handle on the situation, so Bell pointed out the natural strong points in their DZ and told each company commander he expected them to dig in deep, and be prepared to take an assault from any direction.

Major Dan Bradley, as regimental S2, was supposed to brief them on the enemy's likely countermoves. But Danny Boy had been goofing off, and, in all fairness, he wouldn't have known all that much about Field Marshal Model's plans in any case. He'd asked for Hunter's notes and had his clerk type up an impressive dossier which, in truth, contained next to nothing about German positions but at least gave Danny Boy a chance to bone up on what the hell the operation was all about.

Hunter listened, bemused, as Bradley pontificated on outdated enemy dispositions, qualifying each red mark on the acetate by saying, "Of course, we have no way of knowing this unit hasn't moved by now. Radio Orange says the Krauts are running around over there like chickens with their heads cut off."

Hunter had to admit Bradley was good. When he wasn't doping off, Danny Boy adopted an officious air that could convince almost anyone he knew what the hell he was talking about, if they didn't know him.

The opportunistic Bradley waited until the night before they were to load up before he caught up with Hunter and handed him some typed notes and a blue-crayoned map copy, saying, "These are your final jump instructions, buddy boy. I may not get another chance to brief you, so good hunting."

They were alone in the S2 office. Hunter frowned and asked, "What do you mean you won't be able to brief me again? Aren't we all going in the same series?"

Bradley shook his head. "No. I, ah, still have a gimp leg from that last practice jump, so I cleared it with the old man to ride in a Waco with the communications gear. He'll be in his command C-47 of course, and your scouts will drop in two places. Falco's stick will act as pathfinders for regiment. You'll form a screen to our north as indicated there."

Hunter started to ask him what practice jump he was talking about. Then he blinked down at his orders and said, "Wait a minute. This is nuts! You've got me DZed for the village of Uden, nearly five miles north of the Aar!"

"I know where I'm dropping you, buddy boy. You and your scouts will be in a position to make early contact, if the Krauts come down that highway from Nijmegen, see?"

"I *don't* see. For God's sake, you're putting us north of the 501st and I'm not *in* the 501st. Uden's way the hell north of the whole division's DZ!"

"I know. You'll be covering for division I&R. General Taylor's scouts will have enough on their plates securing the HQ area. What's the matter, buddy boy? Getting nervous in the service?"

"No, but this still sounds nuts. If we landed any further north we'd be jumping with the Eighty-second instead of the 101st. It's too far out, Dan. I'll be down with fifteen troopers in the middle of Indian country.

Any contact we'll meet is liable to be between us and the rest of the outfit!"

"So, you'll have your radio, won't you?"

Hunter nodded, but asked, "Does the colonel know about this?"

"The colonel's not running regimental S2. I am. But if you're afraid of the dark you have my permission to run to teacher, buddy boy."

Hunter was tempted. If Bradley wasn't simply stupid he was trying to get rid of half his scouts for some reason. He folded the papers and put them away, saying, "I hope you know what you're doing. You say you'll be with the gliders? They're landing with HQ. How are you going to make it on the ground to the colonel?"

"By jeep, of course. We're landing in style this time. We've even got some field guns in the gliders, remember?"

"Yeah, I'd forgotten how much time you spent, uh, inspecting gliders."

"Was that a crack, buddy boy? I can show you my medical report if you don't believe I sprained my ankle on that last practice jump."

"I don't need a note from your doctor. I was talking about your active sex life, not your legs. I don't give a damn how you cross the channel, just so I don't have to go looking for you again at the last moment."

Danny Boy laughed and said, "Hey, what can I tell you? It's no secret me and Errol Flynn like girls. Maybe after we get things under control over there you can introduce me to some Dutch stuff. Isn't that big blonde of yours dropping with General Taylor?"

"I don't know. She could be on the ground over there already. Prince Bernhard of the Netherlands is up to something with the Dutch resistance, but they never tell us peasants nothing. I have to get back to my men, Dan. Keep your pecker up if I don't see you again this side of Holland."

The major was laughing as Hunter left him. Hunter considered going to the colonel's office down the corridor to check out the strange orders he'd just received. But, hell, he'd wind up looking like an awful sissy if they made sense to old Sam Bell, and not even Danny Boy would deliberately order anyone to commit suicide, right?

Logan Hunter sat near the open hatchway, deafened by the slipstream and the roar of the C-47's twin engines as he watched the light board on the forward bulkhead, dry mouthed with fear. They were alone now, in a bright and clear September sky. He'd watched that same sky blossom with parachutes and flack a few minutes ago as they passed over the last DZ. One of the other transport planes had been trailing smoke the last time he spotted it, for there was no way to move so many planes so far in broad daylight without somebody noticing on the ground. The flack had been heavier than expected. For a disorganized army, the Krauts were shooting pretty good right now.

The alert light winked on. Hunter rose and clipped his static line to the steel cable running the length of the fuselage. He didn't have to yell above the roar. His stick of scouts were trained to follow his lead and did so, hooking up between him and Sergeant Arnold, down at the far end. Hunter moved to the opening and braced himself, keeping one eye on the lights as he tried to spot landmarks on the ground below. They were skimming three hundred feet above the checkerboard fields and red roof-tops of Holland. A canal whipped across his line of vision like a windshield wiper blade and he grunted, "Willems. I hope."

Units of the 501st should be somewhere in the vicinity, but if they'd dropped he couldn't see them. Their kite seemed all alone up here and where was the damned jump light?

Hunter was startled by the sudden sharp noise of flack, sounding as if someone had thrown a bucket of gravel against the metal skin of the lone C-47, and the shock wave tingled the flooring under his boots. He tensed his legs. Why didn't the jump light flash? How long did it take to fly four damn miles?

And then the C-47 shuddered and soared skyward as another burst kicked it in the guts. Hunter saw they were passing over a village and that people down there were waving up at him. Was that Uden? It had to be Uden. How many villages could there be down there? What was the matter with the fly boys? Couldn't they read maps?

And then, as the C-47 began to stall out, Hunter knew why nobody had pushed the jump button.

He dove forward out the opening, cursing as he saw the tilt of the plane had thrown him off balance. He was tumbling head over heels when he hit the end of his static line. The chute blossomed open with his boot heels aimed at the blue sky. The shock snapped his spine like a whip and his webbing almost emasculated him. But he'd gotten his breath back, just as he hit the ground and rolled, spilling his chute. He looked up to see other chutes. He counted fourteen. Only fourteen. Over to the west the plane they'd jumped from was spinning in. As he released his harness and stood up the C-47 hit and exploded in a big ball of flame. Hunter unslung his carbine and headed for the nearest hedgerow, yelling, "Cover on me!" as the others followed.

He flopped behind the hedges and saw the road to Eindhoven ran down the other side. The fields across the way were open and empty. So he could take time out to breathe for a minute.

Sergeant Arnold flopped beside him. "Report," Hunter snapped.

"We're all down except Saunders, sir," Arnold said. "He caught a streamer. He's over on the far side of the DZ, if this is the DZ. What happened up there?"

"Looks like the pilot got hit. We overflew the DZ, but not by much. If that last village was Uden we're maybe a dozen miles north of where we were supposed to land. Hold the stick here while I have a look at Saunders."

As he got to his feet again, Arnold said, "He bought it, sir. I saw him hit." But Hunter started jogging anyway. Sometimes a guy lived a while if he landed on soft ground.

Saunders hadn't. The rookie lay spread-eagled in a patch of marigolds, a bemused smile on his young face as he stared up at the blue sky. He was firmly embedded in the orange flowers. His still useless but now open chute billowed open and shut like a jelly fish at the end of his shrouds. Hunter took out his jump knife and bent to cut the chute free. Then he unstrapped Saunder's carbine, removed the bolt, and drove its muzzle into the earth between the marigolds. He cut the kid's helmet strap and placed the helmet on the carbine's disarmed action. It was all he could do for Saunders. Graves might find him before he rotted or graves might not. Hunter still had his living people to worry about.

He moved back to his improvised position and called, "Cohen, see if you can raise regiment on that R-300. Arnold, I don't see any flank scouts out."

Arnold looked sheepish and yelled, "Spud, move north a hundred yards and take cover. Colsen, south and ditto!"

"I have regiment, sir," Cohen said. "They're asking where the hell we are."

Hunter moved to join Cohen and took the handset with a relieved sigh. He gave his code and said, "We're about a dozen miles north of our assigned DZ. Our kite took a hit but we made it out. Lost one man to a streamer. Over."

Sam Bell answered, "Is that you, Logan? Where the fuck are you? Over."

"Uh, didn't the major brief you on our DZ, sir? Over."

"I don't know where the fuck *he* is, either! I've got your Falco out to my north as my only I&R. I can only hope there's nobody south except division HQ. What series did Bradley fly in, damn it? Over."

Hunter frowned, puzzled by the older officer's confusion. "Didn't he tell you he was crossing in a Waco, sir? Over."

"Waco. What Waco? We're *paratroopers*, damn it! The nearest gliders landed miles from me! But screw Bradley, where the fuck are you? Over!"

Hunter hesitated, aware anyone could be listening in. He chose his words carefully. "We were ordered to drop, uh, ten miles northeast of 501's First Battalion DZ, sir. We overshot by about a dozen. We've made no contact with anybody on either side. Over."

There was a pregnant pause as Bell apparently consulted his own map. Then he snapped, "Somebody has gone out of his cotton picking mind! Who in the hell told you to land way the hell out there? Over!"

"Major Bradley did, sir. He said . . ."

There was a garble of static as the enraged Sam Bell tried to talk while Hunter was still on. Hunter flipped his switch to receive in time to hear, ". . . court-martial the stupid son of a bitch if he ever turns up around here! What the hell's he trying to do, get us all killed? Over."

Hunter was starting to wonder about that too. But all he said was, "I'm waiting for your orders, sir. Over."

"Okay. You say there's nobody up there but you chickens? Over."

"Affirmative, sir. There has to be a flack unit around here somewhere, but we seem to be out in the middle of nowhere much. Flat open fields all around with very little cover. We're on the road that leads your way. Over."

"Okay. Start moving back to us then. But watch your step, Logan. The 501st reports it's already made contact with the enemy at Veghel. So there's heavy action going on between where you are and where we are. Over."

"Roger wilco, sir. Over and out," said Hunter, handing the handset back to his radio man. He stood up and turned to address the others. "Okay, men, here's the situation. We're SNAFU. Regiment wants us to work south a good twenty miles and we've got a canal, two rivers, and a battle between us and regiment. We'll follow the road for now and play by ear as we go. There are marshlands and heaths on both sides of the highway, so flank scouts will just slow us down. Arnold, put two men on point, walking each road shoulder. The rest of us will move staggered on both sides of the highway. Cohen, stay near me with that

R-300 and guard it with your life. Let's form it up and move it out."

As they pushed through the hedges to the hardtop road the wind shifted and Hunter heard a dull rumble of thunder from the south. South was the way he was supposed to take his people, and somebody down the road ahead was getting the crap shot out of them.

Far to the west Major Dan Bradley lay facedown in a water-filled ditch, sobbing with fear and alone somewhere in Holland. Above him a thrush was trilling in a willow tree. But when the wind was right Bradley could hear distant rumbles and crumps he knew wasn't thunder. Nothing seemed to be going on around him anymore, though. So after a time Bradley cautiously rose to his hands and knees and looked around.

He was surrounded by willow trees and cattails. He'd stumbled into some kind of damned old swamp after running a million miles. He had no idea where he was, or where his glider had crashed. Had anybody else gotten out alive? Bradley didn't know. He didn't remember exactly how he'd gotten out of the crumpled Waco after it had spun in like a singed moth to land upside down in those trees. He knew it hadn't landed anywhere near where it had been supposed to, though. He remembered the glider pilot shouting, "Hang on!" and releasing the tow line when their tow plane up ahead burst into flames. After that, things had dissolved in chaos and Bradley was sure he hadn't been the only one who'd been screaming on the way down.

But, what the hell, he was still alive and in one piece, so it was time he started looking out for numero uno. He couldn't do anything for those other clowns, even if he knew where they were. He stood up, soaked, and stepped out of the ditch to get his bearings. He checked his pistol and saw it was still in working condition. Far on the north horizon he saw a tiny church steeple. It didn't tell him much. The British lines were due south. So Bradley started walking that way across a field of knee-high hay.

He came to a road running east and west. He hesitated. He knew there was nothing but the North Sea to his west and the sounds of distant guns were coming from the east. Bradley was about to cross the road to keep moving south when he saw a kid coming from the east on a bike. The Dutch youth spotted him at the same time, hesitated, then pedaled up to Bradley, grinning as he held the handlebar with one hand and made the V sign with the other. As he braked to a stop he said, "Please, Tommy friend, I do not so good the English speak, but I thank God to meet you anyway, ja?"

"I'm American," Bradley said.

"I thank God then two times. You are lost maybe? There are no other soldiers near."

"You know what's going on?" Bradley asked.

"Of course. Radio Orange says we are to stay indoors and out of the way. But I am on my way to join my kommando. We dig up our guns and help you kill Germans, ja?"

"You're with the underground?"

"Ja, I am a corporal. Every Dutchman my age is in or for the underground, unless they have been helping the Germans. Now that Bijitjesday is here we kill *them* too, ja?"

"Sounds swell. Listen, what can you tell me about the 101st American Airborne?"

The Dutch boy looked puzzled and said, "I don't know about numbers. But many paratroopers and gliders have landed over there to the east, north of Eindhoven. This road takes you there. It is maybe fifteen kilometers."

"Jesus, that's a long way to walk. Do you know how they're making out over there?"

"Making out? You mean fighting? Gives much fighting over that way, but the paratroopers are winning. I heard this on the telephone before the Germans cut the lines. The Germans blew up the Son bridge. So the paratroopers are fighting for the one at Best now. The lines went dead before I could find out who is winning. But I think the paratroopers will, ja?"

It was a good question. But, more important, it meant the landings had gone well. If they were already after the crossings, General Taylor's HQ was set up securely in those woods a couple of miles from Best, and his own outfit would be even farther north. Bradley asked the boy, "What's due south of here, kid?"

The Dutch boy smiled grimly. "The German Fifteenth Army. They are falling back from the British, and my kommando means to give them a dusting from their rear, ja?"

"That sounds just keen. Does this road run north of the Wilhelmina Canal?"

"Ja, the canal runs east and west a kilometer to our south. There are no Germans between us and your friends right now."

"That's my best bet then. I'm going to need that bike, kid. Get off."

"My bicycle, please? I can not give it to you. I have to join my kommando now, ja?"

Bradley drew his .45 and said, "You can walk. I'm not about to leg it any fifteen kilometers. Come on, kid. I haven't got all day."

The Dutch boy gasped, "You are a robber! This is most unjust of you!"

"Yeah, it's rough in the ETO. Gimme that bike before I blow your fucking head off!"

The Dutch boy swung his leg off the bike, pale with bewildered anger. As Bradley grasped the handlebar with his free hand, the Dutch boy said, "This is not just. You are as bad as the Germans! I am going to report this to my leader!"

Bradley looked up and down the road, saw nobody was in sight. "Yeah, you probably would do that, wouldn't you?"

Then he raised the .45 and shot the Dutch boy in the face at point-blank range.

The young Dutchman's head flew back like a batted softball. He fell spread-eagled to the road, one leg twitching like the tail of a run-over snake as Bradley pumped two more bullets into him to make sure. Then Bradley forked a leg over the bike and took off, not looking back as he started making up a cover story. He muttered aloud, "Some Kraut must have killed the jerk, right? Yeah, I don't know what happened to him. I just found him laying in the road with this bike and what the hell, I needed the bike. What can they say to that?"

The road did a gentle dogleg and Bradley looked back as he rounded it. The kid he'd shot was a mere speck back there now, and nobody would ever know just what had happened. Wars were confusing that way.

He pedaled on, grinning now, as he realized what a grotesque picture he made riding a bike in his jump suit and helmet. But this sure beat walking, and in a little while he'd be safe at the command post. The colonel would probably be out running around in the bushes, if he knew old Sam Bell. But somebody had to mind the store at the CP and only suckers took chances.

He wondered if the Krauts had killed Hunter by now. Somebody should. The damned lieutenant knew where too many bodies were buried and Sandy was probably right about Hunter not liking him. Old buddy boy Hunter had been giving him a lot of back talk lately, and you had to change your junior officers like socks, before they stunk things up for you.

Bradley repressed a momentary qualm as he considered what he'd have to say if that dumb Hunter somehow made it back alive. But hell, he was covered. He had what seemed to be duplicate maps in his briefcase showing that he'd ordered Hunter to land south of the Drummel and. . . . Jesus! His brief case! He'd left it back there in the wrecked glider!

Bradley stopped pedaling as he fought back a wave of sheer terror. What the hell had made him forget his briefcase like that? It had all his papers in it. Good God, it had some papers he'd been told to get rid of after memorizing! He'd completely forgotten it in his anxiety to get clear of that wrecked Waco. If anybody ever found out he'd done a dumb thing like that. . . But hell, who was ever going to find out? The glider had been a total wipeout. Nobody was going to ask him for the fucking papers. If they did, he could say he left them behind in England for security reasons.

23

IN THE VILLAGE of Uden the people had been told by Radio Orange and their civic officials to stay indoors until further notice. But they hadn't. All morning the sky had been filled with planes and rising columns of orange smoke signals, and Vancouver, the sexton at the church, said he'd seen parachutes coming down just north of town as well. People were up on their rooftops, not caring if they cracked the tiles with their weight as they waved at each other and anything that flew over. The big C-47s were no longer passing over, but every once in a while a flight of P-51s or British Typhoons tore over them just above treetop level and everyone would go crazy for a while. Down in the dry goods store they were having a run on orange ribbon. People bought lengths of orange ribbon, as fast as the three clerks behind the counter could cut them from the roll, and started putting them on inside the store. The women and girls tied orange ribbon in their hair. The men made little bows to wear in their lapels, and more than one man had an old shotgun or hunting rifle cradled in his arm.

The local police chief was no longer there to keep order. Like everyone else in town who'd ever so much as smiled at a German in the past, he was running for his life with his family and belongings stuffed in his overloaded car. In a ditch just outside the south end of town a man in a policeman's uniform lay dead beside his bike. A Dutch farmboy with an ancient fowling piece had remembered the time the policeman had pointed out the only Jewish family in Uden to the Gestapo. The Dutch boy, a member of the Reform Church, hadn't been inducted officially into the local underground because of his youth. But when he'd spotted the fleeing policeman he'd known what he should do. The boy was almost fourteen and today a Dutchman was a Dutchman.

As Hunter and his cut-off stick moved warily along the road from the north, the churchbells started ringing and someone yelled, "They are coming! The British are just outside of town!"

So the whole town of Uden stampeded north to greet the bewildered lost patrol, and there wasn't much Hunter could do about it. It was a weird way to conduct a military operation, but they didn't seem to be Germans, so what the hell.

Hunter asked an English-speaking woman what lay ahead and she kissed him on the cheek and said, "The Germans and their friends are gone from Uden, Tommy! Come, we shall give you a welcome feast, ja?

We don't have any lard or sugar and the coffee is really tulip bulbs, but we will manage to feed you somehow!"

He laughed and said, "We have food. We have to get down to the town of Veghel and—"

"But you *can't* go to Veghel! It is with Germans filled. All *our* Germans went down to, how you say, dig-in with the Germans in Veghel! If you listen you can hear them fighting down that way, ja?"

Hunter turned to Cohen. "You heard the lady, Cohen. Put it on the air." Then he turned back to the woman and said, "I don't have the manpower to take the Germans holding the Veghel Crossing from the rear, ma'am. Is there some way we can work around to cross the Aar and Willems Canal?"

She spoke in Dutch to some of the men around her as they all walked on together into the town. Dutch was close enough to English for him to understand that they thought it was a lousy idea. The woman turned back to him and explained, "Please, Tommy, the banks of the Aar are marsh. Much marsh, in some places very wide. The only crossing for kilometers is the bridge at Veghel, and the Germans are in Veghel, on this side of the water!"

Hunter saw the concerned look in Sergeant Arnold's eyes. He shrugged and said, "The 501st was supposed to drop one battalion on this side. They ought to have the Krauts surrounded by now."

"What if they don't, sir?"

"They'll still be on our side of the crossing. I don't know about you guys, but I'm starting to feel left out. We'll push south and see if we can fall in with the 501st."

The village was only a wide spot in the road. He could see they were within sight of the far side now.

He turned to his volunteer translator and told her, "Ask the people to stay back now, ma'am."

"They don't wish to. They say we will all walk with you a kilometer or so, and then only the men with guns will march with you to Veghel, ja?"

Hunter shook his head. "No deal. It's not that I don't think your men can fight, but my orders are not to pick up irregulars, ma'am. My men and me are in uniform, so the German's can't shoot us if we're captured, but—"

"Hah! You think the Germans care who they shoot? You do not know them or you would not say *can't*, Tommy. The Germans care nothing for the rules of war. Ask the people in Rotterdam. The Germans bombed it flat after the city had surrendered!"

They were still arguing by the time they were going out the south end of town. Hunter didn't know what to do. He knew what you were supposed to do with *Germans* who got in your way, but this was ridiculous.

One of his troopers had handed a cigarette to a pretty girl. Hunter said, "Knock it off, Dalton! We're trying to leave them behind, not adopt them!"

The older woman who spoke English tried to help. She shouted at her fellow villagers in Dutch, but that didn't work either. One of his men had an orange ribbon tied in a bow around the muzzle of his carbine as he walked arm in arm between two girls. Hunter was about to yell at him but gave it up for now. His best bet was to fall back on the training his men had received in the past months. He called out, "Double-time . . . hohhh!" and broke into a jog. These nutty Dutch couldn't possibly be legged-up as well as paratroopers.

And so the stick started jogging down the highway

with the whole damned village of Uden scampering along with them. He saw a fat old woman with orange ribbons in her gray hair galloping happily along and couldn't believe it. Later, some of the Dutch wouldn't believe it either. But they were like kids let out after a long day in school. The Germans had occupied their country since 1940 and they were delirious with joy.

They didn't realize that if the sounds of big guns in the not-so-distant distance meant anything, some of the Germans were still around.

Field Marshal Walter Model was a worried man as he paced back and forth in his field headquarters to the north. Model of course knew Allied paratroopers were landing all around him. He'd even ordered the standard countermoves. But he didn't know what on earth the enemy was up to. He was too smart to think they'd come to dig tulip bulbs. But he still didn't know the objective of Operation Market Garden. For a few panic-stricken moments that morning, as the first reports came in, Model had thought they were after him, personally. Paratroops and gliders had landed all around his forward HQ at Oosterbeek. Every German commander reporting in had the same chaotic tale to tell of skies filled with planes and flack. Many of the enemy planes had been shot down, but most had not, and what in the name of God *were* they after?

Model knew about the bridges and road net, of course, but there were so many bridges in this damned soggy country and he had only so many men. Some vicious fighting was reported around Son, but his engineers had blown the Son bridge and that crossing was obvious, since the observers to the south reported heavy armor pushing north from Belgium. But there were countless other paratroopers far to the north and if he was guessing wrong about Arnhem . . .

An aide came in, smiling, to say, "We just captured some enemy dispatches, Herr Field Marshal. One of our patrols found them in a wrecked glider to our south. They were in a briefcase and—"

Model stopped pacing and snapped, "Never mind what they were in, damn it! Have they been decoded yet?"

"They were not in code, Herr Field Marshal. Just some maps and typewritten tactical instructions. Naturally I had them translated before I came here with them."

Model snatched the papers from his aide and moved to spread them out on a table. He read swiftly, scanned the maps, and read again before he scowled and said, "This has to be a trick. Nobody could be *this* lucky! Tell me more about this crashed glider of yours."

"We thought of a ruse, Herr Field Marshal," the aide said. "Frankly, we don't think they could have meant these plans to fall into our hands. We've a report from the flack crew who shot the glider's tow plane down. It seems legitimate. Also there were bodies in the glider. We think one of the officers who died in the crash must have been very stupid. He was carrying the plans for Operation Market Garden in his briefcase."

Model started to ask what the hell a Market Garden was, but he had a good memory as well as a steel-trap mind. He nodded and said, "So, the Market is our Monty's armored advance and the Garden is the objective of these crazy airborne troops coming down all around us. We have to get out of here before I am captured with all *my* plans! Alert your people that we

295

evacuate in half an hour. Meanwhile I have some phone calls to make."

The field marshal picked up his command phone, all too aware that he could be making a terrible mistake, but with at least *some* plan of counterattack in mind now.

He got his adjutant on the line and snapped, "The objectives are the bridges at Son, Veghel, Nijmegen and, of course, Arnhem. Von Zangen will take command of all Group B west of the enemy corridor from Eindhoven to Arnhem. General Student's First Parachute Army is assigned the eastern flank. What shape is Student in? Has he his reinforcements from the fatherland yet?"

"Yes, Herr Field Marshal, and the II SS Panzer Corps also is at full strength."

"Good. What's the latest from our Fifteenth Army units still near the border?"

"Not too bad, Herr Field Marshal. Across the Schelde, Von Zangen managed to evacuate 82,000 men, 530 guns, 4,600 vehicles, as well as some horse-drawn field artillery."

"So. Combined with units from the Dutch Occupation Army, Group B is in better shape than I thought. All right, alert all units to hold the crossings at all costs for the few hours it will take me to completely reorganize things here. I am on my way to join Bittrich and his SS Panzer. When I hit those swine I mean to hit them hard!"

There was a pause on the other end of the line before his adjutant asked, "Are we not to resist Montgomery's armor from the south, Herr Field Marshal?"

"To hell with Montgomery! If we hold all the crossings, where on earth can the idiot go?"

* * *

By the time they'd jogged a mile Hunter and his men were starting to feel pooped and most of their Dutch fans had dropped behind. But some men were still with them and seemed determined to stay there. Hunter slowed to a walk and yelled at the nearest Dutchman, "Will you guys get out of here?"

The Dutchman grinned and held his rifle up as he said, "Boom boom, ja?"

"Aw, shit," Hunter muttered. "Colson, you're not far enough out on point. Move out and cover that crossroad we seem to be coming to."

The lagging point man trotted wearily forward to pass the other scout out front. As Colson reached the corner of the hedge-lined country lane intersecting with the highway an armored scout car popped out on the hardtop in front of him. Colson gasped at the black cross on its turret and turned his back on it, pumping his carbine over his head in the universal infantry signal for "enemy in sight" as the gunner in the scout car's turret opened up with his heavy machine gun.

Hunter and his men were already crabbing off the road on either side before the German bullets blew Colson in two at the waist. But the Dutch civilians who'd tagged along hadn't been through basic so the machine gun put three of them on the hardtop before the others could make the ditches on either side of the road. Sergeant Arnold rose, shouting, "Bastards!" He emptied his clip at the armored scout car, knocking off some paint but nothing else before Hunter rolled into his knees to spill him as the turret gunner traced a dotted line of death through the space Arnold had just been occupying.

The scout car swung away and burned rubber south as Hunter swore at Arnold and said, "Don't ever do that again!"

"I hit them, sir! I him with at least six rounds!"

"You mean you wasted ammo on Krupp steel, you jerk. Reload your weapon and save it for soft guys, like us. Cohen, haul that R-300 over here and . . . Kee-rist! Everybody *down!*"

A line of medium tanks had followed the scout car out on the hardtop to wheel majestically south, ignoring the shattered body of Colson near the crossroad. Hunter knew the scout car was in radio communication with the tanks and it burned him to be dismissed as so unimportant a target, until he thought about it twice.

As the tanks rumbled away Cohen crawled up to Hunter's position, hauling their own radio. "See if you can raise 501st's S2 for me," Hunter said. He sat up and asked if anyone else had been hit. None of his men had. The chastised Dutch volunteers were moving off, carrying their own dead and wounded. Hunter didn't blame them. But the rules were different for the airborne.

"I've got 501, sir," Cohen said.

Hunter grabbed the handset to say, "This is S2 Lieutenant Hunter, maybe three miles north of Veghel. A Kraut armored scout and four medium tanks just passed us, headed your way. Over."

"This is Floyd with First Battalion. What's your S2 major's nickname? Over."

"Danny Boy. You know me, damn it, Floyd! Over!"

"I do now, good buddy, and I thank you for your words of cheer. What the hell are guys from your outfit doing north of *us*? Over."

"Beats the shit out of me. Those tanks are coming right down your throat. Over."

"We read you and thanks a lot, Hunter. Over and out!"

Hunter turned the set over to Cohen and asked him if they could raise the Eighty-second to the north.

Cohen shook his head. "Not at this range, sir. These things only carry so far."

"Okay, you were in Indian country with me in Normandy, Sergeant. So you know the form. We're moving north, off the road net."

"North, sir? The Eighty-second's a lot further than our own outfit, Lieutenant."

"I know. But they're on our side of the river crossing at Nijmegen. The 101st is on the far side of the battle for Veghel Bridge. So what do you want, egg in your beer?"

"It's still one hell of a walk, sir, but you're the boss. Where can we figure to meet up with the Eighty-second if they haven't taken Nijmegen yet?"

"We're closest to a place called Grave."

"Grave, sir? Pretty spooky name for a DZ, isn't it?"

"Yeah, but come to think of it, *all* the places I've ever landed have been pretty spooky. Let's move it out, Arnold."

The same sun had shone on Paris that morning. But as Ramie Davis stared out the window of the Paris UPI that afternoon she didn't like the look of that sky. Nothing was flying up there that anyone in Paris had to worry about these days, but the sky was turning grey. If the weather turned wet nothing would be flying for or against either side on Market Garden D-2.

Beth Waterman joined her at the window with a tear sheet off the teletype. "Okay, they're still acting awfully stingy with the news up north, Ramie. But it seems the landings went well and the Irish Guards are meeting light resistance on the roads to the DZs."

"Anything about casualties?" Ramie asked bleakly.

Beth shook her head. "You know they never tell us that until years later. They're still trying to sell Pearl Harbor as a nuisance raid. But Monty's supposed to be pretty careful and we still don't know for sure your guy jumped with them, Ramie."

"Logan Hunter's with the 101st and the 101st is down at Eindhoven. But I wish you'd stop calling him my guy, Beth."

"He's not *my* guy, damn it. Who are we trying to kid, Ramie? You've been jumping around like a chick with her head cut off since Market Garden came in over the wire. Are you trying to tell me you're not sweating him out?"

Ramie started to shake her head. Then she sighed and said, "You're right. I keep trying to tell myself he's just a guy-type guy, but I'm going crazy waiting for word. God, Beth, what will I do if it happens again?"

"Again? Wasn't the point of all this unseemly chastity that it *couldn't* happen again if you two kids didn't really mean anything to one another?"

"Yes, and it doesn't seem to be working. My head keeps telling me it's not like we were really lovers, but if that big lug buys the farm I just don't think I can handle it, Beth." She turned from the window and added, "I'm going to the front. Want to come along?"

"You're crazy, Ramie! How on earth would we get to Holland, even if they'd let us?"

"By jeep, of course. It's only about a hundred miles to the Belgian border and we ought to have no trouble getting at least as far as Antwerp."

"Like I said, crazy! It'd be dark by the time we made Antwerp and what are we supposed to do when we get there, Ramie? The fighting's way to the north."

"Come on, we'll wing it with our press passes.

That's if you want to come, of course. I can make it alone if I have to."

Beth looked disgusted and said, "No you can't. You'll need me to flirt with the MPs who like brunettes, and we can spell one another at the wheel. But you know you're not going to find out anything up there near the line that you can't get on the wire sooner here, don't you?"

"I know, Beth. But at least I'll be closer to him."

As the sun went down the sky stayed red over the sausage-shaped battlefield of Market Garden. Dry fields of hay and the heather of the higher moorlands burned under the low overcast, illuminating the Dutch countryside with the dull ruby glow of a photographer's dark room as the 101st dug in for the night. Here and there a brighter glow appeared on the flat horizon. German tanks burned for hours once the Allies managed to set one aflame. It was still up for grabs who controlled the crossings the 101st had landed between. Both Son Of A Bitch and Best Bet had been blown to their south. Flying concrete from the highway bridge at Best had killed or wounded troopers yards from capturing it when the Germans blew it up in their faces. But in the reasonably secure division HQ area only an occasional German shell landed close enough to worry anybody. The wounded off the lines were being tended in sandbagged tents. General Maxwell Taylor ducked under the blackout flap of the tent they said the officers were in and as a medic yelled attention the general said, "As you were. This is a dumb time to try and hit a brace."

There was a low weary chuckle from those wounded in the dimly lit tent who still knew what was going on around them. Taylor spotted a familiar figure on one cot and moved over to him. "Some guys will do anything to get out of KP. How's it going, Sam?"

"It only hurts when I laugh," said Colonel Sam Bell. "Honest to God, Max, have you ever heard of an old soldier like me getting hit by a lousy sniper? I'm so mad I could spit!"

"You ought to be ashamed, too," the general said, "What were you trying to prove, leading that patrol like a damned shave-tail?"

"Somebody had to do it, and I was shorthanded. I had my point men out, but that goddamn crazy Kraut in that tree was taking lessons from the Invisible Man."

"So I heard. Right now he's taking lessons on being dead. We're all shorthanded right now, Sam. So let's not ever do that again. You can consider that an order."

The general straightened up and raised his voice to be heard throughout the tent. "All right, men, here's the scoop on you casualties. Our perimeter's secure and we're expecting advance units of the British armor sometime tomorrow. They radio they've run into scattered resistance and have dug in for the night to move the rest of the way under air cover from those rocket-carrying Typhoons the Limeys like to use on the Krauts. Once the road south is clear we'll evacuate you guys to a field hospital near Paris. So practice up on your ooh-la-las, you lucky bastards!"

There was a chorus of laughter, some of it a little forced. Taylor turned back to Sam Bell. "You know your way around Paris from the last one, you sly old dog. The medics tell me that round you took through the chest didn't hit anything important. So if you don't catch VD in Paris I'll expect you back on the line in six or eight weeks. I'll light a candle in the window for you."

"Jesus, Max, I'm not hurt that bad. Damned sniper just knocked the wind out of me for a spell. Who the hell's watching my store while I'm laying here like a useless sack of shit?"

"Your adjutant, of course. Lieutenant Colonel Lansford's a good man and he's got sense enough to *really* mind the store instead of running up and down the firing line like a Boy Scout. Don't worry, I won't let him steal your job. There'll be plenty of room to promote him without giving him your regiment, at the rate things are going."

"Yeah, I was meaning to ask you about that, Max. How *are* things in tulip land, right now?"

Taylor shrugged and replied, "Beats me. I just heard on the radio that Monty says we're doing great. I don't know what the Brits and the Eighty-second are doing right now, but we seem to be holding our own in a Mexican stand-off. By the way, I'm going to write up your S2 officers for commendations. I guess I'll give your Major Bradley the Legion Of Merit, and Lieutenant Hunter out in the field rates at least a Bronze Star. They saved you guys here from having a lot of company tonight. The 501st set up a lovely tank trap in time to have roast Kraut for lunch!"

Sam Bell tried to sit up, gave it up as a bad idea, and blurted, "What the hell are you talking about, Max? I intend to press charges against that idiot Bradley if he ever shows up around here! I had some men from my reserve battalion looking for the clod to arrest him, but they report he never landed in any of our DZs this morning!"

The general frowned thoughtfully down at Bell.

"Bradley reported in this afternoon, after you were hit. His glider was shot down way off to the west. He worked his way through the Krauts to us on his own. I just finished thanking him for that tip-off on the tanks about to hit 501 on the flank. Their own I&R never spotted them in time, but your Hunter did, and that's all she wrote."

"I should think so! If Bradley had ordered those kids to drop any farther out they'd have been able to tell you what Hitler was eating for breakfast! I was going to have Bradley's ass for that boo-boo!"

General Taylor pursed his lips and said, "Let's back up and reconsider if it was a boo-boo, Sam. I asked Bradley about that when he reported in. I thought it was a pretty odd place to drop scouts too. But Bradley explained about the last-minute G2 tip he received on SS Panzer being somewhere around here, and you can't say his sixth sense didn't pay off!"

Bell grimaced and muttered, "Sixth sense or shit-house luck, you mean!"

"Whatever. The point is that Bradley dropped some scouts where they did us a lot of good. I know you think he's an ass, Sam. I've heard stories about your Danny Boy, too. But to give the devil his due, he made the right move and we'd look pretty silly court-martialing an officer who can produce the whole 501st as defense witnesses."

Bell shrugged with his one good shoulder and said, "Let's not cry over spilled scum, then. The one I'm worried about is Logan Hunter. Have he and his stick made it back yet?"

"Negative, Sam. I worry about good officers, too. So I've got a staff man keeping tabs on Hunter. When last heard from, he was trying to push north to fall in with the eighty-second. He and his men are smack out in the middle of Indian country with Krauts all around them. So he's headed for the high ground."

Sam Bell swore and said, "Christ, it'll take 'em all night to move that far even with nobody shooting at them. What's he running into up that way, Max?"

"Hopefully nothing. The last time Hunter spotted tanks he was able to get out of the way, and that was in broad daylight."

"They got tanks up near Nijmegen?"

Taylor nodded. "You can say that again. The Eighty-second's in worse shape than we are. They're dug in and are yelling for help, under fire from two SS Panzer divisions, Harzer's Ninth and Harmel's Tenth."

"They sound like the Bobbsey Twins. Does Logan Hunter know what he's heading into?"

"Negative. We lost radio contact with him this afternoon. It gets worse, Sam. Radio Orange just flashed us that their agents have spotted Knaust's outfit in the area. My enemy TO has Knaust leading those new Tiger tanks."

24

ALL ROADS LEADING to the front had been coded Red Ball for military traffic only. So Ramie Davis and Beth Waterman were stopped just south of the Belgian border and Ramie spent the next forty-eight hours in hell—or, to be more precise, a sad small French country inn that was doing a land-office business. Montgomery had allowed a British journalist named Alan Wood and a young American correspondent named Walter Cronkite to fly in with the airborne, and Cronkite had almost managed to get himself killed in a glider crash already, so no more correspondents were to go into the battle zone until further notice. Hence the small bar at the inn was crowded with news men and women who'd had the same idea as Ramie, although she doubted many were as emotionally involved with the outcome of Market Garden. The others were only worried about losing the war.

Beth had been right that they'd have been able to follow the battle better from the Paris UPI. News and latrine rumors filtered out of the armageddon to the north in dribs and drabs, wildly distorted. Ramie knew things were going badly when she picked up on the bickering between American and British commanders. The weather had turned bad. The sky was socked in under scattered showers and heavy overcast they all knew favored the Germans. Reinforcements and supplies had been dropped after the first landings on Market Garden D. But the rocket-launching Typhoons that were supposed to take care of German tanks were grounded. Ramie hoped those stories about the new German Tiger tanks were hyperbole. Somebody said the Irish Guards had pushed through at least as far as the 101st, but the main thrust of the combined Canadian and British armor seemed bogged down and the British airborne in Arnhem were yelling for help, loudly. They were surrounded by more Germans than Hitler was supposed to have left and the Germans were throwing ammo into the cut-off Red Devils like it was going out of style.

Beth wanted to return to Paris and at least read the newspapers. But Ramie refused to retreat now that she'd gotten this close to Logan Hunter—wherever in God's name Logan Hunter might be at the moment.

Then vehicles of the Irish Guards started coming back from the front with the wounded, both British and American. When Ramie heard some of the wounded were from the 101st she jumped in her jeep and chased the convey, leaving Beth to her own devices and a cute correspondent from the Manchester *Guardian*.

She caught up with the wounded from Hunter's outfit as they were being unloaded at a field hospital set up in Picardy, across the road from a U.S. military cemetery for the dead of World War One. As she parked her jeep Ramie wondered if this place had been selected with singular lack of sensitivity or pragmatic forethought. The crosses across the road stood stark and white, row on row. Under the occupation the Germans had evidently allowed the French caretakers to keep the grounds neat. Perhaps as a big game hunter keeps his trophies dusted.

The medics were too harassed to question Ramie's press pass and an orderly going somewhere else in a hurry pointed out the way to the ward tent she'd be looking for. Ramie moved down the long row of cots, trying to look invisible as she searched the faces of the wounded men. She asked a man with his leg in traction if he knew a Lieutenant Logan Hunter in the 101st. The wounded trooper shook his head, but said, "That's his CO three bunks over. He might know something."

Ramie made her way to Colonel Bell's side. She introduced herself to old Sam Bell, who said, "Logan didn't come down with us, honey. Are you his girl?"

Ramie hesitated. Then she nodded.

"I'm sorry to hear that," Bell replied, giving her a sympathetic smile. "You're too pretty to fall in love with paratroopers. He and his men were cut off from us while we were waiting for the Limeys to punch through. But the last I heard from the Eighty-second to our north, Logan had made it through to them in one piece. Don't ask me how. General Gavin had lost a couple of S2 officers by then, so he put your Logan to work on I&R with his forward units. He was with the Eighty-second when they grabbed the Nijmegen bridges. Don't ask me how they did that, either. I was talking to an Irish Guards officer in the ambulance coming down. Apparently some advance Guards units made it to the Eighty-second and they say crossing the Waal was a baby Omaha. But they did it."

"Then Logan's still alive!" she gasped, eyes welling with tears.

Sam Bell grimaced and said, "I knew you'd want all the military details. Yeah, the kid's still on his feet, last I heard. I take an interest in Logan Hunter too. His dad and me are old army buddies and I've got the rank to talk a lot on field phones. He was okay as of this afternoon. He's on the far side of the Waal, patroling for the Eighty-second."

"I don't understand," Ramie said, frowning. "Wasn't the bridge at Nijmegen the Eighty-second's objective, Colonel?"

"Those were the good old days. This is not for publication, but since you're his girl I'll trust you to keep a lid on it for now. Market Garden's turning out SNAFU. Somebody on our side screwed up or maybe Model's just a better general than Monty. Anyway, they gave us too much to do with not enough to do it with. 101 has secured their DZ and seems to be holding. Eighty-two is probably going to hold for now, but they've been shot up bad and things could go either way. The Red Devils in Arnhem are in big trouble."

"I heard some of that back at my inn, sir. But what have the British paratroopers to do with Logan and the American Eighty-second Airborne?"

"I wouldn't want this to get around, Miss Davis, but

the British are on our side. What's left of Eighty-two
and the Guards have been ordered to punch through
to Arnhem and see if they can bail the Red Devils out.
They're pinned down east of Arnem on the wrong
side of the Rhine. They're surrounded by heavy German armor and artillery and can't move anywhere on
their own right now. Some of the Free Polish Brigade's
in even worse shape. They dropped on our side of the
Rhine, which would have been better than it sounds
if they weren't cut off from the others. The Poles are
having a Little Big Horn at a place called Driel, so
somebody has to save them too."

"Oh, my God. And Logan and his men are out in
front of the rescue advance?"

"If they're still on their feet they are, Miss Davis.
I said I was sorry when you told me you were his
girl."

The German Tiger smashed through another hedgerow and waddled disdainfully across the open field,
leaving deep muddy ruts in the soft earth with its
wide-cleated tracks as it sniffed for prey with the muzzle of its long-barreled 88. Its crew knew they didn't
have to worry about anything Tommie and Amie had
in this part of Holland, or anywhere else for that
matter. There wasn't an Allied tank that could stand
up to a Tiger's heavy armor and deadly turret gun,
and with the steady drizzle from the sky they didn't
have to worry about planes.

The gun crew could fire that big 88 as flat as a rifle
and they were ready to do so at anything they could
spot. But they didn't spot Hunter and his four other
men as the I&R patrol lay flat in a weed-filled ditch to
let them pass.

As the Tiger rumbled on, Cohen raised his head

from the radio he'd been trying to stick it inside and marveled, "Kee-rist! What was that?"

"It wasn't the Chattanooga Choo Choo," Hunter said. "See if you can raise the Irish Guards. If that town over there is Eist, some light British armor could be in for big trouble."

Cohen nodded and started searching for the right frequency as another trooper asked, "How come we're spotting for the Limeys now, sir?"

It was a stupid question. But Hunter had sent the best recruits on the other diamond patrol under Arnold. "Two reasons," he explained. "Those Krauts are out to shoot anybody who speaks English, and that light British armor is all the armor we've got. The Guards lost a lot of point men getting this far north and somebody'd better tell them about that Tiger. How are we coming, Cohen?"

Cohen said, "I'm on the Guards' frequency, sir. So far all I hear is some guy with a Cockney accent telling me to fuck myself."

Hunter took the hand set and gave his code ID, adding, "You don't have to believe I'm real, Guards. Just keep an eye peeled for heavy stuff coming at you down the Island Highway! Over."

There was a moment of silence before a dry British voice said, "And I'm the Airy Fairy, Jerry! Stuff a sock in it. You're not fooling us with that phoney Yank accent! Over and out, you sod!"

One of the men gasped, "Jesus! Down!" as another Tiger came into view, and then another. Hunter lay flat in the wet grass, keeping his voice down as well when he thumbed the sending switch and said, "Red alert, repeat red alert and this is no drill! This is Lieutenant Logan Hunter of the 101st and I'm speaking to you from beautiful downtown Eist. A whole fucking panzer column is moving in between my position and yours and their 88s are pointed your way! Over!"

There was no answer. Hunter looked bleakly at Cohen, who muttered, "Dumb Limey bastards must have knocked off for tea, sir."

"Here come more tanks," someone said.

"I can hear. Don't anybody move," Hunter replied.

"We can't stay here, sir! We're out in the fucking open!"

"No we're not. We're in a ditch, and they haven't spotted us. Jump up to run and you'll catch an 88 round in your hip pocket, Bronson! Pike, your ass is sticking up. Flatten out, damn it!"

"I'm flat as I can get, Lieutenant! I just naturally come with a big rump!"

Hunter grinned despite the situation. "Take a deep breath then. Heads down. Here comes another Tiger."

One of the men was whimpering like a kicked dog as the ground under them quivered like the floorboards of a Model A with a shot transmission. Hunter was feeling nervous in the service, too. But those Irish Guards moving up the highway to Arnhem were in bigger trouble than he was right now.

Hunter didn't know at the time why the tankers were ignoring all radio messages from people they hadn't gone to school with. Later a lot of armchair generals were going to fault the British Command for issuing such orders. But the airways were cluttered with helpful hints from all sorts of people right now. English-speaking Dutchmen, and/or Germans, were sending messages like, "Tommy! Tommy! The ferry across the Waal at Driel is clear! Why don't you seize it, Tommy?" There was just no way to tell friend from foe.

Sure, the legitimate Dutch underground had code

names to identify themselves, if a harassed lower-level radio man had a code book, but even then one couldn't be sure. A supposed loyal Dutchman code-named King Kong had betrayed his country and Market Garden to the Germans on the first day of the operation and if Monty and Prince Bernhard ever got their hands on King Kong they were going to throw him off the Empire State Building. But meantime nobody was paying much attention to radio messages from the people they didn't know. Some British and American units had already been ambushed that way.

Meanwhile Hunter had his own people to worry about. He started to reach for the map and compass in his side pocket, but he already knew the gross details. He and his half of the stick lay in a drainage ditch running east and west. They were west of the north-south highway between Arnhem and Nijmegen. The tanks had busted through the hedges on the far side of the road to swing south and he couldn't see what, if anything, was following them. There was no cover within a hundred yards of his ditch across the open fallow fields. It was starting to rain harder but visibility was still too good for hundred-yard dashes with possible skirmishing Krauts over there in those goddamn bushes the tanks had burst out of. Sergeant Arnold had to be somewhere to their north and since Hunter couldn't see them, the Germans probably couldn't either. So Arnold could worry about his own ass for now.

Hunter gingerly rose on one stiff arm for a quick look around. Whoever had named this the Low Country hadn't been kidding around. He could see a factory chimney and a haze of smoke from somebody burning trash to his north. The country was more built up this close to the Rhine, but they seemed to be stuck in some sort of green belt south of the industrial zone along the river. Arnold didn't have a radio. Arnold was supposed to be covering down on his leader. But they hadn't been in contact for over an hour and if Hunter pulled out and Arnold didn't know it, the sergeant and his four men would be on their own, six or seven miles north of where the front had been the last time they'd been able to check.

A half track filled with German armored infantry waddled out on the road to swing south after the Tigers. Hunter waited until they were out of sight before he said, "Okay, men, it's creepy-crawly time. Macy, you're point. We'll slither west along this ditch for the cover of that board fence a quarter mile off. Pike, you bring up the rear and keep that big ass down."

"I can't move, sir," Macy whimpered.

"What do you mean you can't move? You haven't been hit and this is a hell of a time to be having the baby! Those Krauts come in sets, Macy. We've got to get the hell clear of that highway before some wise-ass infantry pops out of the bushes at us! Those panzer units are running eager, so they're out ahead of their infantry support right now. But trust me, you'll see some SS on foot around her pronto. So move it out!"

Macy's face was the color of a frog's belly and despite the chill drizzle he was sweating as he shook his head and said, "I can't move, Lieutenant. My legs feel like somebody sucked all the meat out of them. I can't even wiggle my toes . . ."

Cohen, who read *Stars And Stripes*, muttered, "Combat Fatigue."

Hunter unslung his carbine, placed the muzzle against Macy's side, and said, "Okay, Bronson, take the point. Macy and I will follow you. Right, Macy?"

"Please, sir," Macy pleaded, "just let me stay here. I'm just not able to go on. I must be paralyzed or something."

"I'll paralyze you, you asshole! If we leave you here you'll be killed or captured. I'm not as worried about you getting killed as I am about the Krauts taking you alive. If I want them to have my name, rank and serial number I'll give it to them personally. Let's go, Macy."

"I can't move my legs, sir!"

"So, drag 'em, you dumb bastard! I'm not kidding, Macy. If you don't knock this bullshit off I'll leave you here with a bullet in you. I'm not about to leave you here *alive!*"

Macy licked his lips. He made an attempt to roll over but then went limp again and helplessly shook his head.

Cohen whispered, "He's shell shocked, sir."

"Shut up," Hunter growled. "You're a radio man, not a medic. Let's go, Macy."

Macy started to cry. Hunter already had a round in the chamber, but he threw the bolt, ejecting a little .30 to emphasize his point. Macy gasped and suddenly came unstuck to crawl after Bronson along the soggy ditch.

Hunter picked up the still good round and pocketed it as he started crawling after them. Cohen followed, packing the R-300 as he marveled, "Jesus, he was bluffing!"

Hunter didn't answer. He knew poor Macy hadn't been faking his combat fatigue. He'd just needed something more frightening than the Krauts to snap him out of it, for now. Hunter knew the youth could freeze up again if things got rugged. So that meant

Macy couldn't be on point or anywhere else important. They were down to three men and a question mark.

They were almost to the end of the open field when Hunter heard the flat roar of an 88 to his left. A British four-pounder crumped down to geyser muddy earth and sods from the open ground just south of the ditch and Hunter muttered, "You're firing too high, you dumb Limey bastard!"

By the time they reached the fence line, the rain and British shell fire was coming down harder as the tank battle to their south heated up. The ditch ran through a gap in the board fence. So Hunter ordered his men through and rose to his feet for a quick look around.

His view to the south was blocked by more hedges, but something was burning under an oily smoke plume down that way and the woodpecker snarl of a heavy machine gun punctuated the remarks of German 88s and the less powerful British guns. Another shell intended for a Tiger landed too close for comfort and Hunter dove through the gap to flatten out in the wet grass among his men.

"Jesus, why are they shooting at *us*, sir?" Bronson gasped.

"They're not. They're shooting at the Krauts, only the Krauts are between us and our lines. Make for that factory chimney to our north, Bronson."

"Won't that take us toward the Rhine, sir?"

"I sure hope so. Move it out, Bronson!"

They headed north, hugging the fence line as they moved in a low crouch. A farmhouse that looked like it belonged with the fence stood burned to a ruined shell up ahead. As they neared it, Hunter called ahead,

"Check those ruins, Bronson. We'll cover you from here."

"Thanks a lot," Bronson muttered. He peeled away from the fence line to dash over to the nearest open window. A helmeted figure appeared in the window, aiming a carbine as Bronson dove headfirst in the wet grass, yelling, "GI! GI!" The other paratrooper held his fire.

As Bronson got back up, Sergeant Arnold came around the corner of the ruins from the far side and gave the all-clear signal. Hunter jogged over to him and snapped, "Report!"

"Private Green and me are all that's left, Lieutenant," Arnold said, "We stumbled into some SS and the others didn't make it. Neither did the SS. We nailed eight of the bastards, over on the road."

"Is that where you left your dead?"

"Yessir. We didn't have time to mark them. But they're within sight of the road if graves ever makes it up this far."

Hunter moved over to the fence and peered through a gap toward the road. Nothing. All he could see was marigolds. Acres and acres of marigolds. Folks sure picked pretty places to die around here.

He turned back to Arnold and the others. "Okay, we have to get out of range before friendly fire or some more unfriendly SS lands on us. We're about three miles south-southeast of the Rhine crossing at Diel. That looks like our best bet. You and Green fall in with us, Arnold. We're making a nice uncomplicated run for it."

Arnold frowned and said, "The Rhine's eleven miles north of Nijmegen, sir."

"I know that, damn it. Do you want to move south into that tank battle?"

"No, sir. But ain't there a mess of Krauts to the north of us too?"

"To the east and west too. But Major General Sosabowski's Polish Brigade is supposed to be in Diel and I can't think of anyplace better to go, can you?"

"I guess not, sir. But ain't the Poles supposed to be surrounded by the Krauts?"

"Everybody's surrounded by the Krauts. Bronson, take the point again. Let's move it out, men."

They started north, away from the devil they knew in favor of the one who didn't seem to be aiming at them right now. They came to a cinder path and another hedgerow. Bronson scouted it and they moved on. A big Horsa glider lay out in the field to their left flank, crushed like a match box some giant had stepped on. Bloated bodies in British battle dress lay scattered across the emerald green grass like discarded toy soldiers. In a way Hunter supposed they were.

Arnold, trudging at his side, wrinkled his nose and said, "Jesus, they must have bought it the first day, the way they smell. How long's it been, now, Lieutenant?"

"Four or five days. Who counts?"

"I do, sir. I don't know why, but I've always liked to count things. You know, counting the two Krauts on D day I've killed seven guys so far?"

"Goody for you. Stick with me and you may get a baker's dozen."

"I hope so, sir. I sure don't want to have to tell my grandchildren it was seven. They'd think I was full of it, like the Brave Little Tailor. I mean, seven sounds like a guy made it up, see?"

Hunter didn't see. "Tell 'em you nailed eight then.

Eight's a nice authentic-sounding score, Arnold."

"That would be lying, sir. I mean, what's the point of having stories to tell if you're gonna lie?"

"Jesus H. Christ, Arnold, they didn't drop us in this mess to gather material for our memoirs! Stop counting and start looking. You'd better drop back with Pike to cover our rear. He's sort of new at this."

As Arnold fell back Hunter glanced over at the nearby Cohen. "Want me to spell you with the radio pack, Cohen?"

Cohen shook his head. "I'm okay, sir. Do you think Sergeant Arnold is nuts?"

"Why, do you?"

"I'm not sure, sir. I heard Sergeant Falco telling him he was nuts one day. Falco thinks it's nuts to keep counting dead Krauts. He called Arnold Wild Bill Hickock and stuff like that. Some of the other guys think Arnold's sort of trigger happy."

"I don't like that kind of talk behind a man's back, Cohen. Arnold jumped with me in Normandy, which is more than a lot of people can say. For the record, Sergeant Arnold did all right in Normandy, and today he just came through a fire fight in one piece."

"Yessir. *He* did. I'm still glad I was with you and not him when those Krauts came at *us* back there!"

Hunter told him to knock it off, but as they moved on Hunter wondered if Arnold could have avoided the brush with the SS patrol. No patrols on either side were sent out with orders to fight, if they didn't have to. He knew it was a waste of time to ask Arnold if there hadn't been any way to avoid that skirmish. Arnold had obviously thought he and the men under him had to fight, and it was over now, with three dead paratroopers to show for it.

What was all that crap about wanting to tell stories

to his grandchildren? Arnold wasn't even married yet, for God's sake. Hunter knew his own father could have told some lulus about the First World War, but dad had never talked about it much. Hunter wondered how many Krauts his father had killed in that other war, not far from here. Had he killed any at all? What did it matter now? Some of the Germans dad hadn't killed had gone home to father sons of their own, and Hunter had no great desire to meet any of the bastards right now.

25

AT HIS COMMAND post in Brussels Prince Bernhard of the Netherlands was trying to get Monty on the phone. But although Montgomery's Twenty-first Army Group HQ was just up the road Monty wasn't taking calls. He said he was busy. Prince Bernhard was beginning to know why the American general, George Patton, had to be kept away from meetings Monty attended. Everybody kept saying Montgomery was a military genius. Bernhard certainly didn't think of himself as a military genius, but it was his country they were setting on fire, damn it. The least they could do would be to tell him what the hell was going on!

Unlike the Allied High Command, Prince Bernhard listened to the radio reports being sent by his Dutch underground, and they were getting more ominous by

321

the hour. The Germans were already mopping up some freedom fighter kommandos who'd jumped the gun in the first enthusiasm of the massive landings. Now it seemed the British tankers had stopped south of Eist for tea.

And why had the three airborne assaults been so widely spaced in the first place? Prince Bernhard was humble about his modest military education, although he'd received more than a lot of men commanding soldiers in the fields of his homeland at the moment. He didn't consider himself fit to command an airborne division, but he did know his country, and Montgomery had brushed aside suggestions by the prince and other Dutch leaders on the best places to drop. The prince stared morosely out the window at the darkening sky. He knew his Holland's climate too, and could see a North Sea fog was going to blanket the battle zone by morning.

At SHEAF General Eisenhower was better informed about a lot of things than Prince Bernhard. But Monty wouldn't take his calls either. The normally amiable Ike was white-lipped with repressed anger as he studied the acetate overlay of Market Garden. The engineers had run baily bridges across at Son and the Nijmegen Bridge had been taken intact. So why in God's name couldn't those effing tanks push through to the Arnhem Bridgehead? Poor Roy Urquhart had just reported that his Red Devils were taking a hell of a pounding and that they couldn't hold out much longer. The British airborne had been under constant fire for five days now, and aside from the ghastly casualty figures they were running low on ammo. Attempts to drop supplies had gone badly, with more than half the supplies falling behind the German lines, to be gleefully fired into General Urquhart's positions along the Rhine.

Ike had also heard stories about the British tankers stopping beside the road for tea, so when an aide said, "I have Montgomery on the line now, General," Ike's voice was uncharacteristically testy as he grabbed the phone and snapped, "Report!"

A haughty voice replied, "Montgomery here, old boy."

"I know who you are. I've been trying to reach you for hours! What the hell's going on to your north, Monty? You were supposed to be on the Rhine by now!"

"I know, but not to worry, everything's going according to plan."

"Whose plan, yours or Field Marshal Model's? Our kids are getting the shit kicked out of them, Monty! Both the American divisions report casualties I'm never going to explain to Washington and your Urquhart's about to be wiped out any minute!"

"Well, when one makes an omelet, as they say . . . German casualties are very heavy too, you know."

"I don't know. The Dutch underground reports bumper-to-bumper reinforcements streaming in from Germany!"

"Piffle. Jerry's scraping the bottom of his barrel and throwing in cooks and clerks in desperation."

Ike took a deep breath. "Goddamn it, the Germans aren't the only ones who're getting desperate! You still haven't told me where your tanks are, Monty!"

"Well, we seem to have a bit of a snag south of Eist and some heavy panzer is dug in at Oosterhout. My tanks will probably be harboring for the night just north of Nijmegen."

Eisenhower consulted his map and swore. "Monty, your tanks are less than twelve miles south of the Rhine. Can't you punch through?"

"With darkness about to fall? Unthinkable. Can't order one of those gallant charge-of-the-Light-Brigade things this late in the game. We've, ah, taken more losses from those heavy German Tigers than I first allowed for. Perhaps if I could borrow the U.S. Second Armor from your reserves their heavier Shermans could move a bit faster."

Ike's voice went icy calm as he said, "I know this will come as a shock to you, but Market Garden's not the only battle going on in the ETO at the moment. The Second Armor isn't in reserve. It's out killing Krauts between you and the Ninth U.S."

"Oh? Pity. We'll just have to muddle through, I suppose."

Dwight David Eisenhower was normally considered too good-hearted to be a general, but on rare occasions he could turn to granite. Both the flamboyant Patton and the egotistical Montgomery had locked horns with him in the past and discovered to their chagrin that one couldn't really win against a four-star general if he really meant it. So Montgomery knew Ike meant it when he quietly said, "You have until the 25th. That's twice the time you said Market Garden would take."

"I say, Ike. I can't promise a victory by the 25th."

"Who's worried about a victory? I'm thinking of those kids on the ground over there! I doubt like hell Urquhart can hold out at Arnhem that long, but my Eighty-second and 101st can probably hold through this weekend. After that we'll have to cut our losses and pull our finger out of the dike."

"I say, you can't order a withdrawal, Ike!"

"Sure I can. I wear four stars. I don't like retreating any more than you do. But an orderly withdrawal beats a total disaster, and that's what Market Garden is starting to look like!"

As the sun went down Hunter and his men were huddled in a highway culvert south of Driel. Not to get out of the rain but because a German column of armored infantry was using the road right now. The wet walls of the culvert shuddered as the half tracks rumbled over their heads. A man started to say something and Hunter kicked him, brutally, to shut him up. He didn't have to be told they'd be caught like rats in a trap if the Krauts found out they were in here. They'd have been in worse shape if Trooper Pike hadn't spotted the scouts coming up the road behind them on motorbikes before the German point spotted them in open ground.

By the time it was quiet again it was starting to get dark outside. Fog was drifting across the battlefield and things were looking up. If they couldn't see much of anything as they moved out, much of anything wouldn't see them. Hunter slid to the mouth of the culvert, his movements stiff. He was chilled to the bone. He told the others to stay put while he scouted their advance a ways. They'd been following a cinder path beside the highway. There had to be a better way.

Hunter cut away from the highway across a field of wheat stubble. Despite the damp the brittle straw crunched under his boots, as if he was walking over a vast wet welcome mat. But the wheat field hadn't been spread in welcome for the Red Devils who'd come down around here a few days ago. The stubble was pocked by shell craters and the debris of battle.

Abandoned parachute harnesses and empty supply crates lay scattered across the field. He saw a Sten gun clip someone had emptied. A rifle with a British paratrooper's helmet on its stock stood upright near what what looked like a garbage pile. As he moved closer he saw that some of the discarded gear included a swollen corpse in a British jump suit.

"Sorry, guy," he muttered, and moved on. He got to the far side of the field, pushed through waist-high hedges and found himself on a narrow cinder path leading north and south. He nodded and said, "This must be the place." He turned to go back to his men. Then he froze as he heard the sound of a vehicle breaking to a stop on the road over there. Why had they stopped and what was he supposed to do about it?

A million years seemed to pass as he waited for something to happen. Then a German Schmeiser cleared its throat and a big ball of fire rose from his last position, at the culvert. Hunter gagged, "Oh, Jesus!" as he realized what it was. Men were screaming mindlessly as the flame thrower hosed into the culvert at them. Somebody must have made it out the far side, because the submachine gun hammered again in a long burst. Then it got very quiet for another million years as Hunter squatted behind the bushes, heaving but unable to throw up his bile. In the distance someone laughed good-naturedly and called out something in German.

Hunter started running, trying to keep his head below the level of the hedge between him and the German mop-up unit. He realized he was running in blind panic when he tripped over something on the path and sprawled headlong, skinning his palm. He rolled over and looked back to see another swollen corpse in Red Devil kit sprawled across the path. He retched, got to his feet and moved on, under control again, but having no idea at all where he was going, and feeling very, very alone.

Not far to the south a red-faced officer from the Eighty-second was shouting at an officer of the Second Household Cavalry as the latter sat on the hood of his Leyland, heels hooked on the bumper winch, sipping not tea but hot chocolate. The paratrooper was yelling, "You can't harbor for the right now, goddamn it! Those are your own fellow Englishmen up ahead, Major!"

"Orders," the Englishman said. "Can't press on in this fog without heavy infantry support, you know."

"I said I'd *give* you some infantry support, damn it! What do you call my troopers, the Royal Ballet?"

"They're not royal anything. No offense, but you chaps don't know our drill. We started out with some jolly good British Infantry, but we seem to have lost them along the way. Can't advance until replacements get here. Hopefully by morning, what?"

The American shook his head. "You silly prick! It's no wonder you needed us to bail you out of this war! There's a whole division of British soldiers cut off up ahead and nobody seems to be worried about them but us Yanks!"

The Englishman swallowed a thoughtful sip of chocolate before he said, "I don't remember seeing any of you lot about while we stood alone against them for nearly three years."

"Don't give me that shit. I jumped on D day and I just lost a lot of good men here in Holland too!"

The Englishman's voice was calm as he replied, "Before I waste this perfectly good cup by dashing it in your bloody face, perhaps I'd better advise you that I lost some men today too. Before that I lost a mother in the blitz. I shan't go into what I might have done before America saw fit to join us, but my oldest brother died as a commando at Dieppe a year ago and my youngest brother is presently serving with the Red Devils up the road in Arnhem."

The American officer blanched. "Okay, if I was out of line I apologize. But damn it, Major, those guys in Arnhem are in real trouble!"

"I know. We're all in trouble. Can't you see this offensive isn't working the way it was supposed to? My men and I were supposed to be on the Rhine two days ago at the very latest."

"Okay. When do you think your tankers will make it?"

The Englishman finished his cup with a grimace of distaste and answered bleakly. "I doubt if we'll get through at all. But as soon as it's light enough to see again, we'll have to try."

Hunter didn't know the password to give Sosabowski's pickets and the Poles didn't speak enough English to straighten it out right away, but fortunately they decided to capture Hunter instead of shooting him.

They marched him through the ruins of Driest with his hands over his head until a Polish officer recognized his uniform and took him to the CP after giving him back his weapons and wristwatch.

General Stanislaw Sosabowski was a tough-looking middle-aged man who sort of looked like Attila the Hun wearing a red beret. He beamed at Hunter until he found out Hunter didn't seem to have any American troops behind him. Then he sighed and said, "You can call me Stosh anyway, Lieutenant. You say tank battle was in Eist?"

"Not in Eist itself, sir. A couple of miles south of Eist, from the sound of it."

Sosabowski turned wearily to a map hung on the battered wall and muttered to himself in Polish. Then he said, in English, "I don't understand it. The tanks can't be more than six or seven miles from here. Yet you say you saw Tigers earlier today. We can't hold out here much longer. You just saw how easy it is to get through my thin lines."

"I got through some German lines too, sir. I infiltrated between some field artillery and what seemed to be an infantry outfit dug in maybe a mile south."

"I have them on map, here. They may hit us at daybreak. They may just let their big guns pound us a while. They know who we are and they expect us to surrender."

"Are you going to surrender, sir?"

"Don't talk stupid . . . This is D-6, right?"

"I think so, sir. Does it matter?"

"Yes. I'm not supposed to know it, but SHAEF is—how you say—throwing in the towel. You are S2 officer. Look at map and tell me what you think."

Hunter stepped closer and repressed a grimace as he saw the latest blue marks surrounded by so much red. Driel was inside a little blue circle. On the far side of the Rhine a larger blue horseshoe had been drawn west of Arnhem, with its open end against the river. "I thought General Urquhart's Red Devils were holding the town itself, sir."

"Hah, that was ages ago. The Germans have pushed them west almost to due north of us. There are no bridges. German shells have destroyed the ferry. But if we can hold here, men who swim good may have a chance. At least we are on the same side of river as tanks, see?"

Hunter whistled softly. "That's a pretty hairy way to cross a river, General."

"I know. Maybe they can scrape up some boats, like at Dunkerque. That is what Market Garden is turning out to be. Is hairy, as you say, for Urquhart to stay north of Rhine. Forgive Polish writing, but that red arrow up there is the Ninth SS Panzer and more is coming. Do you swim good, Lieutenant?"

"Swim, sir?"

"In water, splash splash like duck, only more quiet because Germans have Rhine zeroed in. I have plan. Too risky to send by radio, now that we know Model has our code and battle plans."

"Model has *what*, General?"

"Everything. Code books, battle plans, everything. Some crazy nut on our side landed with briefcase the Germans captured. But we have spies too. A Dutch Captain Penseel with the underground tipped us off by wireless this morning. Is a little late to make up new codes, but at least we know better than to drop any more information in Model's lap."

"I see. You want a courier who can memorize your plan in English and get over to First Airborne with it, right, sir?"

Sosabowski nodded. "Exactly, and you are going to have to argue like crazy in English too, Lieutenant. General Urquhart outranks us both and is stubborn Scotchman. But if he stays on that side of Rhine he and his men are going to be wiped out, whether the tanks reach me or not!"

26

B Y THAT WEEKEND Ramie Davis and Beth Waterman had finally bulldozed their way through as
far as Brussels. But nobody at Montgomery's
GHQ would tell them anything either. Ambulances
were coming south more often now, and Ramie made
a pest of herself every time she heard they were
carrying men from the 101st.

There were so many casualties from the 101st, and
many of them weren't just wounded. They were
coming down from Eindhoven wrapped in canvas,
some draped over fenders like deer in the hunting
season back home. Ramie couldn't possibly check out
all the dead and wounded, but she kept asking anyone who'd talk to her if they knew Logan Hunter from
S2 until at last a nice Sergeant Falco, sitting with his

arm in a sling by the English driver, told her she was wasting her time.

"He ain't with any of these guys from Eindhoven, miss. Last we heard he was somewhere north of Nijmegen, scouting for the Eighty-second."

"I know," Ramie said, "but some of the men I've seen have been wearing the Double A of the Eighty-second, Sergeant."

"He still ain't coming down this road, miss. Nobody hit north of the Waal is, and nobody's getting hit south of the Waal no more. They've evacuated the wounded from Nijmegen for now."

Ramie's stomach tightened in fear as she licked her lips and asked, "What about the dead, Sergeant?"

Falco shrugged. "I wouldn't know. Graves has hauled a lot in off the line."

"But not all, Sergeant?"

"They can't *get* to some guys, miss. But the Limeys tell me the Krauts have been pretty decent about that. Kraut graves will wire us a list, after. But, hey, what are we talking about? The Kraut ain't been born that can nail the lieutenant. He'll be okay, miss."

Falco's ambulance started with a jolt before Ramie could answer. So she just answered Falco's cheerful wave with one of her own, biting her lip. Another load of wounded troopers went by and someone whistled at her. What was the matter with those kids? Didn't they know there was a war on?

Falco had hardly reassured her, but she saw she was wasting her time by the side of the road, so she went back to join Beth in the improvised press center set up in a Belgian hotel bar. The bar was crowded with other correspondents and someone had installed a bank of field phones. As Ramie joined Beth, Beth said, "Nothing. Monty keeps releasing the same old garbage about everything going according to plan."

"I just saw some of his plan on their way to the hospital or another poppy field. I wonder where they got that guff about the poppies growing row on row? I haven't seen a poppy yet."

"It's not the poppies that grow row on row. It's the crosses. The poppies are supposed to grow between them. Only that's in the spring and this is fall."

Ramis shuddered. "They'll have poppies in the spring, then. Some of us won't be Home Alive in Forty-five after all."

A man from the BBC who'd been buying drinks for Beth came over to them, holding a sheet of foolscap. "I say, Beth, didn't you say you knew an Admiral Kane, RN?"

"We both do. Why?"

"Odd item I just picked up. Royal Marines and Commando Units seem to be getting into Market Garden. Damned if I can see how they fit in."

Ramie looked bleak as she said, "I can. Market Garden's taking to the life boats."

The BBC man frowned and said, "Monty hasn't said anything about pulling out. He seems to be under the impression we're winning."

Ramie shrugged and didn't answer. "Monty would have been issuing those same releases if he'd been with Cornwallis at Yorktown," Beth commented. "I don't think he likes to admit mistakes."

"Oh, I say, Market Garden can't be considered a mistake, as such," the BBC man protested. "Perhaps a bit more than we should have bitten off, but if the German Fifteenth Army hadn't gotten away and if we'd known the Germans still had that many men in Holland and if—"

"If the dog hadn't stopped to sniff it would have caught the rabbit!" Ramie suddenly snapped. Then, mortified at her loss of control, she turned to dash outside again.

"I say, what's gotten into her?" the BBC man asked Beth. "His name is Logan Hunter and he's an S2 lieutenant and he hasn't gotten into her at all, poor thing."

Outside, Ramie lit a cigarette as she stared dully at the passing traffic. A jeep braked to a dusty stop and she heard her name being called.

It was Dan Bradley. The major was on the passenger side of a battered funny-looking jeepish vehicle. As Ramie stepped over to it Bradley grinned and asked, "How do you like my new flivver? We liberated it from the Krauts. The hood's supposed to slant like that. It's a pretty good little car, but now that I've painted its cross out everybody thinks I've been in a wreck."

"Dan, have you seen Logan?" Ramie asked.

Even Bradley had some sensitivity, so he sobered as he shook his head and said, "Not since we took off, honey. He completed the mission I assigned him, but he wound up cut off and had to work his way north."

"Your Colonel Bell told me that back in the Ice Age, Dan. Hasn't there been any news of him since?"

"Hey, no news is good news in Market Garden, Ramie. Everything you hear lately seems to be lousy. I'm on my way to help set up new quarters for the staff in France. I volunteered."

He caught the look on her face and added, "Don't say it. I was under more fire coming down the road than the guys dug in around Eindhoven. "We're holding the roads south of Nijmegen, on paper, but it's cannon to the right of you, cannon to the left of you, like the poem says."

"So you're pulling out?"

"Yeah, and it ain't easy. Looks like most of the Limeys are there to stay. The Household Cav punched through as far as Driel and that's all she wrote. The tanks couldn't get across the river."

"So it's a failure?"

"You could call it that. Disaster is the word you're groping for, doll. We have to go. You want a ride back to France?"

"No. But wait! Colonel Bell said Logan might be with the Eighty-second, Dan. Will they be evacuating down this road?"

"Guess so. It's the only way out and they're rolling us up like a toothpaste tube. I've really gotta go, babe. Maybe I'll take you to Maxim's when we all wind up in Paris, right?"

She didn't answer and he didn't argue. As he drove away Ramie moved to a press jeep parked near the hotel entrance and leaned against it, puffing nervously on her cigarette while she stared at the passing traffic. It was getting heavier even as she watched. A defeated army was passing in review, British and American all mixed up together. How was she going to pick out one face from all those others?

The only advantage she had was that the traffic was crawling; the road from the front had been narrow to begin with and the heavy armor had made a mess of the paving. As an ambulance crawled by she saw a man wearing a red beret riding on the fender, hanging on with his good hand. She ran to catch up, and as she jogged along beside the ambulance she called out, "Are you with the First Airborne?"

The British paratrooper said, "I used to be, love.

There ain't no bloody First Airborne now. My lot made it to the Poles in Driel. But the lads we left north of the bloody Rhine have had it."

"I'm looking for an American officer named Logan Hunter."

"Coo, we was all looking for the ruddy Yanks, but they never made it to us. Sosabowski's engaged in a fighting retreat alongside the Household Guards. Ain't seen many Yanks. They must have run out of Coca Cola, the sods!"

A Red Devil she caught up with an hour later was less critical of his allies but not much more helpful. He was a young officer riding in a jeep with a British tanker and a couple of men from the American Eighty-second. They were bottlenecked in the horrendous traffic south, so Ramie didn't have to run alongside as he answered her desperate questions. "There were *some* Yanks as far north as Driel, miss," he said. "Stragglers from the mess around Nijmegen. The name Hunter doesn't come to mind, though. One might say things are a bit confused to the north at the moment."

One of the men from the Eighty-second said, "You can call it a total SNAFU if you want to be accurate. When we left it all hinged on whether Eighty-two can hold the crossing at Nijmegen until the Poles and some of these other First Airborne who made it back across the river make it. The Arnhem survivors are sort of climbing over Kraut panzer between us and them, but it'll be dark soon, so what the hell."

Ramie turned to the British tanker, but she saw he was staring owlishly right through her. The Red Devil nodded and said, "Shell shock. They asked me to look after him."

Ramie thanked the boys—for anyone younger than

she was had to be a boy—and went back inside. "I'm taking the jeep," she told Beth. "The lane to the front isn't crowded now. Want to come along?"

Beth looked aghast. Then as Ramie turned dully from her, Beth said, "Oh, hell, wait for me. Somebody has to look after you until you start making sense again!"

Logan Hunter and a British paratrooper whose name didn't seem important were sharing a shell hole surrounded by cattails as the sun went down. They were in water up to their hips, for the shell hole was on the mud flats of the lower Rhine. The Red Devil had been hit in the upper left arm with a mortar fragment the day before and it was starting to fester, but he still considered himself lucky when he thought about the rest of his squad. Hunter was finding it hard to think at all. The sun was setting on the eighth day of Operation Market Garden and he'd had maybe three or four hours sleep in all that time. None at all for the past twenty-four hours. He didn't know where they were or what was going on. He'd lost track of the two Poles he'd crossed the river with on that improvised raft the other night. He'd forgotten how he'd wound up on the firing line instead of leading survivors back across the river as he'd planned. He decided he must have volunteered. Nobody around here seemed to be issuing orders that made sense.

It didn't get very dark as the sun went down. Things were burning all around them and the Krauts were firing star shells to light up the river and its banks in eerie chalk-white flare-glow. Somewhere to their east a British Brengun was chatting about the war with a German MG-43. The heavy Brengun growled deep in its throat and the MG-43 snarled with a higher pitched and faster stream of fire, as if it was trying to imitate one of Hitler's speeches. They both winced as somebody yanked a zipper across the sky above them and the Britisher muttered, "88."

Hunter wondered what else was new.

Hunter reached for a smoke. Then he remembered he was out of cigarettes. He would have been out of carbine ammo too, if he'd had his carbine. But he'd lost track of the damned thing after that Screaming Mimi blew him flat back there. He didn't remember crawling away from that position, but he must have, because he was somewhere else now. He still had his pistol. He didn't know what the hell he was supposed to do with it, but he still had it. He drew it and checked the chamber. It was loaded. How about that?

The other man in the soggy hole with him asked, "What's up, Yank?"

Hunter looked dully at him and said, "Nothing. Just wanted to make sure my gun was loaded, like the song says."

"Are you all right, Yank?"

"Sure. In a minute I'm going to say the magic word and turn into Captain Marvel. You see, I'm not really the crippled newsboy everybody thinks I am. I can turn into a big tough bastard in red underwear and fly, if things get really tough."

The Red Devil laughed hollowly. "Right. I read comic books too. You don't have any more practical suggestions, do you?"

"I don't even remember how to turn into Captain Marvel. This mud flat just gets soggier as it runs west and I sure as shit can't see going east."

"You look strong, Yank. Think you could swim the river?"

"Maybe. Could you?"

"Not with this arm. But *you* could try."

Hunter shook his head. "Fuck it. We get out together or we don't get out, right?"

"Garn, you don't owe me, Yank. We're not even from the same mob," the Red Devil said, staring at him in open amazement.

"That's where you're wrong, Limey. Everybody around here who's not a Kraut is in the same outfit tonight."

"You're all right, Yank. By the way, I'm Tom Wilson, Sapper, Airborne Engineers."

"Logan Hunter. First Lieutenant, 101st Airborne."

"Coo, you're a flaming officer?"

"Don't sweat it, Tom. I'm not a very good officer. Lost every fucking man I jumped with, so you can call me Yank if you like. What's that out on the water?"

They both stared from their hiding place as what looked like a big turtle came downstream from the fighting to the east. Wilson said, "It's a rubber raft!" and before Hunter could warn him that those guys aboard could be Krauts he was yelling, "Hoy, you lot on that raft! Over here!"

Germans would have come in shooting, so Hunter got weakly to his feet as the raft moved into the shallows and grounded just beyond the cattails. A voice called, "Shake a leg, lads! We're the last slow boat to China and we really must be on our merry way!"

Hunter and the Red Devil floundered out across the mud. Rough hands dragged them in and down as the Royal Marine in charge snapped, "Shove off, damn it!"

Hunter found himself facedown on wet rubber, wedged between wet muddy boots, with one of his own ankles hooked over the rounded side of the big rubber raft. He thought seriously about sitting up, but he hadn't had any sleep since he couldn't remember when and as he closed his eyes it didn't seem to matter where he was or what was happening.

"What's the matter with him, mate?" one of the marines asked Tom Wilson. "Is he wounded?"

The Red Devil said, "No. He's tired."

"Coo, he picked a funny time and place to turn in, didn't he?"

"Leave him alone. He's all right."

"He's on me bloody feet, you mean. I'll just shift him a bit and—Coo, he ain't—one of your lot. He's a flaming Yank!"

"I said leave him alone and I meant it," the wounded Red Devil growled. "Me and the Yank has been through hell together and I'll cosh the first bloody sod who says he ain't with me, see?"

The marine sergeant at the tiller snapped, "That's enough, lads. Anyone looking for a fight can find all he wants on either bank of this sodding river. Keep your heads and your voices down. We're not out yet by a long shot."

Mollified, Tom Wilson asked, "Where are you taking us, Sarge?"

"Hopefully to our mad Admiral Kane, down the river, if the Jerries haven't sunk him by now."

27

THE GIRLS DIDN'T MAKE IT to the front. They were arrested by Red Ball MPs. Their jeep was shoved in a ditch and they were forced to ride back in a six-by-six full of soldiers too bushed to even get fresh with Beth. Later, Ramie would write a feature story about the chaos all around them, but right now she was too drained to even cry. Logan hadn't made it back from Driel. It seemed pretty certain that everyone still north of there had been killed or captured by now. Beth tried to cheer Ramie up with the rumor that some few survivors had been pulled out by the daring royal marines, but none of the dispatches mentioned any Yanks on the boats bound for England.

At SHAEF General Eisenhower was feeling his age too. Everyone but Monty seemed to know that Market Garden had been a terrible blunder and as the situation map began to restabilize Ike told Monty to go back to old-fashioned soldiering and leave the razzle-dazzle to Patton, who was giving them enough worries for one war.

The mortified Monty proceeded to do as he was told and, despite his supercilious manners, Monty was really a pretty good soldier when he went by the book. The brave Dutch people north of his lines were going to pay for Operation Market Garden with famine and cold in the winter ahead, for the Germans would punish them for all those pretty orange ribbons by seizing most of their food and fuel. But the new northern front now included the southern parts of Holland and as the British dug in to stay Monty suggested it might have turned out worse.

Ike couldn't see how. He'd lost all three and a half airborne divisions he'd had, for at least the rest of the year. The British airborne was almost a total loss. The American Eighty-second and 101st were too decimated to use until new supplies and replacements came over from the Z of I. And with Patton and his other ground commanders screaming for more gas, ammo, *and* replacements, the airbone had low priority for now. Maybe for always, thought Ike. They hadn't worked worth a damn in this war. He was already cannibalizing the air force and quartermaster corps for front-line infantry and it seemed pretty stupid to throw a man who could do a hundred push-ups out of a plane these days.

The remains of the two decimated American airborne divisions were bivouacked west of Paris in the repo depot areas along the Red Ball highways from the beachheads and told to stay out of trouble until Ike figured out something for them to do. Maybe when he was ready to cross the Rhine more sensibly, in maybe '45. Ike told Patton he'd shoot him too if he made any more dumb remarks about the upper Rhine with winter coming on.

When Ramie heard the remains of the 101st were camped north of the Eighty-second within a few hours drive she raced over. A pleasant Lieutenant Colonel Lansford told her he'd just had word that Logan Hunter was safe in England and should be rejoining the outfit any day. When she started to cry he put a fatherly arm around her and made her drink the last of his Canadian Club. When she threw up all over both of their uniforms he was fatherly about that too. He made her lie on a cot in his office while he sent their blouses out to be dunked in gasoline. And he understood when, the next time he looked in on her, she was fast asleep.

He tiptoed out and told his clerk, "The young lady seems nervous in the service. Is there any way we can reach Lieutenant Hunter by phone?"

The clerk said, "Negative, sir. He's on a Free French destroyer, coming across the channel right now. They should be in Le Havre this evening."

So Lansford let Ramie sleep for a couple of hours. He understood all too well how the sudden relief after all those sleepless nights must be hitting her. He'd slept round the clock the first night here in France.

When Ramie woke up she was alone in the little office. Her cleaned uniform blouse hung over a nearby folding chair. She got up, fixed her hair, and put it on. She went out to find Lansford seated at a desk, reading a western magazine. She smiled wanly at him and said, "Heavens, I feel like someone slugged me! How long have I been asleep, Colonel?"

"Couple of hours. I'm taking you over to the mess for some spam and desiccated eggs."

"My God, is it chow time already?"

"No. But a pretty girl can only go so far on black coffee and cigarettes. That booze was pretty dumb of me. But you're starting to look human again. Come on, officer's mess is just down the line."

Ramie shook her head. "I have to get back to Paris and see if I can call Logan."

Lansford got to his feet, saying, "You can't. After we eat we're driving to Le Havre to meet him."

"Do you mean it!" she gasped. "Oh, God, you're an angel, Colonel Lansford!"

The older man laughed. "No I'm not. My oldest daughter's married to an air force navigator, so I've been around this block before."

They were waiting in the staff car parked on the half-ruined quay at Le Havre before Ramie got around to asking Lansford about his married daughter. Seated in the back seat on the long drive down, they'd made small talk Ramie felt safe to handle. He'd told her old Sam Bell was likely to be out of the hospital to resume command in six weeks or so. When she asked about Sergeant Falco he had to think before he remembered who Falco was and assured her Falco's wound had been trivial too. "A lot of the boys will be back in six or eight weeks. Some of them may not want to be, but what the hey, we've probably had it, for the ETO. Hopefully we'll spend some time in the States before they ship us to the Pacific."

Ramie didn't want to think about the Pacific. "You told me your daughter worries about her husband a lot, Colonel. How does she cope with it?"

"What's to cope? She yells and cries like any other

woman. Her mother screams pretty good too. But, hey, my son-in-law just finished his fifty missions and I just wired Doris that I'm still in one piece, so I guess they'll both get some sleep tonight."

Ramie stared at the back of their enlisted driver's head as she murmured, "I thought I was too smart to ever put myself through that again. But it doesn't matter whether you're married to some guys or not. God, when those last Brengun carriers came down from Driel and that nice Polish officer told me they were the last ones out, I felt like I'd been punched in the stomach by Joe Louis!"

The fatherly Lansford nodded and said, "We use a lot of baking soda at my house in Iowa too. My daughter married Jack right after she pinned his wings on him at graduation. Jack told her it might be a good idea if they waited. He's a smart kid, for a fly boy, and he'd heard about the flack over Schweinfurt while he was still a cadet. But she said it would hurt just as bad either way, so they up and tied the knot."

He chuckled and added, "They've had their first kid. A boy. My Doris says I ought to be ashamed, running around in paratroop boots when I'm old enough to be a grandfather."

Ramie laughed. "I think you make a lovely grandfather, Colonel. And her Jack is safe now, right?"

"Well, safe for now. He'll be leaving for the Pacific in a month or so."

Ramie shuddered as she thought of that other girl she'd probably never meet. It felt so strange to know a total stranger so well.

In front of them, the driver said, "Ship coming in, sir. Looks like that destroyer you were talking about."

Ramie opened the door on her side and got out to run down the quay, waving wildly as the little World

War One four stacker moved to meet her, slowly as creeping lava. Sailors with red pom-poms on their hats were waving back at her as they approached and Ramie knew enough French to get what some of them were suggesting. But it didn't matter. She beamed up at them all as the lines were cast ashore and a gangplank slid down to the quay. And then after a maddening number of people had come down the gangplank she saw him, and he saw her. He nearly pushed a field grade officer into the harbor's fetid waters as he bulled down to join her.

For a moment neither spoke as they stood there, oblivious to the men shoving past with duffle bags. Then Ramie said, "I love you."

He nodded gravely. "I love you, too." And then she was in his arms and time stood still for them as the war left them alone for awhile.

When they came up for air, he said, "I never expected to see you here, kitten."

"I was afraid I'd never see you again at all."

"Yeah, it was sort of touch and go for a while. But believe it or not, I wound up boozing with old Admiral Kane and he was asking me about you too. He, ah, asked me what we were going to do about us and I told him you were too scared. Are you still too scared, Ramie?"

"Terribly. Will you marry me, Logan Hunter?"

He laughed and hugged her. "I thought you'd never ask."

They were kissing again when Lieutenant Colonel Lansford joined them to clear his throat and say, "If you lovebirds don't mind, I've got a regiment to run. My car and driver are waiting, son. We'll drop you both off in Paris before I go back to the outfit.

Naturally you'll want some time off, Lieutenant. I'm afraid fifteen days' leave is all I can offer."

"That's very generous of you, sir."

"Nonsense. Looking at you two, I doubt if it'll be nearly enough."

And so Logan Hunter and Ramie Davis were married by an army chaplain and honeymooned in Paris, and if Paris was a little the worse for wear that year it was still the most beautiful city on earth and they were very very happy, while it lasted.

They stayed at Ramie's rented flat near the Opéra. While Ramie's office was within walking distance, UPI insisted on her taking some back vacation leave too.

Songs have been written about Paris in the spring, but autumn in Paris isn't bad either, and the war seemed far away as they walked hand in hand through the Bois de Boulogna, scuffing the fallen leaves like kids. Many of the stores were still boarded up, but the metro was running, and free to anyone in uniform in gratitude for the liberation. They rode out to Luna Park and rode the roller coaster. They bumped each other madly in little electric dodge'em cars. But even in the merry throngs at Luna Park the war had a way of intruding on their thoughts.

There was a ride. A dumb kid's ride. Little airplanes swung round and round on long steel cables and when Logan noticed the French cockades on the stubby little wings he commented on them, saying, "That's funny. Those red, white and blue cockades don't look like they've been painted on too recently. Do you suppose the Germans let them sport their old World War One colors during the occupation?"

"I don't know," Ramie said. "I guess they must have. Why? It seems pretty harmless to me. Those little toy planes couldn't have frightened the Luftwaffe all that much, darling."

He grimaced and said, "I don't know. It just seems kind of funny to think of the Krauts who must have been out here this spring, whizzing around in those same little planes, with French cockades on their wings."

"It's getting cold. Can we go back to my place now?"

He took her arm to lead her toward the metro station. He didn't mention again that she always called it her place, not their place. He guessed it was her place, when you thought about it. But they were married, damn it. Wasn't it his place too?

It wasn't, of course. His place was the BOQ back at HQ & HQ Co. They ate dinner and went to an American movie dubbed in French and then they went home and made love until they were both exhausted. But as he lay there with his wife in his arms Logan Hunter stared up at the ceiling and he didn't feel at home.

He'd thought she was asleep, but, sensing the tension in her man, Ramie raised her head from his shoulder. "What's wrong, darling? Have I done something to upset you?"

He patted her naked back and murmured, "Of course not. I'm just thinking."

"Penny for your thoughts?"

"It's not about us. I mean, not about us exactly. I love you so much I can taste it, and if the sex part was any better it would kill me."

She laughed. "You're pretty sexy, too. But something's eating you."

He hesitated and said, "All right. Don't take this

wrong. I really love you and of course I respect you, but, damn it. I don't feel married. I feel like we're just shacked up!"

She sighed. "You too? I thought I was just being silly. But when you get right down to it, what's married supposed to feel like? I've never been married before."

"That makes two of us. I dunno, Ramie. Maybe it's the, well, lack of anything that feels . . . permanent. I mean, this isn't the kind of place married people belong."

"Lots of married people come to Paris on their honeymoon, darling. It's supposed to be very glamorous."

He stared up at a crack in the ceiling. "I know. I've been telling myself that. But after they have that honeymoon they go home. I meant to a home-type home. There's something, well, missing."

"I feel it too. I know we said no children until after, but if you want—"

"Hey, don't talk dirty, girl! That's one thing I'm not mixed up about! No kid of mine's about to be born before this mess is over. Nobody should have kids until we get those bluebirds over the you-know. That wouldn't make us feel more married. Just more worried."

She nodded and began to fondle him. "I think you've solved the mystery, darling. It's not the surroundings that make a marriage. It's knowing you'll be together a while. I told you I was afraid this would happen."

"Are you sorry, Ramie?"

"That I married you? Of course not, you dope. But if I ever meet Herr Adolf Hitler I mean to give him a good talking-to about the way he's been lousing up my sex life."

As his flesh began to respond to her caressing hand, Hunter said, "I have some hard feelings too, but they're not for Hitler."

She laughed and rolled on her back to open her body to his again. But as he entered her she clutched him tightly and sobbed, "Please don't, Logan! Promise me you won't!"

He frowned, puzzled, and asked, "What's wrong? Am I hurting you?"

She shook her head and said, "No. I love it. Don't stop. Don't ever stop."

He started moving in her, gently, as he persisted, "What was it you didn't want me to do then, Ramie?"

"Nothing. Make love to me. You wouldn't understand."

But he did understand, once he thought about it, and he wanted to promise her he wouldn't. But how could a guy promise a thing like that? He hadn't met a guy in this war yet who'd *volunteered* to get in the mattress cover. All any soldier could promise was that he'd try and keep his ass down and his weapon cleaned and loaded. He knew that wouldn't sound romantic. He knew that all over the world maybe a million other people were feeling the same way tonight. He knew that German and Japanese girls were telling their guys they wanted them to promise too. He knew a lot of them, on both sides, were going to be disappointed if this damned war didn't end soon. But none of those other people were Ramie and Logan Hunter, and thinking about them didn't help. There wasn't anybody in the world who wanted to die in this war but a lot of them were going to.

Neither of them had married as virgins and neither of them were bothered by it, so their lovemaking was skilled as well as passionate. Despite his fatigue,

Logan ejaculated hard in her as Ramie climaxed, sobbing in mingled desire and fear. As he went limp and kissed her tenderly she put her fingers to his face in the dark and murmured, "Logan, are you . . . crying?"

"Must be that time of the month or something."

"Don't be tough, dear. Not with me. We don't need our masks now, do we?"

He kissed her again. "Okay, just call me Mister Softy. I get all choked up when I think about going back to the outfit to do push-ups."

He felt her body stiffen and quickly added, "Push-ups training the new kids in from Z to I, that is. There's no way the 101st is going to see any more action this year."

That was a mask too, and she knew it. But there was a chance he was right. Nobody had ever heard of paratroopers jumping in a snow storm and she'd worry about spring when it got here.

28

THEIR BITTERSWEET HONEYMOON ended all too soon
when Hunter had to go back to his outfit. Yet the
war did seem to have forgotten the young newlyweds for a time as the battered 101st put itself back
together northwest of Paris. The war was constantly in
the news, of course, but no more so in Paris or the
French countryside away from the battle lines than it
seemed in London or even Sioux City as the nights
grew shorter and the last leaves were falling. The rear
area is the rear area and life at the 101st took on a
dreamlike routine quality as petty detail and tiresome
training replaced the gut-wrenching tenseness of the
real thing. The new recruits from the States knew
objectively that they were going through their last
mock battles before the bullets were for real. Their
instructors who'd seen combat tried to pound the

thousand and one things a soldier is supposed to know into them, but a lot of it wasn't taking. They went AWOL and got VD just like back at Benning, and when you tried to stress some important point some joker in the rear ranks still snickered.

Hunter got back to Paris to be with Ramie as often as his duties allowed, albeit not as often as Danny Boy Bradley, who'd heard Admiral Kane was at British HQ in Paris now, and whose redheaded wife, Sandy, had insisted on coming along to try on the new fall Paris fashions, such as they might be.

Replacing the numbers had been easy. But Hunter didn't start to relax about getting the outfit back to fighting strength until some of his combat vets started returning.

The burly Sergeant Falco came back, sporting a cluster to his purple heart and striking terror into fuckups from the Z of I. But, in truth, I&R Platoon would never be the way it was. Scouts didn't come back from hospitals much.

Colonel Sam Bell came back a week after Falco to scare Dan Bradley more than the amiable Lansford had ever managed—although there wasn't a hell of a lot either older officer could do about Danny Boy. A field grade officer isn't a buck private you can tell the first sergeant to keep an eye on. So unless Sam Bell wanted to act as the major's personal keeper Danny Boy still had a lot of built-in leeway, and since getting that medal for sending Hunter's stick into the right place for the wrong reason, Danny Boy was more insufferable than ever.

Hunter could have turned him in more than once, but Bradley knew he wouldn't, and Bradley counted on that when he took off in his "liberated" German jeep to be with Sandy Kane in Paris.

Logan Hunter didn't really give a damn what Danny Boy did. He had his own problems. His new bride wasn't one of them, though. He and Ramie were very much in love and their only marital problems were that he didn't work for UPI and she wasn't allowed to ride in C-47s. But I&R was a mess. It wasn't Hunter's fault. It wasn't even Bradley's fault. I&R scouts were supposed to be the cream of the airborne and the airborne was supposed to be the cream of the army. But they were sending him what seemed to be a mess of silly little kids.

Hunter suspected there were Cub Scout troops back home more fit for combat than the replacements he was getting these days. They popped their gum when he tried to lecture them on map reading and played grab-ass during calijumpics. The army couldn't be seriously considering these smooth-cheeked babies for battle troops. Half of them didn't shave more than twice a week and some were still picking their teenage pimples. Weren't they drafting *men* any more?

Sam Bell, who was older by far than anyone in the regiment, seemed more optimistic when Hunter complained to him about it. He sat Hunter down, poured him a drink, and said, "You're getting to be an ol' sojer, son. How long ago was D day, five whole months?"

"Going on six, sir. But I don't follow you. I jumped with adults on D day!"

Sam shook his head. "No you didn't. I was there when you kids fought your way back. I remember thinking at the time how young you all were. Falco's the old vet of I&R and now some of the new kids are starting to call him Pop behind his back. How old is Falco, Lieutenant?"

"I've forgotten, sir. Thirty or so, I guess."

"Bullshit. Bob Falco's only twenty-seven. I looked it up. Twenty-seven's a baby, to a man my age. You're a baby too. It's a matter of relativity, like Einstein says, see?"

"That may be true, sir. But most of my new scouts aren't old enough to vote and—"

"And your Sergeant Arnold was exactly twenty when he bought the farm on his second combat jump," Bell interrupted. "I know these new kids are green. All of you were green less than six months ago. Wars have always been fought by kids, Logan. They rob the cradle for cannon fodder and if a soldier lasts any time at all they know he must be doing something right, so they promote him and it's his turn to order children in to fight. I know it's shitty, but I'm used to it. You'll get used to it too. So drink up."

Hunter rolled some Canadian down his tongue as he thought and suddenly smiled. "You know, Ramie was telling me one night how old it made her feel to remember the Battle of Britain."

"She's a baby too, in years. But our lives aren't measured in years, Logan. It's the *events* that add up when a guy looks back. Back home in civilian life a guy working in a factory can let a year slip through his fingers like sand. He goes to work every day, sees the same people, waters the same lawn, takes the same kids on the same Sunday drive and, bingo, it's another birthday. Meanwhile, a soldier overseas for a year has lived a lifetime, if he's still alive. Look at yourself, Logan. You haven't been overseas a year yet, but while that Four F has been pissing away his life with a time clock you've been in two battles and gotten married. You've made friends and lost them.

355

You've been to London and you're spending your leaves in Paris and if anybody ever asks you about Holland you can fill 'em in on that too."

"Holland wasn't as much fun, sir. But I think I see what you mean. It does feel like Falco and I are sort of left over from the Civil War after a day trying to drill those new kids just in from Z of I. It's sort of weird when you think back a few short months."

"There you go. In a few more months those new scouts of yours will be staring in wonder at the latest replacements, wondering where the hell their nursemaids were when they got drafted. If you ask your father, he'll tell you he felt the same way. Including about me. Like I said, green troops are always kids. There's just no way to draft green vets."

Hunter finished his drink and thanked the older officer for the insight as he left. Falco had the platoon out on the firing range, familiarizing them with captured German small arms, so he was free for the moment to call Ramie in Paris. He headed up the company street as a six-by-six stopped to drop off some enlisted men. Hunter walked toward them, wondering where they'd come from and how many of them still slept with teddy bears. A familiar figure carrying a duffle bag caught his eye and Hunter stopped, jaw agape, as they both said at once, "My God, I thought you were dead!"

It was Sergeant Arnold.

Hunter ran up to him, ignoring the salute, and grabbed Arnold by the arms, gasping, "Jesus H. Christ! How did you get out alive? The last time I saw you they were hosing you down with a flame thrower!"

"Yessir. It was sort of messy. I went back, after, when I couldn't find you. Cohen picked something

up on the R-300 and said I'd rather get you back
to talk to some brass. So I'd just ducked out of that
culvert when some Krauts stopped on the road. I
flopped by a dead Limey out in the open and pretended I was dead too. If you saw what they did
with that flame thrower you know what I found when
they left. I yelled for you, but you didn't answer.
So I figured you must have taken off. I did some
taking off myself, after that. But what happened to
you, sir?"

"Long story. Leave your duffle bag here and come
over to the club with me while I tell you over a
beer."

Arnold frowned and asked, "Officer's club, sir?"

"It's all right. You're my guest. Jesus Christ, Arnold,
you don't know how good it feels to see you!"

He led the dubious sergeant down the line to the
pre-fab officer's club as he briefly filled him in on his
own escape. The club was nearly empty at this time of
day. A rifle platoon leader Hunter knew to nod to was
seated on a sofa near the far wall, nursing a drink and
last month's *Esquire*. Neither he nor the enlisted bartender saw fit to comment on Hunter's guest. The
officer's club was funded by the officers themselves,
not the taxpayer, so it was up to the members themselves who they invited in. Enlisted guests were not
encouraged, but Hunter was within his rights. He
ordered a couple of beers and demanded to know
how Arnold had gotten away and why it had taken
him all this time to get back to the outfit. The rifle
officer across the room put down his magazine to listen
too as Arnold repeated what had happened back at
the culvert. "I played dead 'til I was sure the Krauts
were gone, sir. Then I crawled back where I left the
others. It was awful. The guys in the culvert looked

like big burned match heads, you know? Pike made it out the other end with his clothes on fire I guess. They machine-gunned him. Then they drove off, laughing, the sons of bitches!"

"What did you do then, Sergeant?"

"I shit my pants. I mean, no kidding, when I stopped running there was something in my pants around my boot top. So I unbloused it and a couple of turds fell out. I might have pissed my pants, too, only I was so wet you couldn't tell. I remembered what you'd said about not running more than you could help it, so I started walking. I tried to work south with my compass, but every time I did there was firing ahead of me. So I knew I couldn't get back to Nijmegen and I knew there were more Krauts north of me and that Germany was east, so I started walking west."

The rifle officer came over and said, "That's what I'd have done. Next round's on me, guys. I want to hear the rest of this."

Hunter introduced them and the rifle officer offered a handshake as he said, "Keep going, Sergeant. I know you never *walked* across the North Sea."

Arnold said, "Nosir. I damned near did, though. I walked through the night, hitting the dirt every time somebody seemed to be moving around me. And, Jesus, a lot of things were moving that night. As the sun came up I found myself wandering around in sand dunes. I didn't know where the hell I was. There were sand dunes as far as you could see. Then this bunch of Dutchmen came along. Dutch kids, really. They were all pretty young. They had orange armbands and guns and at first they were going to kill me 'cause they thought I was a Kraut. But a couple of them spoke English and we got that straightened out. They gave me something to eat and some water. Jesus, that water tasted good. They said they were the local kommando and that I should stick with them. So I did. The leader was a kid called Kay. I thought it was a dumb name for a guy, but old Kay was a fighting son of a bitch. Hey, you know I got three more Krauts now, Lieutenant?"

Hunter nodded approvingly and asked, "Is that where you've been all this time, Sergeant?"

"Nosir. Me and that kommando ran around hitting stray Krauts until we got word that the rest of you were pulling out and that the Krauts were winning. Old Kay didn't like that much. He said he couldn't go home if the Krauts were in his village. It seems he shot a cop or something back there the first day we dropped in. We started working south, toward the British lines. That's when I got my last Kraut, personal. We ran into some counter-guerrilla SS guys that specialize in guys like I was with. We were holed up in this barn for the night and old Kay said we could trust the Dutch farmer who owned it, but I dunno, there was something I didn't like about the setup. The farmer talked sneaky. Or maybe he talked right in words and I picked up something because the words meant nothing and I was only looking at his eyes. Anyway, I didn't like it. It wasn't raining that night. So when the other guys bedded down in the barn I went out to a haystack in the field to flip out solo. Next thing I knew all hell was breaking loose! I sat up to see the barn was on fire and all these guys in Kraut helmets were hosing down the flames with machine gun fire. So I left the haystack by the back door. That's when I ran into this Kraut. He was alone too. I guess somebody told him to look around out there, or maybe he was taking a piss. I didn't ask. I just killed the mother and kept going."

"Didn't the others hear the gunfire, Arnold?"

"What gunfire, sir? I swung my carbine like Babe Ruth and knocked his damned head half off! I don't know if they heard that or not, but I just kept going until I was clear. I moved all night and holed up in some willow trees all the next day. I kept this up I don't know how long and then one morning as I came out of some reeds I stumbled into a patrol and some bastard shot me in the thigh. Only it was a British patrol and they said they were sorry and took me back with them. I got out of the hospital yesterday. The medics said it was only a flesh wound and that I'd have to try harder if I wanted to be shipped Z of I."

The two officers laughed and the rifleman clapped Arnold on the back and said, "By God, I wish I had you leading one of my squads, Sergeant!"

"I saw him first," Hunter said. "That makes your score ten now, right, Arnold?"

Arnold nodded with a frown and said, "Yessir. I've gotta do something about that. Ten sounds like you made it up. If I could just get me one more I could say I nailed eleven and everybody would believe me, see?"

When the rifleman looked puzzled, Hunter explained, "He counts."

Before he could elaborate, Major Dan Bradley came in. Danny Boy was not alone. He'd brought Sandy Kane on base with him. The redhead looked like butter wouldn't melt in her mouth as the two of them came to the bar. A female guest was not unheard of, but Hunter repressed an impulse to ask Bradley if he was smoking funny cigarettes these days. The stupid bastard was openly flaunting his relationship with the wife of a senior officer in front of God and everybody.

Bradley smirked and said, "Afternoon, buddy boy. You remember Sandy here, don't you?"

Hunter managed not to smile as he said, "Yes. Last time we met was just before Market Garden. New dress, Sandy?"

"As a matter of fact, it is. New Paris designer named Dior just opened up."

Bradley suddenly noticed the stripes on young Arnold's sleeve. "What's *he* doing here?"

"Surely you remember Sergeant Arnold, Dan," Hunter said. "I had him down as KIA. He just came back to us from the dead and we've been having a drink on it."

Bradley sniffed. "Marvelous. But I wasn't aware this was the enlisted men's club. You're both way out of line, Lieutenant."

Hunter hit him.

Hunter hit him with everything he had and Danny Boy flew ass over teakettle across a nearby table to land on his hands and knees as Sandy screamed and Hunter moved around the table to do it again because it felt so good. Hunter was aware that somebody was yelling, "Gentlemen, gentlemen, please!" but he didn't care.

Bradley did. Bradley rose to his feet with blood in his eye as well as running from the corner of his big mouth. He dropped into a fighting crouch and put up his dukes as they met head-on. And the fight, while it lasted, was something to write home about.

No man with Danny Boy Bradley's obnoxious personality got through puberty without learning how to fight, and, like Hunter, Bradley was a trained paratrooper. Hunter had intended to just punch him out until he saw Bradley wanted to use his boots too. So after that it started to get rough. The average barroom brawler wouldn't have lasted long against either of them and the fight was rough as hell on the furniture as they knocked each other all over the club room. Hunter was in better shape, but Bradley was heavier and nastier by nature, so they were about even when the room filled up with enough other paratroopers to pile on and pry them apart. The friendly rifle officer slapped Hunter gently to gain his attention and shouted, "Knock it off, you dumb jerk!"

Hunter nodded and relaxed, looking around in wonder at the wreckage. Some others had Bradley in a far corner, holding a wet bar towel to his battered face. Both Arnold and Sandy had had sense enough to duck out.

"Let me go. I'm okay," Hunter muttered. The rifle officer nodded to the men holding him. As they released Hunter he took a deep breath and called across to Bradley, "Want to call it quits, Major?"

"Bullshit! I'm pressing charges, Hunter. You cold cocked me for no reason at all and I've got witnesses!"

The bartender looked at the ceiling thoughtfully, as if he'd just noticed something interesting up there. The rifle platoon leader said, "He had a pretty *good* reason, if you ask me, Major. But you won't be calling on *me* to testify, will you?"

Before Bradley could answer, Colonel Bell came in. He stood in the doorway for a moment as he surveyed the wreckage. Then he snapped, "All right, both of you, in the back room, *alone*, and *now*!"

As soon as he had the two of them in a storage room behind the bar Sam Bell said, "All right, from the bruises I see it looks like a draw. You're both chipping in for the wrecked furniture. Agreed?"

Bradley pointed his finger at Hunter and said,

"Colonel, I want that man arrested and court-martialed for striking a superior officer!"

Sam Bell said, "I'm sure you do. I won't go into who's the superior officer. You've both made blithering idiots of yourselves. But the regiment cleans its own dirty linen. Do you read me, Major?"

Bradley shook his head stubbornly and insisted, "I'm within my rights under the ARs, sir! I'll take it all the way to division if I have to!"

"No you won't," Bell said. "General Taylor drinks with Admiral Kane, you asshole!"

Bradley fell silent as if someone had pulled his plug. He stared openmouthed at the older man as Sam Bell nodded and said, "I know, she's a great lay. Apparently I'm the only white man in the ETO who hasn't found that out for himself by personal experience. And if you ever bring a married woman on my post again no junior officer is going to have to hit you. I'll personally kick the shit right out of you!"

Bradley licked his split lips and blustered, "My personal life has nothing to do with the fact that I was just assaulted, Colonel!"

"You're wrong," said Bell. "If you thought with your brains instead of your glands you'd see it has everything to do with it. How the hell are you going to press charges against Hunter here without the TJA asking all sorts of people who that redhead in the bar with you at the time might have been? The case is closed, Major. That's a direct order, for the good of the service."

Bradley looked sullenly at Hunter as he muttered, "Then teacher's pet gets off scott free?"

Bell's voice was icy as he said, "You make one more crack like that and I'll frog march you to the guard house on a charge of insubordination. I told you regiment washes its own linen. I didn't say it was open season on field grade officers around here."

Bell turned to Hunter. "I don't know why you've started hitting superior officers again, Lieutenant. But it's a nasty habit and I've already told you not to do it anymore. You're confined to base until further notice."

"But, sir, I told my wife I could spend the weekend with her in Paris."

"Tough shit. Call her and tell her you can't. But make it snappy. You're pulling OD tonight. I had assigned it to another officer, but he knows how to behave himself and he has things to do in Paris too. Is there to be any further discussion on who's running this goddamn regiment?"

Neither younger man answered, so Bell said, "All right. Bradley, get the hell out of my sight. Hunter, call your wife and tell her not to hold supper for you. Then get back to me in time for guard mount. Like I said, the case is closed."

29

IT WAS SNOWING in Paris, just starting to stick as Ramie stared out her window, alone, hating old Sam Bell only a little less than she hated Adolf Hitler. Her Logan had called to tell her he was pulling OD again that weekend, as he had the two weekends before. Even Ramie knew that the ARs decreed no officer pulled officer of the day two nights in a row. But Colonel Bell said self-contained junior officers deserved weekends in Paris more than fuck-ups who clobbered field grade officers in front of witnesses, and that if Hunter wanted to take the extra duty up with division it was his own ass.

Ramie of course couldn't know that Sam Bell had stuck his own neck out far indeed by covering an offense calling for a general court-martial with what he called washing their own linen.

The phone rang and Ramie snatched it up eagerly, hoping against hope that the old ogre had relented. But it was Beth Waterman on the line. Beth said, "There's something going on at the front, Ramie. You'd better get back here. It looks like we might be on the wires a lot tonight."

"What's happened? Has Patton made it to the upper Rhine?"

"It's more to the north. Up on the First Army's front. The first reports are sort of confusing, but something big seems to be happening up in Belgium, in the Ardennes sector."

Ramie said, "I'm on my way," and hung up, wondering what was going on.

What was going on was called Operation Christ Rose by the Germans. It would be called the Von Rundstedt Offensive, to the considerable annoyance of Field Marshal Gerd von Rundstedt who thought it was a crazy idea and was one of the few remaining German generals who could talk to Hitler like that. General Baron Hasso von Manteuffel, who actually led Operation Christ Rose, thought it was crazy too, but the Germans had to do something, and fast. And so, spearheaded by the Panzer Lehr Division and the Panthers and Tigers of the crack Second Panzer "Adolf Hitler" Division, Manteuffel threw all the weight of his last reserves and any kitchen sinks he could find at the weakest link in the Allied lines.

The war was grinding to a lull as winter set in, and since everybody except the Germans knew the Ardennes was lousy tank country the Americans in the hilly wooded Ardennes had been ordered to dig in and hold until the spring fighting weather. By luck or devilish ingenuity, the German spearhead made contact exactly where green troops just arriving at the front were still setting up shop, unprepared and perhaps overconfident after being told they'd been given a quiet sector to hold until they got used to things over here.

The panzer columns moved under an eerie artificial moonlight manufactured by shining German searchlights on the low overcast that kept Allied air support grounded on snow-covered fields for far too long. The Germans didn't alert their victims with the usual artillery barrage. They just rolled forward through the swirling snow, their cleats and engines muffled to a low ominous rumble that seemed to come from anywhere to the nervous green troops ahead of them. White-clad German ski troopers slid between the wide-spread tanks, like ghosts armed with machine pistols, and the next forty-eight hours were sheer chaos for everybody, and hell for the Americans caught napping, as Operation Christ Rose burst through the Allied lines like a blow torch through butter, splitting the Allied armies in two very confused groups with the German advance patrols running wild behind their lines.

As always in any war, there were heroes and cowards on both sides. In some sectors whole Allied units simply cut and ran, while in others the GIs dug in and fought to the last man in scattered lonely Alamos. At a place called Malmedy a whole battalion of American artillerymen surrendered to sixty SS men without firing a shot, and were herded into a snow-covered field and massacred by machine gun fire for their trust in man and the Geneva Conventions. At another Belgian place called St.-Vith, Major Don Boyer and a hundred men of the Seventh U.S. Armored would hold like a rock for the better half of a week and at last escape the Nazis surrounding them.

Scattered like chaff before the massive German assault, communications chaotic or completely cut off, the disorganized Americans did what they could to survive on their own from moment to moment, and though a lot of them were cut off and killed or captured, some made the right moves, either by accident or design as the lay of the land began to dictate the almost hydraulic flow of men and machines, as it does the flood waters of any unexpected deluge.

In dribs and drabs, battered units started falling into the grip of a traffic whirlpool created by the position of a Belgian town called Bastogne, at the hub of the Ardennes road net. Afoot or in vehicles, in company strength or in little lost groups of less than a squad, and sometimes quite alone, GIs found themselves converging on Bastogne, simply because, like Rome, all roads seemed to lead there sooner or later.

The remains of the shot-up Tenth U.S. Armored found themselves in Bastogne and, not knowing what else to do, dug in. They were joined by a battery of lost Negro artillerymen who, lacking orders or directions, had hung on to their big Long Toms and the ammo that went with them.

Fourteen M-4 tanks of the Ninth Armored had fought their way out of a panzer trap at Longvilly to make it as far as Bastogne where they stopped, out of gas but still full of fight.

The 705th Tank Destroyer Battalion had found stopping a Tiger a bit much, but as they reeled back they wound up in Bastogne too, and dug in with the other survivors. Other GIs wandered in until, unplanned and hardly noticed at first, the little Belgian town began to justify its name, which, in English, meant bastion. In the Middle Ages it had controlled the routes through the Ardennes. As the snow and

German shells fell on its quaint rooftops Bastogne proved its site had been well chosen by some long dead baron in another kind of armor.

It was Montgomery who first saw what was going on. Everyone else, on both sides, was pretty confused about Operation Christ Rose as they stared at the total confusion of their respective situation maps. Christ Rose wasn't coming up roses for the Germans either. Their own paratroops had landed in the wrong places and the panzer columns were taking on odd kinks that hadn't been intended on the map as they were forced to move around unexpected weakness and knifed through soft spots that shouldn't have been there. Eisenhower couldn't see what the Germans thought they were doing either. But Monty had been brooding about the one serious blunder of his career for months, and reliving Market Garden in his nightmares as he tried to explain it away as somebody else's fault. By now there wasn't a move, good or bad, that had been made in Market Garden that Monty didn't have etched in his brain with acid. So, as he found himself cut off in the north with his own and some American units placed under his command for the emergency, Montgomery studied his own situation maps, blinked a couple of times, and called Ike to say, "It's Market Garden, in reverse!"

Ike had enough to worry about, but he was a polite man, so he listened as Monty said, "Instead of an airborne assault backed by armor they've sent armor with a spot of airborne to confuse us."

"They're confusing us pretty good," said Ike.

"I say, isn't it obvious? Their main objective is Antwerp, cutting supplies for all of us and isolating my lot to spoil my spring advance across the Rhine. Look at the shape of that bulge and forget the way it's pointing. It's Market Garden's salient into Holland, all over again."

"Monty, that's crazy. Holland was dead flat, cut by canals. This bulge of yours is in high country, cut up by ridges, damn it!"

"I said it was Market Garden in *reverse*, old boy. The lay of the land is different, but the same traffic rules apply. Look at that bottleneck at Bastogne and tell me what you see?"

Ike looked, and because he wasn't as dumb as Monty thought, he gasped and said, "*Arnhem*! I see what you mean!"

"I thought you would. Market Garden failed because we couldn't take and hold Arnhem. If the Germans fail to take Bastogne, they'll be in the same perishing boat they put us in this fall!"

Ike said he'd get back to Monty and hung up. He turned to an aide and snapped, "I want at least a division into Bastogne before the enemy can cut that north-south road into it from France. I mean right now! What reserve division do we have close enough to the Belgian border to make a run for it?"

"What about the 101st airborne, sir? They're almost back to full strength and they're the closest. But their commanding officer's in England at the moment and they don't have air transport ready."

"Shove 'em in trucks and let their second in command lead 'em! What are you waiting for? Do it!"

The aide nodded and picked up a phone. "Patch me through to general McAuliffe at Division HQ, 101st Airborne."

There was a maddening delay. The aide cupped his hand over the mouthpiece and said, "They're calling him to the phone, sir."

Eisenhower grabbed the phone and said, "Hello,

Tony? Ike, here. Listen, I've got a little job for you."

Phones started ringing all over the ETO that night as the 101st found itself back in business. In Paris Major Dan Bradley shot a warning glance at the naked woman in bed beside him as he reached across her for the phone. They were at his hotel for a change because Sandy's husband was in town to attend some sort of meeting at Paris GHQ. She'd jarred hell out of him a couple of times by picking up a phone he'd left listed with the outfit.

A voice he recognized as Logan Hunter's said, "Sorry to disturb you, Major, but it's a red alert. All leaves are canceled and they want you back here on the double."

"I'm driving an open jeep and it's snowing, buddy boy. What the hell's going on?"

"We're moving out. I mean *now*! The colonel says if any officers don't make it back by the time we're loaded we'll have to leave without them."

"Okay, I'll try, I'll try. But this has to be a drill, buddy boy! Nobody's sending us anywhere to jump in a goddamn blizzard!"

"We're not jumping. We're moving to the line by truck, and that's all I can tell you on this wire. You'd better move it if you don't want to miss the show, Major. Got to hang up. Other guys to call!"

As the line went dead Bradley reached across Sandy again to cradle it. Then he dropped the hand on her nude breast, tweaking her nipple as he said, "This is your lucky night, doll face."

"I hope so. What was that all about, lover?"

"Oh, the outfit's going someplace. We don't have to worry about it."

As a navy wife, even Sandy had some sense. She

frowned up at him and asked, "Won't you get in trouble if you're AWOL when your regiment runs off wherever without you?"

"Hey, what AWOL? I signed out like a good little boy and even left 'em this number. Is it my fault the roads are slippery tonight? Hell, I can always say I tried."

He leaned over to kiss her as he ran his hand down her torso to cup her mons. "Oh, I like a man who tries," she purred. "But when do you have to go back to your regiment?"

"How should I know? That wise-ass Hunter didn't even tell me where they were headed. It's his fault, not mine, if it takes me a week or so to catch up with them, right?"

She laughed and said, "You're incredible. But I can't spend the weekend with you. I told you my husband is in town."

"Yeah. Why don't you divorce the old bastard if he's so lousy in bed?"

"Nobody is that lousy in bed when he's very rich and old enough to leave me a very well-off widow in a few years. What's the matter, are you getting jealous?"

"Jealous of that old fart? You gotta be kidding! Can he even get it up these days?"

She began to respond to his hand as she purred, "Not as well as some crude Yanks I know. But not to worry, his demands are modest and there's enough of what you're teasing to go around. Would you eat me again, Danny? I love it when you eat me first."

"Jesus, you call *me* crude? First you remind me I'm going sloppy seconds with that old Limey bastard and now you want to lick it clean!"

"You *are* jealous!"

"Shit, maybe I'm just delicate by nature. You wanna screw or do you wanna tell me about your fucking old husband?"

Not waiting for an answer, he rolled over to mount her. She responded hungrily, thrilled as always by the gross vulgarity of her brutal lover. Danny Boy really was an animal, she thought, as he began to pound her. Sandy knew her own perverse nature well enough to understand why this longer than usual affair was so stimulating. It was the sheer contrast between the two men with whom she was sharing her body. She knew she could never tell this oaf that her husband was really a better lover, or the lover she preferred. Her Ivor was still a handsome virile man, and a far more considerate sex partner. But it was so much more fun to go to bed with her husband after a roll in the gutter with some sweaty animal like this one. She didn't know why she enjoyed being dirty in every way, but she did. It made her feel even cleaner to bathe and perfume herself for Ivor after spending part of her day in dirty underwear, and when Ivor kissed her between the thighs after she'd just been with another man it drove her wilder than it ever had before she'd discovered the forbidden fruits of afternoon adultery. Dan Bradley ejaculated in her and said, "Turn over. I want to give it to you Greek."

She hesitated, for she really didn't get much more than discomfort out of anal sex. But she'd be with Ivor tomorrow night and she knew the memory of giving herself totally to a man her husband would despise—with justice—would offer a perverse thrill. So she rolled over, took a deep breath, and tried to relax her anal muscles as he wet a finger with saliva to lubricate her there. But, damn it, it hurt when he thrust into her like that. As he started to sodomize her

Sandy decided to bitch him too by saying conversationally, "They tell me you're afraid to jump."

He muttered, "What the hell are you talking about?" as he stared down between their bodies, enjoying the view.

She yawned, not attempting to pretend enjoyment as she started getting used to what was a pretty silly thing when one thought about it. "That fight you had with Logan Hunter seems to have stirred up a bit of resentment among the other officers. Stirred up old memories too, one gathers. I overheard a couple of them talking about you at a party the other evening. Is it true you never really jumped in Sicily, that you came in later as a replacement?"

"Don't be an asshole."

"I didn't want to be. This was your idea. I gather some of your comrades consider you a bit of a fraud, Dan. They were probably feeling sorry for the newlyweds when they said you were, well, yellow."

He was sweating as he tried to maintain his erection despite her remarks. He growled, "Hey, I dropped in Market Garden, right?"

"If you say so. But you seem to be avoiding whatever the 101st is up to at the moment."

He withdrew angrily, and slapped her bare bottom. "Shit, you want me to leave? I can still get back in time, if I leave right now."

She rolled over and smiled up at him. "Actually, I wanted that thing out of my perishing arse. But you've warmed me up now, so let's do it right."

"Okay, let me wash it off then."

"No, don't wash it off, Dan. Put it in me dirty. I love it when you make me feel absolutely filthy."

He shook his head in wonder as he lowered himself

374

onto her. "You sure are a funny little broad, Sandy. Sometimes I don't understand you at all."

"I don't think you'd understand a pig. But you'd no doubt rut with it if it let you."

He kissed her throat as he started moving faster, muttering, "You're all the pig I need. But listen, if I'm stuck in Paris we gotta work out some way for us to do this more often."

She started to say it was out of the question, with her husband in town. But then Sandy thought of a rather shocking French bedroom farce and said, "Hmm, it might be interesting to play musical beds at that. I could send our maid away and her bedroom's right down the hall."

"Jesus, Sandy, isn't that cutting it sort of thin? I'm not afraid of the old fart, but you're just asking to get caught."

"I never get caught. But *almost* getting caught is a terrific thrill."

30

THE AMERICAN six-by-six was an unsung deadly weapon of World War Two. Rugged as a dollar alarm clock, the big truck had six wheels and six speeds forward. It could carry two and a half tons of almost anything almost anywhere. So over fifteen thousand men of the 101st Airborne were crammed in like sardines with their baggage and weapons to race the south flank of Operation Christ Rose for Bastogne.

They just made it. Ten minutes after Brigadier Tony McAuliffe's jeep tore over the Neufchâteau Highway into Bastogne on December 19 an advance panzer column cut the last road link into the little town and Bastogne was surrounded.

Monty was terribly pleased.

He wasn't crazy. He read maps well. The cut-off

but now strongly garrisoned road juncture formed a festering boil on the finger the Germans had poked through the Allied lines. To the north and south, the Allied generals started wheeling their units to slowly form what in the end would resemble the jaws of a nutcracker with Operation Christ Rose as the nut.

But it was a tough nut, and the Allies needed time to shift the huge amounts of men and materiel in the lousy weather they were having. If Bastogne could hold until the Allies were ready to counterattack, it would be very painful indeed for the Germans. All units, British and American, who'd been cut off north of the bulge were placed under Montgomery. In the south Omar Bradley, with George Patton carrying the ball, wheeled to form the bottom jaw of the nutcracker. It hurts bad enough to have one's finger in a nutcracker. Picture the finger with a throbbing cyst against the bone and put yourself in General Manteuffel's place.

The German traffic could and did flow around Bastogne, of course, just as commuters could somehow work around Times Square or Piccadilly should some unpleasant mob occupy either during the morning rush hour. It took more than Hitler's speeches to keep a German army moving. They needed Hermann and Otto. Hermann was ammunition and Otto was fuel and the supply problem was already bad enough without the traffic jams Bastogne was causing. So as our hypothetic commuters would have called for the cops, Manteuffel ordered Bastogne taken. Troops and tanks vital to the German thrust west were diverted to enclose the hitherto unknown little Belgian town and the "Battered Bastards of Bastogne" were born.

* * *

Colonel Bell set up his CP in the basement of a bakery, closed for the duration. Since Major Bradley hadn't made it back in time, Logan Hunter was given his job as regimental S2 and old Sam Bell swore that if they lived he meant to see that the job and rank that went with it would be Hunter's to keep. Sam Bell was feeling guilty about confining Hunter to the post so that he'd lost those last weeks with his new bride. But he was awfully glad Hunter had been on base when the orders flashed down from SHAEF. Many officers and men of the reserve division had been on leave when the balloon went up, and though few had deliberately failed to make it back in time the outfit was shorthanded.

Hunter was feeling guilty too. He'd called Ramie's place in Paris a couple of times before he'd had to move out. But she hadn't been in. When he'd gotten through to her office Beth Waterman had told him Ramie was out in the snow somewhere in her UPI jeep. She was trying to get an interview with Patton, if she could find him. Hardly anyone knew where Patton might turn up these days.

Hunter felt even more guilty as he called Sergeant Falco into his improvised S2 office and said, "Congratulations, you just made lieutenant. The rank's temporary, of course, but if you do it right the colonel says he can swing a battlefield commission. Can you do my old job right, Falco?"

"No," Falco said, "and I don't want to be no fucking officer. I don't like fucking officers, present company excepted. Who's gonna take my place as platoon sergeant if I get bumped up, Lieutenant?"

"Captain. I just made captain and I'm bucking for major, Lieutenant Falco. Arnold will have to be platoon sergeant. He's the only noncom we have with combat experience."

When Falco scowled Hunter said, "I know, he's just a kid and he counts. But do you have anyone else in mind for the job?"

"I guess not, sir. We know Arnold's a survivor. I notice he sort of tends to survive alone, though. We got thirty green kids to worry about. That means every squad leader's a greenhorn too."

"Robert E. Lee and even Colonel Bell must have started out as greenhorns. Isn't on-the-job-training fun?"

As if he'd heard his name, Colonel Bell came in, stamping snow off his boots. He nodded at Falco and said to Hunter, "Jesus, it's cold as a witch's tit outside. McAuliffe's taken command and he's giving us one of those colored Long Tom crews to hold this sector of the perimeter."

As Hunter noted that on his spread-out situation map, Bell frowned down at it and said, "I don't see much red out there in Indian country, Logan."

"I'm organizing I&R now with Lieutenant Falco, sir."

"Well, shake a leg then. I hate blank maps. I know how we did it in the last war and I know how they've been doing up to now in this one. The big question is how those purple-pissing Nazis out there in the snow mean to set up their siege. They might dig in for some old-fashioned trench warfare. They might circle us like Indians to keep us from zeroing in on steady targets. They might do a little of both. If I was on the other side I'd have my artillery back and dug in while my tanks and infantry skirmished razzle dazzle, probing for weak links in our defenses." Bell stabbed a finger down on the map and asked, "Are those fields out in front of us really open or was the mapmaker too lazy to draw trees?"

"We'll check that out, sir," Hunter said. "It's hard to see far in this snowstorm so I'll send out patrols."

"Order them to try and take some prisoners too. Or if they have to kill the bastards they run into, make sure we get some paybooks and shoulder straps. It helps to be able to look up the guys you're fighting in the Enemy Order of Battle books."

"Roger Wilco, sir. Falco, you heard what the colonel wants. Get on it."

Falco gulped and blurted, "Hey, Lieutenant, I mean Captain, I don't know shit about running I&R!"

"Learn then. Let's not show stage fright, Falco. You've been at my side in the field often enough to know my old job. Until we know what's out there you'd better run strong combined combat and intelligence patrols. You take half the scouts and give the other half to Arnold. That way the new squad leaders can pick up a few pointers before they have to lead their own diamonds. What are you waiting for, a goodbye kiss? You can make it to the school bus without momma holding you by the hand. Move it out, Falco."

Falco left, muttering to himself. Sam Bell chuckled and said, "Welcome to the club. You're shaping up to be a really chicken-shit command officer, son. I'm glad that asshole Bradley didn't make it back."

"I'm not. I'm worried about those children of mine. What's going to happen to Danny Boy, Colonel?"

"Nothing, probably. He called in just as I was loading up back there in France. Said he was calling from some farmhouse halfway back from Paris. Seems his jeep got stuck in a snow drift."

"Do you believe that, sir?"

"No. But how is anyone ever going to prove it? What really gripes my ass is that now the bastard's sure to live through the war. This is the big one, Logan. Hitler's shot his wad and all the battles after this one figure to be downhill sledding. Ike will never need us when he crosses the Rhine now."

"The Rhine's a long ways off, sir."

"Not that far. And the Krauts have committed their best and last reserves on this side of the Rhine, the stupid bastards. I was just looking at the large-scale map in Tony McAuliffe's CP. Monty must be hugging himself right now and George Patton's probably jerking off. If we can hold this bottleneck until the other kids can reshuffle, the Krauts are in for a disaster that will make Market Garden look like a noisy tea party!"

"I see the strategic position of Bastogne, sir. But how long will we have to hold out here?"

Bell shrugged and said, "That's the sixty-four dollar question. Patton won't be allowed to move until Montgomery's in position and Monty moves like a cat shitting through a funnel. Let's say six weeks to be on the safe side."

Hunter gasped and said, "They expect us to hold this position for six whole fucking weeks? That takes us into 1945, Colonel!"

Bell nodded grimly. "Yeah, Merry Christmas and Happy New Year. Meanwhile, let's get some I&R on the bastards surrounding us and see if it looks like we can do it."

They could do it. As his S2 maps began to flesh out with blue and red crayon marks Hunter gained a new perspective on the desk work he despised. A much better officer than the AWOL Bradley, Hunter didn't just make pretty marks as his scouts brought in odds and ends of I&R. Like a chess master playing in semi-darkness Hunter had to make out patterns in the shifting blue and red marks on his map. The Germans encircling the town and its outskirts moved constantly to avoid becoming tempting targets for the defender's artillery, which had surprised hell out of them. The black Long Tom gunners now under McAuliffe's command were well trained and hot as hell. The Americans had other big guns. The trapped tanks couldn't go anywhere, but the M-4s fired 75s and of course the tank destroyer units had brought their big stuff in with them. Each battalion of the 101st had a heavy weapons company to lob mortar rounds at any German dumb enough to stay in one place long enough for them to range on it. When one added all the rifle companies and machine gun crews encircled in Bastogne, a frontal assault became out of the question. So the Germans figured their best bet was to pound the place down around the Americans and the almost forgotten civilian population of Bastogne.

Hunter's blue marks moved a lot on the acetate as the Battered Bastards of Bastogne learned the dangers of staying too long in one position too. Every German artillery shell lobbed into Bastogne meant one they'd be short of in the final rounds of the war. But meanwhile it was hell on the people they were landing on.

One didn't need to be from the 101st, or even another American GI to qualify as a Battered Bastard of Bastogne. Roughly four thousand Belgian men, women, and children had been trapped inside the German ring of infantry, armor, and artillery, and as death rained down on them the gallant citizens did their own war duties.

A lot of this consisted in trying to stay the hell out

of the way. The women tended the children and the wounded in the cellers of Bastogne as the walls of their homes began to crumble away under constant harassing fire. The Belgian town officials kept order, which wasn't always easy when a salvo of 155s came lancing down out of the leaden overcast. Civilians and soldiers shared such food as had been in Bastogne in the beginning or trucked in with the 101st. The nasty weather settled in for one of the snowiest winters the Belgians could recall in this century, so air cover as well as air drops were out of the question for the moment. Belgian children chewed American gum in the cellers of Bastogne as GIs learned how well some Belgian women cooked. C rations with a soupçon of kitchen herbs tossed in were one hell of an improvement over what came out of the cans originally.

Belgian men and boys served as runners, litter bearers, and vital extra hands as the GIs shifted positions or repaired shell damages. The unsung Bastogne fire department saved the place from burning down more than once. And thus the town held out, with ground and airborne, black and white, civilian and military fighting side by side.

The snow stopped falling for a time. The German general who'd been told to reduce the bottleneck or else wasn't about to attack in clear visibility across open snow-covered fields. So he sent in a message under a flag of truce. It read:

Dec. 22, 1944.
To: The U.S.A. Commander:
The fortune of war is changing. This time the U.S.A. Forces in and near Bastogne have been encircled by strong German armored units . . .
There is only one possibility to save the en-

circled U.S.A. troops from total annihilation; that is the honorable surrender of the town . . .

If this proposal should be rejected, one German artillery corps and six heavy A.A. 88 battalions are ready to annihilate the U.S.A. troops in and near Bastogne . . .

All the serious civilian losses caused by this artillery fire would not correspond with the well-known American humanity.

The German Commander

The German parley team was sent back with a shorter message from Tony McAuliffe. It read:
Nuts.

31

CHRISTMAS EVE in Paris found Beth Waterman alone and feeling blue. Ramie was somewhere at the front with Patton, wherever the front was these days. Beth was worried about Ramie's husband too, of course, but she couldn't really tell at her UPI desk what was going on up there in Belgium save for the fact that it seemed terribly important that some dinky little town called Bastogne be kept from falling into German hands. No phone or V mail messages were going in or out of Bastogne. But no news was good news from the front. Graves was very conscientious about informing widows they were due that ten thousand dollars.

Beth had been invited to a party over in the posh Neuilly district. But it was awfully cold out and Neuilly was pretty far from the center of Paris. So Beth decided she'd ask that cute new reporter just in from the States if he'd like to come home with her to share the fruit cake mom had sent her for Christmas. The cake would probably be hard as a rock, but they could work something out.

The party Beth had decided to skip was at the private house leased by the Kanes, near a loop of the Seine. If Beth couldn't make it, Dan Bradley could. If the admiral was surprised to see an officer of the 101st in Paris when the news from Bastogne was so grim, he was too polite to say so. The two men didn't say much of anything to each other; they mingled with other guests at opposite sides of the room. Sandy of course was in her element, shining her teeth at one and all in her new Paris frock of what was either hoarded white silk or a salvaged parachute.

Danny Boy found parties boring if he wasn't hunting, and he already had his bed partner for the night, if Sandy was right about her husband having to leave early for a meeting—and if the old bastard would only go.

He drank more than he should have to pass the time, but he was still in pretty good shape when the admiral excused himself and Sandy came over to Bradley to warn, "Cut down on the inky-pooh, dear. You know what it does to your erection."

He laughed and said, "I'll show you an erection, soon as we get rid of these other bastards."

That didn't take long. The other guests had made their own plans for Christmas Eve. As she let the last couple out, Sandy told the servants they could clean up another time and gave them the night off to do whatever Frogs were supposed to do on Christmas Eve.

As they found themselves alone at last, Bradley took

Sandy in his arms and said, "It's about time. Where's the bedroom?"

"I've a better idea. Let's do it right here, on the floor."

"You mean, here in the middle of the fucking living room?"

"Yes, it's never been a fucking room before. Come on, we'll leave the lights on and have a floor show."

"Floor show? Yeah, I bet you would like to tear off a piece in front of an audience, wouldn't you?"

A voice from the doorway near the bar said dryly, "As a matter of fact, she almost has, more than once."

It was Ivor Kane. The admiral came to join them in the center of the room as Sandy gasped, "Darling! I thought you were on your way to meet Mountbatten!"

"I daresay. You didn't really think they wouldn't give me Christmas Eve off to be with my adoring faithful wife, did you, Sandy? No, I suppose you didn't. Thinking doesn't seem to be your strong point."

"I can explain, Admiral," Bradley said.

Kane looked at him as if he'd just noticed a speck of lint on his navy blue and said flatly, "Stay out of this, you twit. I'm speaking to my wife. As a matter of fact I think you'd better leave, don't you?"

Bradley was tempted. But he saw the pleading look in Sandy's eyes and blustered, "Not until I know she's safe. You seem to be overreacting to a harmless bit of fun."

Kane looked sincerely puzzled as he muttered, "Safe? My God, do you actually think I'd strike a woman? You must have been brought up in a rather ordinary pig pen, Major. I'll be the judge of how one should or should not react to what you two call harmless fun. You did say you were on your way out, didn't you?"

Bradley sneered and asked, "What can you do if I say no, throw me out?"

"If I have to," Kane answered mildly.

Sandy knew her husband better than her lover did. She nervously licked her lips and said, "Dan, you'd better go."

But Bradley had mistaken the older man's manners for softness. As the natural bully he was, Bradley said, "No, I think we'll just see if this old fart has enough hair on his chest to take on the U.S. Airborne."

Ivor Kane stared morosely at the young braggart for a long moment as Sandy edged back toward a couch against the wall. Kane sighed, said, "Very well"—and kicked Bradley, hard, in the groin.

As Bradley gasped in pain and clutched at his crotch with both hands the admiral moved in, leading with his left, and broke Bradley's nose with a vicious left hook, followed by a right cross that split Bradley's lip and loosened a tooth as it sent him sprawling on the rug.

The admiral stood politely, guard up, to say lightly, "Sandy, you stay right where you are. I'll deal with you after we see what this strange young man of yours means to do next. Where on earth did you ever find such a silly sod?"

Bradley rolled over, groaning. He still could have crawled out. Admiral Kane was too polite to kick a man when he was down. But Bradley was almost as physically tough as he thought he was. So he made the mistake of rolling to the fireplace and getting to his feet, with a poker in his hand. He shook his head like a bull and roared, "I'll kill you!" as he came at the admiral, poker raised to strike.

Admiral Kane dodged as gracefully as a matador

and rabbit-punched the charging paratrooper as he went by. Bradley sprawled headlong on the rug as the admiral landed in the small of his back with both heels, bounced off, and kicked the poker over toward's Sandy's feet. He moved her way, saying, "Hand me that, will you?" When she didn't move or answer he stooped to retrieve the weapon himself and turned back to face Bradley.

Kane saw the paratrooper wasn't moving. He rolled Bradley over with his foot and knelt to feel the side of Danny Boy's throat. He got to his feet with a sigh and took the poker back to the fireplace to hang it back in place before he turned to his wife. "He seems to be dead," he said, his eyes leveling on hers.

Sandy gasped, "Oh, God, he can't be!"

"Afraid he is, my dear. But not to worry, you'll no doubt find someone as uncouth to muck about with. You always have."

He went to the sideboard to pour himself a drink. "I'd say this just about tears it, Alexandra. I've put up with a lot from you in the past, for you are a rather fantastic little thing in bed, despite your, ah, lack of breeding. But a man in my position can hardly afford a wife who gets him into fist fights like a common seaman. I'm going to have to ask you for a divorce."

"Are you mad? This is no time to talk about divorce! You just killed a man!"

"Yes, sorry about that. But the river's not far and I'll have some of my lads clean up this mess. We'll say the Frogs must have done it, should anyone ask. As I recall he left our party with the others quite some time ago."

"You're going to be sent to prison, you maniac!"

He sipped his drink with a slight frown. "Prison, for a rear admiral on Montbatten's staff? Don't talk rubbish. About the divorce, I'm sorry but I don't mean to be the guilty party. My solicitors will try to keep it out of the *Mirror*, but I fear we really will have to charge you with, ah, casual adultery. No need to name names if you don't contest the action, of course."

Sandy's gutter-fighter instincts were returning to her as she saw she wasn't in any physical danger after all. "Don't be an ass, Ivor. I'd be a fool to give you a divorce. What would become of me?"

He pursed his lips judiciously and said, "Well, you are getting a bit long in the tooth to go back to being a show girl at the Windmill, and I understand trade has been falling off around Trafalgar Square these days. But cats land on their feet and you are a bit of an alley cat, you know."

Sandy pointed at the body on the floor as she shook her head stubbornly and insisted, "I'll not be cast aside like an old shoe! If you accuse me of adultery I've some countercharges you'll have to answer for, peer or not!"

Kane raised an eyebrow. "I might keep an old shoe. But you've become a rather filthy little tart since I made the mistake of spoiling you. You're being very silly about this rather unpleasant American chap. I told you I'd have no trouble sweeping him under the rug. But it would be most unpleasant to have you running about shouting all sorts of accusations. Perhaps I'd better have you shot."

She looked up at him with a puzzled smile and he nodded and said, "I could, you know. I can prove you spent some time in bed with Evans, the German spy who worked for us for a time. Some of the information he had on that microfilm would have been rather difficult for him to have gotten, had not a faithless wife provided access to certain drawers in our private bedroom."

"Ivor! That's monstrous! You know perfectly well I had no idea Evans was an enemy agent!"

"Perhaps," he said with a shrug. "Nonetheless, you did invite him into our bedroom and he did get into my private drawers as well as you. Do you really want to explain your messy sex life to a military court when I'm perfectly willing to settle for an uncontested divorce, my dear?"

She didn't answer. She couldn't answer as she stared in dawning horror into her husband's unwinking ice-cold eyes and realized fully for the first time why Louis Montbatten had once called Ivor one of the toughest men in the Royal Navy.

Kane nodded and said flatly, "I didn't think you'd want to be charged as this war's answer to Mata Hari, even though one assumes you've slept with as many Allied officers as she did. Do I have your undivided attention, my dear?"

She nodded, numbly.

"Good! Now I'm going to tell you exactly what we're both going to do and say about this little mess of yours, unless you want to be shot."

32

THE NEXT MORNING, *north* of Bastogne, the Hell On Wheels U.S. Second Armored delivered a Christmas present. It was the *German* Second Armored, stalled along the road west of Bastogne as it waited for more fuel. The German supply column was caught in a horrendous traffic jam near Bastogne, under fire from the long-range Long Toms those segregated but smart black gunners had thought to drag along with them. So as the Tigers and Panthers stood helpless on the road shoulder, with their fuel going up in smoke far behind them, the lighter M-4 tanks of their oddly matching U.S. division hit them and proceeded to roll the panzer column up like a big tube of toothpaste. But what Hell On Wheels was squeezing out was hardly toothpaste. It was blood and fire, a lot of blood and fire, stretching over ten miles under dense black clouds of billowing smoke.

The Germans were starting to hurt in lots of other places, and the Allies were getting a grip on the bulge as the jaws of the nutcracker began to close. The victory of the U.S. Second Armored was only a foretaste of what was to come if they didn't do something fast about their hopelessly snarled traffic. The Germans surrounding Bastogne were in the position now of a doughnut rather than a nut in a nutcracker, with the hard steel ball of Bastogne where the hole should be, giving them no room to maneuvre as Monty began his lavalike advance from their north flank, while Patton, starting farther from the battlefield, tore across France to hit them from the south. The sensible thing for them to be doing by now would be a planned withdrawal, while they still had time. But Adolf Hitler wasn't making much sense these days, and the men of Operation Christ Rose were ordered to hold their salient at all costs.

They couldn't do that with Bastogne smack in the middle of the bulge, lobbing shells at anything and everything that tried to pass either way along the spider web of roads with Bastogne at its hub.

Manteuffel was a better strategist than Hitler. His enlisted driver was a better strategist than Hitler. It was even rumored in the German army that the young American actress, Miss Shirley Temple, knew at least as much about winning a war as Adolf Hitler. But the German officers who'd tried to get rid of Hitler last summer were all dead now, so what was a poor German general to do when the boss insisted on the impossible?

They tried the impossible, of course. Sick at heart,

Manteuffel diverted vital reserves and impossible-to-replace war materiel to the reduction of Bastogne. And Bastogne held, not like a rock, but like a big thirsty sponge that soaked up fire power the Germans could have put to much better use at other times and places.

Baron Von der Heydte's German airborne was fighting for its life as it pleaded for supplies and reinforcements. Bully Boy Sepp Dietrich and his SS men were supposed to have linked up with the scattered German paratroops by this time, but, as in Market Garden, the ground forces just couldn't get through as planned. Bogged down at the Elsenborn Ridge rather than at Arnhem Bridge, the SS could only show their German Kultur by burning farms and butchering POWs or, apparently just for the hell of it, Belgian civilians.

In another sector near Stoumont another SS leader wasn't worried about German Kultur. He was out of gas. His name was Jochen Peiper and although the hatchet-faced Peiper was a much nicer man about the Geneva Conventions than Dietrich he was said to be a fighting son of a bitch, giving anything to fight with. But his Kampfgruppe was running low on ammo too. The pigs he radioed for Hermann and Otto kept telling him the Allies still had that highway blocked behind him but that Bastogne would fall any day now. Colonel Peiper didn't have that many days. Those maniacs in Bastogne were no longer the only enemy troops he had to worry about. The U.S. Thirtieth Infantry had moved into the bulge and was said to be less than fifteen miles from his position, with ammo and gas to spare. American tank destroyers were coming at him from the south. British Tommies were moving from the north in that slow but ominous way that Tommy moved. Without supplies—and he wasn't getting any supplies—Colonel Peiper was no longer interested in making it to Antwerp. If he abandoned his vehicles and ran like hell on foot toward the Rhine there was an outside chance they'd make it.

All over the chaotic battle zone other German commanders were sending the same plaintive messages. "Low on Hermann. Out of Otto. Under increasing enemy fire. What shall we do?" And the harassed General Manteuffel didn't have any answers. No sensible answers, anyway. Obviously, if bogged down German crews stayed with their stalled tanks until some American or British tank got to it, they'd be cooked alive in their helpless Tiger or Panther. On the other hand, Hitler had ordered any German crew allowing a German tank to fall into Allied hands without a fight executed as traitors to the Third Reich.

Manteuffel told his field commanders he was not accepting excuses either. He wanted them to lance that boil at Bastogne and he wanted them to do it now. So the ghostly white-clad infantry and Krupp-clad tanks all around Bastogne took a deep breath, took off the gloves, and moved in shooting from the hip.

But the Battered Bastards beat them back, littering the snow-covered slopes all around Bastogne with white-clad bodies and burning tanks.

This was largely because the Germans were attacking some of the best trained fighters in the U.S. Army over open ground, with the defenders dug in and with their weapons zeroed.

The zeroing of defensive weapons firing from fixed positions sounds arcane but is really very simple. If you have a machine gun, a mortar, or a cannon all set up, and you know where a possible target is going to be in the near future, you don't have to wait and aim at the moving target. You can set the sights on a cross road, a ditch, a shell crater, or other likely cover your enemy figures to use. Then, when his attack commences, you just leave your weapon the way it is and proceed to fire it every time some suckers land in your pre-determined killing zone.

Choosing these killing zones fell to Logan and other S2 officers around the perimeter of Bastogne's defenses, of course. As a man who'd landed in some killing zones himself in the past, Hunter could spot many out there in the snow fields just by looking through his field glasses. But at night he'd sent patrols out to move between the German lines toward his, putting themselves in the German's shoes as they pretended they were sneaking into town.

All his scouts found some. Falco had a knack for spotting where a tank would move over or between natural obstacles. But young Sergeant Arnold was fiendishly good as he slithered through the snow, finding the safest ways in and then noting each on Hunter's S2 map as a swell place to lob a mortar round. It was Arnold who found a tight culvert under a road running at right angles to the American field of fire. "It's not on the map, sir," he said. "But it's right here, by this shattered tree. Their ski troopers will flatten out behind the lip of that road to get their breath for the last charge. Some wise-ass is bound to spot the culvert entrance and send a scout through it down this snowed-over stream bed, see?"

Hunter nodded and made a note that a 75 trained there would play hell with Krauts bunched up near the culvert, while a dotted line of mortar aiming points was indicated for the far side of that barely noticeable snow-covered roadway. A heavy machine gun of course was zeroed in to dust up any Krauts who survived the mortar fire and were still dumb enough to come over the top.

One of the new kids, a teen-aged rather shy-looking Texan named Verdugo, surprised Hunter by turning out to be surprisingly good at collecting enemy pay books. Verdugo liked to scout alone and he was sort of vague on his methods, but with Falco's grudging permission Verdugo would slip out at night and come back with pay books, regimental badges and officer's pistols. Verdugo insisted the pistols were his to keep. A Walthers P-38 was worth sixty dollars on the war souvenir market and Hunter agreed he'd earned them.

The Germans tried again from another angle. But the other regiments also had good S2, and when the lead tanks started catching point-blank Long Tom fire not even a Tiger had been designed to take, they fell back out of range, leaving those slopes littered too, as they licked their wounds and hammered the town with heavy, almost hysterical artillery barrages.

The heavy German barrages cost the Germans more, strategically, than they cost the defenders of Bastogne —although, of course, it was sometimes hard to understand this when a 155 or Screaming Mimi lands on women and children or even troops.

General McAuliffe knew his troops were tough enough to take such casualties as the expensively erratic German shelling was inflicting. Neither his Screaming Eagles nor the others who'd fought their way into Bastogne could be considered sissies. But the Belgian civilians hadn't volunteered for this battle. They just woke up one morning in their own homes to find it going on all around them.

He called the community leaders together for a meeting. He told them he might be able to arrange a truce with the Krauts allowing him to evacuate non-combatants. If anyone wanted out.

They didn't. Belgium had been occupied by Germans in two wars now, and there wasn't much you could tell a Belgian about German Kultur. They knew all too well what could happen to women and children behind the German lines even when there was food and shelter from the bitter cold. And besides, they told him, Bastogne was their town, not the Germans', and they were damned if they were ever going to let a German swagger down their streets again.

Tony McAuliffe had already made his position clear to the Krauts, so the matter was settled. The Battered Bastards of Bastogne would just hang in there, for as long as they had to.

They had to, longer than either they or the Germans had expected.

The Allied armies north and south of the bulge had restabilized their fronts and were winning skirmish after skirmish as the jaws of the nutcracker closed. But the bulge was large and the weather stayed rotten, forcing even the flamboyant Patton to watch his step as his Third Army inched forward through heavy snow drifts with no air cover.

But it was obvious to Manteuffel by now that Operation Christ Rose was a costly failure no matter how Der Adolf ranted and raved about treason.

The young Prussian general didn't consider it treason to save his army and possibly a Third Reich that was going to need one hell of a lot of men and materiel if they were to stop the enemy at the Rhine. So, having lost all his airborne and a heartbreaking amount of armor, Manteuffel ordered an orderly "strategic withdrawal to prepared positions," which was as close as he could get to saying retreat without getting shot.

But now the Bastogne bottleneck that had impeded the German thrust to the west became a big fish hook snagged in their flesh as they tried to pull back. Bastogne hadn't shrunk as the bulge was being squeezed smaller, and as routes north and south of Bastogne were lost to the Germans the ones near Bastogne became even more vital. The German units besieging Bastogne were told to try harder, and were reinforced with others pulled back from the other fronts, mad as hornets whose nest was being slowly crushed.

The fighting at Bastogne ebbed and flowed, like a pounding surf. The sky stayed overcast but the snow storms came and went. The Germans attacked in their white overalls when the visibility was poor, then fell back to pound the town with long-range guns when it was clear. There were lulls when nothing at all was going on, and these quiet times while the enemy took time out were as hard on the nerves of the Battered Bastards as the fighting.

As always in a war, one noticed the little irritations that formed a constant part of life on the line more than the short heady minutes of actual fighting. It was possible to shave or even take a quick bath in Bastogne, which was more than the Germans all around had going for them. But by now everyone in town smelled pretty gamey. Bodies buried under rubble were of course dug out and buried within hours, but the spoiled food and shattered sewer lines under all that rubble filled the air with eye-watering fumes when the heat of fermentation overcame the cold in the air above.

With the sky socked in, air drops were out of the question and so mail call became a dimly remembered luxury. Hunter was only one among many who had to just sit and wonder about his wife and family back home. They received almost no news from the outside world, if there was an outside world anymore. They could listen to news broadcasts on the radio, of course, but the news was censored and SHAEF was playing down the bulge. Neither Bastogne nor its gallant defenders were mentioned as the Armed Forces Network prattled on about supposedly more important actions to the north and south.

This didn't bother Logan Hunter as much as it did some of the more recent arrivals from the States. Even before he'd married a war correspondent Hunter had noticed the news media didn't know their ass from their elbow about the war. The best civilian reporter tended to get confused about the significance of what was going on all around. The military was confusing even to those who were in it. That was why they sent officers to school first. Many draftees would fight all through the war, or die in it, without the vaguest idea where they were or what was really going on. That was why privates were supposed to take orders from the officers.

They didn't always, and that was why even at Bastogne there were MPs and court-martials. Be it recorded there was not one case of misbehavior before the enemy, and of course desertion or AWOL just couldn't happen. But as the weeks wore on there were disciplinary problems. In a town of four thousand one can always find a bottle somewhere and though ninety percent or more of the civilian population were devout and decent country types, there were always some naughty girls. Three sisters dwelling in the ruins near the center of town gained a certain notoriety and the title of "Division Punch Board" as they and a few others catered to the carnal appetites of men not presently engaged with the enemy. But there were over twenty thousand healthy young men in Bastogne, not counting the unwed civilians, and so there were fights. Fist fights for the most part, but some ugly incidents with knives and even guns as well. One soldier raped a Belgian girl. His company CO saw no need to pester the general with formal procedure at a time like this. His outraged buddies took him into an alley, shot him, and reported him killed in action.

During a shelling one of Hunter's squad leaders was killed. As soon as it was safe to discuss the matter with Falco again, Hunter suggested young Verdugo to replace him. Falco shook his head and said, "I don't think so, Captain. The Mex is a hell of a scout. But he's a lone wolf. You gotta have a guy who worries about the guys around him."

So Hunter went through the 201 files and called in a nineteen-year-old kid named Dalman. "Dalman, I've been going over your records and I see you took ROTC in high school. What's this about you speaking a little German?"

Dalman blinked and said, "Did they put that down, sir? When I was at the induction center some sergeant asked me if I spoke any foreign languages and I said I had a German grandmother and knew a few words. I don't really speak German."

"You speak more than anyone else in your squad. I'm making you the leader of the second squad. Pick out your own assistant squad leader. You know your men better than I do."

Dalman gulped and said, "I don't know nothing about leading a squad, Captain! I just came overseas!"

"Welcome to the club. You've been in combat over a month now. That's more than a lot of guys could say when they led their squads into D day and Market Garden. I know what they taught you in high school ROTC. It was chocolate soldier bullshit, but at least they taught you something. You're dismissed, Sergeant Dalman."

"Begging the captain's pardon, I'm only a Pfc."

"Not anymore. Don't sew on the stripes, though. Just tell your guys you're a sergeant for now and let Kraut snipers guess. I said dismissed."

As Dalman left him alone with his maps and his thoughts, Hunter felt a hundred years old. There were so many things like that to be decided, fast, and if he'd made a mistake it could cost him a third of his scouts. How the hell did the top brass take this pressure? Did they just block it out that human lives hung in the balance every time they issued a command? It was no wonder the colonel kept a bottle in his file cabinet, or that Patton was a crazy son of a bitch. It took a guy half drunk or just a plain sadistic bastard to run this war.

Hunter lit a smoke and got up to study his S2 charts. The regiment was taking a lot of rocket fire that seemed to be coming from those woods to the northeast of their front. He didn't have the position of that Screaming Mimi battery marked. But that colored artillery officer said he could knock it out with his Long Tom if somebody could pinpoint its position a little better.

Hunter puffed nervously as he juggled the odds in his head. Falco had come back from his last patrol with a touch of frostbite. It would have to be Arnold. But Arnold was a lot like Verdugo. He was a natural survivor on his own, but he tended to lose track of his flank men moving in the dark.

Hunter took a deep drag, picked up a pencil stub and started picking names from his duty roster. His best bet was a small diamond of picked scouts. Arnold with Verdugo on point. Trooper Masters was steady under fire. Okay, Masters on right flank, that big kid Brown on the left. Trooper Hollis looked like a good runner. He'd be getaway man. It was a good diamond. It ought to work. If it didn't work . . . ? Tough shit. It was rough in the ETO.

"Shit," Tex Verdugo muttered under his breath as he lay flat on his belly in a snow bank. The snow storm they'd started out in was beginning to taper off and despite the darkness of the night Verdugo knew he'd stand out like a sore thumb if some son-of-a-bitch Nazi fired a flare about now. He'd asked the gringo captain if he could have that Belgian girl sew him some white camouflage from old sheets, but Hunter had said no. It made the 101 pickets nervous when guys crawled back to them dressed in white, even if they yelled the password a lot. Verdugo understood the S2 officer's point, but damn it, that big gringo didn't have to flounder around out here like a fucking seal on an ice floe, dressed in fucking OD. Verdugo wondered how you got to be an officer. Old Hunter was okay, for one of them, but you'd think they'd let guys who'd seen some *action* run things.

Verdugo flinched as something touched his boot heel. He coiled like a rattler as he looked back, trench knife raised to strike. Then he growled, "Don't ever do that again, Sarge. What the fuck are you doing here on point with me?"

"I thought something happened to you," Arnold said. "You haven't moved for hours!"

"More like three minutes. I've been studying those trees ahead."

Arnold peered past him at the tree line, which was actually only visible as a slightly darker shade of blackness against the dark slate color of snow at midnight. "I don't see a damned thing," Arnold said.

"Neither do I. That's why I'm studying. The Krauts should have pickets along the tree line. I haven't spotted shit. They must be half-buried in this snow in them white pajamas of theirs."

"If we can't see them," said Arnold, "they can't see us, right?"

"Wrong. We're in the open and if we move in on a picket he'll spot us."

"Okay, what can we do about it? We gotta find that Kraut battery and get back before daybreak."

"I said I was studying," Verdugo said. "Where are the other guys?"

"Where they're supposed to be. You want me to take the point?"

"No, I want to get back alive. Don't be so fucking eager, Sarge. We got plenty of time to do it right."

Arnold started to say something and Verdugo kicked him and hissed, "Bingo! Over to the right. Stay here." Then he was crawling away, trending to the left. Arnold stared in the direction the Texan had indicated. He didn't see anything at first. And then it did seem as if a paler blur had moved again at the tree line. Arnold studied it, eyes narrowed. He just couldn't tell. That Mex had eyes like a cat if he'd really seen anything over that way, and now Arnold couldn't spot Verdugo either. Where the hell was he?

A voice from behind him whispered, "You okay, Sarge?"

Arnold whispered back, "Yeah. Get back where

you belong, Hollis. You're supposed to stay farthest down the slope at all times."

"I thought maybe something was wrong."

"Something's always wrong. Getaway on point is wrong too, so move it!"

Trooper Hollis did as he was told. The sarge had jumped in Normandy and Holland, so he must know what he was doing.

Something was crawling toward Arnold from the tree line and he stiffened, easing his carbine into position. He had exactly ten Krauts now. If this guy was a Kraut he'd have eleven. Arnold wanted eleven. Ten sounded dumb.

Verdugo called out softly, "We're clear. I got 'em. Their pay books say Panzer Lehr Division. Ain't that a new outfit in this neck of the woods?"

"Yeah, they must have pulled back to join the fun and games. What do you mean you got 'em? I didn't hear no fighting."

"I didn't *want* anybody to hear no fighting. I used my knife. Got around behind 'em and that's all she wrote. The captain says their pickets should be posted every hundred yards or so. We can move into the woods now, if we keep it down to a roar."

"Okay, take the point and we'll follow. But what if their OD finds 'em before we come back?"

"Jesus, were you figuring on coming back the same way? Look, you want me on point or don't you? I know how to get in and out, damn it."

Arnold told him to quit his bitching and move out. He gave Verdugo a good lead and then used his little toy cricket to signal the others they were moving forward.

Once they were in the trees they could stand up and walk. The snow wasn't as deep but the darkness was deeper. Arnold took out his pocket compass and read the radium dial. He had his bearings back when Verdugo materialized beside him and said, "Okay, we can go home now. I've got that Screaming Mimi on my field map."

"You what? I haven't seen a fucking thing!"

"That's 'cause they're over the next ridge. That colored looie was right about them rockets not carrying far. They got the launchers lined up on a secondary road through the woods. They're bunched like suckers too. Couple of Long Tom rounds oughtta take out the whole outfit. You know what they was doing when I peeked in on 'em? They was standing around a fire like a bunch of Boy Scouts. Ain't that a bitch? I couldda peppered half the assholes with one burst. They don't even have a perimeter guard. They must be green as hell. Let's get back and tell them colored guys where to send the mail."

Arnold nodded. Then he hesitated. "Wait a minute. We've got a clean beeline getaway route and Hitler owes me at least one more Kraut."

"You're bucking for Section 8! We're scouts, not rifle. It's not our job to smoke up that rocket battery. We were told to find it for the artillery, not take it out ourselves!"

"Yeah, but you say they're sitting ducks. Come on, let's just empty a couple of clips into them for laughs and run like hell!"

Verdugo stubbornly shook his head. "Them sitting ducks have guns, Sarge."

"Are you yellow?"

"No, but you're sure talking stupid. The captain said not to take no chances. He wants I&R, not O.K. Corral bullshit!"

"Cover me," Arnold said. "I'm going over the ridge for a look-see."

He started forward as Verdugo followed, muttering to himself. Arnold moved up a sudden rise in the snow-covered ground in a low crouch. Sure enough, on the far side he saw the orange glow of an oil-drum fire. He eased closer to see the white-clad figures clustered around the meagre warmth, their vehicles on the far side and the cluster-barrel rocket launchers outlined black on his side of the foolish illumination. Arnold raised his carbine as he told Verdugo, "Okay, start running!" and pulled the trigger.

It only took a few seconds to empty his banana clip as the startled Germans scattered in all directions, leaving two men near the fire on the ground. But a few seconds are a long time in a fire fight and as Arnold turned to run after the others he was slammed across the back and sent sprawling headlong in the snow. He rose on his arms, staring numbly at the little pinwheeling stars before his eyes. "Hey," he muttered, "I'm hit. But it hardly hurts at all. How about that?" And then he fell forward, dead.

He'd killed two more Germans, making it an even dozen, and an even dozen didn't sound right either. But Arnold was never going to tell any war stories to his grandchildren, so it really didn't matter.

Verdugo and the others got back. Hunter gave the position of the rocket battery to the young black artillery officer and before dawn the Long Tom had cratered the position into a snowy moonscape. But of course by then the Germans, knowing they'd been spotted, had moved their Screaming Mimies somewhere else.

Arnold hadn't just gotten himself killed as an eager

beaver. He'd done a piss-poor job of I&R. Hunter told Falco they'd been wrong about Verdugo. Verdungo had done it by the book. So Verdugo was promoted to the late Sergeant Arnold's vacant spot on the TO.

33

ONE DAY, six long weeks after they'd been trucked into Bastogne, a trooper pissing in a snow bank saw his shadow as the sun rose. He looked up and the sky was clear. By the time word got around, the first Allied fighter planes were dropping out of the blue bowl above Bastogne to add to the Third Reich's troubles. American P-51s and barrel chested P-47s skimmed along the ridges surrounding Bastogne, strafing and bombing German positions. Not to be outdone, British Spitfires, Typhoons, and the deadly Mosquitos that could double as bomber or fighter hit the Germans as the Yanks headed home for more ammo and fuel. On the ramparts of Bastogne, soldiers and civilians waved and cheered, ignoring the occasional round of 88 or Screaming Mimi lobbed at them by poor losers.

Later a flight of C-47s came over to drop fresh supplies and a message that Patton was coming, fast, and that air recon showed the Germans pulling east. Operations Christ Rose was ending for the Germans as Market Garden had for the Allies.

But Tony McAuliffe wasn't content to just sit there like a bump on a log until the tankers arrived. He called his staff in and went over the S2 maps Hunter and the others had prepared. Then he stabbed his finger at the nearby but withdrawing Panzer Lehr Division. "These guys are abandoning their armor and pulling out on foot. Let's *get* the sons of bitches!"

So they did. Keeping enough reserves to hold the town if somebody was mistaken about the German rout, McAuliffe sent a spearhead of his 501st regiment out across the snow to hit the disorganized Panzer Lehr, and it was the U.S. Airborne's turn to win a viciously one-sided battle.

The German tankers and even their armored infantry just weren't legged up to fight in knee-deep snow, while the paratroopers were the best-trained infantry in the U.S. Army. So they didn't just maul the German withdrawal, they wiped them damned near out. Long before Patton could "rescue" the Battered Bastards of Bastogne, they were in full control of the surrounding countryside within artillery range of the town.

To the south, George Patton told his lead tanks to step on the gas as the bulge fell apart ahead of his advance. He hadn't driven all this way to congratulate anyone, damn it. He wanted to *kill* the purple-pissing Nazis, not wave bye-bye to them. And that's just what the Third Army started doing as they lanced into the chaos Operation Christ Rose had become.

In a reversal of the first terrible days of the German offensive, when Americans had run around like decapitated chickens, bewildered Germans tore all over, cut off, lost, out of communication with one another. Some units surrendered to the first American they could find. Some dug in to fight bitterly to the end. Most just tried to somehow make it out, wherever out might be these days. With Monty chewing at them from the north, with the U.S. Second Armored as his longest sharpest fang, and Patton streamrollering from the south behind a rolling wave of heavy long-range artillery, and the Battered Bastards holding a spreading hole in the center of the burning rug, going anywhere wasn't easy.

With the weather now favoring Allied air superiority, the Germans had to move at night when they could move at all. All a smart German could do in broad daylight was hole up and keep his head down. So crusty George Patton was riding near the head of his advance column as he neared Bastogne, disdainful of possible sniper fire as he stared loftily out across the snow-covered fields.

Not far behind him Ramie Hunter née Davis had hitched a ride in a weapons carrier. She'd been covering Patton's advance for weeks now, and the general no longer called her a cunt. He liked the way she wrote about him these days and she'd decided he wasn't really a maniac. Maybe a little weird, but a man racing to save her husband couldn't be all bad.

Her husband had his own duties that day and the last person he was expecting to meet as he led a heavy combat patrol out of Bastogne to mop up snipers who might be along Patton's route was the young wife he'd left in Paris. They hadn't found any snipers. Hunter was on a snow-covered ridge reporting to Colonel Bell by radio when one of his men shouted. He looked up, and said, "We've spotted Third Army,

411

Colonel. It's beautiful! They're coming up the valley like they're on parade and, Jesus, Patton really does ride a white tank, like they say! Over!"

Hunter turned the R-300 over to his T/5 and stood up to join the other troopers waving by the side of the road. The scout cars out in front pulled over to let the tall white tank take the lead. Patton's tank stopped near Hunter and the general glared down at Hunter and snapped, "Report!"

"Captain Hunter, 101st Airborne. Welcome to Bastogne, General."

"I know which side *you're* on, goddamn your eyes! Where are the purple-pissing *Nazis?*"

Hunter pointed east with his finger. "They went thataway, General. You can head 'em off at the pass."

Patton didn't think it was funny. "All you men are out of uniform! You all need shaves and haircuts! Who do you think you are, Willy and Joe?"

"No sir. We're the 101st Airborne and we've no excuse for our appearance."

"Well, get these men cleaned up and ready for inspection, goddamn it. I'm driving on to meet with General McAuliffe. You can hitch a ride with my support vehicles."

"Begging the general's pardon, we're on patrol. We'll get ready for inspection as soon as we *walk* back to Bastogne, sir."

"Very well," said Patton. Then a twinkle in his eye betrayed him as he asked, "By the way, did Tony McAuliffe really say nuts to the Germans?"

"He did, sir. I was there."

"Jesus, I wish I'd said that! Carry on, Captain."

Hunter watched, smiling as the white tank moved on. Then a small uniformed figure was running across the snow at him, shouting his name. He recognized Ramie as her helmet fell off, and he ran to meet her. He took her in his arms and kissed her. Then he held her at arms' length and asked, laughing, "How the hell did *you* get here?"

"I was going to ask you the same thing, and don't you ever do it again. My God, you smell like a goat. The beard's sort of becoming, though."

Lieutenant Falco came over to them, eyes merry but face impassive as he said, "I can handle the patrol, sir. If you two wanna grab a ride in."

Hunter glanced over at the long passing column and said, "Negative. I'm sorry, Ramie, but I've got to finish this sweep and report the area secured. Suppose we flag down a ride for you? You can wait for me in town."

"Suppose we don't and say we did? I've never had a chance to file a story on . . . whatever this is. Where's my damned helmet?"

Verdugo had picked it up and was bringing it over to them. Hunter said, "I wish you'd do as I say, honey. We're not expecting any trouble, but you never know."

She took the helmet with a nod of thanks to the grinning Verdugo, put it firmly on, and said, "Negative, as you big tough GIs say. If I can ride with Patton I guess I can march with the 101st Airborne, damn it."

Hunter laughed. "Okay, but stay close to me. Verdugo, take your squad out on point. If we don't meet anybody in the next couple of miles we'll know it's over, for now."

As the patrol moved out, Ramie walked at her man's side, saying, "Oh, I've so many things to tell you. Beth's engaged and the French police found Dan

Bradley in the river and the Kanes are getting a divorce and—"

"Later, Kitten," he cut in, aware of the other men around them. He explained gently, "This is a combat patrol. No talking allowed."

She fell silent as they trudged along. She had on a pair of the new infantry boots but her feet were already getting cold and it was hard going in this crusty stuff. She started making mental notes for her feature as her husband snapped absolutely unintelligible orders and his men did things she didn't see the point of, at first. But by the time they stopped on a hard-packed road and she could stamp the snow off her boots Ramie was beginning to grasp the essentials. Hunter called out, "That's all she wrote. Route-step back to the outskirts of Bastogne, but we'd better fall in and march in cadence past that silly white tank."

As the men laughed and they started back, Ramie said, "Can I talk now?"

"Yes," he said, and added in a whisper, "I love you."

"Me, too. I think I see what we were supposed to be doing just now. If this war keeps up much longer *everybody* will understand it!"

He sighed and said, "Nobody will ever understand it. But not to worry. It can't last much longer. Hitler just threw away the last cream of his army. If the Krauts don't fold this coming spring I'll eat this tin hat."

"We heard you people did a great job here. Are you very pleased?"

"Well, very pleased is putting it kind of strong. Let's say I'm just pleased. We *did* it, Ramie! We showed everybody we weren't just a bunch of guys in pretty boots. They mauled us good on D day and they damned near wiped us out in Holland. But this time we won big. And, yeah, I'm pleased."

"And you've been promoted too! Uh, does that mean you might have to fight again?"

"I don't know, Ramie. At our last staff meeting General McAuliffe said we'd be pulled back in reserve to shape up again and that Ike had earmarked us and the Second Armored for the occupation of Berlin. I know that sounds a little optimistic, but the war should be over before we're ready to go in again— knock wood."

She rapped her knuckles on the stock of his slung carbine as she asked, "Do you suppose the occupation army will provide married quarters for their captains, dear?"

"I can do better than that. Half of Bastogne's still standing. So we ought to be able to wrangle our own bedroom tonight. Like you said, we've got a lot of talking to catch up on."

"We'll have a lifetime to *talk* about this stupid war. Let's just find that bedroom, for now."